WINDFALL

DESMOND BAGLEY was born in 1923 in Kendal, Westmorland, and was brought up in Blackpool. He began his working life at 14 as a printers' devil and then did a variety of jobs until going into an aircraft factory at the start of World War II.

When the war ended he decided to travel to southern Africa, going overland through Europe and the Sahara. He worked for a time in Uganda, then in Kenya and on a Rhodesian asbestos mine before he reached South Africa in 1951.

He became a freelance journalist in Johannesburg and wrote his first published novel, *The Golden Keel*, in 1962. In 1964 he returned to England and lived in Totnes, Devon, for twelve years. He and his wife then moved to their present home in Guernsey in the Channel Islands. Here he has found the ideal place for combining his writing with his other interests, which include computers, mathematics, military history, and entertaining friends from all over the world.

In *Windfall*, Desmond Bagley has written another of his inimitable thrillers, but he has also produced a thoughtful novel of present-day Kenya; a novel of insight and humour that explores the intricate interrelationships of the Africans, Asians and Europeans who live and work there, and share a common love of their country.

DESMOND BAGLEY

Windfall

FONTANA/Collins

First published by William Collins Sons & Co. Ltd 1982
This continental edition first issued in Fontana
Paperbacks 1982

Made and printed in Great Britain by
William Collins Sons & Co. Ltd, Glasgow

TO
JAN HEMSING
and an unknown number of Kenyan cats

It is difficult to know when this business began. Certainly it was not with Ben Hardin. But possibly it began when Jomo Kenyatta instructed the Kenyan delegation to the United Nations to lead a move to expel South Africa from the UN. That was on the 25th of October, 1974, and it was probably soon thereafter that the South Africans decided they had to do something about it.

Max Stafford himself dated his involvement to the first day back at the London office after an exhaustive, and exhausting, trip around Europe – Paris, Frankfurt, Hamburg, Amsterdam, Milan. Three years earlier he had decided that since his clients were multinational he, perforce, would also have to go multinational. It had been a hard slog setting up the European offices but now Stafford Security Consultants, as well as sporting the tag 'Ltd' after the company name, had added 'S.A.', 'GmbH', 'SpA' and a couple of other assortments of initials. Stafford was now looking with a speculative eye across the Atlantic in the hope of adding 'Inc'.

He paused in the ante-room of his office. 'Is Mr Ellis around?'

Joyce, his secretary, said, 'I saw him five minutes ago. Did you have a good trip?'

'Wearing, but good.' He put a small package on her desk. 'Your favourite man-bait from Paris; Canal something-or-other. I'll be in Mr Ellis's office until further notice.'

Joyce squeaked. 'Thanks, Mr Stafford.'

Jack Ellis ran the United Kingdom operation. He was young, but coming along nicely, and ran a taut ship. Stafford had promoted him to the position when he had made the decision to move into Europe. It had been risky using so young a man in a top post where he would have to negotiate with some of the stuffier and elderly Chairmen of companies, but it had worked out and Stafford had never regretted it.

They talked for a while about the European trip and then Ellis looked at his watch. 'Bernstein will be here any minute.' He gestured to a side table on which lay several fat files. 'Have you read the reports?'

Stafford grimaced. 'Not in detail.' Having determined to expand he had gone the whole hog and commissioned an independent company to do a world-wide investigation into possibilities. It was costing a lot but he thought it would be worthwhile in the long run. However, he liked to deal with people rather than paper and he wanted to match the man against the words he had written. He said, 'We'll go over it once lightly with Bernstein.'

Two hours later he was satisfied. Bernstein, an American, was acute and sensible; he had both feet firmly planted on the ground and was not a man to indulge in impossible blue sky speculation. Stafford thought he could trust his written reports.

Bernstein tossed a file aside. 'So much for Australasia. Now we come to Africa.' He picked up another file. 'The problem in general with Africa is political instability.'

Stafford said, 'Stick to the English-speaking countries. We're not ready to go into francophone Africa.' He paused. 'Not yet.'

Bernstein nodded. 'That means the ex-British colonies. South Africa, of course, is the big one.' They discussed South Africa for some time and Bernstein made some interesting suggestions. Then he said, 'Next is Zimbabwe. It's just attained independence with a black government. Nobody knows which way it's going to go right now and I wouldn't recommend it for you. Tanzania is out; the country is virtually bankrupt and there's no free enterprise. The same goes for Uganda. Now, Kenya is different.'

'How?' asked Ellis.

Bernstein turned several pages. 'It has a mixed economy,

very much like Britain. The government is moderate and there is less corruption than is usual in Africa. The Western banks think highly of Kenya and there's a lot of money going into the country to build up the infrastructure – modernization of the road system, for instance.' He looked up. 'Of course, you'd have competition – Securicor is already established there.'

Securicor was Stafford's biggest competitor in Britain. He smiled and said, 'I can get along with that.' Then he frowned. 'But is Kenya really stable? What about that Mau-Mau business some years ago?'

'That was quite a while ago,' said Bernstein. 'When the British were still there. Anyway, there are a lot of misconceptions about the Mau-Mau insurrection. It was blown up in the Western press as a rebellion against the British and even the black Kenyans have done some rewriting of history because they like to think of that period as when they got rid of the British oppressor. The fact remains that in the seven years of the Mau-Mau rebellion only thirty-eight whites were killed. If it was a rebellion against the British it was goddamn inefficient.'

'You surprise me,' said Ellis. 'Then what was it all about?'

Bernstein tented his fingers. 'Everyone knew the British would be giving up jurisdiction over Kenya – the tide of history was running against the British Empire. The Mau-Mau insurrection was a private fight among black Kenyans, mainly along tribal lines, to figure out who'd be on top when the British abdicated. A lot of people died and the few whites were killed mainly because they happened to be caught in the middle – in the wrong place at the wrong time. When it was all over, the British knew who was going to hold the reins of government. Jomo Kenyatta was intelligent, educated and had all the qualifications to be the leader of a country, including the prime qualification.'

'What was that?' asked Ellis.

Bernstein smiled. 'He'd served time in a British jail,' he said dryly. 'Kenyatta proved to be surprisingly moderate. He didn't go hog-wild like some of the other African leaders. He encouraged the whites to stay because he knew he needed their skills, and he built up the trade of the country. A while ago there was considerable speculation as to what would happen when he died. People expected another civil war on the lines of the Mau-Mau but, surprisingly, the transition was orderly in the democratic manner and Moi became President. Tribalism is officially discouraged and, yes, I'd say Kenya is a stable country.' He flicked the pages he held. 'It's all here in detail.'

'All right,' said Stafford. 'What's next?'

'Now we turn to Nigeria.'

The discussion continued for another hour and then Stafford checked the time. 'We'll have to call a halt now. I have a luncheon appointment.' He looked with some distaste at the foot-thick stack of papers on the desk. 'It'll take some time to get through that lot. Thanks for your help, Mr Bernstein; you've been very efficient.'

'Anything you can't figure out, come right back at me,' said Bernstein.

'I think we'll give Africa a miss,' said Stafford thoughtfully. 'My inclination is to set up in the States and then, perhaps, in Australia. But I'm lunching with a South African. Perhaps he'll change my mind.'

* * *

Stafford's appointment was with Alix and Dirk Hendriks. He had met Alix a few years earlier when she had been Alix Aarvik, the daughter of an English mother and a Norwegian father who had been killed during the war. It was in the course of a professional investigation and, one thing leading to another, he had gone to North Africa to return to Britain with a bullet wound in the shoulder and a sizeable fortune for Alix Aarvik. His divorce was ratified about that time and he had contemplated marrying Alix, but there was not that spark between them and he had not pursued the idea although they remained good friends.

Since then she had married Dirk Hendriks. Stafford did not think a great deal of Hendriks. He distrusted the superficial veneer of charm and suspected that Hendriks had married Alix for her money. Certainly Hendriks did not appear to be gainfully employed. Still, Stafford was honest enough to admit to himself that his dislike of Hendriks might be motivated by an all-too-human dog in the manger attitude. Alix was expecting a baby.

Over lunch Alix complained that she did not see enough of him. 'You suddenly dropped out of my life.'

'For men must work,' said Stafford lightly, not worrying too much that his remark was a direct dig at Dirk Hendriks. 'I've been scurrying around Europe, making the fortunes of a couple of air lines.'

'Still intent on expansion, I see.'

'As long as people have secrets to protect there'll be work for people like me. I'm thinking of moving into the States.' He leaned back to let a waiter remove a plate. 'A chap this morning recommended that we expand our activities into South Africa. What do you think about that, Dirk?'

Hendriks laughed. 'Plenty of secrets in South Africa. It's not a bad idea.'

Stafford shook his head. 'I've decided to keep out of Africa altogether. There's plenty of scope in other directions and the Dark Continent doesn't appeal to me.'

He was to remember that remark with bitterness in the not too distant future.

2

Three thousand miles away Ben Hardin knew nothing about Max Stafford and Kenya was the last thing on his mind. And he was in total ignorance of the fact that, in more senses than one, he was the man in the middle. True, he had been in Kenya back in 1974, but it was in another job and in quite a different connection. Yet he was the unwitting key which unlocked the door to reveal the whole damn mess.

It was one of those hot, sticky days in late July when New York fries. Hardin had taken time off to visit his favourite bar to sink a couple of welcome cold beers and, when he got back to the office, Jack Richardson at the next desk said, 'Gunnarsson has been asking for you.'

'Oh; what does he want?'

Richardson shrugged. 'He didn't say.'

Hardin paused in the act of taking off his jacket and put it back on. 'When does he want to see me?'

'Yesterday,' said Richardson dryly. 'He sounded mad.'

'Then I guess I'd better see the old bastard,' said Hardin sourly.

Gunnarsson greeted him with, 'Where the hell have you been?'

'Checking a contact on the Myerson case,' said Hardin inventively, making a mental note to record the visit in the Myerson file. Gunnarsson sometimes checked back.

Gunnarsson put his hands flat on the desk and glowered at him. He was a burly, square man who looked as though he had been hacked out of a block of granite and in spite of the heat he wore his coat. Rumour had it that Gunnarsson lacked sweat glands. He said, 'You can forget that, Ben; I'm taking you off the case. I have something else for you.'

'Okay,' said Hardin.

Gunnarsson tossed a thin file across the desk. 'Let's get this straight. You clear this one and you get a bonus. You crap on it and you get canned. We've been carrying you long enough.'

Hardin looked at him levelly. 'You make yourself clear. How important is this one?'

Gunnarsson flapped his hand. 'I wouldn't know. A Limey lawyer wants an answer. You're to find out what happened to a South African called Adriaan Hendriks who came to the States some time in the 1930s. Find out all about him, especially whether he married and had kids. Find them, too.'

'That's going to take some legwork,' said Hardin thoughtfully. 'Who can I use?'

'No one; you use your own damn legs.' Gunnarsson was blunt. 'If you can't clear us a pisswilly job like this then I'll know you're no use to Gunnarsson Associates. Now you'll do it this way. You take your car and you go on the road and you find what happened to this guy. And you do it yourself. If you have to leave New York I don't want you going near any of the regional offices.'

'Why not?'

'Because that's the way I want it. And I'm the boss. Now get going.'

So Hardin went away and, as he laid the file on his desk, he thought glumly that he had just received an ultimatum. He sat down, opened the file, and found the reason for its lack of bulk. It contained a single sheet of computer print-out which told him nothing that Gunnarsson had not already told him; that a man called Adriaan Hendriks was believed to have entered the United States in the late thirties. The port of entry was not even recorded.

'Jesus wept!' said Hardin.

* * *

Ben Hardin wished, for perhaps the thousandth time, or it could have been the ten thousandth, that he was in another line of work. Every morning when he woke up in whatever crummy motel room it happened to be it was the thought that came into his mind: 'I wish I was doing something else.' And that was followed by the automatic: 'Goddamn that bastard, Gunnarsson,' and by the equally automatic first cigarette of the day which made him cough.

And every morning when he was confronted by breakfast, invariably the junk food of the interstate highways, the same thought came into his mind. And when he knocked on a door, any door, to ask the questions, the thought was fleetingly at the back of his mind. As with the Frenchman who said that everything reminded him of sex so everything reminded Hardin of the cruel condition of his life, and it had made him an irritable and cynical man.

On the occasion of the latest reiteration of his wish he was beset by water. The rain poured from the sky, not in drops but in a steady sheet. It swirled along the gutters a foot or more deep because the drains were unable to cope, and Hardin had the impression that his car was in imminent danger of being swept away. Trapped in the metal box of the car he could only wait until the downpour ceased. He was certainly not going to get out because he would be soaked to the skin and damn near drowned in ten seconds flat.

And this was happening in California – in Los Angeles, the City of the Angels. No more angels, he thought; the birds will all have drowned. He visualized a crowd of angels sitting on a dark cloud, their wings bedraggled, and managed a tired grin. They said that what California did today New York would do tomorrow. If that was true someone in New York should be building a goddamn Ark. He wondered if there was a Mr Noah in the New York telephone book.

While he waited he looked back on the last few weeks. The first and obvious step had been to check with the Immigration and Naturalization Service. He found that the 1930s had been a lean decade for immigrants – there were a mere 528,431 fortunate people admitted into the country. McDowell, the immigration officer he checked with, observed dryly that

Hardin was lucky – in the 1920s the crop had been over four million. Hardin doubted his luck.

'South Africa,' said McDowell. 'That won't be too bad. Not many South Africans emigrate.'

A check through the files proved him right – but there was no one called Adriaan Hendriks.

'They change their names,' said McDowell some time later. 'Sometimes to Americanize the spelling. There's a guy here called Adrian Hendrix . . .' He spelled it out. 'Would that be the guy you want? He entered the country in New Orleans.'

'That's my man,' said Hardin with satisfaction.

The search so far had taken two weeks.

Further searches revealed that Hendrix had taken out naturalization papers eight years later in Clarksville, Tennessee. More to the point he had married there. Establishing these simple facts took another three weeks and a fair amount of mileage.

Adrian Hendrix had married the daughter of a grain and feed merchant and seemed in a fair way to prosper had it not been for his one fault. On the death of his father-in-law in 1950 he proceeded to drink away the profits of the business he had inherited and died therefrom but not before he sired a son, Henry Hendrix.

Hardin looked at his notebook bleakly. The substitution of the son for the father had not made his task any easier. He had reported to Gunnarsson only to be told abruptly to find young Hendrix and to stop belly-aching, and there followed further weeks of searching because Henry Hendrix had become a drop-out – an undocumented man – after leaving high school, but a combination of legwork, persistence and luck had brought Hardin to the San Fernando Valley in California where he was marooned in his car.

It was nearly three-quarters of an hour before the rain eased off and he decided to take a chance and get out. He swore as he put his foot into six inches of water and then squelched across the street towards the neat white house. He sheltered on the porch, shaking the wetness from his coat, then pressed the bell and heard chimes.

Presently the door opened cautiously, held by a chain, and an eye and a nose appeared at the narrow opening. 'I'm looking for Henry Hendrix,' Hardin said, and flipped open a notebook. 'I'm told he lives here.'

'No one by that name here.' The door began to close.

Hardin said quickly, 'This *is* 82, Thorndale?'

'Yeah, but my name's Parker. No one called Hendrix here.'

'How long have you lived here, Mr Parker?'

'Who wants to know?'

'I'm sorry.' Hardin extracted a card from his wallet and poked it at the three-inch crack in the doorway. 'My name is Hardin.'

The card was taken in two fingers and vanished. Parker said, 'Gunnarsson Associates. You a private dick?'

'I guess you could call me that,' said Hardin tiredly.

'This Hendrix in trouble?'

'Not that I know of, Mr Parker. Could be the other way round, from what I hear. Could be good news for Hendrix.'

'Well, I'll tell you,' said Parker. 'We've lived here eight months.'

'Who did you buy the house from?'

'Didn't buy,' said Parker. 'We rent. The owner's an old biddy who lives in Pasadena.'

'And you don't know the name of the previous tenant? He left no forwarding address?' There was not much hope in Hardin's voice.

'Nope.' Parker paused. ''Course, my wife might know. She did all the renting business.'

'Would it be possible to ask her?'

'I guess so. Wait a minute.' The door closed leaving Hardin looking at a peeling wooden panel. He heard a murmur of voices from inside the house and presently the door opened again and a woman peered at him then disappeared. He heard her say, 'Take the chain off the door, Pete.'

'Hell, Milly; you know what they told us about L.A.'

16

'Take the chain off,' said Milly firmly. 'What kind of a life is it living behind bolts and bars?'

The door closed, there was a rattle, and then it opened wide. 'Come on in,' said Mrs Parker. 'It ain't fit for a dog being out today.'

Thankfully Hardin stepped over the threshold. Parker was a burly man of about forty-five with a closed, tight face, but Milly Parker smiled at Hardin. 'You want to know about the Hendersons, Mr Hardin?'

Hardin repressed the sinking feeling. 'Hendrix, Mrs Parker.'

'Could have sworn it was Henderson. But come into the living room and sit down.'

Hardin shook his head. 'I'm wet; don't want to mess up your furniture. Besides, I won't take up too much of your time. You think the previous tenant was called Henderson?'

'That's what I thought. I could have been wrong.' She laughed merrily. 'I often am.'

'Was there a forwarding address?'

'I guess so; there was a piece of paper,' she said vaguely. 'I'll look in the bureau.' She went away.

Hardin looked at Parker and tried to make light conversation. 'Get this kind of weather often?'

'I wouldn't know,' said Parker briefly. 'Haven't been here long.'

Hardin heard drawers open in the next room and there was the rustle of papers. 'The way I hear it this is supposed to be the Sunshine State. Or is that Florida?'

Parker grunted. 'Rains both places; but you wouldn't know to hear the Chambers of Commerce tell it.'

Mrs Parker came back. 'Can't find it,' she announced. 'It was just a little bitty piece of paper.' She frowned. 'Seems I recollect an address. I know it was off Ventura Boulevard; perhaps in Sherman Oaks or, maybe, Encino.'

Hardin winced; Ventura Boulevard was a hundred miles long. Parker said abruptly, 'Didn't you give the paper to that other guy?'

'What other guy?' asked Hardin.

'Why, yes; I think I did,' said Mrs Parker. 'Now I think of it. A nice young man. He was looking for Henderson, too.'

Hardin sighed. 'Hendrix,' he said. 'Who was this young man?'

'Didn't bother to ask,' said Parker. 'But he was a foreigner – not American. He had a funny accent like I've never heard before.'

Hardin questioned them further but got nothing more, then said, 'Well, could I have the address of the owner of the house. She might know.' He got the address and also the address of the local realtor who had negotiated the rental. He looked at his watch and found it was late. 'Looks like the day's shot. Know of a good motel around here?'

'Why, yes,' she said. 'Go south until you hit Riverside, then turn west. There are a couple along there before you hit the turning to Laurel Canyon.'

He thanked them and left, hearing the door slam behind him and the rattle of the chain. It was still raining; not so hard as before but still enough to drench him before he reached the shelter of his car. He was wet and gloomy as he drove away.

* * *

His motel room was standard issue and dry. He took off his wet suit and hung it over the bath, regarded it critically, and decided it needed pressing. He wondered if Gunnarsson would stand for that on the expense account. Then he took off his shirt, hung it next to the suit, and padded into the bedroom in his underwear. He sat at the table, opened his briefcase, and took out a sheaf of papers which he spread out and regarded dispiritedly. His shoulders sagged and he looked exactly what he was – a failure. A man pushing fifty-five with a pot belly, his once muscular body now running to fat, his brains turning to mush, and the damned dandruff was making his hair fall out. Every time he looked at his comb he was disgusted.

Ben Hardin once had such high hopes. He had majored in languages at the University of Illinois and when he had been approached by the recruiter he had been flattered. Although the approach had been subtle he was not fooled; the campus was rife with rumours about the recruiters and everyone knew what they were recruiting for. And so he had fallen for the flattery and responded to the appeals to his patriotism because this was the height of the Cold War and everyone knew the Reds were the enemy.

So they had taken him and taught him to shoot – handgun, rifle, machine-gun – taught him unarmed combat, how to hold his liquor and how to make others drunk. They told him of drops and cut-outs, of codes and cyphers, how to operate a radio and many other more esoteric things. Then he had reported to Langley as a fully fledged member of the CIA only to be told bluntly that he knew nothing and was the lowest of the low on the totem pole.

In the years that followed he gained in experience. He worked in Australia, England, Germany and East Africa. Sometimes he found himself working inside his own country which he found strange because the continental United States was supposed to be the stamping ground of the FBI and off-limits to the CIA. But he obeyed orders and did what he was told and eventually found that more than half his work was in the United States.

Then came Watergate and everything broke loose. The Company sprang more holes than a sieve and everyone rushed to plug up the leaks, but there seemed to be more informers than loyal Company men. Newspaper pages looked like extracts from the CIA files, and the shit began to fly. There were violent upheavals as the top brass defended themselves against the politicians, director followed director, each one publicly dedicated to cleaning house, and heads duly rolled, Hardin's among them.

He had been genuinely shocked at what had happened to the Company and to himself. In his view he had been a loyal servant of his country and now his country had turned against him. He was in despair, and it was then that Gunnarsson approached him. They met by appointment in a Washington bar which claimed to sell every brand of beer made in the world. He arrived early and, while waiting for Gunnarsson, ordered a bottle of Swan for which he had developed a taste in Australia.

When Gunnarsson arrived they talked for a while of how the country was going to hell in a handcart and of the current situation at Langley. Then Gunnarsson said, 'What are you going to do now, Ben?'

Hardin shrugged. 'What's to do? I'm a trained agent, that's all. Not many skills for civilian life.'

'Don't you believe it,' said Gunnarsson earnestly. 'Look, Fletcher and I are setting up shop in New York.'

'Doing what?'

'Same racket, but in civilian form. The big corporations are no different than countries. Why, some of the internationals are bigger than goddamn countries, and they've all got secrets to protect – and secrets to find. My God, Ben; the field's wide open but we've got to get in fast before some of the other guys who were canned from Langley have the same idea. We wait too long the competition could be fierce. If this Watergate bullshit goes on much longer retired spooks will be a drug on the market.'

Hardin took a swig of beer. 'You want me in?'

'Yeah. I'm getting together a few guys, all hand picked, and you are one of them – if you want in. With our experience we ought to clean up.' He grinned 'Our experience and the pipelines we've still got into Langley.'

'Sounds good,' said Hardin.

'Only thing is it'll take dough,' said Gunnarsson. 'How much can you chip in?'

Money and Hardin bore a curious relationship. A dollar bill and Hardin were separated by some form of anti-glue – they never could get together. He had tried; God, how he had tried. But his bets never came off, his investments failed, and Hardin was the centre of a circle surrounded by dollar bills moving away by some sort of centrifugal force. He had once been married and the marriage had failed as much by his inability to keep money as by the strain imposed by his work. The alimony payments now due each quarter merely added to the centrifugal force.

Now he shook his head. 'Not a thin dime,' he said. 'I'm broke and getting broker. Annette's cheque is due Tuesday and I don't know how I'm going to meet that.'

Gunnarsson looked disappointed. 'As bad as that?'

'Worse,' said Hardin glumly. 'I've got to get a job fast and I have to sweet talk Annette. Those two things are holding my whole attention.'

'Gee, Ben; I was hoping you'd be in with us. There's nobody I'd rather have along, and Fletcher agrees with me. Only the other day he was talking about how ingeniously you shafted that guy in Dar-es-Salaam.' He drummed his fingers on the table. 'Okay, you don't have money, but maybe something can be worked out. It won't be as sweet a deal as if you came in as a partner but it'll be better than anything else you can get. And we still want you along because we think you're a good guy and you know the business.'

So a deal had been worked out and Hardin went to work for Gunnarsson and Fletcher Inc. not as a partner but as an employee with a reasonable salary. At first he was happy, but over the years things began to go wrong. Gunnarsson became increasingly hard-nosed and the so-called partnership fell apart. Fletcher was squeezed out and Gunnarsson and Fletcher Inc. became Gunnarsson Associates. Gunnarsson was the ramrod and let no one forget it.

And Hardin himself lost his drive and initiative. No longer buoyed by patriotism he became increasingly dissatisfied with the work he was doing which in his view fulfilled no more elevating a function than to increase the dividends of shareholders and buttress the positions of corporate fatcats. And he was uneasy because a lot of it was downright illegal.

He fell down on a couple of jobs and Gunnarsson turned frosty and from then on he noted that he had been downgraded as a field agent and was relegated to the minor investigations about which no one gave a damn. Like the Hendrix case.

Hardin lay on the bed in the motel and blew a smoke ring at the ceiling. Come on, Hardin, he thought. You've nearly got a Hendrix – you're nearly there, man. Think of the bonus Gunnarsson will pay you. Think of Annette's alimony.

He smiled wryly as he remembered that Parker had referred to him as a 'private dick'. Parker had been reading too many mysteries. Natural enough, though; wasn't this Chandler country; Philip Marlowe country; 'down these mean streets a man must go' country? Come on, you imitation Marlowe, he said to himself. Get off your ass and do something.

He swung his legs sideways, sat on the edge of the bed, and reached for the telephone. From what he had gathered the owner of the Parker house operated from her home in Pasadena, and it was still not too late in the evening to talk to her. He checked the number in his notebook and dialled. After a few buzzes a voice said in his ear, 'The White residence.'

The White House! He suppressed an inane chuckle, and said, 'Mrs White?'

'It is she speaking.'

'My name is Hardin, and I represent Gunnarsson Associates of New York. I understand you own a house in North Hollywood.'

'I own several houses in North Hollywood,' she said. 'To which do you refer?'

'It would be 82, Thorndale; at present rented by Mr Parker.'

'Yes, I own that property, but it is rented to Mrs Parker.'

'I see; but I have no interest in the Parkers, Mrs White. I am interested in a previous tenant, a man called Hendrix. Henry Hendrix.'

'Oh, him!' There was a sudden sharpness to Mrs White's voice. 'What is your business, Mr Hardin?'

'I'm a private investigator.'

'A private eye,' said Mrs White, confirming his theory that he was in mystery readers' country. 'Very interesting, I must say. What do you want *him* for? Nothing trivial, I hope.'

He explored the nuances of her voice, and said, 'I can't tell you, Mrs White. I just find them; what happens to them is out of my hands.'

'Well, I hope that young man gets his comeuppance,' she said bitterly. 'He *wrecked* that house. It took me thirty-five hundred dollars to repair the damage done by him and his friends.'

'I'm sorry to hear that,' said Hardin, injecting sincerity into his voice. 'How did it happen?'

'He – Hendrix, I mean – rented the house and agreed to abide by all the conditions. What I didn't know was that he was leader of what they call a commune. You *know*; those young people who go around with dirty feet and the men wearing head bands.' Hardin smiled. 'Mrs Parker tells me the place still stinks of marijuana. And the filth they left there you wouldn't believe.'

'And when did they leave?'

'They didn't *leave*, they were thrown out,' said Mrs White triumphantly. 'I had to call the Sheriff's Department.'

'But when was this?'

'Must be nine . . . no, ten months ago.'

'Any idea where they went?'

'I don't know, and I don't care. For all I care they could go drown, only it would dirty up the ocean.'

'You say Hendrix was the leader of the commune?'

'He paid the rent.' Mrs White paused. 'But no; I don't reckon he was the leader. I think they used him as a front man because he was cleanest. The leader was a man they called Biggie. Big man – tall as a skyscraper and wide as a barn door.'

Hardin made a note. 'Do you know his name – his last name?'

'No; they just called him Biggie. He had long blond hair,' she said. 'Hadn't been washed for months. Kept it out of his eyes with one of those head bands. Shaggy beard. He walked around with his shirt open to the waist. Disgusting! Oh, and he wore something funny round his neck.'

'What sort of funny?'

'A cross. Not a decent Christian cross but a funny cross with a loop at the top. It looked like gold and he wore it on a chain. You couldn't help but notice it the way he wore his shirt open.'

'Were there any women in the commune, Mrs White?'

'There were. A lot of brazen hussies. But I didn't have any truck with them. But I'll tell you something, Mr Hardin. There were so many of those folks in that little house they must have slept head-to-foot. I don't think there could have been a virgin among them, and I don't think they were married, either.'

'You're probably right,' said Hardin.

'Orgies!' said Mrs White, relishing the word. 'We found a lot of incense sticks in the house and some funny statues, and they weren't made in the way God made man. I knew then I was right to get rid of that man. Could have been another Charles Manson. You heard of him back East?'

'Yes, I've heard of Charles Manson.' Hardin closed his notebook. 'Thank you for your information, Mrs White; you've been very co-operative.'

'Are you going to put those folks in jail where they belong?'

'I'm a private investigator, Mrs White; but if I find evidence of wrongdoing I'll pass the information on to the authorities. Thanks for your help.'

He put down the telephone, lit another cigarette, and lay back on the bed. Incense sticks and strange statues! And the funny cross with the loop at the top was probably an Egyptian ankh. He shook his head. God, the things the kids were up to these days.

He wondered briefly who else was looking for Hendrix and then closed his eyes.

3

Hardin walked out of his room next morning into a day that was rainwashed and crisp. He put his bags into his car and drove to the front of the motel. As he got out he looked in astonishment towards the north. There, stretched across the horizon, was a range of mountains with snow-capped peaks rising to a height of maybe 10,000 feet. They had not been there the previous day and they looked like a theatrical backdrop.

'Hollywood!' he muttered, as he went into the inside for breakfast.

Later, as he was tucking his credit card back into his wallet, he said, 'What are those mountains out there?'

The woman behind the desk did not raise her head. 'What mountains?' she asked in an uninterested way.

'That range of mountains with snow on the top.'

She looked up. 'Are you kidding, mister? There are no mountains out there.'

He said irritably, 'Goddamn it! They're practically on your doorstep. I'm not kidding.'

'This I've got to see.' She came from behind the desk and accompanied him to the door where she stopped and gasped. 'Jesus, those are the San Gabriels! I haven't seen them in ten years.'

'Now who's kidding who?' asked Hardin. 'How could you miss a thing like that?'

Her eyes were shining. 'Musta been the rain,' she said. 'Washed all the smog outa the air. Mister, take a good look; you ain't likely to see a sight like that for a long time.'

'Nuts!' said Hardin shaking his head, and walked towards his car.

As he drove downtown he pondered on the peculiarities of Los Angeles. Any community that could lose a range of mountains 10,000 feet high and 40 miles long was definitely out of whack. Hardin disliked Los Angeles and would not visit it for pleasure. He did not like the urban sprawl, so featureless and monotonous that any section of the city was like any other section. He did not like the nutty architecture; for his money it was a waste of time to drive down to Anaheim to visit Disneyland – you could see Disneyland anywhere in L.A. And he did not like the Los Angeles version of the much lauded Californian climate. The smog veiled the sun and set up irritation in his mucous membranes. If it did not rain, bush fires raged over the hills burning out whole tracts of houses. When it rained you got a year's supply inside twelve hours and mud slides pushed houses into the sea at Malibu. And any day now the San Andreas Fault was expected to crack and rip the whole tacky place apart. Who would voluntarily live in such a hell of a city?

Answer: five million nuts. Which brought his mind back smartly to Hendrix, Biggie and the commune. To hell with Gunnarsson; he would go see Charlie Wainwright.

The Los Angeles office of Gunnarsson Associates was on Hollywood Boulevard at the corner of Highland, near Grauman's Chinese Theatre. His card got him in to see Charlie Wainwright, boss of the West Coast region, who said, 'Hi, Ben; what are you doing over here?'

'Slumming,' said Hardin as he sat down. 'You don't think I'd come here if I had a choice?'

'Still the same old grouch.' Wainwright waved his hand to the window. 'What's wrong with this? It's a beautiful day.'

'Yeah; and the last for ten years,' said Hardin. 'I had that on authority. I'll give you a tip, Charlie. You can get a hell of a view of the San Gabriels today from the top of Mullholland Drive. But don't wait too long; they'll be gone by tomorrow.'

'Maybe I'll take a drive up there.' Wainwright leaned back in his chair. 'What can we do for you, Ben?'

'Have you got a pipeline into the Sheriff's office?'

'That depends on what you want to come down it,' said Wainwright cautiously.

Hardin decided not to mention Hendrix. 'I'm looking for a guy called Biggie. Seems he's mixed up in a commune. They were busted by sheriff's deputies about ten months ago over in North Hollywood.'

'Not the L.A.P.D.?' queried Wainwright. 'Don't they have jurisdiction in North Hollywood?'

Hardin was sure Mrs White had not mentioned the Los Angeles Police Department, but he checked his notebook. 'No; my informant referred to the Sheriff's Department.'

'So what do you want?'

Hardin looked at Wainwright in silence for a moment before saying patiently, 'I want Biggie.'

'That shouldn't be too difficult to arrange.' Wainwright thought a while. 'Might take a little time.'

'Not too long, I hope.' Hardin stood up. 'And do me a favour, Charlie; you haven't seen me. I haven't been here. Especially if Gunnarsson wants to know. He's playing this one close to his chest.'

'How are you getting on with the old bastard?'

'Not bad,' said Hardin noncommittally.

* * *

Two hours later he was in a coffee shop across from City Hall waiting for a deputy from the Sheriff's Department. Wainwright had said, 'Better not see him in his office – might compromise him. You don't have an investigator's licence for this state. What's Gunnarsson up to, Ben? He's not done this before. These things are usually handled by the local office.'

'Maybe he doesn't like me,' said Hardin feelingly, thinking of the miles of interstate highways he had driven.

He was about to order another coffee when a shadow fell across the table. 'You the guy looking for Olaf Hamsun?'

Hardin looked up and saw a tall, lean man in uniform. '*Who?*'

27

'Also known as Biggie,' said the deputy. 'Big blond Scandahoovian – monster size.'

'That's the guy.' He held out his hand. 'I'm Ben Hardin. Coffee?' At the deputy's nod he held up two fingers to a passing waitress.

The deputy sat opposite. 'Jack Sawyer. What do you want with Biggie?'

'Nothing at all. But he's running with Henry Hendrix, and I want to visit with Hank.'

'Hendrix,' said Sawyer ruminatively. 'Youngish – say, twenty-six or twenty-seven; height about five, ten; small scar above left eyebrow.'

'That's probably my boy.'

'What do you want with him?'

'Just to establish that he's his father's son, and then report back to New York.'

'Who wants to know?'

'Some British lawyer according to my boss. That's all I know; Gunnarsson doesn't confide in me. Operates on need to know.'

'Just like all the other ex-CIA cloak and dagger boys,' said Sawyer scornfully. He looked at Hardin carefully. 'You were a Company man, too, weren't you?'

'Don't hold it against me,' said Hardin, forcing a grin.

'Even if I don't that doesn't mean I have to like it. And you don't have an investigator's licence good in California. If I didn't owe Charlie Wainwright a couple I wouldn't be here now. I don't like you guys and I never have.'

'Now wait a minute,' said Hardin. 'What's eating you?'

'I'll tell you.' Sawyer leaned forward. 'Last year we busted a gang smuggling cocaine from Mexico. Turned out that half of them were bastards from the CIA. *They* claimed we'd wrecked one of their best Mexican operations. *We* said they were breaking the law of the United States and we were going to jail them. But do you think we could? Those sons of bitches are walking around free as air right now.'

Hardin said, 'You can't blame that on me.'

'I guess not,' said Sawyer tiredly. 'Okay, I'll tell you where to find Biggie.' He stuck out his forefinger. 'But step out of line one inch and I'll nail your hide to the barn door, even if it's for spitting on the sidewalk.'

'Thanks,' said Hardin ironically.

'You'll find the gang down at Playa del Rey. If they're not there try Santa Monica, down near the Bristol Pier. There's a greasy spoon called Bernie's where they hang out.'

Hardin wrote in his notebook. 'Does Hendrix have a record? Or Hamsun?'

'Hamsun's been busted for peddling pot. He had a fraction under an ounce on him, so it didn't come to much. Nothing on Hendrix; at least, not here.'

'I've been wondering about something,' said Hardin, putting away his notebook. 'When you cracked down on the commune in North Hollywood you found some funny things in the house, I hear. Statues of some kind, and not the kind a good, Christian woman would like.'

'The good, Christian woman being Mrs White,' said Sawyer ironically. 'The old witch. There's nothing to it, Hardin. It's just that the kids tried their hand at pottery; reckoned they could sell the stuff at the Farmer's Market and make a few dollars. That pottery kiln did most of the damage to the house when it blew up.'

'Is that all?'

'That's all,' said Sawyer, and laughed. 'Turned out they weren't very good at sculpting. They didn't know enough anatomy; least, not the kind you need for sculpting.' He became philosophical. 'They're not a bad crowd of kids, not as things are these days. Sure, they smoke pot, but who doesn't. I bet my own kids do when I'm not around. They're just mostly beach bums, and that's not illegal yet.'

'Sure,' said Hardin. He had a sudden thought. 'Does Biggie still wear the ankh?'

'The *what*?'

'The ankh.' He sketched it on the back of the menu.

'Yeah, he still wears that thing. Didn't know it had a name.

It should be valuable. It's big and looks as though it's solid gold. But it would take some real crazy guy to rip it off Biggie.'

* * *

Hardin spent two days at Playa del Rey and drew a blank, so he went up the coast to Santa Monica. He found Bernie's and had a cup of coffee, steering clear of the hamburgers. The place stank of rancid oil and he judged the level of hygiene was good for a jail sentence. The coffee was lousy, too, and there was lipstick on his cup.

He questioned the harassed waitress intermittently as she passed and repassed his table and again drew a blank. Yes, she knew Biggie but had not seen him for some time. No, she didn't know anyone called Hendrix. Hardin pushed aside the unfinished coffee and left.

For another two days he roamed the Santa Monica water front, questioning the kids – the beach bums and surfing freaks – and made little progress. Biggie was well known but no one had seen him around. Hendrix was less known and no one had seen him, either. Hardin looked gloomily at the offshore oil rigs which periodically sprang leaks to poison the fish and kill the seabirds, and he cursed Gunnarsson.

On the evening of the second day he checked again at Bernie's. As he stared distastefully at the grease floating on the surface of his coffee a girl sidled up next to him. 'You the guy looking for Biggie?'

He turned his head. Her long uncombed hair was a dirty blonde and her make-up had been applied sloppily so that she looked like a kid who had just used the contents of her mother's dressing table for the first time. 'I'm the guy,' he said briefly.

'He don't like it.'

'I'm broken-hearted.'

She made a face. 'But he'll talk to you.'

'When and where?'

'Tonight – eight o'clock. There's an old warehouse on

Twenty-seventh Street at Carlyle. He'll be there.'

'Look,' said Hardin. 'I'm not interested in Biggie, but he has a sidekick called Hendrix – Hank Hendrix. Know him?'

'Sure.'

'He's the guy I want to talk with. Let him be at the warehouse. I don't give a damn about Biggie.'

The girl shrugged. 'I'll pass the word.'

* * *

Hardin was at the rendezvous an hour early. The abandoned warehouse was in a depressed area long overdue for urban renewal; the few windows still intact were grimy, and the place looked as though it would collapse if an over-zealous puff of air blew in from the Pacific. He tested a door, found it unlocked, and went inside.

It took only a few minutes to find that the building was empty. He explored thoroughly, his footsteps echoing in the cavernous interior, and found a locked door at the back. He unlocked it and returned to his car where he sat with a good view of the front entrance and lit a cigarette.

Biggie and Hendrix showed up halfway through the third cigarette. Biggie was unmistakable; tall and broad he looked like a circus strong man, and there was a glint of gold on his bare chest. Hendrix, who walked next to him, was no lightweight but next to Biggie he looked like a midget. They went into the warehouse and Hardin finished his cigarette before getting out of the car and crossing the road.

He entered the warehouse and found Biggie sitting on a crate. Hendrix was nowhere to be seen. Biggie stood up as he approached. 'I'm Ben Hardin. You'll be Olaf Hamsun, right?'

'Could be,' conceded Biggie.

'Where's Hendrix?'

Biggie ignored the question. 'You a pig?' he asked.

Hardin suppressed an insane desire to giggle; the thought of describing himself as a private pig was crazy. Instead, he said mildly, 'Watch your mouth.'

Biggie shrugged. 'Just a manner of speaking. No offence meant. What do you want with Hank?'

'If he wants you to know he'll tell you. Where is he?'

Biggie jerked his thumb over his shoulder. 'Back there. But you talk to me.'

'No way,' said Hardin decidedly.

'Suit yourself. Now shut up and listen to me, buster. I don't like creeps like you asking questions around town. Christ, every Joe I've talked to in the last couple days tells me I'm a wanted man. Hurts my reputation, see?'

'You shouldn't be hard to find.'

'I'm not hiding,' said Biggie. 'But you and your foreign friend bug me.'

'I don't have a foreign friend,' said Hardin.

'No? Then how come he's been asking around, too?'

Hardin frowned. 'Tell me more,' he said. 'How do you know he's foreign?'

'His accent, dummy.'

'I told you to watch your mouth,' said Hardin sharply. He thought for a moment and remembered that Gunnarsson had mentioned a British lawyer. 'Could it be a British accent?'

'You mean like we hear on those longhair programs on TV?' Biggie shook his head. 'No; not like that. This guy has a real foreign accent.' He paused. 'Could be a Kraut,' he offered.

'So you've talked with him.'

'Naw. I had a friend talk with him at Bernie's. I was in the next booth.'

'What did he want?'

'Same as you. He wants to visit with Hank.'

'Can you describe him?'

'Sure. Big guy, well set up; looks like he can handle himself. Short hair, crewcut like a soldier boy.' Biggie scratched his chest absently, his hand moving the golden ankh aside. 'Scar on his cheek.'

'Which side?'

'Left.'

Hardin pondered. All this was adding up to the classic picture of a German soldier except that ritual duelling was no longer acceptable. 'How old is he?'

'Thirty-five – maybe forty. Not more. So you really don't know the guy.'

'I don't give a damn about him and I don't give a damn about you. All I want is to talk to Hendrix. Go get him.'

'You don't give a damn about me, and you don't listen good.' Biggie stuck out his forefinger then tapped himself on the chest. 'The only way to get to Hendrix is through me.'

'Does he know that?' asked Hardin. 'What is he, anyway? Your fancy boy?'

'Christ, that does it,' said Biggie, enraged.

'Oh, shit!' said Hardin resignedly as Biggie flexed his muscles. 'I'm not mad at you, Biggie; I don't want to fight.'

'Well, I want to fight you.' Biggie plunged forward.

It was no contest. Hardin was full of frustrations; his angers at Gunnarsson, the weary miles of travel, his sense of personal failure – all these he worked out on Biggie. He had several advantages; one was that Biggie had never learned how to fight – he never had to because what idiot would want to tangle with a man who was obviously a meat grinder? The idiot was Hardin who had been trained in unarmed combat by experts. In spite of his age and flabbiness he still knew the chopping places and pressure points, the vulnerable parts of a man's body, and he used his knowledge mercilessly. It was only by a deliberate act of will that he restrained himself from the final deadly blow that would have killed.

Breathing heavily he bent down and reached for the pulse at the side of Biggie's neck and sighed with relief as he felt it beating strongly. Then he straightened and turned to see Hendrix watching him.

'Jesus!' said Hendrix. He was wide-eyed as he stared at the prostrate Biggie. 'I didn't think you could beat him.'

'I've taken a lot of shit on this job,' said Hardin, and found his voice was shaking. 'But I wasn't going to take any from him.' He bent down and ripped the golden ankh from

Biggie's neck, breaking the chain. 'And I've been insulted by a cop, a cop who told me this couldn't be done.' He tossed the golden cross down by Biggie's side. 'Now let's you and me talk.'

Hendrix eyed him warily. 'What about?'

'You can start off by telling me your father's name.'

'What's my old man got to do with anything?' said Hendrix in surprise.

'His name, sonny,' said Hardin impatiently.

'Hendrix, of course. Adrian Hendrix.'

'Where was he born?'

'Africa. Some place in South Africa. But he's dead.'

Hardin took a deep breath. This was the one; this was the right Hendrix. 'You got brothers? Sisters? Your Mom still alive?'

'No. What's this all about?'

Hardin said, 'I wouldn't know, but a man in New York called Gunnarsson wants to know.'

'Why?'

'Because a British lawyer wants to know. Maybe you're inheriting something. What about going to New York with me to find out?'

Hendrix scratched his jaw. 'Gee, I don't know. I don't like the East much.'

'Expenses paid,' said Hardin.

Biggie stirred and groaned, and Hendrix looked down at him. 'I guess Biggie will be hard to live with now,' he said reflectively. 'He won't want anyone around who's seen him slaughtered like that. Might not be a bad idea to split for a while.'

'Okay,' said Hardin. 'Is there anything you want to take?'

'Not much,' said Hendrix, and grinned. 'I have a good surfboard but that won't be much use in New York. I'd better take some clothes, though.'

'I'll come help you pack,' said Hardin, and added pointedly, 'I've had a hard time finding you, and I don't want to lose you now.'

4

Hendrix told Hardin where he lived and, as he drove, Hardin thought about the other man looking for Hendrix. Or other men. The man described by Biggie was hardly likely to be the 'nice young man' as described by Mrs Parker. All right, then; two or more men. He said, 'Did Biggie ever say anything about another guy looking for you? Could be a German.'

'Yeah.' Hendrix lit a cigarette. 'He told me. He thought you were together but he wanted to make sure first before...' He broke off suddenly.

'Before what?'

Hendrix laughed shortly. 'Biggie thought there might be some dough in it somewhere. If you and the foreign guy were together, then okay; but if you weren't he figured he could make a trade.'

'Sell you off to the highest bidder?' Hardin grimaced. 'What did you think of that?'

Hendrix shrugged. 'Biggie's all right. It's just that he was short of dough, that's all. We're all short of dough.'

'All?'

'The gang.' He sighed. 'Things haven't been the same since we were busted over in the San Fernando Valley.'

'When you blew up Mrs White's house?'

Hendrix turned his head sharply. 'You've been getting around.' He sounded as though he did not like it. 'But it wasn't all that much. Just some smoky walls and busted glass.'

Hardin came back to his main problem. 'The foreigner. Did you ever meet him?'

'No. Biggie set up a meeting for tonight in case he had something to trade. That's why he wanted to blow you off fast.'

'Where's the meeting?'

'I don't know – we didn't get that far. Man, you sure cooled him.' He pointed. 'That's our place.'

Hardin drew up in front of the dilapidated house. 'I'll come in with you.' He escorted Hendrix to the door and they went in. In the narrow hall they met the girl who had set up the meeting with Biggie. She looked at Hardin with surprise and he thought he detected something of alarm in her eyes.

She turned to Hendrix. 'Where's Biggie?'

'He'll be along. He . . . uh . . . had something to attend to,' said Hendrix. 'Come on, Mr Hardin; we'd better make this fast.'

As they climbed the stairs Hardin thought with amusement that Hendrix had every reason for speed. If Biggie came back and found him in the act of packing he would want to know why and Hendrix would not want to tell him. 'How many in the gang?' he asked.

'It varies; there's six of us now. Have been as many as twelve.' Hendrix opened the door of a room. 'This won't take long.'

It took less time than Hardin would have thought. Hendrix was a nomad and had few possessions, all of which went into a metal-framed backpack. He lifted it effortlessly and then looked regretfully at the surfboard lying against the wall behind the unmade bed. 'Can't take that along, I guess. You sure there are dollars in this, Mr Hardin?'

'No,' said Hardin honestly. 'But I can't think of anything else.'

'You said a British lawyer. I don't know any Britishers and I've never been out of the States.' Hendrix shook his head. 'Still, you said you'll pay my way so it's worth a chance.'

They went downstairs and met the blonde girl again. 'When'll Biggie be back?' she asked.

'He didn't say,' said Hendrix briefly.

She looked at the backpack. 'You going some place?'

'Not far.' Hendrix coughed. 'Just down to . . . uh . .

Mexico, Mr Hardin and me. Got to pick up a package in Tijuana.'

She nodded understandingly. 'Be careful. Those Customs bastards are real nosy. What is it? Pot or snow?'

'Snow,' he said. 'Come on, Mr Hardin.' As they got into the car Hendrix forced a smile. 'No use in letting the world know where we're going.'

'Sure,' said Hardin. 'No point at all.' He switched on the ignition and, as he took off the handbrake, something whined like a bee in front of his nose. Hendrix gave a sharp cry, and Hardin shot a glance at him. He had his hand to his shoulder and blood was oozing through his fingers.

Hardin had been shot at before. He took off, burning rubber, and turned the first corner at top speed. Only then did he look in the mirror to check for pursuers. The corner receded behind him and nothing came into sight so he slowed until he was just below the speed limit. Then he said, 'You all right, Hank?'

'What the hell!' said Hendrix, looking unbelievingly at the blood on his hand. 'What happened?'

'You were stung by a bee,' said Hardin. 'From a silenced gun. Hurt much?'

'You mean I've been shot?' said Hendrix incredulously. 'Who'd want to shoot me?'

'Maybe a guy with a German accent and a scar on his left cheek. Perhaps it's just as well you and Biggie couldn't keep that appointment tonight. How do you feel?'

'Numb,' said Hendrix. 'My shoulder feels numb.'

'The pain comes later.' Hardin still watched the mirror. Everything behind still seemed normal. But he made a couple of random turns before he said, 'We've got to get you off the streets. Can you hold on for a few more minutes?'

'I guess so.'

'There's Kleenex in the glove compartment. Put a pad of it over the wound.'

Hardin drove on to the Santa Monica Freeway and made the interchange on to the San Diego Freeway heading north.

As he drove his mind was busy with speculations. Who had fired the shot? And why? And who was the intended victim? He said, 'I don't know of anyone who wants to kill me. How about you, Hank?'

Hendrix was holding the pad of tissues to his shoulder beneath his shirt. His face was pale. 'Hell, no!'

'You told the girl back there we were going to Tijuana to pick up a package of cocaine.'

'Ella? I had to tell her something to put Biggie off.'

'She didn't seem surprised. You've done that often? The cocaine bit, I mean.'

'A couple of times,' Hendrix admitted. 'But it's small time stuff.'

'A man can make enemies that way,' said Hardin. 'You might have stepped on someone's turf. The big boys don't like that and they don't forget.'

'No way,' said Hendrix. 'The last time I did it was over a year ago.' He nursed his shoulder. 'What the hell are you getting me into, Hardin?'

'I'm not getting you into anything; I'm doing my best to get you out.'

They were silent for a long time after that, each busy with his thoughts. Hardin changed on to the Ventura Freeway and headed east. 'Where are we going?' asked Hendrix.

'To a motel. But we'll stop by a drugstore first and pick up some bandages and medication.'

'Jesus! I need a doctor.'

'We'll see about that when you're under cover and rested.' Hardin did not add that gunshot wounds had to be reported to the police. He had to think about that.

He pulled into the motel on Riverside Drive where he had stayed before and booked two rooms. The woman behind the desk was the one he had seen before. He said casually, 'The San Gabriels have vanished again.'

'Yeah; it's a damn shame,' she said, a little forlornly. 'I bet we don't see them again for another ten years.'

He smiled. 'Still, it's nice to see the air we're breathing.'

He got Hendrix into his room, examined his shoulder, and was relieved by what he saw. It was a flesh wound and the bullet had missed the bone; however, it had not come out the other side and was still in Hendrix. He said, 'You'll live. It's only a · 22 – a pee-wee.'

Hendrix grunted. 'It feels like I've been kicked by a horse.'

As he dressed the wound Hardin puzzled over the calibre of the bullet. It could mean one of two things; the gun had been fired either by an amateur or a very good professional. Only a good professional killer would use a · 22, a man who could put his bullets where he wanted them. He tied the last knot and adjusted the sling. 'I have a bottle in my bag,' he said. 'I guess we both need a drink.'

He brought the whiskey and some ice and made two drinks, then he departed for his own room, the glass still in his hand. 'Stick around,' he said on leaving. 'Lie low like Brer Rabbit. I won't be long.' He wanted to talk to Gunnarsson.

'Where would I go?' asked Hendrix plaintively.

* * *

On the telephone Gunnarsson was brusque. 'Make it quick, Ben; I'm busy.'

'I've got young Hendrix,' said Hardin without preamble. 'Only trouble is someone just put a bullet in him.'

'God damn it!' said Gunnarsson explosively. 'When?'

'Less than an hour ago. I'd just picked him up.'

'How bad is he?'

'He's okay, but the slug's still in him. It's only a · 22 but the wound might go bad. He needs a doctor.'

'Is he mobile?'

'Sure,' said Hardin. 'He can't run a four-minute mile but he can move. It's a flesh wound in the shoulder.'

There was a pause before Gunnarsson said, 'Who knows about this?'

'You, me, Hendrix and the guy who shot him,' said Hardin factually.

'And who the hell was that?'

'I don't know. Someone else is looking for Hendrix; I've crossed his tracks a couple of times. A foreign guy – could be German. That's all I know.' Hardin sipped his whiskey. 'What is all this with Hendrix? Is there something I should know that you haven't told me? I wouldn't like that.'

'Ben; it beats me, it really does,' said Gunnarsson sincerely. 'Now, look, Ben; no doctor. Get that kid to New York as fast as you can. Come by air. I'll have a doctor standing by here.'

'But what about my car?'

'You'll get it back,' said Gunnarsson soothingly. 'The company will pay for delivery.'

Hardin did not like that idea. The car would be entrusted to some punk kid who would drive too fast, mis-treat the engine, forget to check the oil, and most likely end up in a total wreck. 'All right,' he said reluctantly. 'But I won't fly from Los Angeles. I think there's more than one guy looking for Hendrix and the airport might be covered. I'll drive up to San Francisco and fly from there. You'll have your boy the day after tomorrow.'

'Good thinking, Ben,' said Gunnarsson, and rang off.

* * *

They left for San Francisco early next morning. It was over 300 miles but Hardin made good time on Interstate 5 ignoring the 55 mph speed limit like everyone else. He went with the traffic flow, only slowing a little when he had the road to himself. If you stayed inside the speed limit you could get run down, and modern cars were not designed to travel so slowly on good roads.

Hendrix seemed all right although he favoured his wounded shoulder. He had complained about not being seen by a doctor, but shut up when Hardin said, 'That means getting into a hassle with the law. You want that?' Apparently not, and neither did Hardin. He had not forgotten what Deputy Sawyer had said about spitting on the sidewalk.

Hendrix had also been naturally curious about why he was

being taken to New York. 'Don't ask me questions, son,' Hardin said, 'because I don't know the answers. I just do what the man says.'

He was irked himself at not knowing the answers so, when they stopped for gas, he took Hendrix into a Howard Johnson for coffee and doughnuts and did a little pumping of his own. Although he knew the answer he said, 'Maybe your old man left you a pile.'

'Fat chance,' said Hendrix. 'He died years ago when I was a kid.' He shook his head. 'Mom said he was a deadbeat, anyway.'

'You said she was dead too, right?'

'Yeah.' Hendrix smiled wryly. 'I guess you could call me an orphan.'

'Got any other folks? Uncles, maybe?'

'No.' Hendrix paused as he stirred his coffee. 'Yeah, I have a cousin in England. He wrote to me when I was in high school, said he was coming to the States and would like to meet me. He never did, but he wrote a couple more times. Not lately, though. I guess he's lost track of me. I've been moving around.'

'What's his name?'

'Funny thing about that. Same as mine but spelled differently. Dirk Hendriks. H-E-N-D-R-I-K-S.'

'Your father spelled his name the same way when he was in South Africa,' said Hardin. 'Have you got your cousin's address?'

'Somewhere in London, that's all I know. I had it written down but I lost it. You know how it is when you're moving around.'

'Yeah,' said Hardin. 'Maybe he's died and left you something. Or maybe he's just looking for you.'

Hendrix felt his shoulder. 'Someone sure is,' he said.

* * *

So it was that Hardin saw Gunnarsson sooner than he expected. Hardin and Hendrix took a cab from Kennedy

Airport direct to Gunnarsson Associates and he was shown into Gunnarsson's office fast. Gunnarsson was sitting behind his desk and asked abruptly, 'You've got the Hendrix kid?'

'He's right there in your outer office. You got a doctor? He's in pain.'

Gunnarsson laughed. 'I've got something to cure his pain. Are you sure he's the guy?'

'He checks out right down the line.'

Gunnarsson frowned. 'You're sure.'

'I'm sure. But you'll check yourself, of course.'

'Yeah,' said Gunnarsson. 'I'll check.' He doodled on a piece of paper. 'Does the guy have kids?'

'None that he'll plead guilty to – he's not married.' Hardin was wondering why Gunnarsson did not invite him to sit.

Gunnarsson said, 'Now tell me how Hendrix got shot.'

So Hardin told it all in detail and they kicked it around for a while. At last he said, 'I guess I earned that bonus. This case got a mite tough at the end.'

'What bonus?'

Hardin stared. 'You said I'd get a bonus if I tracked down any Hendrixes.'

Gunnarsson was blank-faced. 'That's not my recollection.'

'Well, I'll be goddamned,' said Hardin softly. 'My memory isn't that bad.'

'Why would I offer you a bonus?' asked Gunnarsson. 'You know damned well we've been carrying you the last couple of years. Some of the guys have been bending my ear about it; they said they were tired of carrying a passenger.'

'Which guys?' demanded Hardin. 'Name the names.'

'You're on the wrong side of the desk to be asking the questions.'

Hardin was trembling. He could not remember when he had been so angry. He said tightly, 'As you get older you become more of a cheapskate, Gunnarsson.'

'That I don't have to take.' Gunnarsson put his hands flat on the desk. 'You're fired. By the time you've cleaned out your desk the cashier will have your severance pay ready.

Now get the hell out of my office.' As he picked up the telephone Hardin turned away blindly. The door slammed and Gunnarsson snorted in derision.

* * *

Hardin took the elevator to the lobby and crossed the street to the Irish bar where, in the past, he had spent more time than was good for either his liver or his wallet. He sat on a stool and said brusquely, 'Double bourbon.'

Over the drink he brooded on his fate. Damn Gunnarsson! It had never been Hardin's style to complain that life was unfair; in his view life was what you made it. Yet now he thought that Gunnarsson had not only been unfair but vindictive. Canned and out on his ear after five minutes' conversation – the bum's rush.

He viewed the future glumly. What was a man aged fifty-five with no particular marketable skills to do? He could set up on his own, he supposed; find an office, put some ads in the paper, and sit back and wait for clients – a seedy Sam Spade. Likely he'd have to wait a long time and starve while waiting. More likely he'd end up carrying a gun for Brinks or become a bank guard and get corns on his feet from too much standing.

And his car, goddamn it! He and his car were separated by three thousand miles. He knew that if he went back to Gunnarsson and reminded him of the promise to bring the car back to New York Gunnarsson would laugh in his face.

He ordered another drink and went over the events of the last few weeks. Gunnarsson *had* promised him a bonus if he cracked the Hendrix case, so why had he reneged on the offer? It wasn't as though Gunnarsson Associates were broke – the money was rolling in as though there was a pipeline from Fort Knox. There had to be a definite reason.

Come to think of it the Hendrix case had been a funny one right from the beginning. It was not Gunnarsson Associates' style to send a man freelancing all over the country – not when they had all those regional offices. So why had

43

Gunnarsson handled it that way? And the way he had been fired was too damned fast. Gunnarsson had deliberately needled him, forcing an argument and wanting Hardin to blow his top. Any boss was entitled to fire a man who called him a cheapskate.

Dim suspicions burgeoned in Hardin's mind.

His musings were interrupted by a hand on his shoulder and a voice said, 'Hi, Ben; I thought you were on the West Coast.'

Hardin turned his head and saw Jack Richardson. 'I was,' he said sourly. 'But how did you know?'

'I had to call the Los Angeles office this morning. Wainwright said you'd been around. What's your poison?'

'Make it bourbon.' So Wainwright couldn't keep his big mouth shut after all. Richardson ran the files at Gunnarsson Associates; the records were totally computerized and Richardson knew which buttons to push. Now Hardin regarded him with interest. 'Jack, did you hear any of the guys in the office beefing about me? Complaining of how I do my work, for instance?'

Richardson looked surprised. 'Not around me. No more than the usual anyway. Everyone beefs some, you know that.'

'Yeah.' Hardin sipped his whiskey. 'Gunnarsson canned me this morning.'

Richardson whistled. 'Just like that?'

Hardin snapped his fingers. 'Just like that. Took him about thirty seconds.'

'Why?'

'I called him a cheapskate for one thing.'

'I'd have liked to have seen his face,' said Richardson. 'No wonder he fired you.'

'I don't think it was the reason,' said Hardin. 'I think it was something else. Could you do me a favour?'

'I might, depending on what it is. Don't ask for dough, Ben. I'm broke.'

'Who isn't?' said Hardin feelingly. 'I'd like you to ask your

44

metal friend across the street for the name and address of the British lawyer who started the Hendrix case.'

'The Hendrix case,' repeated Richardson, and frowned. 'Gunnarsson seems to be keeping that one under wraps. He says he's handling it personally. I don't have any information on it so far.'

Hardin found that interesting but he made no comment. 'But the details of the original letter from England should be in the files.'

'I guess so,' said Richardson without enthusiasm. 'But you know how Gunnarsson is about security. The computer logs every inquiry into any case and Gunnarsson checks the log.'

'He can't check every log; he'd be doing nothing else.'

'Spot checks mostly,' admitted Richardson. 'But if he's handling the Hendrix case personally that's one log he might very well check. I can't risk it, Ben. I don't want to get fired, too.'

'For Christ's sake!' said Hardin in disgust. 'You know enough about the computer to gimmick a log. You wrote the goddamn programs for the data base.'

'What's your interest in this?'

'I'm damned if I know; I've got to do some hard thinking. There's something wrong somewhere. I feel it in my bones. But, for your information, Gunnarsson isn't handling the Hendrix case. I've been handling it, and I cracked it. Then I get fired. I'd like to figure out why I was fired.'

'Okay, Ben; I'll see what I can do,' said Richardson. 'But you don't talk about this. You keep your mouth zipped.'

'Who would I talk to? When can I have it?'

'I'll see what I can do tomorrow. I'll meet you in here at midday.'

'That's fine,' said Hardin and drained his glass. 'This one's on me. Then I'll go clean out my desk like a good boy.' He signalled the bartender. 'I wonder what Gunnarsson's idea of severance pay is.'

5

Gunnarson's idea of severance pay made Hardin madder than ever. He tried to complain but could not get past the acidulated spinster who guarded Gunnarsson's office, and neither could he get through on the phone. Gunnarsson's castle was impregnable.

But Richardson came up with the information he needed next day. He gave Hardin an evelope and said, 'You don't know where you got it.'

'Okay.' Hardin opened the envelope and took out a single piece of paper. 'This isn't a computer print-out.'

'You're damned right it isn't,' said Richardson. 'If Gunnarsson found a print-out with that information floating loose he'd head straight for me. Is it what you want?'

Hardin scanned it. A London inquiry agency, Peacemore, Willis and Franks, requested Gunnarsson Associates to search for any living relatives of Jan-Willem Hendrykxx -- Hardin blinked at the spelling – and to pass the word back. Hendrykxx was reputed to have married in South Africa and to have had two sons, one of whom was believed to have emigrated to the United States in the 1930s. There was also the address and telephone number of a lawyer in Jersey.

It told Hardin nothing he did not know already except for the unusual spelling of Hendrix, and the Jersey address confused him until he realized that it referred to the original Jersey in the Channel Islands and not the state of New Jersey. He nodded. 'This is it.' There was something more. Peacemore, Willis and Franks was the British end of Gunnarsson Associates, a fact not generally known. It meant that Gunnarsson had been in it right from the start, whatever 'it' was. 'Thanks. It's worth a drink, Jack.'

If Hardin was mad at Gunnarsson he was also broke. He moved out of his apartment on the East Side and into a rooming house in the Bronx. It cost more in subway and bus fares to get into Manhattan but it was still cheaper. He wired instructions to San Francisco to sell his car and wire the money. He did not expect much but he needed the cash, and a car was a needless luxury in the city.

He carefully maintained his pipelines into the offices of Gunnarsson Associates, mainly through Jack Richardson, although there were a couple of secretaries whom he took to frugal lunches and pumped carefully, trying to get a line on what Gunnarsson was doing in the matter of Hank Hendrix. The answer, apparently, was nothing at all. Worse still, Hendrix had vanished.

'Maybe Gunnarsson sent him to England,' Richardson said one day.

'You can check that,' said Hardin thoughtfully. 'There'll be an expense account for the air fare. Do me a favour.'

'Goddamn it!' said Richardson heatedly. 'You'll get me fired.' But he checked and found no record of transatlantic flights since Hendrix had arrived in New York. On his own initiative he checked for any record of medical expenses paid out for the treatment of Hendrix's wound and, again, found nothing. He was a good friend to Hardin.

'Gunnarsson is playing this one close,' commented Hardin. 'He's usually damned hot on record keeping. I'm more and more convinced that the bastard's up to no good. But what the hell is it?'

Richardson had no suggestions.

Probably Hardin would not have pressed on but for a genuine stroke of luck. Nearly a month had passed and he knew he had to get a job. His resentment at Gunnarsson had fuelled him thus far but an eroding bank account was a stronger argument. He had set aside enough for Annette's next payment and that he would not touch, but his own reserves were melting.

Then he got a wire from Annette. 'GOT MARRIED THIS

'Thank God!' he said to Richardson. 'Now some other guy can maintain her.' Briefly he wondered what sort of a man this stranger, Kreiss, was then put the matter out of his mind. For he was now the master of unexpected wealth and his heart was filled with jubilation. 'Now I can do it,' he said.

'Do what?' asked Richardson.

'I'm flying to England.'

'You're nuts!' Richardson protested. 'Ben, this obsession is doing you no good. What can you do in England?'

'I don't know,' said Hardin cheerfully. 'But I'll find out when I get there. I haven't had a vacation in years.'

Before leaving for England he flew to Washington on the shuttle where he renewed acquaintance with some of his old buddies in the Company and armed himself with some British addresses, and he visited the British Embassy where he ran into problems. No one knew much about Jersey.

'They're autonomous,' he was told. 'They have their own way of doing things. You say you want to know about a will?'

'That's right.'

'In London a copy would be kept in Somerset House,' said the attaché. 'But I don't think that applies to Jersey wills.' He thought for a moment then his face lightened. 'I do believe we have someone who would know.' He picked up a telephone and dialled, then said, 'Pearson here. Mark, you're a Jerseyman, aren't you? Yes I thought so. Would you mind popping in here for a moment?' Pearson put down the telephone. 'Mark le Tissier should know about it.'

And Mark le Tissier did. 'Wills are kept in the Greffe,' he said.

'The *what*?'

'The Greffe.' Le Tissier smiled. 'The Public Records Office. I had the same problem a couple of years ago. They'll give you a copy.'

'All I have to do is to go to this place, the Greffe, and ask?'

'Oh you don't have to *go*. Just drop a line to the Greffier. We'll go into the library and dig out his address.'

So Hardin went back to New York and wrote to Jersey, giving as return address *poste restante* at the London office of American Express. A few days later he flew and the day he left from Kennedy Airport the rooming house in the Bronx in which he lived burned to the ground though he did not know about it until long after. Still, it could have been chance; there are, after all, whole blocks burned out in the Bronx.

* * *

In the employment of Gunnarsson Associates Hardin had learned how to travel light. He freshened up before landing at Heathrow in the early morning and cleared Customs quickly while the rest of the passengers were waiting for their baggage, then took the Underground into London where he registered at an inexpensive hotel near Victoria Station. He then walked through St James's Park towards the Haymarket where he picked up his mail.

He enjoyed the walk. The sun was shining and he felt oddly contented and in a holiday mood as he strolled by the lake. It was true that it had been some years since he had taken a real vacation. Perhaps he had been getting in a rut and the split with Gunnarsson was to be good for him in the long run. He had little money and no prospects but he was happy.

After leaving the American Express Office Hardin bought a street plan of London from a news vendor because, although he was no stranger to London, it was many years since he had been there. Then he went into a pub to inspect the single letter he had received. The envelope was bulky and bore Jersey stamps. He ordered a half pint of beer at the bar and took it to a corner table, then opened the envelope.

The will was seven pages long. Jan-Willem Hendrykxx had left £10,000 to Dr Morton, his physician, as a token of esteem for keeping him alive so long, £20,000 to Mr and

Mrs Adams, his butler and housekeeper, and various sums of between £1,000 and £4,000 to various members of his staff, which appeared to be large.

Detailed instructions were given for the sale of his real property of which he had a plenitude; a house in Jersey, another in the South of France, yet another in Belgium, and a whole island in the Caribbean. The sums arising from these sales and from the sale of his other possessions were to be added to the main part of his estate. Hendrykxx had evidently been a careful man because the will was up-to-date and he had estimated the current market values of his properties. Thenceforth the terms were expressed in percentages; 85 per cent of his estate was to go to the Ol Njorowa Foundation of Kenya, and 15 per cent to be divided equally among his living descendants.

The name of the executor was given as Harold Farrar of the firm of Farrar, Windsor and Markham, a Jersey law firm. Hardin made a note of the address and the telephone number. His hand trembled a little as he noted the size of the estate.

It was estimated at forty million pounds sterling.

*　*　*

Hardin drank his beer, ordered another, and contemplated what he had discovered. Hank Hendrix and Dirk Hendriks, if he was still around, stood to split £6 million between them. He translated it into more familiar terms. The rate of the dollar to the pound sterling had been volatile of late but had settled at about two to one. That made twelve million bucks to split between two if there were no other heirs and he knew of none, unless Dirk Hendriks had children. That dope-smuggling drop-out, Hank Hendrix, was a multi-millionaire. The main bulk of the fortune might be going to the foundation with the funny name but the residue was not peanuts.

Hardin smiled to himself. No wonder Gunnarsson had been so interested. He always knew the value of a dollar and would not resist the temptation to put himself alongside six million of them in the hope of cutting himself a slice. He had isolated Hendrix and that young man would be no match for Gunnarsson who could charm birds from a tree when he wanted to. Gunnarsson would cook up some kind of deal to guarantee that some of those dollars would stick to his fingers.

So what was the next step? Hardin walked to the corner of the bar where there was a telephone and checked the directory which lay on a shelf next to it. He turned to 'H' and found the Hendriks's; there were more than he expected of that spelling, perhaps fifteen. He ran his finger down the column and found 'Hendriks, D.' On impulse he checked the variant spelling of 'Hendrykxx' but found no entry.

He returned to his table and consulted the street map. The address was near Sloane Square and the map of the London Underground gave his route. He patted his jacket over his breast pocket where he had put the will. Then he finished his drink and went on his way.

Coming up from the subway at Sloane Square he discovered himself in what was obviously an upper class section of London comparable to the 70s and 80s of Manhattan's East Side. He found the street he was looking for, and then the house, and gave a low whistle. If Dirk Hendriks lived in this style he was in no particular need of a few extra millions.

Hardin hesitated, feeling a bit of a fool. He had found what he wanted to know – why Gunnarsson had been so secretive – and there was nothing in it for him. He shrugged and thought that perhaps Hank was in there with his cousin; the place looked big enough to hold an army of Hendrixes. He would like to see the kid again. After saving his life and ministering to his wounds he felt a proprietary interest. He walked up the short flight of steps to the front door and put his finger on the bellpush.

The door was opened by a young woman in a nurse's uniform. Someone sick? 'I'd like to see Mr Hendriks – Dirk Hendriks,' he said.

The young woman looked doubtful. 'Er . . . I don't think

he's here,' she said. 'You see, I'm new. I haven't been here long.'

Hardin said, 'What about Henry Hendrix?'

She shook her head. 'There's no one of the name here,' she said. 'I'd know that. Would you like to see Mrs Hendriks? She's been resting but she's up now.'

'Is she sick? I wouldn't want to disturb her.'

The nurse laughed. 'She's just had a baby, Mr ... er ...'

'Sorry. Hardin, Ben Hardin.'

She opened the door wider. 'If you come in I'll tell her you're here, Mr Hardin.'

Hardin waited in a spacious hall which showed all the evidences of casual wealth. Presently the nurse came back. 'Come this way, Mr Hardin.' She led him up the wide stairs and into a room which had large windows overlooking a small park. 'Mrs Hendriks; this is Mr Hardin.' The nurse withdrew.

Mrs Hendriks was a woman in her mid-thirties. She was short and dark, not particularly beautiful but not unattractive, either. She used make-up well. As they shook hands she said, 'I'm sorry my husband isn't here, Mr Hardin. You've missed him by twenty-four hours. He went to South Africa yesterday. Do you know my husband?'

'Not personally,' said Hardin.

'Then you may not know that he's a South African.' She gestured. 'Please sit down.'

Hardin sat in the easy chair. 'It's not your husband I really want to see,' said Hardin. 'It's Han ... Henry Hendrix I'd like to visit with.'

'Henry?' she said doubtfully.

'Your husband's cousin.'

She shook her head. 'I think you're mistaken. My husband has no cousin.'

Hardin smiled. 'You may not know of him. He's an American and they've never met. Least, that's what Hank told me. That's how he's known back home. Hank Hendrix; only the name is spelled different with an 'X' at the end.'

'I see. But I still think you're mistaken, Mr Hardin. I'm sure my husband would have told me.'

'They've never met. A few letters is all, and those some years ago.' Hardin was vaguely troubled. 'Then Hank hasn't been here?'

'Of course not.' She paused. 'He might have come when I was in confinement. I've just had a baby, Mr Hardin, and modern doctors prefer maternity wards.'

'The nurse told me,' said Hardin. 'Congratulations! Boy or girl?'

'I have a son,' she said proudly. 'Thank you, Mr Hardin.' She reverted to the problem. 'But Dirk would have told me, I'm sure, if a long-lost cousin had arrived out of the blue.'

'I'm sure he would have,' said Hardin sincerely, and his sense of trouble deepened. If Hank had come to England he would have certainly looked Dirk up; all it took was a phone book. Damn it, the Jersey lawyer would have certainly introduced them. Jack Richardson had checked that flight tickets had not been bought, so where in hell was Hank and what game was Gunnarsson playing?

His worry must have shown on his face because Mrs Hendriks said gently, 'You look troubled, Mr Hardin. Is there anything I can do to help?'

Hardin felt the copy of the will in his pocket. At least that was real. He said, 'Has Mr Hendriks heard from a lawyer about his grandfather's will?'

Mrs Hendriks was astonished. 'His grandfather! My husband's grandfather died years ago in South Africa. Or, at least, I've always assumed so. Dirk has never mentioned him.'

Hardin took a deep breath. 'Mrs Hendriks; I have something to tell you and it may take a while. It's like this . . .'

6

Max Stafford was contemplating the tag end of the day and thinking about going home when his telephone rang. It was Joyce, his secretary. 'Mrs Hendriks is on the line and wants to talk to you.'

'Put her through.'

There was a click. 'Max?'

'Hello, Alix. How is motherhood suiting you?'

'Great. I'm blooming. Thank you for the christening mug you sent young Max. A *very* elegant piece of Georgian silver. He'll drink your health from it on his coming-of-age.'

Stafford smiled. 'Is it eighteen or twenty-one these days? I'll be a bit long in the tooth then.'

She laughed. 'But that's not why I rang; there's a proper "Thank you" letter in the post. Max, I need your advice. A man, an American called Hardin, came to me yesterday with a strange story concerning Dirk. Now, Dirk isn't here – he's in South Africa. I tried to ring him last night but he seems to be on the move and no one knows exactly where he is. I'd like you to see this man before he goes back to America.'

'What sort of strange yarn is he spinning?'

'It's a bit difficult to explain and I probably wouldn't get it right. It's complicated. Please see him, Max.'

Stafford pondered for a moment. 'Is Dirk in trouble?'

'Nothing like that. In fact it might be the other way round. Dirk might inherit something according to Hardin, but there's something odd going on.'

'How odd?'

'I don't know,' she said. 'I can't get the hang of it.'

'When is Hardin going back to the States?'

'Tomorrow or the day after. I don't think he can afford to stay.' She hesitated. 'I would like your advice, Max; you've always been wise. Things have been difficult lately. Dirk has been broody for quite a while – ever since I told him I was pregnant. It's been worrying me. And now this.'

'This Hardin character isn't blackmailing you, is he?'

'It's nothing like that,' she protested. 'Can you come to lunch? I'll see that Hardin is here.'

Stafford thought about it. His in-tray was overflowing and Joyce was a strict secretary. Still, this might be something he could sort out in an hour. 'All right,' he said. 'I'll be with you at twelve-thirty.'

'Thank you, Max,' said Alix warmly. 'I knew I could depend on you.'

Stafford put down the telephone and sat thinking. Presently he became aware that Ellis was standing before him snapping his fingers. 'Come out of your trance. Got a problem?'

Stafford started. 'Not me – Alix Hendriks. It seems that Dirk doesn't relish being a father. He's whistled off to South Africa and left Alix holding the three-week-old baby which I consider bloody inconsiderate. And now she's come up against someone who sounds like a con man, and Dirk isn't around. She wants my advice.'

'The last time you helped Alix you came to the office with your arm in a sling,' said Ellis. 'Watch it, Max.'

'That kind of lightning doesn't strike twice,' said Stafford.

* * *

Stafford soon found that the problem presented by Alix was not to be sorted out in an hour. He arrived on time at the house in Belgravia and found Hardin already there, a balding man in his mid-fifties with a pot belly like a football. To Stafford's eye he looked seedy and rundown. After gravely inspecting and admiring Stafford's three-week-old namesake the three of them adjourned to the dining room for lunch and Hardin retold his story.

It was three in the afternoon when Stafford held up the

sheaf of papers. 'And this is purported to be the will?'

Hardin's face reddened. 'It *is* the goddamn will. If you don't believe me you can get your own copy. Hell, I'll even stand the cost myself.'

'All right, Mr Hardin; cool down.'

During Hardin's narrative Stafford had been revising his opinion of the man. If this was a con trick he found it difficult to see the point because there was nothing in it for Hardin. The will was obviously genuine because its source could be so easily checked and the passing of a fake will through the Probate Court was inconceivable. Besides, there was Gunnarsson.

He said, 'What do you think Gunnarsson has done with Hendrix?'

Hardin shrugged. 'I wouldn't know.'

'Would you call Gunnarsson an ethical man?'

'Christ, no!'

'Neither would I,' said Stafford dryly.

'You know him?' said Hardin in surprise.

'Not personally, but he has caused me a considerable amount of trouble in the past. We happen to be in the same line of business but reverse sides of the coin, as you might say. I run Stafford Security Consultants.'

Hardin was even more surprised. 'You're *that* Stafford? Well I'll be damned!'

Stafford inspected the will. 'Old Hendrykxx was either wise or had good advice.'

Alix poured more coffee. 'Why?'

'Setting up in the Channel Islands. No death duties, capital gains tax or capital transfer tax. It looks as though Dirk will get about three million quid free and clear. I know quite a bit about that aspect. When we went multinational we began to put our business through the Channel Islands.' He laid the will on the table. 'Who do you think shot Hendrix in Los Angeles?'

'That I don't know, either,' said Hardin. 'I can only guess. There were other guys looking for Hendrix besides me. I told you that.'

'Who could be German,' said Stafford. 'All right, Mr Hardin; why did you come to England?'

'I was so mad about the way Gunnarsson shafted me that I wanted to do something about it. Call it revenge, if you like. I drew a blank in New York and when I got a few unexpected dollars I came over here.' Hardin shrugged and pointed at the will. 'When I saw that, I knew damn well what Gunnarsson was doing, but there's not a thing I can do about it. But I came here to see Hank and to tell him to watch his step with Gunnarsson and to put a zipper on his wallet.'

Stafford was pensive for a while. At last he said, 'How long are you staying in England?'

'I'm leaving tomorrow or maybe the day after. Depends on when I can get a reservation.' Hardin smiled wryly. 'I have to get home and go back to earning a living.'

'I'd like you to stay a little longer. Your expenses will be paid, of course.' Stafford glanced at Alix, who nodded. He did not know exactly why he wanted Hardin to stay. He just had an obscure feeling that the man would be handy to have around.

'I don't mind staying on that basis,' said Hardin.

Stafford stood up. 'If you let me have the name of your hotel I'll be in touch.'

'I have it,' said Alix.

'Then that's it for the moment. Thank you, Mr Hardin.' When Hardin had gone Stafford said, 'May I use your phone?'

Alix looked up from clearing away the coffee cups. 'Of course. You know where it is.'

Stafford was absent for five minutes. When he came back he said, 'Jan-Willem Hendrykxx really did exist. I've been talking to my man in Jersey who looked him up in the telephone book. His name is still listed. I think Hendrykxx is a Flemish name.' He picked up the will. 'That would account for the house in Belgium. I've asked my chap to give me a discreet report on the executor of the estate and to find out when and

57

how Hendrykxx died.'

Alix frowned. 'You don't suspect anything . . . ? I mean he must have been an old man.'

Stafford smiled. 'I was trained in military intelligence. You never know when a bit of apparently irrelevant information will fit into the jigsaw.' He scanned the will. 'The Ol Njorowa Foundation stands to inherit about thirty-four million pounds. I wonder what it does?' He sat down. 'Alix, what's this with you and Dirk? You sounded a shade drear on the phone this morning.'

She looked unhappy. 'I can't make him out, Max. I don't think fatherhood suits him. We were happy enough until I got in the family way and then he changed.'

'In what way?'

'He became moody and abstracted. And now he's pushed off back to South Africa just when I need him. The baby's just three weeks old – you'd think he'd stay around, wouldn't you?'

'Um,' said Stafford obscurely. 'He never mentioned his grandfather at any time?'

'Not that I can remember.' She made a sudden gesture as if brushing away an inopportune fly. 'Oh, Max; this is ridiculous. This man – this Fleming with the funny way of spelling his name – is probably no relation at all. It must be a case of mistaken identity.'

'I don't think so. Hardin came straight to this house like a homing pigeon.' Stafford ticked off points on his fingers. 'The American, Hank Hendrix, told him that Dirk was his cousin; Hardin saw the instructions to Gunnarsson from Peacemore, Willis and Franks to turn up descendants of Jan-Willem Hendrykxx with the funny name; in doing so Hardin turns up Hank Hendrix. It's a perfectly logical chain.'

'I suppose so,' said Alix. 'But can you tell me why I'm worried about Dirk inheriting millions?'

'I think I can,' he said. 'You're worried about a bit that doesn't seem to fit. The shooting of Hank Hendrix in Los

Angeles. And I've got one other thing on my mind. Why haven't the Peacemore mob turned up Dirk? Hardin did it in thirty seconds.'

* * *

Curtis, Stafford's manservant, was mildly surprised at seeing him. 'The Colonel is back early,' he observed.

'Yes, I got sidetracked. It wasn't worth going back to the office.'

'Would the Colonel like afternoon tea?'

'No; but you can bring me a scotch in the study.'

'As the Colonel wishes,' said Curtis with a disapproving air which stopped just short of insolence.

Curtis was a combination of butler, valet, chauffeur, handyman and nanny. He was ex-Royal Marines, having joined in 1943 and electing to stay in the service after the war. A 37-year man. At the statutory retiring age of 55 he had been tossed into the strange civilian world of the 1980s, no longer a Colour-Sergeant with authority but just another man-in-the-street. A fish out of water and somewhat baffled by the indiscipline of civilian life. He was a widower, his wife Amy having died five years before of cancer; and his only daughter was married, living in Australia, and about to present him with a third grandchild.

When Stafford had divorced his wife he had stayed at his club before moving into a smaller flat more suitable for a bachelor. It was then that he remembered Curtis whom he had known from the days when he had been a young officer serving with the British Army of the Rhine. One night, in one of the lesser salubrious quarters of Hamburg, he had found himself in a tight spot from which he had been rescued by a tough, hammer-fisted Marine sergeant. He had never forgotten Curtis and they had kept in touch, and so he acquired Curtis – or did Curtis acquire Stafford? Whichever way it was they suited each other; Curtis finding a congenial niche in a strange world, and Stafford lucky enough to have an efficient, if somewhat military, Jeeves. Curtis's only fault was that he would persist in addressing Stafford in the third person by his army title.

Stafford looked at the chunky, hard man with something approaching affection. 'How's your daughter, Sergeant?'

'I had a letter this morning. She says she's well, sir.'

'What will it be? Boy or girl?'

'Just so that it has one head and the usual number of arms, legs and fingers. Boy or girl – either will suit me.'

'Tell me when it comes. We must send a suitable christening present.'

'Thank you, sir. When would the Colonel like his bath drawn?'

'At the usual time. Let me have that scotch now.' Stafford went into his study.

He sat at his desk and thought about Gunnarsson. He had never met Gunnarsson but had sampled his methods through the machinations of Peacemore, Willis and Franks which was the wholly-owned London subsidiary of Gunnarsson Associates, and what he had found he did not like.

It was the work of Stafford Security Consultants to protect the secrets of the organizations which were their clients. A lot of people imagine security to be a matter of patrolling guards and heavy mesh fencing but that is only a part of it. The weakest part of any organization is the people in it, from the boss at the top down to the charwomen who scrub the floors. A Managing Director making an indiscreet remark at his golf club could blow a secret worth millions. A charwoman suborned can find lots of interesting items in waste paper baskets.

It followed that if the firm of Stafford Security Consultants were making a profit out of guarding secrets – and it was making a handsome profit – then others were equally interested in ferreting them out, and the people who employed Gunnarsson Associates were the sort who were not too fussy about the methods used. And that went for the Peacemore mob in the United Kingdom.

Stafford remembered a conversation he had had with Jack

Ellis just before he left for the Continent. 'We've had trouble with the Peacemore crowd,' said Ellis. 'They penetrated Electronomics just before the merger when Electronomics was taken over. Got right through our defences.'

'How?'

Jack shrugged. 'We can guard against everything but stupidity. They got the goods on Pascoe, the General Manager. In bed with a gilded youth. Filthy pictures, the lot. Of course, it was a Peacemore set-up, but I'd have a hell of a job proving it.'

'In this permissive age homosexuality isn't the handle it once was,' observed Stafford.

'It was a good handle this time. Pascoe's wife didn't know he was double-gaited. He has teenage daughters and it would have ruined his marriage so he caved in. After the merger we lost the Electronomics contract, of course. Peacemore got it.'

'And Pascoe's peccadilloes came to light anyway.'

'Sure. After the merger he was fired and they gave full reasons. He'd proved he couldn't be trusted.'

'The bastards have no mercy,' said Stafford.

Industrial espionage is not much different from the work of that department called MI6 which the British government refuses to admit exists, or the KGB which everyone knows to exist, or the CIA which is practically an open book. A car company would find it useful to know the opposition's designs years in advance. One airline, after planning an advertising campaign costing half a million, was taken very much by surprise when its principal rival came out with the identical campaign a week before its own was due to start.

A company wanting to take over another, as in the Electronomics case, would like to know the victim's defensive strategy. Someone wanted to know what bid price Electronomics would jib at, and employed Peacemore to find out.

Of course, no one on the Board comes right out and says, 'Let's run an espionage exercise against so-and-so.' The Chairman or Managing Director might be thinking aloud and says dreamily, 'Wouldn't it be nice if we knew what so-and-so are doing.' Sharp ears pick up the wishful think and the second echelon boys get to work, the hatchet men hungry for promotion. Intermediaries are used, analogous to the cut-outs used in military and political intelligence, the job gets done with no one on the Board getting his hands dirty, and an under-manager becomes a manager.

Defence is difficult because the espionage boys go for the jugular. All the security guards in creation are of no avail against human weakness. So Stafford Security Consultants investigated the personnel of their clients, weeding out doubtful characters, and if that was an offence against human rights it was too bad.

And sometimes we fail, thought Stafford.

He sighed and picked up the neglected whisky which Curtis had brought in. And now Gunnarsson was mixed up in the affairs of a friend. Not that Stafford felt particularly friendly towards Dirk Hendriks, but Alix was his friend and he did not want her hurt in any way. And Gunnarsson was not acting in a straightforward manner. Why had he not produced the missing heirs?

Stafford checked the time. It was probably after office hours in Jersey but he would try to talk with the Jersey law firm. There was no reply.

7

The next morning, just after he arrived at the office, Stafford took a call from Peter Hartwell, the director of the Jersey holding company whom he had queried the day before. Hartwell said, 'Your man, Hendrykxx, died a little over four months ago. The body was cremated. I checked the newspapers and it went unreported except for the usual formal announcement.'

'What was the cause of death?'

'Heart attack. It was expected; he had a history of heart trouble. I discovered we shared the same doctor so I was able to ask a few questions. I went to the Greffe and saw the will. Makes bloody interesting reading, doesn't it?'

Stafford said, 'I'm surprised the newspapers didn't get hold of it. It's not often multimillionaires hop their twig.'

Hartwell laughed. 'Millionaires are not uncommon here – they're just plain, ordinary folk. Besides, Hendrykxx lived very quietly and didn't make waves. The news boys don't read every will deposited in the Greffe, anyway.'

'How long had he lived on Jersey?' asked Stafford.

'He came in 1974 – not all that long ago.'

'What about the executor? What's he like?'

'Old Farrar? Good man, but damned stuffy. What's your interest in this, Max? Isn't it a bit out of your line?'

'Just doing a favour for a friend. Thanks, Peter; I'll get back to you if I need anything more.'

'There is one odd point,' said Hartwell. 'The clerk in the Greffe said there's been quite a run on copies of that particular will. One from England, two from America and another from South Africa.' Hartwell laughed. 'He said he was considering printing a limited edition.'

After he put down the phone Stafford leaned back and thought for a moment. So far, so uninteresting, except possibly for the requests for copies of the will. He snapped a switch, and said, 'Joyce, get me Mr Farrar of Farrar, Windsor and Markham, St. Helier, Jersey. It's a law firm.'

Five minutes later he was speaking to Farrar. He introduced himself, then said, 'I'm interested in the late Mr Jan-Willem Hendrykxx. He died about four months ago.'

'That is correct.'

'I believe you are having difficulty in tracing the heirs.'

'In that you are mistaken,' said Farrar. He had a dry, pedantic voice.

Stafford waited for him to continue but Farrar remained silent. Well, Hartwell had said he was stuffy. Stafford said, 'I take it you refer to Henry Hendrix of Los Angeles and Dirk Hendriks of London.'

'You appear to be well informed. May I ask how you obtained your information?'

'I've been reading the will.'

'That would not give you the names,' said Farrar dryly. 'But essentially you are correct. Mr Henry Hendrix is flying from the United States tomorrow, and Mr Dirk Hendriks has been informed.' Farrar paused. 'It is true that I was surprised at the length of time taken by . . .' He stopped as though aware of being on the edge of an unlawyerly indiscretion. 'May I ask your interest in this matter, Mr Stafford?'

Stafford sighed. 'My interest has just evaporated. Thanks for letting me take up your time, Mr Farrar.' He hung up.

The telephone rang almost immediately and Alix came on the line. 'It's true, Max,' she said excitedly. 'It's all true.'

'If you mean about Dirk's inheritance, I know. I've just been talking to Farrar.'

'Who?'

'The executor of the estate. The Jersey solicitor.'

'That's funny. The letter came from a solicitor called Mandeville in the City.' Alix hurried on. 'Dirk knew all the time. He said he didn't want to excite me when I was having

64

the baby. He had to go to South Africa to collect evidence of identity. He got back this morning and he's seeing the solicitor tomorrow. And there *is* a long-lost cousin, Max. He'll be there too.'

'All very exciting,' said Stafford unemotionally. 'Congratulations.' He paused. 'What do you want me to do about Hardin?'

'What would you suggest?'

'He strikes me as being an honest man,' said Stafford. 'From the way it looked there *could* have been jiggery-pokery, and Hardin did his best to put it right at considerable personal effort. I suggest you pay his London expenses and his total air fare. And you might add a small honorarium. Shall I take care of it?'

'If you would,' she said. 'Send me the bill.'

'I'll break the news to him at lunch. 'Bye.' He rung off, asked Joyce to make a lunch appointment with Hardin, and then sat back, his fingers drumming on the desk, to consider the matter.

There did not seem much to consider. Mandeville was probably Farrar's London correspondent; law firms did arrange their affairs that way. Stafford wondered why Dirk Hendriks had not told Alix before he went to South Africa – she had had the baby by then – but he always had been an inconsiderate bastard. There were a couple of minor points that did not add up. Who shot Hendrix and why? And why hadn't Gunnarsson produced Hendrix in England as soon as he had been found? But he had only Hardin's word for those events. Perhaps Hardin really was a con man and playing his own devious game. Stafford who prided himself on being a good judge of men shook his head in perplexity.

He got on with his work.

* * *

Stafford stood Hardin to lunch in a good restaurant. The news may have been good for Hendrykxx's heirs but it was bad news for Hardin, and he judged a good meal would make the medicine go down better. Hardin said ruefully, 'I guess I made a fool of myself.'

'The man who never made a mistake never made anything,' said Stafford unoriginally. 'Mrs Hendriks doesn't want you to be out of pocket because of this affair. How long is it since you left Gunnarsson Associates?'

'Just about a month.'

'What did he pay you?'

'Thirty thousand bucks a year, plus bonuses.' Hardin shrugged. 'The bonuses got a little thin towards the end, but in good years I averaged forty thousand.'

'All right.' Stafford took out his chequebook. 'Mrs Hendriks will stand your air fare both ways, your London expenses, and a month's standard pay. Does that suit you?'

'That's generous and unexpected,' said Hardin sincerely.

Again Stafford wondered about Hardin, then reflected that sincerity was the con man's stock in trade. They settled the amount in dollars, Stafford rounded it up to the nearest thousand, converted it into sterling, and wrote the cheque. As Hardin put it into his wallet he said, 'This will keep me going until I get settled again back home.'

'When will you be leaving?'

'Nothing to keep me here now. Maybe tomorrow if I can get a seat.'

'Well, good luck,' said Stafford, and changed the subject.

Over the rest of lunch they talked of other things. Hardin learned that Stafford had been in Military Intelligence and opened up a bit on his own experiences in the CIA. He said he had worked in England, Germany and Africa; but he talked in generalities, was discreet, and told no tales out of school. 'I can't talk much about that,' he said frankly. 'I'm not one of the kiss-and-tell guys who sprang out of the woodwork with Watergate.'

Stafford silently approved, his judgment of Hardin oscillating rapidly.

Lunch over, Stafford paid the bill and they left the restaurant, pausing for a final handshake on the pavement. Stafford watched Hardin walk away, a somehow pathetic figure, and wondered what was to become of him.

* * *

Dirk Hendriks rang up next day, and Stafford sighed in exasperation; he was becoming fed up with *l'affaire* Hendriks. Dirk's voice came over strongly and Stafford noted yet again that the telephone tends to accentuate accent. 'I've seen the solicitor, Max. We're going to Jersey tomorrow to see Farrar, the executor.'

'We?'

'Me and my unexpected cousin. I met him in Mandeville's office.'

'Happy family reunion,' said Stafford. 'What's your cousin like?'

'Seems a nice enough chap. Very American, of course. He was wearing the damnedest gaudy broadcheck jacket you've ever seen.'

'Three million will cure any eyestrain, Dirk,' said Stafford dryly. 'Did you find out about the Ol Njorowa Foundation?'

'Yes. It's some sort of agricultural college and experimental farm in Kenya.' Hendriks hesitated. 'There's a funny condition to the will. I have to spend one month each year working for the Foundation. What do you make of that?'

Stafford had noted that clause. His tone became drier. 'A month a year isn't much to pay for three million quid.'

'I suppose not. Look, Max; this character, Hardin. What did you make of him?'

Stafford decided to give Hardin the benefit of the doubt. 'Seems a good chap.'

'So Alix says. She liked him. When is he going back to the States?'

'He's probably gone by now. He said there wasn't anything to keep him here, and he has to find a job.'

'I see. Could you give me his address in New York? He

must have run up some expenses and I'd like to reimburse him.'

'It's all taken care of, Dirk,' said Stafford. 'I'll send you the bill; you can afford it now. In any case, he didn't leave an address.'

'Oh!' In that brief monosyllable Stafford thought he detected disappointment. There was an appreciable pause before Hendriks said, 'Thanks, Max.' He went on more briskly, 'I must get on now. We've just left Mandeville who seems satisfied, and Cousin Henry, Alix and I are having a celebratory drink. Why don't you join us?'

'Sorry, Dirk; I'm not a bloated millionaire and I have work to do.'

'All right, then. I'll see you around.' Hendriks rang off.

Stafford had told a white lie. Already he was packing papers into a briefcase in preparation to go home. There was a Test match that afternoon and he rather thought England would beat Australia this time. He wanted to watch it on television.

He walked into his flat and found Curtis waiting for him. 'The Colonel has a visitor. An American gentleman, name of Mr Hardin. I rang the office but the Colonel had already left.'

'Oh! Where is he?'

'I settled him in the living room with a highball.'

Stafford looked at Curtis sharply. 'What the devil do you know about highballs?'

'I have been drunk with the United States Navy on many occasions, sir,' said Curtis with a straight face. 'That was in my younger days.'

'Well, I'll join Mr Hardin with my usual scotch.'

Stafford found Hardin nursing a depleted drink and examining the book shelves. 'I thought you'd have gone by now.'

'I almost made it, but I decided to stay.' Hardin straightened. 'Did Hank Hendrix arrive?'

'Yes; I had a call from Dirk. They met the lawyer this afternoon. He seemed satisfied with their credentials, so Dirk says.'

'The lawyer's name being Mandeville?'

'Yes. How do you know that?'

Stafford had thought Hardin had appeared strained but now he looked cheerful. 'I bumped into Gunnarsson this morning at Heathrow Airport. Well, not bumped exactly – I don't think he saw me. I decided not to leave right then because I wanted to follow him.'

Curtis came in with a tray and Stafford reached for his whisky. 'Why?'

'Because the young guy with him wasn't the Hank Hendrix I picked up in Los Angeles.'

Stafford was so startled that he almost dropped the glass. 'Wasn't he, by God?'

Hardin shook his head decidedly. 'No way. Same height, same colouring – a good lookalike but not Hank Hendrix.'

Stafford thought of his conversation with Dirk. 'What was the colour of his jacket?'

Hardin grinned crookedly. 'You couldn't mistake him for anyone but an American – Joseph's coat of many colours.'

That did it. Curtis was about to leave the room and Stafford said abruptly, 'Stick around, Sergeant, and listen to this. It might save a lot of explanations later. But first get Mr Hardin another highball, and you might as well have one yourself. Mr Hardin; this is Colour-Sergeant Curtis, late of the Royal Marines.'

Hardin gave Stafford a curious look then stood up and held out his hand. 'Glad to know you, Sergeant Curtis.'

'Likewise, Mr Hardin.' They shook hands then Curtis turned to Stafford. 'If the Colonel doesn't mind I'd rather have a beer.'

Stafford nodded and Curtis left to return two minutes later with the drinks. Stafford said, 'So you followed Gunnarsson?'

'Yeah. Your London taxi drivers don't surprise worth a damn. I told mine that if he kept track of Gunnarsson's cab it was worth an extra tip. He said he could do better than that – they were on the same radio net. Five minutes later he said Gunnarsson was going to the Dorchester. I got there before him and had the cab wait. It ran up quite a tab on the meter.'

'You'll get your expenses.'

Hardin grinned. 'It's on the house, Mr Stafford. Because I'm feeling so good.'

He sipped his replenished highball. 'Gunnarsson and the other guy registered at the desk and then went upstairs. They were up there nearly two hours while I was sitting in the lobby getting callouses on my butt and hoping that the house dick wouldn't latch on to me and throw me out. When they came down I followed them again and they took me to Lincoln's Inn Fields.'

'Where Mandeville has his chambers. Right? That's where you got the name.'

'Right. I still kept the cab and hung on for a while. Gunnarsson came out just as Mrs Hendriks went in with a guy. Would he be Dirk Hendriks?'

'Big broad-shouldered man built like a tank?' Like a lot of South Africans Hendriks was designed to play rugby scrum half.

'That's the guy.' Stafford nodded sharply, and Hardin said, 'They went into the same place. I followed Gunnarsson to the office of Peacemore, Willis and Franks. I didn't think I could do much more so I came here and paid off the taxi.' He looked up. 'I thought it was better I came here instead of your office.'

Stafford nodded absently, mulling it over, then he said, 'All right; let's do a reconstruction. You found Henry Hendrix and took him to Gunnarsson in New York. Gunnarsson, who had been hoping for a gold mine, realised he'd found it. Hendrix had no family, he'd never been out of the States, and it wouldn't be too hard to drain him of information and put someone else in as a substitute here in London.'

Curtis coughed. 'I don't really know what this is about yet, but where is the real Henry Hendrix?'

Hardin gave him a sideways glance. 'I wouldn't care to guess.' There was a silence while they digested that, then he asked, 'So what do we do now?'

'I suppose I should tell Farrar he's being taken,' Stafford said slowly. 'But I'm not going to.' Hardin brightened. 'If I do then Gunnarsson can slide right out from under.'

'Yeah,' said Hardin. 'The young guy takes his lumps for being an impostor, and Gunnarsson spreads his hands and says he's been as deceived as anyone else. All injured innocence.'

'And no one would believe you,' commented Stafford. 'He'd call you a liar; a disgruntled ex-employee who was fired for incompetence.'

'That he would.' Hardin scratched his jaw. 'There's still Biggie and the commune. They'd know this guy isn't Hank.'

'Christ, they're seven thousand miles away,' said Stafford irritably. 'This man, whoever he is, has committed no crime in the States. He'd be tried here under British law or perhaps Jersey law, for all I know.'

'What's the sentence for impersonation over here?'

'It wouldn't be much. Maybe two years.'

Hardin snorted, but Stafford ignored him. He was deep in thought and looked upon Hardin with new eyes. The man had proved to be right, after all, and here he had at hand an unemployed Intelligence agent and a man who hated Gunnarsson's guts. If Stafford was going against Gunnarsson it occurred to him that Hardin would be handy to have around. He knew Gunnarsson and how he operated, and the first rule of any kind of warfare is: 'Know your enemy'.

He said, 'You told me you worked in Africa. Do you know Kenya?'

'Sure.' Hardin shrugged. 'It will have changed since I was there, but I know Kenya.'

'Are you *persona grata*?'

'I'm okay in Kenya.' He smiled. 'I wouldn't like to say what would happen if I stuck my nose into Tanzania.'

Stafford said, 'You told me your salary at Gunnarsson Associates. I think we can match that, and maybe a bit more. How would you like to work for Stafford Security Consultants?'

Hardin did not jump at it. 'Are you in the same business as Gunnarsson?'

'Not exactly. We try to stop the bastards.'

Hardin held out his hand. 'I'm your man. Thanks, Mr Stafford.'

Stafford smiled. 'I'm Max, you are Ben, and the Sergeant is the Sergeant.'

Hardin had given up his hotel room so Stafford told him he could use the spare bedroom until he got fixed up. 'You can pay your rent by briefing Sergeant Cùrtis on this thing.'

'What's this with Kenya?'

Stafford said, 'That's where I think the action will be.' He was thinking that an awful lot of money was going to the Ol Njorowa Foundation, a hell of a lot more than the six million dollars going to the fake Hendrix. The Foundation would be awash with cash – something like seventy million American dollars – and he was sure that Gunnarsson had got the heady scent of it in his nostrils.

8

Stafford discussed the Gunnarsson affair with Jack Ellis who was the next biggest shareholder in Stafford Security after himself. He felt he could not run up costs on the firm without informing Ellis. He outlined the situation and Ellis said thoughtfully, 'Gunnarsson. He's the Peacemore mob, isn't he?'

'That's right.'

'We've been having trouble with that crowd. Remember Electronomics?'

'All too clearly,' said Stafford. 'Jack, our next logical expansion is into the States. We're going to come up slap hard against Gunnarsson sooner or later. I'd rather it was sooner, before we set up operations over there. I want to go after him now when he's not on his home ground.'

Ellis nodded. 'That should make it easier. Who knows about all this? I mean that Gunnarsson has run in a substitute for Hendrix.'

'Just four; you, me, Hardin and the Sergeant.'

'Not Alix Hendriks?'

Stafford shook his head. 'Nor Dirk. I want to keep this tight.'

'And why Kenya?'

Stafford said, 'There was once an American bank robber called Willie Sutton. Someone asked him why he robbed banks. He looked a bit disgusted, and said, "That's where the money is." There's a hell of a lot of money going into Kenya. Gunnarsson will go where the money is.'

'What do we know about this Foundation in Kenya?'

'Not a damned thing; but that can be cured.'

'And you want to handle this personally?'

'With help.' Stafford shrugged. 'I've been working damned hard in Europe, and I haven't had a holiday for three years. Let's call this paid leave of absence.'

Ellis smiled wryly. 'I have an odd feeling of *déjà vu* as though we've had this conversation before.'

Stafford said, 'Make no mistake, Jack; this isn't a favour for Alix Hendriks. This is for the future benefit of Stafford Security.'

Ellis agreed.

* * *

Stafford sent Hardin to Kenya as a one man advance party. He did not want Hardin to meet either Gunnarsson or Hendrix by accident and, although there are eight million people in London, he was taking no chances. The West End covers a comparatively small area and it would be plain bad luck if they met face to face in, say, Jermyn Street. In Kenya Hardin was to arrange hotel accommodation and hire cars. He was also to do a preliminary check into the Ol Njorowa Foundation.

Gunnarsson and the fake Hendrix were kept under discreet observation. Stafford arranged to get a look at them so that he would know them again when he saw them. Gunnarsson did nothing much; he frequented the offices of Peacemore, Willis and Franks, which was natural since he owned the place, and he gambled in casinos, winning often. His luck was uncanny. Hendrix, after looking around London, hired a car and went on a tour of the West Country.

It was then that Stafford invited Alix and Dirk Hendriks to dinner; they were his spies behind the enemy lines. Over the aperitifs he said, 'How did you get on in Jersey?'

Dirk laughed. 'I signed a lot of papers and got writer's cramp. The old man had a fantastic head for business. His investments are widespread.'

'Did you know your grandfather?'

Dirk shook his head, and Alix said, 'You've never mentioned him, Dirk.'

'I thought he was killed in the Red Revolt of 1922,' said

Dirk. 'There was a revolution on the Rand, a real civil war which Smuts put down with artillery and bombers. That's when he disappeared, or so I was told. It's a bit spooky to know that he really died only a few months ago.'

'And your grandmother – did you know her?' asked Stafford.

'I have vague recollections,' said Dirk, frowning. 'She used to tell me stories. It must have been she who told me about my grandfather. She died when I was a kid. They all did.'

'All?' said Alix questioningly.

'Both my parents, my sister and my grandmother were killed in a car crash. The only reason I wasn't in the car was because I was in hospital. Scarlet fever, I believe. I was six years old.' He put on a mock lugubrious expression. 'I'm a lone orphan.'

Alix put her hand over his. 'My poor darling. I didn't know.'

Stafford thought it odd that Dirk had not told Alix this before but made no comment. Instead he said, 'What's this Foundation in Kenya?'

'Ol Njorowa?' Dirk shook his head. 'I don't know much about it other than what I've already told you. We're going out next Wednesday to inspect it. Since I have to spend a month a year there I'd better learn about it. The Director is a man called Brice. Mandeville thinks a lot of him.'

'How does Mandeville come into it? He's a Q.C., isn't he? I thought Farrar was the executor.' Stafford held up a finger to a passing waiter.

'He did a lot of legal work for my grandfather. Apparently they were on terms of friendship because he said he used to stay at my grandfather's house whenever he went to Jersey.'

'Is he going to Kenya with you?'

Dirk laughed. 'Lord, no! He's a bigwig; he doesn't go to people – they go to him. But Farrar is coming along; he has business to discuss with Brice.'

Stafford turned to Alix. 'Are you going, too?'

She smiled ruefully. 'I'd like to, but I couldn't take young Max. Perhaps we'll go next time.'

'And Henry Hendrix is going, of course. Where is he, by the way? I thought you'd be together.'

'He's sightseeing in the country,' said Dirk, and added tartly, 'We're not going to live in each other's pockets. It's only now that I appreciate the saying, "You can choose your friends but not your relatives".'

'Don't you like him?'

'He's not my type,' said Dirk briefly. 'I think we'll choose different months to stay at Ol Njorowa. But, yes; he will be going with Farrar and me.'

'I might bump into you in Nairobi,' said Stafford casually. 'I'm taking a holiday out there. My flight is on Tuesday.'

'Oh?' Dirk looked at him intently. 'When did you decide that?'

'I booked the trip a couple of weeks ago – at least, my secretary did.'

The waiter came up, and Alix said, 'I won't have another drink, Max.'

'Then we'll go in to dine,' he said, and rose, satisfied with his probing.

* * *

Next day he learned that Gunnarsson had visited a travel agent and a discreet enquiry elicited his destination – Nairobi. Stafford had Curtis book two seats on the Tuesday flight and cabled Hardin, advising him to lie low. Curtis said, 'Am I going, sir?'

'Yes; I might want someone to hang my trousers. What kind of natty gent's clothing would be suitable for Kenya?'

'The Colonel doesn't want to trouble his head about that. Any of the Indian stores will make him up a suit within twenty-four hours. Cheap too, and good for the climate.'

'You're a mine of information, Sergeant. Where did you pick up that bit?'

'I've been there,' Curtis said unexpectedly. 'I was in Mombasa a few years ago during the Mau-Mau business. I got a bit of travel up-country to Nairobi and beyond.' He paused.

'What kind of trouble is the Colonel expecting – fisticuffs or guns?' Stafford regarded him thoughtfully, and Curtis said, 'It's just that I'd like to know what preparations to make.'

Stafford said, 'You know as much as I do. Make what preparations you think advisable.' The first thing any green lieutenant learns is when to say "Carry on, Sergeant". The non-commissioned officers of any service run the nuts and bolts of the outfit and the wise officer knows it.

Curtis said, 'Then have I the Colonel's permission to take the afternoon off? I have things to do.'

'Yes; but don't tell me what they are. I don't want to know.'

The only matter of consequence that happened before they went to Kenya was that Hendrix crashed his car when careering down a steep hill in Cornwall near Tintagel. He came out with a few scratches but the car was a total write-off.

* * *

They flew to Nairobi first class on the night flight. Curtis was a big man and Stafford no midget and he saw no reason to be cramped in economy class where the seats are tailored for the inhabitants of Munchkinland. If all went well Gunnarsson would be paying ultimately. Stafford resisted the attempts of the cabin staff to anaesthetize him with alcohol so he would be less trouble but, since he found it difficult to sleep on aircraft, at 3 a.m. he went to the upstairs lounge where he read a thriller over a long, cold beer while intermittently watching the chief steward jiggle the accounts. The thriller had a hero who always knew when he was being followed by a prickling at the nape of his neck; this handy accomplishment helped the plot along on no fewer than four occasions.

Curtis slept like a baby.

They landed just after eight in the morning and, even at that early hour, the sun was like a hammer. Stafford sniffed and caught the faintly spicy, dusty smell he had first encountered in Algeria – the smell of Africa. They went through Immigration and Customs and found Hardin waiting. ''Lo, Max; 'lo, Sergeant. Have a good flight?'

'Not bad.' Stafford felt the bristles on his jaw. 'A day flight would have been better.'

'The pilots don't like that,' said Hardin. 'This airport is nearly six thousand feet high and the midday air is hot and thin. They reckon it's a bit risky landing at noon.'

Stafford's eyes felt gritty. 'You're as bad as the Sergeant, here, for unexpected nuggets of information.'

'I have wheels outside. Let me help with your bags. Don't let these porters get their hands on them; they want an arm and a leg for a tip.'

They followed Hardin and Stafford stared unbelievingly at the vehicle to which he was led. It was a Nissan van, an eight-seater with an opening roof, and it was dazzlingly painted in zebra stripes barely veiled in a thin film of dust. He said, 'For Christ's sake, Ben! We're trying to be inconspicuous and you get us a circus van. That thing shouts at you from a bloody mile away.'

'Don't worry,' Hardin said reassuringly. 'These safari trucks are as common as fleas on a dog out here, and they'll go anywhere. We're disguised as tourists. You'll see.'

Hardin drove, Stafford sat next to him, and Curtis got in the back. There was an unexpectedly good divided highway. Stafford said, 'How far is the city?'

'About seven miles.' Hardin jerked his thumb. 'See that fence? On the other side is the Nairobi National Game Park. Lots of animals back there.' He laughed. 'It's goddamn funny to see giraffes roaming free with skyscrapers in the background.'

'I didn't send you here to look at animals.'

'Hell, it was Sunday morning. My way of going to church. Don't be a grouch, Max.'

Hardin had a point. 'Sorry, Ben. I suppose it's the lack of sleep.'

'That's okay.' Hardin was silent for a while, then he said, 'I was talking to one of the local inhabitants in the bar of the Hilton. He lives at Langata, that's a suburb of Nairobi. He said all hell had broken loose early that morning because a lion had taken a horse from the riding stables next door. Even in Manhattan we don't live that dangerously.'

Stafford thought Hardin had turned into the perfect goggling tourist. He was not there to hear small talk about lions. He said, 'What about the Foundation?'

Hardin caught the acerbity in Stafford's voice and gave him a sideways glance. He said quietly, 'Yeah, I got some information on that from the same guy who told me about the lion. He's one of the Trustees; Indian guy called Patterjee.'

Stafford sighed. 'Sorry again, Ben. This doesn't seem to be my day.'

'That's okay. We all have off days.'

'Did you get anything interesting out of Patterjee?'

'A few names – members of the Board and so on. He gave me a printed handout which describes the work of the Foundation. It runs agricultural schools, experimental laboratories – things like that. And a Co-operative. The Director responsible to the Board is called Brice; he's not in Nairobi – he's at Ol Njorowa. That's near Naivasha in the Rift Valley, about fifty miles from here.'

'Who started the Foundation – and when?'

'It was started just after the war, in the fifties. The handout doesn't say who by. I did some poking around Naivasha but I didn't see Brice; I thought I'd leave him for you. He's English and I thought you'd handle him better, maybe.'

'Did Patterjee say anything about the Hendrykxx inheritance?'

'Not a murmur. But he wasn't likely to talk about that to a stranger he met in a bar. The news isn't out yet. I checked the back issues in a newspaper office.'

They were coming into the city. Stafford had not known what to expect but was mildly surprised. He knew enough not to expect mud huts but the buildings were high rise and modern and the streets were well kept. Hardin braked hard. 'When you're driving around here watch out for guys on bicycles. They think traffic lights don't apply to them.'

The lights changed and Hardin let out the clutch. 'We're on

Uhuru Highway. Over to the left is Uhuru Park.' Stafford saw black schoolgirls dressed in gym slips playing handball. There were flowers everywhere in a riot of colour. They turned a corner and then another, and Hardin said, 'Harry Thuku Road, named after a revolutionary hero who got on the wrong side of the British in colonial days. And there's the Norfolk where we're staying.'

He put the vehicle into a slot between two identically zebra-striped Nissans. 'One of those is ours. I thought we'd better have two sets of wheels.'

'Good thinking.' Stafford twisted and looked back at Curtis. 'You're very loquacious, Sergeant; you've been positively babbling. Anything on your mind?'

'Got things to do if the Colonel will excuse me,' he said stolidly. 'I could do with a street map.'

'I have one here,' said Hardin. 'But you'd better register first.'

They went into the hotel as a horde of porters descended on the Nissan. After registering Curtis gave Stafford a brief nod and went away, walking out of the hotel and into the street. Hardin stared after him. 'The strong, silent type,' he commented. 'Where's he going?'

'Better you not ask,' said Stafford. 'He's going his mysterious ways his wonders to perform.'

Their rooms were across an inner courtyard alive with the noise of birds from two large aviaries. 'The Sergeant is bunking in with me,' said Hardin. 'You're on your own. I've ordered breakfast in your room; I reckoned you might be tired and not want to use the dining room.' They ascended stairs and he opened a door. 'Here you are.'

A waiter was stooping over a loaded tray which he had just set down. He straightened and said, with a wide grin, 'Breakfast, sah; guaranteed finest English breakfast.'

Hardin tipped him and he left. 'The refrigerator is full of booze.'

Stafford shuddered. 'Too early in the morning.'

'Tell me something,' said Hardin. 'What's with you and the

Sergeant? I thought you had the class system in England. It doesn't show with you two.'

'I don't happen to believe in the class system,' said Stafford, uncovering a dish to reveal bacon and eggs. He picked up a glass of orange juice and sipped it, noting appreciatively that it was freshly squeezed. 'Have you anything more to tell me before I demolish this lot and fall on that bed?'

'Yeah. The name of the Foundation. Ol Njorowa is the name of a place near Naivasha. It's Masai. I don't know what the translation into English would be but the British settlers call it Hell's Gate. When do you want to be wakened?'

'Twelve-thirty.'

Stafford had breakfast and went to bed thinking of Hell's Gate. It was a hell of a name to give to a charitable foundation.

9

Hardin woke Stafford on time. He felt hot and sticky but a shower washed away the sweat. As he came out of the bathroom Hardin said, 'The Sergeant is back – with friends.'

'What friends?'

'You'll see them in the Delamere Bar.'

Stafford dressed and they went downstairs. As they crossed the courtyard in the midday sun Stafford felt the sweat break out again, and made a note to ask Curtis about his tailor.

The Delamere Bar was a large patio at the front of the hotel scattered with tables, each individually shaded, from which one could survey the passing throng. It was crowded, but the Sergeant had secured a table. He stood up as they approached. 'I would like the Colonel to meet Pete Chipende and Nair Singh.'

They shook hands. Chipende was a black African who offered a grin full of white teeth. 'Call me Chip; everyone does.' His English was almost accentless; just a hint of East African sing-song. Nair Singh was a turbanned Sikh with a ferocious black beard and a gentle smile.

As Stafford sat down Hardin said, 'The beer's not bad; cold and not too alcoholic.'

'Okay, a beer.' Stafford noted that it was probably too alcoholic for the Sikh who sat in front of a soft drink. He looked at Curtis and raised his eyebrows.

Curtis said, 'Back in London I thought we might need friends who know the territory and the language, so I made a few enquiries and got an address.'

'Our address,' said Chip. 'We work well; turn our hands to anything.'

Stafford kept his eye on Curtis. 'Where did you get the address?'

He shrugged. 'Friends, and friends of friends,' he said carelessly.

'You have useful friends.' Curtis was playing the old soldier, and Stafford knew he would get nothing more out of him – not then. He turned to the others. 'Do you know the score?'

Nair said, 'You want people watched.'

'Unobtrusively,' added Chip. He paused. 'And maybe you'll want more.'

'Maybe.' A waiter put down glasses and beer bottles. 'All right. A man arrives tomorrow from London. Gunnarsson, an American. I want to know where he goes and what he does.'

Chip poured himself some beer. 'Can be done.'

'There'll be two others; Hendrix, another American; and Farrar, an Englishman. Hendrix is important – Farrar less so. And there'll be another man – also Hendriks, but spelled differently.' He explained the difference.

Hardin said, 'You want Dirk tailed?' His voice held mild surprise.

'Why not?' Stafford poured beer, tasted it and found it refreshingly cold. 'Does anyone know anything about the Ol Njorowa Foundation?'

'Ol Njorowa?' said Chip. The name slipped more smoothly off his tongue than it had off Stafford's. 'That's near Naivasha.'

'An agricultural college,' said Nair. 'Doing good work, so I hear. I know someone there; a scientist called Hunt.'

That interested Stafford. 'How well do you know him?'

'We were at university together.' Nair pointed. 'Across the road there. We drank too much beer in this place.' He smiled. 'That was before I returned to my religion. I see him from time to time.'

'Could you introduce me? In an unobtrusive way?'

Nair thought for a moment. 'It's possible. When?'

'Today, if you can. I'd like to find out more about the Foundation before Gunnarsson arrives.'

'It will have to be at Naivasha. Who will be going apart from you?'

'Ben will be along. The Sergeant and Chip will stay to look after Gunnarsson tomorrow morning.'

Nair nodded and stood up. 'I'll make the arrangements. Be back soon.'

Stafford took a bigger sample of beer. 'Sergeant; I need suitable clothing or I'll melt away.'

He said, 'I'll see that the Colonel is fitted out.'

'You want a safari suit like this,' said Chip, fingering his own jacket. He smiled. 'You'd better go with Nair after lunch. You look too much the tourist. He'll get you a better price.'

Hardin handed Stafford a menu. 'Talking about lunch . . .'

They ordered lunch and another beer each all round – a soft drink for Nair. When he came back he said, 'Everything fixed. We'll have dinner with Alan Hunt and his sister at the Lake Naivasha Hotel. It's part of the same chain as the Norfolk so I booked rooms for tonight. Is that all right?'

'That's fine.'

Lunch arrived and they got down to it.

* * *

That afternoon Stafford was fitted out with a safari suit in less than an hour in one of the Indian shops near the market. Nair did the chaffering and brought the price down to a remarkably low level. Stafford ordered two more suits, then they set out for Naivasha, Nair driving and Hardin sitting in the back of the Nissan.

Outside town the road deteriorated, becoming pot-holed with badly repaired patches. When Stafford commented on this Nair said ruefully, 'It is not good. You would not think that this is an arterial highway – the main road to Uganda. The government should repair it properly and stop the big trucks.'

'Yeah,' said Hardin. 'The main liquids in this country seem to be beer and gasoline.'

Stafford found what he meant when they passed Limuru and started the descent of the escarpment into the Rift Valley.

The drop was precipitous and the road wound tortuously round hairpin bends. They were stuck behind a petrol tanker and in front of that was a big truck and trailer loaded with Tusker beer. The Nissan ground down in low gear, unable to overtake in safety, until Nair made a sound of exasperation and pulled off the road.

'We'll let them get ahead,' he said. 'This low gear work makes the engine overheat.' He opened the door of the car. 'I will show you something spectacular.'

Stafford and Hardin followed him through trees to the edge of a cliff. He waved. 'The Rift!'

It was a tremendous gash in the earth's surface as though a giant had struck with a cleaver. Stafford estimated a width of twenty miles or more. In the distance the waters of a lake glinted. Nair pointed to the hills on the other side. 'The Mau Escarpment – and that is Lake Naivasha. The mountain there is Longonot, a volcano, and the Ol Njorowa College is just the other side. You can't see the buildings from this angle.'

'How far does the Rift stretch?' asked Hardin.

Nair laughed. 'A long way. Four thousand miles, from the Lebanon to Mozambique. It's the biggest geological scar on the face of the earth. Gregory, the first white man to identify it, said it would be visible from the moon. Neil Armstrong proved it. Here, at this place, Africa is being torn in two.' He caught Stafford eyeing him speculatively. 'I studied geology at university,' he said dryly.

'And what do you do now, Nair?'

'I'm a courier, showing tourists around Kenya.' He turned. 'The road should be clear now.'

As Stafford walked back to the car he wondered about that courier bit. Perhaps it was true, perhaps not. And perhaps it was true but not the entire truth. This friend of a friend of Sergeant Curtis was a shade too enigmatic for his liking. 'And Chip? Is he a courier, too?'

'Why, yes,' said Nair.

They got to the floor of the Rift Valley unhampered by beer trucks, although a steady procession was grinding up the hill, going the other way. Once on the level Nair increased speed. They passed a road going off to the left across the valley. Nair said, 'That's the road to Narok and the Masai Mara. You ought to go there – many animals.'

Stafford grunted. 'I'm not here for sightseeing.' Thereafter Nair was silent until they arrived at the hotel.

It was a low-slung building, painted white with a red, tiled roof and, but for the row of rooms set to one side, it could have been a gentleman's country house. They registered and found their rooms. Stafford shared with Hardin and, as soon as they were alone, he said, 'What do you know about this pair – Chip and Nair?'

Hardin shrugged. 'No more than you. The Sergeant was tight-mouthed.'

'He said he had connections here, but that was a long time ago, during the Mau-Mau business. At that time Chip and Nair wouldn't have been long out of kindergarten. I think I'll have to have a serious talk with him when we get back to Nairobi.'

Stafford had a quick shower before they assembled on the lawn in front of the hotel. It was six o'clock, the cocktail hour, and groups of guests were sitting at tables knocking back the pre-prandial booze while watching the sun dip below the Mau Escarpment beyond the lake. He ordered gin and tonic, Hardin had a Seagram's, while Nair stuck to his lemon squash.

A dachshund was chasing large black and white birds quite unsuccessfully; they avoided his mad rushes contemptuously. Nair said, 'Those are ibis; quite a lot of them around here. There are also pelicans, marabou storks and cormorants all around the lake.' He pointed at an incredibly multi-coloured bird, gleaming iridescently in blues, greens and reds, which was hopping among the tables. 'And that's a superb starling.'

'You seem to know a lot about birds,' Stafford said. 'For a geologist.'

'A courier must know a lot if he's to please his clients,' Nair said blandly. 'Will you need a cover story for Alan Hunt?'

The switch in subject matter was startling. Stafford looked

at him thoughtfully, and said, 'I thought Hunt was your friend. Would you con him?'

Nair shrugged, 'As I said, I try to please my clients. I told him you were about to visit the geo-thermal project at Ol Karia; that's about two kilometres the other side of Hell's Gate.'

'But I know damn-all about it.'

'You don't have to know anything. You're going there as a vaguely interested visitor. They're drilling for steam to power an electricity generating plant. It's very interesting.'

'No doubt. Tell me, Nair; why are you doing this for me? Why are you playing along?'

He toyed with the iron bangle he wore on his wrist. 'Because I was asked,' he said. 'By a good friend in England.'

Stafford looked at Hardin. 'What do you think of that?'

He grinned. 'Not much.'

Nair said earnestly, 'Just be thankful that we're here to help you, Mr Stafford.'

Stafford sighed. 'Since we're on first name terms you'd better call me Max.' He added something pungent in Punjabi. Nair lit up and responded with Punjabi in full flow. Stafford said, 'Whoa, there! I wasn't in the Punjab long enough to learn more than the swear words. I was there for a short time as a boy just after the war; my father was in the Army. It was at the time of Partition.'

'That must have been a bad time,' Nair said seriously. 'But I've never been to India; I was born in Kenya.' He looked over Stafford's shoulder. 'Here is Alan Hunt now.'

Hunt was a tall, tanned man, blond with hair bleached almost white by the sun. He was accompanied by his sister, a shade darker but not much. Nair made the introductions and Stafford found her name was Judy. A hovering waiter took the order for another round of drinks.

'Is this your first visit to Kenya?' asked Judy, launching into the inevitable introductory smalltalk.

'Yes.' Stafford looked at his watch. 'I've been here about ten hours.'

'You get around quickly.'

'The car is a great invention.' Alan Hunt was talking to Nair. 'Are you with your brother at the Ol Njorowa College?'

'Yes; I'm an agronomist and Alan is a soil scientist. I suppose we complement each other. What do you do, Mr Stafford?'

'Max, please. I'm your original City of London business-man.' He tugged at the sleeve of his jacket. 'When I'm not wearing this I'm kitted out in a black suit, bowler hat and umbrella.'

She laughed. 'I don't believe it.'

'Take my word for it. It's still *de rigueur*.'

'I've never been to England,' she said a little wistfully.

'It's cold and wet,' Stafford said. 'You're better off here. Tell me something. I've been hearing about Hell's Gate – that's Ol Njorowa, isn't it?'

'In a way. It's what the English call it.'

'It sounds like the entrance to Dante's Inferno. What is it really?'

'It's a pass which runs along the western flank of Longonot; that's the big volcano near here. There are a lot of hot springs and steam vents which gave it its name, I suppose. But really it used to be an outlet for Lake Naivasha when the lake was a lot bigger than it is now.'

'How long ago was that?'

She smiled. She had a good smile. 'I wouldn't know. Maybe a million years.'

Nair stood up. 'We'd better go inside. The lake flies will be coming out now the sun has set.'

'Bad?' asked Hardin.

'Definitely not good,' said Hunt.

* * *

Over dinner Stafford got to know something about Hunt – and the Foundation. Hunt told about his work as a soil scientist. 'Jack of all trades,' he said. 'Something of geology, something of botany, something of microbiology, a smidgin

88

of chemistry. Its a wide field.' He had been with the Foundation for two years and was enthusiastic about it. 'We're doing good work, but it's slow. You can't transform a people in a generation.'

When Stafford asked what he meant he said, 'Well, the tribes here were subsistence farmers; the growing of cash crops is a different matter. It demands better land management and a touch of science. But they're learning.'

Stafford looked across at Judy. 'Don't they object to being taught by a woman?'

Hunt laughed. 'Just the opposite. You see, the Kikuyu women are traditionally the cultivators of land and Judy gets on well with them. Her problem is that she loses her young, unmarried women too fast.'

'How come?'

'They marry Masai men. The Masai are to the south of here – nomadic cattle breeders. Their women won't cultivate so the men like to marry Kikuyu women who will take care of their patches of maize and millet.'

Stafford smiled. 'An unexpected problem.'

'There are many problems,' Hunt said seriously. 'But we're licking them. The Commonwealth Development Corporation and the World Bank are funding projects. Up near Baringo there's a CDC outfit doing the same thing among the Njemps. It's a matter of finding the right crops to suit the soil. Our Foundation is more of a home grown project and we're a bit squeezed for cash, although there's a rumour going around that the Foundation has been left a bit of money.'

Not for long, Stafford thought. He said, 'When was the Foundation started?'

'Just after the war. It took a knock during the Mau-Mau troubles, went moribund and nearly died on its feet, but it perked up five or six years ago when Brice came. He's our Director.'

'A good man?'

'The best; a real live wire – a good administrator even though he doesn't know much about agriculture. But he has the sense to leave that to those who do. You must come to see us while you're here. Combine it with your visit to Ol Karia.'

'I'd like that,' said Stafford. He did not want to be at Ol Njorowa when Dirk Hendriks was around because his curiosity might arouse comment. 'Could we make it next week?'

'Of course. Give me a ring.'

They went into the lounge for coffee and brandy. Hunt was about to sit down when he paused. 'There's Brice now, having a drink with Patterson. He's one of the animal study boys. I can clear your visit to the College right away.' He went over and talked with Brice then he turned and beckoned.

He introduced Stafford and Hardin to Brice who was a square man of medium height and with a skin tanned to the colour of cordovan leather. His speech was *almost* standard Oxford English but there was a barely perceptible broadening of the vowels which betrayed his Southern Africa origins. It was so faint that Hardin could be excused for identifying him as English.

He shook hands with a muscular grip. 'Glad to have you with us, Mr Stafford; we don't get too many visitors from England. Have you been in Kenya long?' The standard ice-breaking question.

'I arrived this morning. It's a beautiful country.'

'Indeed it is,' Brice said. 'It's not my own country – not yet – but I like it.'

Judy said questioningly, 'Not yet?'

Brice laughed jovially. 'I'm taking out Kenya citizenship. My papers should be through in a couple of months.'

'Then you're English,' Stafford said.

He laughed again. 'Not me; I'm Rhodesian. Can't you tell by my accent?' He raised his eyebrows at Stafford's silence. 'No? Well, I lived in England a while, so I suppose I've lost it. I got out of Rhodesia when that idiot Smith took over with UDI.'

'What's that?' asked Hardin.

'The Unilateral Declaration of Independence.' Brice smiled.

90

'I believe you Americans made a similar Declaration a couple of hundred years ago.'

'Of course,' said Hardin. 'I was here in Africa when it happened, but I never got that far south. How did it come out in the end? African affairs aren't very well reported back home.'

'It couldn't last,' said Brice. 'You couldn't have a hundred thousand whites ruling millions of blacks and make it stick. There was a period of guerilla warfare and then the whites caved in. The British government supervised elections and the Prime Minister is now Mugabe, a black; and the name of the country is now Zimbabwe.'

'Do you have any intention of going back now that Mugabe is in command?' asked Stafford.

Brice shook his head. 'No,' he said. 'Never go back – that's my motto. Besides, I have precious little to go back to. I had a farm up near Umtali, and that's where the war was.' His face hardened. 'My parents were killed and I heard that the farm-house my father built was burned out – a total loss. No, this will be my country from now on.' He sipped from his glass. 'Mind you, I couldn't leave Africa. I didn't like England; it was too bloody cold for my liking.'

He turned to Hunt. 'I don't see any reason why Mr Stafford shouldn't take a look at the College. When would that be?'

'Some time next week?' suggested Stafford.

They arranged a day and Brice noted it in his diary. He smiled, and said, 'That will probably be the day I kill the rumours.'

Stafford lifted his eyebrows. 'What rumours?'

'About the unexpected inflow of cash,' said Hunt. He looked at Brice. 'Is it true?'

'Quite true,' said Brice. 'An unexpected windfall. Could be as much as six or seven million.'

'Kenya shillings?' queried Hunt.

Brice laughed. 'Pounds sterling,' he said, and Hunt gave a long whistle.

Stafford kept a poker face and wondered what had happened to the rest of the cash. There was a shortfall of about twenty-seven million.

Brice said, 'Keep it under your hat, Alan, until I make the official announcement. I'm seeing the Trustees and a lawyer in the next few days.'

They had a few more moments of conversation and then Stafford and Hunt returned to their own table. Stafford was abstracted, mulling over what Brice had said, but presently he got talking to Judy. 'If you're coming to the College you must go ballooning with us,' she said.

He stared at her. 'Ballooning! You must be kidding.'

'No, I'm not. Alan has a hot air balloon. He *says* he finds it useful in his work.' She laughed. 'I think that is just an excuse, though; it's for the sport mostly. It's great fun. A good way of spotting animals.'

'Can you steer it?'

'Not very well. You go where the wind listeth, like a thistledown. Alan talks learnedly about wind shear and other technicalities, and says he can go pretty much where he wants. But I don't think he has all that much control.'

'What happens if you blow over the lake?'

'You don't go up if the wind is in that direction; but if it changes you swim until the chase boat catches up, and you hope there aren't any crocodiles about.'

Stafford said, 'I call that living dangerously.'

'It's not really dangerous; we haven't had as much as a sprained wrist yet. Alan caught the ballooning bug from another Alan – Alan Root. Have you heard of him?'

'The wildlife man? Yes; I've seen him on television back home.'

'He lives near here,' said Judy. 'He does a lot of filming from his balloon. And he went over Kilimanjaro. Ballooning is becoming popular here. Down at Keekorok in the Masai Mara they take tourists up and call it a balloon safari.'

It was pleasant sitting there chatting. Stafford learned a bit more about the Foundation, but not much, and was sorry when the Hunts departed at about eleven, their parting words urging him to come back soon. When they had gone he, Hardin and Nair pooled their knowledge and found it wouldn't fill an egg-cup.

Stafford said, 'Ben, I'm sending you back to England to do something we should have done before. In any case you're too conspicuous here; Nairobi is a small town and you could come face to face with Gunnarsson all too easily.'

'Yeah,' he said. 'I suppose I am your hole card. What do I do in England?'

'You study the life and times of Jan-Willem Hendrykxx. I could bear to know how he made his boodle and why he left it to the Ol Njorowa Foundation. Find the Kenya connection, Ben. And nose around Jersey while Farrar is away. The old man must have talked to *someone* in the seven years he was there.'

'When do I leave?'

'Tomorrow.' Stafford turned to Nair. 'And I'd like to know more about the Foundation. Can you dig out anything on it?'

He nodded. 'That should be easy.'

'Then we leave for Nairobi immediately after breakfast tomorrow'

10

They got back to Nairobi just after eleven next morning and, as Nair parked the car outside the Norfolk, Stafford saw Curtis in the Delamere Bar sinking a beer. He said to Hardin, 'Tell the Sergeant I'll see him in my room now.'

'Okay,' said Hardin.

'I'll find Chip,' said Nair.

Stafford nodded and got out of the car. He went into the bar to buy cigarettes and then went up to his room where Curtis and Hardin awaited him. He looked at Curtis and said, 'Where's Gunnarsson?'

'At the Hilton,' said Curtis. 'Chip is covering him.'

'Chip is covering him,' Stafford repeated. 'All right, Sergeant; exactly who are Chip and Nair?'

He wore an injured look. 'I told you.'

'Don't come the old soldier with me,' said Stafford. 'I've had better men than you booked for dumb insolence. You've told me nothing. Now, out with it. I want to know if I can trust them. I want to know if they'll sell me should Gunnarsson offer a higher price. How much are we paying them, anyway?'

'Nothing,' Curtis said. 'It's a favour.'

Stafford looked at him in silence for a while, then said. 'That does it. Now you've *got* to tell me.'

'I'm a mite interested, too,' said Hardin.

Curtis sighed. 'All right; but I don't want anyone getting into trouble. No names, no pack drill; see? I told the Colonel I'd been in Kenya before, but that wasn't the only time. I spent a leave here in 1973. The Colonel knows how it's done.'

'You talked to a Chief Petty Officer and came over as a supernumerary in one of Her Majesty's ships. A free ride.'

He nodded. 'She was one of the ships on the Beira patrol.'

'What's that?' asked Hardin.

'A blockade of Beira to try to stop oil getting into Rhodesia,' said Stafford. 'And bloody ineffectual it was. Carry on Sergeant.'

Curtis said, 'I went ashore at Mombasa, had a look around there, then came up here on the train. I'd been here three or four days when I went to have a look at that big building – the tall round one.'

'The Kenyatta Conference Centre,' said Hardin.

'That's it,' said Curtis. 'It wasn't finished then. There was a lot of builder's junk around; it was a mess. I'd left it a bit late in the day and before I knew it the twilight had come, and that doesn't last long here. Anyway I heard a scuffle and when I turned a corner I saw four black Africans attacking an old Indian and a girl. They'd beat up the old man and he was lying on the ground, and now they were taking care of the girl. It was going to be a gang rape, I reckon. It didn't happen.' He held up his fists. 'I'm pretty good with these.'

Stafford knew that; Curtis had been runner-up in the Marine Boxing Championships in his time. And a tough Marine Colour-Sergeant would be more than a match for four unskilled yobbos. 'Go on.'

'The girl was fifteen years old, and the man was her grandfather. The girl was unhurt if scared, but the old man had been badly beaten-up. Anyway the upshot of it was that I took them home. They made quite a fuss of me then – gave me a meal. It was good curry,' he said reminiscently.

'We'll leave your gourmet experiences until later,' Stafford said. 'What next?'

'The Indians were in a bad way then. Kenyatta had declared that holders of British passports must turn them in for Kenyan passports.'

'It was the Kenya for the Kenyans bit,' remarked Hardin. 'I was here then. The word for it was "localization".'

'The Indians didn't want to give up their British passports but they knew that if they didn't the government would deport them,' Curtis said. 'India wouldn't have them and the only place they could go to was the UK. They didn't mind that but they weren't allowed to take any currency with them, and their baggage was searched for valuables before leaving.'

'Yeah,' said Hardin. 'They were between the rock and a hard place.' He shrugged. 'But I don't know that you could blame Kenyatta. He didn't want a big foreign enclave in the country. It applied to the British, too, you know. Become Kenyans or leave.'

Curtis said, 'They asked me to help them. I'd told them how I had come to Kenya and they wanted me to take something back to England.'

'What was it?' Stafford asked.

He sketched a small package in the air. 'A small box sewn up in leather.'

'What was in it?'

'I don't know. I didn't open it.'

'What do you think was in it?'

Curtis hesitated, then said, 'I reckon diamonds.'

Stafford said, 'Sergeant, you were a damned fool. If you'd have been caught you'd have been jailed and lost your service pension. So you took it to England.'

'Yes. Landed at Portsmouth and then went up to London to an address in the East End.'

'What did you charge for your services?'

He looked surprised. 'Nothing, sir.' Stafford regarded him thoughtfully, and Curtis said, 'They were good people. You see, they got to England and settled. And after that my Amy was a fearsome time in dying and I had a hard officer. I applied for compassionate leave and he wouldn't let me have it. I got it at the end, though; I was there when she died. And I found those Indians had been looking after her – taking flowers and fruit and things to the hospital. Seeing she was eased.' He was silent for a while, then repeated, 'Good people.'

Stafford sighed and went to the refrigerator. He broke the paper seal and took out a bottle. 'Have a beer, Sergeant.'

'Thank you, sir.'

He gave another to Hardin and opened one for himself. 'So when you knew we were coming to Kenya you went and asked for assistance. Is that it?'

'Yes, sir.'

'What's the name of this Indian family?' Curtis held his silence, and Stafford said gently, 'It's safe with me, Sergeant.'

Reluctantly he said, 'Pillay.'

A snort came from Hardin. 'Every second Gujarati is called Pillay; those that aren't are called Patel. It's like meeting a Britisher called Smith or Jones.'

Stafford paused in the pouring of the beer. 'Gujarati! This is where it stops making sense. Nair Singh is a Sikh, and since when have Sikhs and Gujaratis been chums? Not to mention Pete Chipende – he's a black African and that's a combination even less likely. And you say these two are helping us free of charge? Come *on*, Sergeant!'

'Hold it a minute,' said Hardin. 'Max, you need a short course in Kenyan political history. I was working here, remember? The Company was very interested in political activities in Kenya, and I was in it up to my neck so I know the score.'

'Well?'

He held up a finger. 'A one party state – the Kenya African National Union; that's KANU. Kenyatta was President, and the vice-President was Oginga Odinga. But even in a one party state there are factions, and Odinga broke away and formed the Kenya People's Union – the KPU. Kenyatta wasn't having that. There was a power struggle and, in the end, the KPU was banned. Odinga spent quite a time in jail. That was back in 1969. Of course, being Africa the brawl was about tribal loyalties as much as anything else. Kenyatta was a Kikuyu and Odinga a Luo. I've been keeping my ear to the ground while I've been here, and even now KANU is losing ground among the Luos. Of course, there's ideology involved, too.'

'So what's this got to do with anything?'

'Odinga had to get his money from somewhere; he had to

have a war chest. I know he got some from the Chinese and some from the Russians. Kenyatta wasn't having anything to do with the Commies – he closed down their embassies – so they'd do anything to embarrass him. But there was a strong feeling that Odinga was getting funds from the expatriate Indian community in Britain. They'd been thrown out and they didn't bear Kenyatta any love, either.'

'So what's your conclusion?'

'My guess is that Chip and Nair are Odinga's supporters, KPU men. The KPU is banned but it's still going strong underground. If a source of UK funds should request a favour it wouldn't be refused.'

"Damn!' said Stafford. 'Bloody politics is the last thing I want to get mixed up in.'

'You're not mixing in politics,' said Hardin. 'You're not attacking the government. Just accept the favour and keep your mouth shut. Those guys could be useful. They *are* being useful.'

Curtis looked woebegone. Stafford smiled, and said, 'Cheer up, Sergeant; the Good Samaritan nearly always gets the chop in this weary world. It's really my fault. I told you back in England that I didn't want to know what you were up to.'

Curtis drank some beer and Stafford could see him take heart. Hardin said, 'You can bet there'll be more than Chip and Nair. They may not show but they'll be there.'

'What tells you that?'

'Past experience,' he said, and drained his glass.

*   *   *

So that was that. Stafford had allies thrust upon him that he could very well do without. But Hardin was right – they could be useful. He determined to accept their help up to a point and to keep his mouth shut as Hardin advised. Hear no evil, see no evil, speak no evil. But trust them he would not.

Chip showed up early in the afternoon. It seemed that Gunnarsson was doing what Stafford had done – sleeping away his travel weariness. But he had not appeared for lunch and had a meal sent up to his room. 'Who is keeping an eye on him now?'

Chip showed a mouthful of teeth. 'Don't worry. He's being watched.'

So Hardin was right; Chip and Nair were not alone. Chip said, 'Mr Farrar's party is coming in from London on the morning flight.'

'How do you know?'

Again the teeth. 'My brother-in-law is an official at the airport.'

Nair turned up a few minutes later. He brought with him a thick envelope which he handed to Stafford. It proved to be a rundown on the Ol Njorowa Foundation. It was quite detailed and he wondered how Nair had got hold of all this information at such short notice. Very efficient.

There were five Trustees; K. J. Patterjee, B. J. Peters, D. W. Ngotho, Col. S. T. Lovejoy and the Rev. A. T. Peacock. He said, 'Who are these people?'

Chip lounged over and looked over his shoulder. 'One Indian, a Parsee; three Brits and a black Kenyan.'

'People of influence? Of standing in the community?'

Stafford heard a chuckle and looked up to see that Nair's face was wreathed in a smile as well as a beard. Chip said, 'We wouldn't go as far as to say that; would we, Nair?'

Nair laughed outright. 'I don't think so.'

Chip's hand came over Stafford's shoulder and tapped on the paper. 'Patterjee was jailed for trying to smuggle 12,000 kilogrammes of cloves from Mombasa. That's highly illegal in this country. Peters was convicted of evading currency regulations and jailed. Ngotho was convicted of being a business prostitute; also jailed.'

'What the hell is a business prostitute?'

Nair said, 'Non-citizens cannot hold controlling interests in businesses in Kenya. There was a brisk trade in front men – Kenyans who would apparently own shares but who did not actually do so. Pure legal fakery. It was Mzee Kenyatta

99

who coined the phrase, "business prostitute", wasn't it?'

'That's right,' said Chip. 'He made it illegal. Colonel Lovejoy is okay, though; he's been in Kenya forever. An old man now. Peacock is a missionary.'

Stafford was baffled. It was a curious mixture. 'How in hell did three crooks get made Trustees of the Ol Njorowa Foundation?'

'It *is* odd,' agreed Chip. 'What is your interest in the Foundation, Max?'

'I don't know that I have any interest in the Foundation itself. The Foundation is peripheral to my investigation.'

'I wonder . . .' mused Nair.

Chip said, 'You wonder what?'

'If the Foundation is really peripheral to Max's investigation.'

'Since we don't know what Max is investigating that's hard to say,' observed Chip judiciously.

Stafford sighed and leaned back in his chair. 'All right, boys; suppose we stop talking with forked tongues.'

Chip said, 'Well, if we knew what we were doing it would help. Wouldn't it, Nair?'

'I should think so.'

Stafford said, 'I'll think about it. Meanwhile, if you cross-talk comedians will allow me, I'll get on with this.' He turned pages. There were plans of the College which appeared to be quite extensive, involving lecture rooms, laboratories, studies, a library and a residential area. There were sports facilities including a swimming pool, tennis courts and a football field. There was also a large area devoted to experimental plots, something like British garden allotments but more scientific.

Stafford flipped a few pages and found a list of the faculty and caught the name of Alan Hunt. He tapped the name at the top of the page. 'This man, Brice, the Director. Your friend, Hunt, seems to think he's a good man, good for the Foundation. Would you agree?'

'Yes, I would. He's built up the place since he's been there.

He works in well with the agronomists at the University, too.' Nair shrugged. 'I think the University – and the Government – are pleased that the Foundation can take up some of the financial load. Research is expensive.'

But Hunt had said that cash was tight. Stafford ignored that for the moment and flipped back the pages to the beginning – to the Trustees. 'How long have these three jokers been on the Board of Trustees?'

'I don't know,' said Chip. 'But we can find out. Can't we, Nair?'

'I should think so,' said Nair. 'Not much difficulty there.'

The telephone rang and Stafford picked it up, then held it out to Chip. 'For you.'

He listened, answering in monosyllables and not speaking English. Then he put down the phone, and said, 'Gunnarsson is up and about. He's at the New Stanley, having a coffee at the Thorn Tree.' He stood up. 'I'll be about his business. Coming, Nair?'

'Might as well. Nothing to do here except drink Max's beer, and I can't.' He joined Chip at the door.

Chip turned, and said softly, 'I hope you'll make up your mind about telling us what this is about, Max. It would be better for all of us.' The door closed behind them.

Stafford seriously doubted that. If Hardin was right and a proscribed political party was looking for loot to replenish its war chest there was too much of it about floating relatively loose for him to take chances. He spent the rest of the afternoon concocting a suitable story which would satisfy Chip and Nair, and then went to see Hardin who was in his room packing.

* * *

Hardin went back to London. Farrar duly arrived and wasted no time. He whisked the two heirs down to Naivasha. Unknown to him Gunnarsson went, too, and they all stayed at the Lake Naivasha Hotel. And, unknown to any of them, Chip and Nair were there. A real cosy gathering. Stafford stayed in Nairobi digging a little deeper into the curious matter of the Trustees, although he would dearly have liked to be a fly on the wall when Farrar, Hendrix, Hendriks and Brice got together in Brice's office.

They stayed in Naivasha for a total of three days and then returned to Nairobi. Farrar and Dirk took the night flight to London, and Stafford wired Hardin to expect them. Gunnarsson moved into the New Stanley with Hendrix, and Stafford sat back wondering what was to happen next. Sooner or later he would have to make a move, but he didn't know the move to make. It was like playing chess blindfold, but he knew he would have to do something before distribution of the estate was made and Gunnarsson and Hendrix departed over the horizon, disappearing with three million pounds. Stafford badly needed ammunition – bullets to shoot – and he hoped Hardin would find something.

Chip came to see him. 'You wanted to know when the various Trustees of the Foundation were appointed.'

'I could bear to know.'

Chip grinned. 'Lovejoy and Peacock are founder Trustees; they've been on the Board since 1950. The others all came on at the same time in 1975.'

Stafford sat back to think. 'When did Brice take over as Director? When exactly?'

Chip said, 'Early 1976.'

'Interesting. Try this on for size, Chip. The Foundation was started in the 1950s but, according to Alan Hunt, it went moribund just after Kenya went independent. But that doesn't mean to say it had no money. I'll bet it had more than ever. The Charities Commission in the UK has done a survey and found scores of charities not doing what their charters have called for, but piling up investment money. No jiggery-pokery intended, just apathy and laxity on the part of the Trustees.'

'So?'

'So the Foundation *must* have had money. Where else could Brice have got it for his revitalizing programme? Now, take three vultures called Patterjee, Peters and Ngotho who realize there's a fat pigeon to be picked over. Somehow, I don't know how, they get themselves elected on to the Board of Trustees. They appoint as Director a non-Kenyan, a stranger called Brice, a man who doesn't know the country or its customs and they think they can pull the wool over his eyes.'

'While they milk the Foundation?' said Chip. He nodded. 'It would fit. But what about Lovejoy and Peacock?'

'I've done a little check on that pair,' said Stafford. 'Colonel Lovejoy is, as you say, an old man. He's eighty-two and senile, and no longer takes any active role in any business. Peacock, the missionary, used to be active in the Naivasha area but he moved to Uganda when Amin was kicked out. Now he's doing famine relief work there up in Karamoja. I don't think they'd be any problem to our thieves. But Brice is too sharp. He's no figurehead; he's proved that while he's been Director. Our trio have hardly got their hands into the cash register before he's really taken charge. He's got his hands on the accounts and they can't do a damned thing about it.'

'And they couldn't fire him,' said Chip. He laughed. 'If he caught them at it he'd have them by the short and curlies. And if he was sharp enough he'd keep them on as Trustees. That would put him in as top dog in the Foundation. He wouldn't want a stronger Board – it might get in his way.'

'Maybe he'd sweeten them by letting them take a healthy honorarium this side of larceny. That's what I'd do,' said Stafford. 'Just to keep them really quiet.'

Chip said, 'Max, you have a devious mind. You could just be right about this.'

'And what it means is that Brice is an honest man. The take could have been split four ways instead of three, but he really built up the Foundation into a going concern. I'd like to see this man; I have a standing invitation from Alan Hunt.' Stafford looked at his watch. 'I'll ring him now.'

'I'll drive you to Naivasha,' Chip offered.

'No, I'll go alone. But stay in touch. And keep a careful eye on Gunnarsson and Hendrix. If they move I want to know.'

11

Ol Njorowa College was about twelve kilometres from the Lake Naivasha Hotel. Stafford showered to wash away the travel stains and then drove there, first along the all-weather road that skirted the lake, and then along the rough track which would, no doubt, be dicey in wet weather. He found the College under the slopes of brooding Longonot.

There was a heavy meshed high fence and a gatehouse with closed gates, which surprised him. A toot on the horn brought a man running, and he wound the window right down as the man approached. He stooped and brought a gnarled, lined face to Stafford's level. 'Yes, sah?'

'Max Stafford to see Mr Hunt.'

'Dr Hunt? Yes, sah.' The lines of suspicion smoothed from the face. 'You're expected.' He straightened, issued a piercing whistle, then bent again. 'Straight through, sah, and follow the arrows. You can't miss it.'

The gates were opening so Stafford let out the clutch and drove through the gateway. The road inside the College grounds was asphalted and in good condition. There were 'sleeping policemen' every fifty yards, humps right across the road to cut down the speed of cars. They did, and as Stafford bumped over the first he checked the rear view mirror; the gates were closing behind and there was no evidence of anyone pushing them. Most of the buildings were long, low structures but there was a two-storey building ahead. The grounds were kept in good condition with mown lawns, and flowering trees were everywhere, bougainvillea and jacaranda.

Outside the big building he put the car into a slot between neatly painted white lines. When he got out he felt the hammer blow of the sun striking vertically on to his head. Because the elevation cut the heat one tended to forget that this was equatorial Africa, with the Equator not very far away. Hunt was waiting in the shade under the portico at the entrance and came forward.

They shook hands. 'Glad you could come.'

'Glad to be here.' Stafford looked around. 'Nice place you have.'

Hunt nodded. 'We like to think so. I'll give you the Grand Tour. Would you like it before or after a beer?'

'Lead me to your beer,' Stafford said fervently, and Hunt chuckled.

As they went inside he said, 'This block is mostly for administration, offices and so on. Plus those laboratories that need special facilities such as refrigeration. We have our own diesel-electric generators at the back.'

'Then you're not on mains power? That surprises me. I saw a lot of high tension pylons as I drove around the lake. Big ones.'

'Those are the new ones from the geothermal electric plant at Ol Karia. It's not on line yet. The power lines are being erected by the Japanese, and the geothermal project has advisors from Iceland and New Zealand. Those boys know about geothermal stuff. Have you been out there yet?'

'It's next on my list.'

'When we get mains power we'll still keep our own generators for standby in case of a power cut.' He opened a door. 'This way.'

He led Stafford into a recreation room. There was a half-size billiards table, a ping-pong table, several card tables scattered about, and comfortable armchairs. At the far end there was a bar behind which stood a black Kenyan in a white coat polishing a glass. Hunt walked forward and flopped into a chair. 'Billy,' he called. 'Two beers.'

'Yes, sah; two beers coming. Premium?'

'*Hapana*; White Cap.' Hunt gave Stafford a half smile. 'Premium is a bit too strong if we're going to walk in the midday sun.'

'Mad dogs and Englishmen,' Stafford suggested.

'Something like that.' Hunt laughed. 'You know, the Victorians had entirely the wrong idea, what with their pith helmets and flannel spinal pads. They were more likely to get heatstroke indoors than outdoors in their day; their roofs were of corrugated iron and they cooked on wood-burning stoves. The rooms must have been like ovens.'

Stafford looked at Hunt's sun-bleached hair. 'So you're not worried about sunstroke?'

'You're all right once you're acclimatized and as long as you don't overdo it.' The bartender put a tray on the table. 'Put it on my chit,' said Hunt. He poured his beer. 'Cheers!'

Stafford waited until he had swallowed the first stinging, cold freshness before he said, 'Tell me something. Isn't a place like this eligible for a government grant?'

Hunt stretched his legs and absently rubbed a red scratch on his thigh. 'Oh, we get a grant but it doesn't go far enough. They never do. But things are changing. You heard what Brice said the other day. He still hasn't made the official announcement, though.'

Hunt said, 'Anyway, it was enough to bring the Trustees out of the woodwork. They came this week and it's the first time I've seen them here, and that's been two years.'

Stafford said, 'I'd have thought, if money was tight, they'd have been in your hair seeing there wasn't any wastage.'

'Oh, Brice keeps them informed.' There was a slight hesitation as though he had meant to say something else, and Stafford guessed it was that Brice kept the Trustees in line. 'I wouldn't say he's machiavellian about it, but it suits me if I never see the Trustees. I have enough to bother about.' He looked up and waved. 'Here's Judy and Jim Odhiambo.'

Stafford stood up but Judy waved him back into the chair. 'Sit down, Max. I'd give my soul for an ice-cold tonic.'

He was introduced. Odhiambo was a short and stocky black with muscular arms. Hunt said, 'Dr Odhiambo is our resident expert on cereals – maize, millet, wheat – you name it.'

'Dr Hunt exaggerates,' said Odhiambo deprecatingly.

He ordered a beer for himself and a tonic for Judy. Hunt said, 'I've got something for you, Jim. I came across a paper in the Abstracts about primitive, ancestral forms of maize in Peru and I remembered what you said about preserving the gene pool. If you're interested I'll dig it out.'

Within two minutes they were engaged in a technical conversation. Judy said ruefully, 'This must be very dull for you.'

'Not at all,' Stafford said lightly. 'I like to hear experts talk, even though I don't understand one word in ten.' He looked at the bubbles rising in his glass. 'Alan has been telling me about the Foundation's good fortune.'

She lit up. 'Yes, isn't it wonderful.' And more soberly she said, 'Not that I'm cheering about the death of an old man in England, but I never knew him, and we can do so much good with the money here.'

'Who was he?'

'I haven't the slightest idea.'

A cul-de-sac. A bit of offensive was needed or he would never get anywhere. 'Why the fortifications?'

Judy wrinkled her brow, 'What fortifications?'

Stafford said, 'The fence around the grounds, and the gatehouse with closed gates.'

'Oh, that.' Her voice was rueful again. 'We like to give visitors to Kenya a good impression, but there are some awfully light-fingered people around here. We were losing things; not much – just minor agricultural implements, seeds, petrol – stuff like that. Most of it didn't matter very much, but when Jim Odhiambo breeds a special kind of maize for a certain soil and the seed is stolen and probably ends up in the stewpot of some ignorant *wananchi* then it hurts. It really does.'

'*Wananchi*?'

'Indigenous Kenyan. You can't really blame them, I suppose. The seed would look like any other seed, and they don't really understand what we're doing here.' She shook her head. 'Anyway, with the fence and the gates we tightened security.'

Hunt drained his glass. 'Come and see my little empire, Max. The bit of it that's upstairs.'

Stafford followed him and, on the way, said, 'Is Brice here today?'

'You'll probably meet him at lunch.' Hunt led the way along a corridor. 'Here we are.' He opened a door.

It was a laboratory filled with incomprehensible equipment and instruments the uses of which Hunt explained with gusto and, although much of it was over Stafford's head, he could not but admire Hunt's enthusiasm. 'Perhaps, with this new money, I can get the gas chromatograph I've been pushing for,' Hunt said. 'I need it to identify trace elements.'

Stafford wandered over to the window. Being on the top storey he had quite an extensive view. Away in the distance he could see the fence around the College grounds, and there was a man walking along it as though on patrol. He wore a rifle slung over his shoulder. He said, 'Why do you need armed guards?'

Hunt stopped in full spate. 'Huh?'

'Armed guards; why do you need them?'

'We don't.'

Stafford pointed. 'Then what's he doing out there?'

Hunt crossed to the window. 'Oh, we've been having a problem with a leopard lately, but how the devil it gets over the fence we don't know. It's taken a couple of dogs and the resident staff are disturbed – some of them have children here just about the size to attract a leopard.'

'And you don't know how it gets in?'

'Brice thinks there must be a tree, probably an acacia, which is growing too near the fence. He was organizing an exploration of the perimeter this morning. That's why he wasn't around.'

'How long is your perimeter?'

'I wouldn't know,' said Hunt lightly. 'I haven't measured it.'

* * *

Lunch was in the staff canteen which would not have disgraced a moderately good hotel as a dining room. It was spacious with good napery and silverware, and the food was very good. It seemed to Stafford that for a Foundation supposed to be hard up for money the senior staff did themselves well.

He was introduced to most of the staff over a pre-lunch drink at the bar. Their names and faces were forgotten as soon as the introductions were made, as usually happens on these occasions, but he estimated that they were black Kenyans, Indians and whites in roughly equal proportions, and honorifics like 'Doctor' and 'Professor' were bandied about with enthusiasm.

Hunt grinned at him, and said *sotto voce*, 'We have an almost Germanic regard for academic titles out here. You don't happen to be a Ph.D., do you?'

'Not a hope.'

'Pity.'

Stafford was re-introduced to Brice who said, 'Is Alan looking after you, Mr Stafford?'

Stafford smiled. 'Like royalty.'

They had a few moments more of conversation and then Brice drifted away, going easily from group to group with a word and a laugh for everyone. A jovial man with an instinct for leadership. Stafford had it himself to some degree and recognized it in another.

A few minutes later they adjourned for lunch and he found himself sitting with the Hunts and Odhiambo. He nodded towards Brice who was at what could be called the top table. 'Nice chap.'

Odhiambo nodded. 'For a non-scientist.' He leaned forward. 'Do you know he hardly understands a thing about what we're doing here. Odd in such an intelligent man. But he's a good administrator.'

Judy said, 'But, Jim, you don't really understand literature, do you?'

'I appreciate it,' he said stiffly. 'Even if I don't wholly

understand it. But Brice doesn't *want* to know about our work.' He shook his head and looked at Stafford. 'We have a review meeting each week for the senior staff which Brice used to chair. It was impossible because he simply didn't understand. In the end he gave up and left it to us.'

Alan Hunt said, 'You must agree he knows his limitations and leaves us alone.'

'There is that,' agreed Odhiambo.

'Then who does the forward planning?' Stafford asked. 'The scientific work, I mean.'

'The weekly meeting reviews progress and decides on what must be done,' said Odhiambo.

'That's right,' said Hunt. 'Brice only digs his heels in when it comes to a matter of costs. He runs the financial end. I must say he does it very well.'

The meal was very good. They were ending with fresh fruit when Brice tapped on a glass with the edge of a knife and the hum of conversation quietened. He stood up. 'Ladies and gentlemen, friends and colleagues. I understand that certain rumours are circulating about a change in the fortunes of our College – a favourable change, I might add. I don't like rumours – they add to the uncertainty of life – and so this is to be regarded as an official statement.'

He paused and there was dead silence. 'The Foundation is the fortunate recipient of a certain sum of money from a gentleman in Europe now dead. The sum involved is five, perhaps six, maybe even seven . . .' He paused again with a fine sense of timing. '. . . million pounds sterling.'

Pandemonium erupted. There was a storm of applause and everyone stood, clapping and cheering. Stafford joined in, smiling as much as anyone, but wondering what had happened to the rest of the loot. Judy, her eyes shining, said, 'Isn't it just great?'

'Great,' he agreed.

Brice held up his hands and the applause died away. 'Now that doesn't mean you can go hog-wild on your financial requisitions,' he said genially, and there was a murmur of amusement. 'There are legal procedures before we get the money and it may be some months yet. So, for the time being, we carry on as usual.' He sat down and a hubbub of noisy conversation arose again.

Stafford was still puzzled. He had assessed Brice, on his record, as being an honest man. Under the will 85 per cent of more than forty million pounds was to go to the Foundation so why was Brice lying? Or was he? Could it be that the Hendrykxx estate was being looted by someone else? Farrar, perhaps. A crooked lawyer was not entirely unknown – someone had once made the crack that the term 'criminal lawyer' is a tautology.

Hunt said something, rousing Stafford from his abstraction. 'What's that?'

'I'll show you around the College,' he repeated.

'All right.'

* * *

They did the rounds in a Land-Rover and Stafford found the place to be more extensive than he had thought. The research was not only into agricultural science concerning the growing of crops, but animal husbandry was involved and also a small amount of arboriculture. Hunt said, 'We're trying to develop better shrubs to give ground cover in the dry lands. Once the cover is destroyed the land just blows away.' He laughed. 'There's a chap here trying to develop a shrub that the bloody goats won't eat. Good luck to him.'

An extensive area was given over to experimental plots which looked like a patchwork quilt. Hunt said, 'It's based on a Graeco-Latin square,' and when Stafford asked what that was Hunt launched into an explanation replete with mathematics which was entirely beyond him, but he gathered it had something to do with the design of experiments. He commented that mathematics seemed to enter everything these days.

They were on their way back to the Admin Block when his attention was caught by something not usually associated with an agricultural college – a dish antenna about twelve feet across and looking up almost vertically. 'Stop a minute,' he said. 'What's that for?'

Hunt braked. 'Oh, that's the animal boys. It's a bit peripheral to us.'

'That,' Stafford said positively, 'is a radar dish and nothing to do with bloody animals,'

'Wrong,' said Hunt. 'It's a transmitter-receiver in communication with a satellite up there.' He jerked his thumb upwards. 'And it has everything to do with animals.'

'All right; I'll buy it.'

'Well, it's no use us developing super crops if animals wreck the fields. You've no idea how much damage an elephant can do, and hippos are even worse. A hippo going through a maize field is like a combine harvester, and what it doesn't eat it tramples. So there's basic research going on into the movement of animals; we want to know how far they move, and where they're likely to move, and when. Selected animals are tagged with a small radio, and a geo-stationary satellite traces their movements.'

'What will you scientists get up to next?'

Hunt shrugged. 'It's of more use in tracing truly migratory animals like the Alaskan caribou. They used this method when they were planning the oil pipeline across Alaska. An elephant doesn't migrate in the true sense of the word although the herds do get around, and a hippo might go on a twenty-mile stomp.' He nodded towards the dish on the top of the building. 'But they're also using this to trace the annual migration of wildebeest from the Serengeti.' He released the brake.

'That's in Tanzania, isn't it?'

'Yes; but wildebeest don't respect national boundaries.'

Stafford laughed. 'Neither do radio waves.'

As they drove off Hunt said, 'I'd take you in there but there's no one about right now. As I said, it's peripheral to our work here. The radio crowd isn't financed by the Foundation; we just give them space here. They're a bit clannish; too; they don't mix well. We very rarely see them.'

He pulled up in front of the Admin Block, and Stafford said, 'Thanks for the guided tour. What about coming to the hotel for dinner?'

Hunt shook his head regretfully. 'Sorry, I've got something else on – a committee meeting. But what about coming up with me in the balloon tomorrow? Jim Odhiambo wants me to do some photography.'

Always something new. 'I'd like that,' said Stafford.

'I'll pick you up at the hotel – seven o'clock.'

* * *

Stafford drove back to the hotel and found a message waiting. Ring Curtis. He used the telephone in his room and got Curtis on the line who said, 'Chip wants to speak with the Colonel if the Colonel will hold on a minute.'

Stafford held on. Presently Chip said, 'Max?'

'Speaking.'

'Gunnarsson and Hendrix are going on safari.'

'And just what does that mean?'

'Going to a game lodge to see animals. Our main tourist attraction. They've booked with a tour group going to the Masai Mara down on the Tanzanian border. They'll be staying at the lodge at Keekorok. Don't worry; we'll be keeping an eye on them. No need for you to change any plans.'

Stafford said, 'Are you sure this is just an ordinary tour group?'

'Sure,' said Chip soothingly. 'I used to do the courier bit with them. It's standard operational procedure for tourists, showing them the big five – lion, leopard, elephant, rhino and buffalo.' He laughed. 'If they're lucky they see the lot; sometimes they aren't lucky.'

'What have our pair been doing?'

'Sightseeing around town. They had lunch once in the revolving restaurant on top of the Kenyatta Conference Centre. Gunnarsson's been playing the tables in the International Casino. Just the usual tourist stuff.'

'When are they going on safari?'

'Day after tomorrow.'

Stafford made up his mind. 'Can you lay me alongside Gunnarsson? I'd like to get a closer look at him.'

'You want to go to the Mara?' Chip paused. 'Sure, that can be arranged. When?'

'I'd like to be there when Gunnarsson arrives.'

'Stay where you are. We'll pick you up tomorrow morning.'

'Bring the Sergeant,' said Stafford, and hung up.

He had no idea why he wanted to see Gunnarsson but inactivity irked him, and he wanted to know why Gunnarsson was sticking around. It could not be to see animals – he doubted if Gunnarsson was a wild life enthusiast – so he was possibly waiting for something. If so, what? Anyway, this was more important than ballooning so Stafford picked up the telephone to cancel the appointment with Hunt.

12

Chip came early next morning accompanied by Nair and Curtis. 'We won't need two trucks,' he said to Stafford. 'We'll leave yours here and pick it up on the way back.'

Stafford took Curtis on one side. 'Any problems, Sergeant?'

'No, sir.'

'I hope you've been keeping your ears open. Did Chip or Nair let anything drop to give a reason why they're being so bloody helpful?'

'Nothing I heard, sir.' Curtis paused, waiting for Stafford to continue, then he said, 'I'll pack the Colonel's case.'

Stafford had already packed so they wasted no time and were soon on the road. It was a good road, if narrow, and went straight as an arrow across the Rift Valley, and they made good time. They skirted the Mau Escarpment and eventually arrived at Narok which was nothing more than a village.

On the way Chip probed a little. 'Did you find what you wanted to know about Brice?'

'Not exactly,' said Stafford. 'He tells me he's applying for Kenyan citizenship. I would have thought a White colonial Rhodesian would be *persona non grata* here.'

'Normally you'd be right,' said Chip. 'But Brice's credentials are impeccable. He was anti-UDI, anti-Smith, anti-white rule. He left Zimbabwe – Rhodesia as it was then – at the right time. Brice is a liberal of the liberals, isn't that so, Nair?'

'Oh, yes; he's very liberal,' said Nair.

'You seem to know a lot about him,' observed Stafford.

'Just interested,' said Chip. 'He's not a secretive man. He talks a lot and we listen. We listen to lots of people, including you. But you don't say anything.'

'I don't go much for light conversation.'

'No, you don't,' he agreed. 'But some things don't need words. That scar on your shoulder, for instance. I saw it this morning before you put your shirt on. A bullet wound, of course.'

Stafford's hand automatically went up to touch his shoulder. 'Not unusual in a soldier,' he said. Actually the bullet had been taken out three years before by Dr Fahkri in Algiers; he had not done a good job and the wound had gone bad in England and so the scarring was particularly noticeable.

'You left the army ten years ago,' said Chip. 'That scar is more recent.'

Stafford looked sideways at him. 'Then you *have* been investigating me.'

Chip shrugged. 'To protect our own interests. That's all.'

'I hope I came out clean.'

'As much as anyone can. What's your interest in Brice?'

'He's come into a lot of money,' said Stafford. 'Or the Foundation has.'

'We know,' said Nair. 'It's in today's *Standard*.' He passed the newspaper forward from the back seat.

It was on the front page. The Ol Njorowa Foundation had inherited a sum of money from the estate of Jan-Willem Hendrykxx, a mysterious millionaire. The exact amount was not yet known but was believed to be in the region of £7 million. It was a thin story which told Stafford nothing he did not know already except that someone was pulling a fast one.

Chip said, 'Yet another spelling of the name. Are they all connected?'

Stafford nodded. 'Dirk Hendriks and Henry Hendrix are both heirs under the Hendrykxx estate.'

'A South African and an American,' said Chip thoughtfully. 'Sounds improbable, doesn't it, Nair?'

'Highly improbable,' said Nair, the eternal echo.

'They're both grandsons of old Hendrykxx,' said Stafford.

'The family got scattered and the names got changed. Nothing impossible about that.'

'I didn't say impossible,' said Chip, and added, 'Seven million sterling is a lot of money. I wonder what the Trustees think of it, Nair.'

Nair smiled through his beard. 'I should think they are delighted.'

Stafford said, 'I wish I could check out Brice; he seems too good to be true.'

'What would you want to know?' asked Chip.

'I'd like to know if Mr and Mrs Brice had a farm near Umtali in Zimbabwe. I'd like to know if the farm was burned and the Brices killed by guerillas. I'd like to know if their son . . . what's his name, anyway?'

'Charles,' said Nair. 'Charles Brice.'

'I'd like to know if their son, Charlie, left when he says he did.'

'I think we could find that out,' said Chip seriously.

'How?'

'I think our brothers in Zimbabwe would co-operate. Wouldn't you say so, Nair?'

'I think they would,' said Nair. 'I'll see to it.'

Stafford took a deep breath. 'You boys seem to have an extensive organization.'

'People are supposed to help and support each other,' said Chip, smiling. 'Isn't that what Christianity teaches? So we're helping *you*.'

'At the request of some Indian in London?' said Stafford incredulously. 'At the request of Curtis? Pull the other leg, it's got bells on it. What do you think, Sergeant?'

'It does seem rum, sir,' said Curtis.

Chip looked hurt. 'I don't think Max appreciates us, Nair.'

Nair said, 'Suspicion corrodes the soul, Max.'

'Oh, balls!' he said. 'Look, I appreciate your help but I doubt your motives. I'll be quite plain about that. I don't know who you are and I don't know what you want. The helping hand you are so kindly offering is bloody unnatural, and Christianity hasn't got a damned thing to do with it. Nair isn't even a Christian, and I doubt if you are, Chip.'

Chip smiled. ' "Him that is weak in the faith receive ye, but not to doubtful disputations." Romans 14:1. I was educated in a mission school, Max; I'll bet I know more of the Bible than you. Don't be weak in the faith, Max; and let's not have any doubtful disputations. Just accept.'

'Chip is right,' said Nair. 'Is there anything else you'd like us to do?'

It was obvious to Stafford that he was not going to get anything out of this pair that they did not want him to know. If they were members of a banned political organization then it was obvious they would be careful. But he wished he knew why they were being so damned helpful. He was sure it was not because they liked the colour of his eyes.

* * *

Chip had been driving but at Narok Nair took over. Chip said, 'He's the better driver.'

'Will a better driver be needed?'

'You'll see.'

After Narok they left the asphalt and encountered the most God-awful road it had been Stafford's fate to be driven over. He had been more comfortable in a tank going across country in NATO exercises in Germany. Where heavy rains had washed gullies across the road they had not been filled in and repaired, and the traffic of heavy trucks had worn deep longitudinal grooves. Several times Nair got stuck in those and Stafford heard the underside of the chassis scraping the ground.

'Manufacturers of exhausts must do a roaring trade out here.' He looked back and saw they were creating a long rooster's tail of dust. 'Why the hell don't they repair this road? Don't they encourage visitors to Masai Mara?'

Chip said, 'Narok District and the Government are having an argument about who pays. So far no one pays – except to the repair shops.'

Stafford took out the map he had bought in Nairobi and discovered they were driving across the Loita Plains. Every so often they passed villages of huts and sometimes a herdsman with his cattle. They were tall men with even taller spears and dressed in long gowns. Chip said they were Masai.

'What tribe are you?' Stafford asked.

'Kikuyu.'

Stafford remembered Hardin's lecture on African tribal politics. 'Not Luo?'

Chip slanted his eyes at Stafford. 'What makes you think I'd be Luo?'

'I haven't the slightest idea.' Chip frowned but said nothing.

They passed a petrol tanker that had not made it. It was overturned by the side of the road and burnt out. They crossed a narrow bridge and Stafford checked the map. There were only two bridges marked and, after the second, the road changed status from being a main road to a secondary road. He commented on this with feeling and Nair burst out laughing.

Oddly enough, after the second bridge the road improved somewhat. Game began to appear, small herds of antelope and zebra and some ostriches. Chip played courier to the ignorant tourist and identified them. 'Impala,' he would say, or 'Thomson's gazelle.' There were also eland and kongoni.

'Are we in the Reserve yet?' Stafford asked.

'Not until we pass the Police Post.'

'Then there are more animals in the Reserve than here?'

'More?' Chip laughed. 'Two million wildebeest make the migration from the Serengeti to the Mara every year.' Stafford thought that was a lot of venison on the hoof. Chip rummaged around and found a map. 'Here's a map of the Mara. I thought you'd like to see what you're getting into.'

At first glance Stafford thought he was not getting into much. He checked the scale and found there were large chunks of damn-all cut through by what were described as 'motorable tracks.' Since the horrible road from Narok had been described as a main road he regarded that with reservation. There were two lodges, Keekorok and Mara Serena, and Governor's Camp; also about a dozen camp sites scattered mainly in the north. Streams and rivers abounded, there were a couple of swamps thrown in and, as Chip had said, a couple of million wildebeest and an unknown number of other animals, some of which were illustrated on the map.

He said, 'Is there really a bird called a drongo? I thought that was an Australian epithet.'

They arrived at the Police Post at the Olemelepo Gate and Nair drew to a halt. Chip said, 'I'll see to it. Be my guest.' He got out and strolled across to the police officer who sat at a table outside the Post.

Stafford got out to stretch his legs and when he slapped his jacket a cloud of dust arose. Curtis joined him. 'Enjoying yourself, Sergeant?'

Curtis brushed himself down and said ironically, 'Not so dusty.'

'People pay thousands for what you're going through.'

'If I have a beer it'll hiss going down.'

Stafford unfolded the map and checked the distance to Keekorok Lodge. 'Not long to go – only eight miles to your beer.'

Chip came back and they started off again and well within the hour the beer was hissing in the Sergeant's throat.

13

Keekorok was 105 miles south of the Equator and at an altitude of 5,258 feet; there was a sign at the front of the Lodge which said so. It was a pleasant sprawling place with an unbuttoned air about it, a place to relax and be comfortable. There was a patio with a bar overlooking a wide lawn and that evening Stafford and Chip sat over drinks chatting desultorily while watching vervet monkeys scamper about in the fading light of sunset.

'We might as well do the tourist bit tomorrow,' said Chip. 'We'll go and look at animals. I'll be courier – I know the Mara well.'

Stafford said, 'I want to be here when Gunnarsson and Hendrix arrive.'

'They won't be here until six in the evening.'

'How do you know?'

'Because that's what the courier has been told,' said Chip patiently.

Stafford sat up straight. 'What do you mean by that?'

'I mean that Adam Muliro, the driver, has been told when to deliver the party. I told him.' Chip paused and added with a grin, 'He's my brother-in-law.'

'Another?' said Stafford sceptically.

'You know us Third World people – we believe in the extended family. Now take it easy, Max.' He spread out a map on the table. 'I'll show you hippo here, at Mara New Bridge.' He tapped his finger on the map.

The River Mara ran a twisting course north to south and the place where it was bridged was close to the Tanzanian border. If the scale of the map was anything to go by the road ran within three hundred yards of the border. Stafford thought of the different political philosophies of the two countries; the Marxist state of Tanzania and Kenya with its mixed economy. He had heard there was no love lost between them. 'Does Kenya have problems with Tanzania?'

Chip shrugged. 'The border is closed from time to time. There's a bit of friction; nothing much. Some poaching. There's an anti-poaching post here at Ngiro Are.' He spoke of the collapse of the East African Federation; the attempt of the three ex-British African nations to work in unison. 'It couldn't work – the ideas were too different. Tanzania went socialist – a totally different political philosophy from ours. As for Uganda . . .' He made a dismissive gesture. 'With Amin in power it was impossible.' He tapped the map again. 'You see the problem?'

Stafford frowned. 'Not really.'

'I have my finger on it,' Chip said. 'South of the border is Tanzania. Until 1918 it was German East Africa, then it was British Tanganyika, and now Tanzania. But look at the border – a line drawn straight with a ruler by nineteenth-century European bureaucrats. The country is the same on both sides and so are the people. Here they are Masai.' His finger moved south to Tanzania. 'And there they are Masai. A people separated by nineteenth-century politics.' He sounded bitter. 'That's why we have the Shifta trouble in the north.'

'What's the Shifta trouble?'

'The same thing. A line drawn with a ruler. On one side the Somali Republic, on the other side, Kenya; on both sides, Somalis. There's been a civil war running up there ever since I can remember. Nobody talks about it much. It's referred to in the press as Shifta trouble – banditry. Cattle raids and so forth. What it is really is an attempt to get a United Somalia.' Chip smiled grimly. 'Tourists aren't welcome on the North East Frontier.'

There was a diversion. In the fading light a bull elephant had come up from the river and was now strolling on the lawn, making its way purposefully towards the swimming pool. There were cries of alarm and then white-coated staff erupted from the kitchen, clattering spoons on saucepans.

The elephant stopped uncertainly and then backed away, its ears flapping. Ponderously it turned and lumbered away back to the river.

Stafford said, 'That's one problem we don't have in English gardens.' He realized that the elephant had crossed the path he would have to walk to go to his room that night. 'Are those things dangerous?'

'Not if you don't get too close. But you're quite safe.' Chip jerked his head. 'Look.'

Stafford turned and saw a man in uniform standing on the edge of the patio who was holding a rifle unobtrusively, and thought that if Stafford Security Consultants were to move into Africa they would have to learn new tricks and techniques.

* * *

So next day they went to look at animals and saw them in profusion; wildebeest, impala, gazelle, topi, zebra. Also lion, elephant and giraffe. Stafford was astonished to realize that what he saw was but a fraction of the vast herds which roamed the plains in the nineteenth-century. Although he was not in Kenya as a sightseer he found that he really enjoyed the day, and Chip, whatever he might be otherwise, knew his stuff as a guide.

They returned to Keekorok at five in the afternoon and, after cleaning away the travel stains, Stafford settled down to wait for Gunnarsson and Hendrix while settling the dust in his throat with the inevitable and welcome cold beer. They arrived on time in a party of six travelling in the usual zebra-striped Nissan, booked in at the desk and then went to the room they shared. Stafford marked it.

Later they appeared on the patio for drinks and he was able to assess them close at hand for the first time. Gunnarsson looked to be in his mid-fifties and his hair was turning iron-grey. He was a hard-looking man with a flat belly and appeared to be in good physical condition. His height was an even six feet and what there was on his bones was muscle and not fat. His eyes were pale blue and watchful, constantly on the move. He looked formidable.

The fake Hendrix was in his late twenties, a gangling and loose-jointed young man with a fresh face and innocent expression, and stood about five feet, nine inches. He was blond with a fair complexion and if he missed shaving one day no one would notice, unlike Gunnarsson who had a blue chin.

Chip joined Stafford at his table. 'So they're here. Now what?'

Stafford sighed. 'I don't know.'

'Max, for God's sake!' he said exasperatedly. 'I'm doing my best to help but what can I do if you don't trust me? Nair is becoming really annoyed. He thinks you're wasting our time and we should quit. I'm beginning to agree with him.'

During the past couple of days Stafford had come to like Chip; his style was easy and his conversation intelligent. He didn't want Chip to leave because he suspected he would need someone who really knew his way about Kenya. That was the role he had planned for Hardin but Hardin wasn't around.

He said, 'All right; I'll tell you. That young man has just come into a fortune – three million pounds sterling from the Hendrykxx estate.'

Chip whistled. 'And you want to take it from him?'

'Don't be a damned fool,' Stafford said without heat.

Chip grinned. 'Sorry. I really didn't put you down as a crook.'

'The whole point is that he isn't Hendrix. He's a fake rung in by Gunnarsson.' He told Chip the story.

'But why didn't you just tell the police in London?' asked Chip.

'Because Gunnarsson would have slid out from under, all injured innocence, and I want Gunnarsson. He's a cheap, unethical bastard who has got in my way before, and I want his hide. The trouble is I can't find a way of doing it. I've been beating my brains silly.'

'I'll have to think about this,' said Chip. 'This is a big one.'

Stafford watched Hendrix. He was chatting up a girl who was in his party. 'Who is she? Do you know?'

'Her name is Michele Roche. She's doing the tour with her parents. They're French. Her father's a retired businessman from Bordeaux; he was in the wine trade until six months ago.'

'You don't miss much,' Stafford said.

Chip grinned widely. 'I told Adam Muliro to find out as much as he could. The other member of the tour group is a young Dutchman called Kosters, Frederik Kosters. He and Hendrix don't like each other. They're both trying to get to know Michele better and they get in each other's way. Kosters is something in the diamond business in Amsterdam. Here he comes now.'

Stafford turned and looked at the young man making his way to the bar. He greeted the girl and she smiled at him warmly. Chip said, 'Kosters speaks French which gives him an advantage.'

'Your Adam Muliro is a fund of information. What did he find out about Gunnarsson?'

'He's an insurance broker from New York.'

'In a pig's eye. He runs an industrial espionage outfit. He's ex-CIA.'

'Is he, now?' said Chip thoughtfully. 'That's interesting.'

'And Hendrix; what about him?'

'According to Adam he smokes bhang. You'll know it better as marijuana. That's an offence in Kenya, of course, but it could be useful. If you want him held at any time the police could be tipped off. I could make sure that bhang would be found in his possession.'

'And you accused me of having a devious mind,' Stafford remarked. 'Anything else? Is he bragging about new found wealth, for instance?'

'Not according to Adam. He doesn't talk much about himself.'

'I don't suppose he can, seeing that he's someone else.'

Chip nodded. 'Adam says that Gunnarsson jumped on Hendrix a couple of times and made a change of subject but he didn't know why. We know why now.'

'Yes,' said Stafford. 'Hendrix must have been opening his mouth a bit too wide. Making trifling errors and in danger of blowing his cover. It must be wearing for Gunnarsson to be riding shotgun on three million pounds.'

'When is Hendrix getting the money?'

'I don't know, but it will be very soon. Farrar is fixing that now.' Stafford shook his head. 'I'd like to know why Gunnarsson and Hendrix are hanging about here in Kenya when the cash is in England. If I were Hendrix I'd be twisting Farrar's arm; urging him to get a move on.'

'You would if you were innocent,' said Chip. 'But Hendrix isn't. Perhaps Gunnarsson thinks he can keep closer to Hendrix here than in England. I wouldn't suppose there's all that much trust between them.'

'No honour among thieves? That might be it. Gunnarsson won't want Hendrix vanishing with the loot as soon as he lays hands on it. He's certainly sticking close to him now.'

Chip stretched his arms. 'Now I understand your problem better, but I don't know how to solve it. What do we do?'

'What we've been doing; we watch and wait. I can't think of anything else.'

* * *

Next day they went game spotting again, but this time with a difference; they stayed within easy reach of Gunnarsson's tour group. That was not difficult because Adam Muliro co-operated, never getting too far away. If Gunnarsson spotted them they would just be another group in the distance, and they were careful never to get too close. Stafford did not know why he was taking the trouble because it was a pretty pointless exercise. Action for the sake of action and born out of frustration.

And, of course, they saw animals – sometimes. Stafford found how difficult it is to see an unmoving animal, even one so grotesque as a giraffe. Once Nair pointed out a giraffe and he could not see it until it moved and he found he had been staring between its legs. And the grass was long and the exact colour of a lion. Of them all it was, oddly enough, Curtis who was the best at game spotting.

They were on the way back to Keekorok when Nair braked to a halt. 'We're getting too close,' he said. The Nissan ahead of them topped a rise and disappeared over the other side. 'We'll be able to see it when it rounds the bend over there.' He pointed to where the road curved about a mile away.

Stafford produced a packet of cigarettes and offered them around. Chip said, 'This isn't getting us far, Max.'

Nair smiled. 'Call it a holiday, Chip. Look at the pretty impala over there.'

Curtis said, 'With due respect I think the Colonel is wasting his time.'

Those were strong words coming from the Sergeant who had few words to spare at any time. Stafford said, 'And what would you suggest?'

'Get hold of Hendrix on his own and beat the bejesus out him until he admits he's an impostor,' he said bluntly.

'Sergeant Curtis has a point,' said Chip.

'It's an idea,' said Stafford. 'The problem will be to separate him from Gunnarsson. I don't want to tip him off.' Or anyone else, he thought. There was the peculiar conduct of Brice back at Ol Njorowa College; Stafford had not told Chip about the twenty-seven or so million pounds unaccounted for. That did not tie in at all.

They kicked it around a while, then Nair said, 'Funny. They're not in sight yet.' There was no sign of the Nissan that had gone ahead.

'They've probably found a lion over the hill,' said Chip. 'Tourists stop a long time with lions. They're probably making a fortune for Kodak.'

'Not Gunnarsson and Hendrix,' said Nair.

They talked some more and then Nair moved restlessly. 'Still no sign of them. A long time even for lion.'

'Perhaps there's a track leading off the road just over the hill,' said Stafford.

'No track,' said Nair positively.

He said, 'Then he's gone off the road, track or no track.'

'Adam wouldn't do that; not without giving us a signal.' Chip stubbed out his cigarette. 'Let's move it, Nair. Just to the top there.'

Nair turned the key in the ignition and they moved off. At the top of the rise they stopped and looked down into the little valley. The Nissan was standing in the centre of the road below them about 400 yards away. There was nothing unusual about that; tour buses stood stationary like that all over the Reserve and it was normally the sign that something unusual had been spotted – a kill, perhaps.

Chip took binoculars and scanned the vehicle. 'Get down there, Nair,' he said quietly.

They coasted down the hill and came to a halt next to the Nissan. There was not a living soul in it.

* * *

The first bizarre thought that came into Stafford's head was the story of the *Mary Celeste*. Chip shot a spate of words to Nair in a language he did not understand, probably Swahili, and they both got out, ignoring the deserted vehicle and looking about at the landscape. There must have been a watercourse in the valley, now dried up, because there was a small culvert to take water under the road, and the bush was particularly thick and green.

Stafford and Curtis got out to join them, and Chip said sharply, 'Don't come closer.'

Stafford said, 'Where the hell have they all gone?' It was an offence to get out of a car in the Reserve; you could lose tourists that way, and that would be bad for business.

Chip stooped and picked up something which glittered in the sun – a pair of dark glasses with one lens broken. 'They didn't go voluntarily.'

'Kidnapped!' Stafford said incredulously. 'Who'd want to do that?'

'The *Jeshi la Mgambo*,' said Nair. 'Right, Chip?'

'I'd say so.' Chip opened the door of the Nissan and looked

inside. 'It's stripped,' he said. 'No cameras, binoculars or anything else. Everything gone.'

Nair looked back along the road. 'They'll have had a man up there watching us.' He turned and pointed. 'Up there, too. They could still be around.'

'Too damned right,' said Chip. He moved quickly to their own Nissan and opened the door at the back. Stafford had inspected the vehicle so he did not know where he got them but when he turned around Chip was holding two rifles. He tossed one to Nair and said to Stafford, 'Can you use one of these?'

'I have been known to,' Stafford said dryly. 'Now will you kindly tell me what's happening?'

'Later,' Chip said, and gave him the rifle.

'I can use one of those, too,' said Curtis.

'You're going to Keekorok as fast as you can drive,' said Chip. He took a notebook and pen from his pocket and scribbled rapidly. 'Give this to the manager of the Lodge; he'll radio the Police Post at Mara New Bridge.' Going to the driver's seat he fished out the map of Masai Mara and marked it. 'That's where we are now. Okay, Sergeant; move!'

Curtis looked at Stafford, who nodded. 'Which truck?' he asked.

'Ours,' said Chip. 'But wait.' He went to the back again and when he straightened he was holding a sub-machine-gun, one of the little Israeli Uzis which are supposed to be one of the best designs in the world. He also had two packs of rifle ammunition and a spare magazine for the Uzi. 'On your way,' he said. 'Don't stop for anyone. If anyone tries, keep your head down and run them over.'

The crackle of authority in Chip's voice brought an automatic, 'Yes, sir,' from Curtis. He climbed behind the driver's seat, the wheels spun, and he was away in a cloud of dust.

Stafford checked the rifle. A sporting and not a military weapon, it was bolt action with a five round magazine. The magazine was full so he put a round up the spout, set the safety catch, took out the magazine to put another round in, then put the rest of the ammunition into his pockets. Chip watched and nodded approvingly. 'You've been there before,' he said.

Nair was kneeling by the Nissan looked at the dusty road. 'Six of them,' he said. 'Six, I think.'

'Six of who?' Stafford demanded irascibly.

'*Jeshi la Mgambo*,' said Chip. 'Tanzanians. The so-called Tanzanian Police Reserve. A paramilitary force with bad discipline. This has happened three or four times before. They come across the border, pick up a busload of tourists, and hustle them across the border. Then they're picked clean of everything they've got and left to walk back to Keekorok. The government has sent several protest notes to the Tanzanians.' He shrugged. 'It stops for a while but then they start again.'

'And they're armed?'

His reply was brief and chilling. 'Kalashnikovs.'

Stafford winced and looked down at the rifle he held. The Russian Kalashnikov is a fully automatic weapon which can spew out bullets as water from a hosepipe. The sporting rifle, while not exactly a toy, was not in the same league. 'And we're going after them?'

Chip gave him a quick glance. 'What else would you suggest? Curtis is the oldest; nearly sixty. That's why I sent him back. It could be a rough trip.'

Stafford said mildly, 'On those grounds Curtis could have given you an argument.'

'Besides, we have only three guns.'

Nair said, 'The border is over there – two miles. They can't have got much of a start and the prisoners will slow them down. Also they'll have to cross the Losemai.'

'Easy at this time of year,' said Chip. 'Let's go.'

They went on foot because to track from a Nissan is impossible, and it was Chip who did the tracking. He went confidently, going by signs which eluded Stafford and as he marched behind he wondered about these men who could produce an armoury at the drop of a hat. An Uzi isn't something you pick up casually at the corner shop.

14

In the African bush there is a species of acacia known as the wait-a-bit thorn. It is well named. Chip and Nair knew enough to avoid them while Stafford, trailing in the rear, did not. He found it was like being trapped in barbed wire and his temper suffered, as did his suit and his skin.

After a while he got the hang of it and learned to travel in the master's footsteps and then it became better. Chip kept up a cracking pace, stopping occasionally to cast around. Twice he pointed out the signs of passage of those they were pursuing – footprints on the dusty earth. Nair nodded, and said in a low voice, 'Military boots.'

Once Chip threw his arms wide and the party came to a sudden halt. He waved and they made a wide circuit of a patch of ground on which Stafford saw a snake, not very long but with a body as thick as a man's brawny arm. Afterwards Chip told him it was a puff adder, and added, 'Most snakes get out of the way when they sense you're coming, but not the puff adder – he's lazy. So, if you're not careful you tread on him and he strikes. Very poisonous. Don't walk about at night.'

It was hot and Stafford sweated copiously. Heavy physical exercise on the Equator at an altitude of 5,000 feet is not to be recommended if you are not acclimatized. The Kenyan Olympics Team has a training camp at 9,000 feet where the oxygen is thin and the body becomes accustomed to its lack. When they go to sea level that gives a competitive edge, an advantage over the others. But Stafford was a reverse case and he suffered, while Chip and Nair were in better shape.

The terrain consisted of rolling plains with an occasional

outcrop of rock. The trees, mostly flat-topped acacias, were scattered except where they tended to grow more thickly in the now dry watercourses, and the grass was waist high. The ground was so open that anyone looking back would surely see a long way.

Consequently they made good time in the valleys between the ridges but slowed as they came to a crest, creeping on their bellies to peer into the next shallow valley. As they came up to the top of one such ridge Chip said quietly, 'We're in Tanzania. There's the Losemai.'

Ahead, stretching widely, was a green belt of thicker vegetation which marked the Losemai River. It looked no different than any similar place in the Kenyan Masai Mara. Chip took his binoculars, and said, 'Hold up your hand to shade these from the sun.'

Stafford put up his hand to cast a shadow on the lenses, and reflected that Chip was up to all the tricks of the trade. He didn't want a warning flash of light to be reflected; it would have been like a semaphore signal. He wondered where Chip had learned his trade. More and more there were certain things about Chip and Nair which didn't add up into anything that made sense.

Chip surveyed the land ahead, the binoculars moving in a slow arc. Suddenly he stopped, pointing like a hunting dog. 'There – entering the trees at two o'clock.' Another military expression.

Away in the distance Stafford saw the minute dots and strained his eyes to count. Chip said, 'I make it thirteen. You were right, Nair; *Jeshi la Mgambo*, six of them. And six in the tour group plus Adam. They're all there.'

Nair said, 'Do you think they'll stop at the Losemai? What happened before?'

'They might,' said Chip. 'They've got good cover down there and it's a convenient place to strip the tourists.'

Stafford said, 'It seems a lot of trouble for little profit.'

Chip snorted. 'Oh, there's profit. Take your tourist; he comes here to photograph animals so he usually has a good camera, still or cine. Plus telephoto lenses and other goodies such as a wristwatch. He also has money, traveller's cheques and credit cards, and there's a good trade in cheques and cards. A tourist, particularly a German or American, can be worth up to £1,000 on the hoof, and that's a damn sight more than the average Tanzanian makes in a year.'

'Don't bother about convincing Max of what he can see with his eyes,' said Nair acidly. 'How do we get there?'

'The last of them has gone into the trees,' said Chip. He took the glasses from his eyes, withdrew from the top of the ridge and rolled over on to his back, then looked about him. He jerked his thumb. 'We can't follow them that way; they might have someone keeping watch. I know they're undisciplined, but we can't take that chance.'

Nair looked along the ridge. 'That thin line of trees there might be a stream going down to join the Losemai. It could give cover.'

'We'll take a look,' said Chip.

They went along the ridge, keeping below the crest, and found that it was a stream or, rather, it would be when the rains came. Now it was dusty and dry although if one dug deep enough one would find dampness, enough to keep the acacias green in the dry season. The force of rushing water during the rains had carved into the soft soil making a channel which averaged a couple of feet deep. It would provide cover of a minimal kind.

So they went down on their bellies, following the winding of the watercourse. It was something Stafford had not done since his early days in the Army and he was out of practice. Once he jerked his hand up as he was about to put it on something which moved. It scuttled away and he saw it was a scorpion. He sweated and it was not all because of the African heat.

It took a long time but finally they got down to the shelter of the trees which fringed the Losemai and were able to stand up. Chip put his fingers to his lips and cautiously they made their way to the river and lay close to the bank, hidden by tall grass. Stafford parted the stems and looked to the other side.

It was not a big river by any standards; the depth at that time of year was minimal and Stafford supposed one could cross dry shod by jumping from sandbank to sandbank. The flow of water was turgidly slow and muddy brown. In a clearing on the other side a giraffe was at the water's edge, legs astraddle and drinking. Something on a sandbank moved and he saw a crocodile slip into the water with barely a ripple, and changed his mind about jumping from sandbank to sandbank.

Chip said softly, 'I don't think they've crossed; that giraffe wouldn't be there. We'll go up river on this side very slowly.'

They went up river in military formation. Chip, with the sub-machine-gun, was point; behind him Stafford was back-up, and Nair was flanker, moving parallel but about fifty yards away and only visible momentarily as he flitted among the trees, his rifle at high port.

It was very slow and very sweaty work. The river bank was full of noises; the croaking of frogs and the chirping of grass-hoppers and cicadas. Occasionally Stafford jerked as he caught a movement out of the corner of his eye but always it was the quick flash of a brightly coloured bird crossing the river. Once there was a splash from the water and he saw a small brown animal swimming away because Chip had disturbed it in its waterside home.

Suddenly Chip went down on one knee and held the Uzi over his head with both hands. Stafford stopped and snapped off the safety catch on the rifle. Chip motioned him forward so he went up to him and knelt beside him. There was a distant murmur of voices and a louder burst of laughter. 'Cover me,' said Chip, and went forward on his belly.

For a moment Stafford lost sight of him in the long grass, then he came into view again. Chip beckoned and Stafford dropped flat and went to join him. Chip had parted the grass and was staring at something. 'Take a look,' he said quietly. The voices were louder.

Stafford parted the stems of grass and found that he was looking into a clearing by the river. They were all there, the Tanzanians and the tour group. The Tanzanians wore camouflaged battle fatigues and were all armed with automatic rifles. Two of them wore grenades attached to their belts and one, with sergeant's stripes, had a pistol in a holster.

The tour group was in a bad way. They had been stripped of most of their clothing and Mam'selle and Madame Roche were down to their bras and panties. Madame Roche's face was blotchy as though she had been crying and her husband, a ridiculous figure with his big belly swelling over his underpants, was trying to comfort her. Michele Roche had paled under her tan so that her face was a jaundiced yellow. She looked scared, and young Kosters was talking quietly to her, his hand on her arm.

If Gunnarsson was frightened he did not show it. His face was dark with anger as he stooped to pick up a shoe and as a rifle was nudged into his back he straightened with a quick truculence and shouted, 'Goddamn it, you've gotta leave us shoes.' The answer was a shake of the head and another dig with the rifle. He dropped the shoe and glowered.

Hendrix, also stripped, was standing separately from the group flanked by two Tanzanians. The young black sitting on the ground with a set, expressionless face would be Adam Muliro, the courier. Before him, striking dazzling reflections from the sun, was the loot – cameras, lenses, binoculars and other equipment, together with a pile of clothing.

Slowly Stafford let the grass escape from his fingers to form a screen. Chip put his mouth to Stafford's ear. 'We can do nothing. We could cause a massacre.'

That was certainly true. Those Kalashnikov rifles scared Stafford and the sight of the grenades frightened him even more. He had been a soldier and he knew what those weapons could do. If, as had happened before, the prisoners were turned loose to walk back to Keekorok, the only discomfort they would suffer would be sunburn and cut and sore feet. Under the circumstances a shooting match was out of the question. They were outnumbered and outgunned and the safety of the prisoners could not be risked.

Chip indicated that Stafford should withdraw so he wriggled backwards and then turned, still lying flat. Then he looked back to see Chip running towards him at a crouch. Chip waved his arm wildly as he passed and then flung himself headlong into a thick patch of long grass and vanished from sight. Stafford got the message and picked himself up and ran for the nearest tree.

Just as he got there he heard voices. The tree trunk was not as thick as his body and he set himself edge on to it, moving slowly around so as to keep it between him and the approaching men. They came closer and he could distinguish a baritone and a lighter voice; and could even catch words but did not understand the language. As they went by he risked a glance. Hendrix was hobbling by the river bank, walking painfully because of his bare feet. He was clad only in his underpants and behind him came two Tanzanians, one of them prodding him in the back with a rifle. They disappeared from view.

Chip's head came out of the grass. He waved his arm in a wide circle and then ran to the river bank and began to follow. Stafford turned to find Nair and saw him emerge from hiding. He waved him to follow Chip and then took off, making a wide circle. Chip was still at the point, Stafford was now flanker and Nair was rearguard. Stafford stayed about fifty or sixty yards from the river and kept parallel with it, occasionally going in as closely as he dared to keep track of Hendrix and his captors.

Once he got close enough to hear Hendrix wail, 'Where are you taking me? What have I done?' There was a thump and a muffled grunt and a short silence before he said desolately, 'Christ! Oh, my Christ!' Stafford guessed he had been hit in the kidneys by a rifle butt but did not risk going close enough to see.

They went on this manner for quite a distance, perhaps half a mile, and then Stafford lost them. He backtracked a hundred yards and found that they had stopped. Hendrix was standing quite close to the edge of the river facing the Tanzanians, one quite young, the other an older man. The young one had Hendrix at rifle point keeping him covered; the other had his rifle slung and was smoking. He took the cigarette stub from his mouth, examined it critically, then casually dropped it and put his foot on it before he unslung his rifle. He lifted it to his shoulder and aimed at Hendrix, his finger on the trigger.

Hastily Stafford brought up his own rifle but it was then that Chip cut loose with the Uzi. The burst of fire caught the man in the back and he was flung forward. The young Tanzanian whirled around and Stafford shot him in the head. He grew a third eye in the middle of his forehead and staggered back and fell into the river with a splash. After that sudden outburst of noise there was a silence broken only by insect noises and the whimpering of Hendrix who was on his knees staring unbelievingly at the sprawling body before him.

Chip came into sight, gun first and cautiously, and then Nair. Stafford went to join them. He said, 'The bastard was going to shoot Hendrix,' and heard the incredulity in his own voice. He snapped his fingers. 'Just like that.'

Chip stirred the body with his foot, then bent down to check the pulse at the side of the neck. He straightened up. 'They've gone crazy,' he said blankly. 'They've never tried anything like this before.' He turned to Nair. 'Get back there – about a hundred yards – and keep watch.'

Stafford went over to Hendrix. Tears streaked his face and he was making gagging noises at the back of his throat. Stafford tried to help him to his feet but he went limp and lay down in a foetal position. 'For God's sake, man,' said Stafford. 'Get up. Do you *want* to be killed?'

'He's been nearly frightened to death,' said Chip.

'He'll be the death of us if he doesn't move,' Stafford said grimly. 'They'll have heard those shots.'

'They were expecting to hear shots,' said Chip. 'Let's hope they can't tell the difference between an Uzi and a

Kalashnikov. But they're pretty far away.' He bent down and began going through the pockets of the dead man.

Stafford walked to the river bank which here was about six feet high. The river moved sluggishly and the body of the man he had shot had not drifted far. He was the first man Stafford had ever killed as far as he knew and he felt a little sick. His soldiering had been mostly in peacetime and even in those faraway days in Korea it was surprising how rarely you saw the enemy you were shooting at. And later they did not go too much for bodies in Military Intelligence.

Chip said, 'No identification; just this.' He held up a wad of currency. 'Kenya twenty-shilling notes.' He put them into his pocket. 'Help me get his clothes off.'

'Why strip him?'

Chip nodded towards Hendrix. 'He's not going to move far or fast without clothes and boots. And we don't have much time; not more than a few minutes. These men will be expected back and when they don't show someone will come looking.'

While Stafford was unlacing the Tanzanian's boots Chip stripped him of his bloody and bullet-ripped jacket and, together, they took off his trousers. Undressing a dead man is peculiarly difficult. He does not co-operate. Then they rolled the body to the edge of the bank and dropped it over the side. It fell with a splash into the muddy water. The other body had gone.

'No one will find them now,' said Chip. 'This looks like a likely pool for crocodiles. The crocs will take them and wedge them under water until they ripen enough to eat.' It was a gruesome thought.

They dressed Hendrix and he did not co-operate, either. He was almost in a state of catatonia. Stafford noted that Hendrix had no scar on either shoulder, a scar which ought to have been there. He said nothing, and looked up when Chip said, 'One of your problems is solved; you've separated Hendrix from Gunnarsson. How long do you want to keep it that way?'

That hadn't occurred to Stafford. He said, 'We'll discuss it later. Let's get the hell out of here.'

They hoisted Hendrix to his feet and Stafford slapped his face hard twice with an open palm. Hendrix shook his head and put up his hand to rub his cheek. 'What did you do that for?' he asked, but the imbecilic vacuous look in his eyes was fading.

'To pound some sense into you,' Stafford said. 'If you don't want to die you've got to move.'

A slow comprehension came to him. 'Christ, yes!' he said.

Chip was brushing the ground with a leafy branch, scattering dust over the few bloodstains and eliminating all signs of their presence. He walked over to where he had fired the sub-machine-gun and picked up all the cartridge cases he could find, then he tossed them and the two Kalashnikovs into the river. 'Let's get Nair,' he said, so Stafford picked up his rifle and they went from that place.

They struck away from the river and headed north-east for the border, going up the narrow gully they had come down until they got to the comparative safety of the other side of the ridge where they rested a while and had a brief council of war. At a gesture from Chip Nair stood guard on Hendrix and he and Stafford withdrew from earshot. 'What now?' said Chip.

Up to that moment Stafford had had no opportunity for constructive thinking; all his efforts had been bent on staying alive and out of trouble and he had not considered the implications of what he had seen. Those people stripped to trek back to Keekorok troubled him. If they travelled when the sun was up they would get terribly sun-burned, and Chip had indicated that travel at night could be dangerous. He said, 'How far is it to Keekorok from here?'

'About eleven or twelve miles – in a straight line. But no one travels in a straight line in the bush. Say fifteen miles.'

That was a long way; a day's march. Stafford was not worried about Gunnarsson or Kosters. Gunnarson was tough enough and the young Dutchman looked fit. Michele

Roche could probably take it, too, but her parents were something else. A sedentary wine merchant who looked as though he liked to sample his own product freely and his elderly wife were going to have a hell of a tough time. He said, 'This is a funny one, Chip. These border raids: has anyone been killed previously?'

Chip shook his head. 'Just robbery. No deaths and not even a rape. They took three Nissans full of Germans about a year ago but they all came back safely.'

'Then why this time?' asked Stafford. 'That was nearly a deliberate murder. It looked almost like a bloody execution.'

'I don't know,' Chip said. 'It beats me.'

'That charming scene in the clearing when Gunnarsson wanted his shoes. Did you notice anything about Hendrix?'

'Yes, he was separated from the others.'

'And under guard. Now, why should Tanzanians want to cut Hendrix from the herd to kill him? If you could give me the answer to that I'd be very happy because I think it would give us an answer to this whole mess.'

'I don't *have* an answer,' Chip said frankly.

'Neither do I,' said Stafford, and brooded for a while.

'Well; you've got Hendrix now,' said Chip. 'If you want to question him now's the time to do it before he joins the others.'

'Whoever wanted Hendrix out of the way wanted it to be bloody permanent,' Stafford said ruminatively. 'And it wasn't a matter of secrecy, either. Chip, supposing you were in that tour group and you saw Hendrix marched away. A little later you hear shots, and then the Tanzanians who took Hendrix away return wearing broad grins. What would you think?'

'I'd think Hendrix had been shot, probably trying to escape.'

'So would I,' said Stafford. 'And that's probably what the rest of the group think right now, except that Hendrix's guards didn't return. But they'll have heard the shots. Does that sound reasonable?'

'It could be.'

Nair gave a peculiar warbling whistle and beckoned. They went back to the crest of the ridge and Nair pointed to the belt of trees by the Losemai. 'They're coming out.'

Minute figures were emerging on to the open plain. Chip, his binoculars to his eyes, counted them. '. . . four . . . five . . . six.'

'No more.'

'No more. Just the group minus Hendrix. The Tanzanians have sent them home.' He looked at the setting sun. 'They won't make good time, not without shoes. They'll be spending a night in the bush.'

'Dangerous?'

He shook his head. 'Not if they're careful; just scary. But Adam will look after them if they have the sense to let him. We'll wait for them up here.'

Stafford said, 'Let's have a chat.'

Hendrix stirred at Nair's side. 'Say, who *are* you guys?'

'Lifesavers,' said Stafford. 'Your life. Now shut up.' He looked at Nair. 'Keep him quiet. If he doesn't want to be quiet then quieten him.' He did not want Hendrix to get any wrong ideas about his rescuers. He wanted him softened up and it was best that Hendrix should think he'd jumped out of a moderately warm frying pan into a bloody hot fire.

Stafford jerked his head at Chip and they walked away again. He said, 'I don't know the motives for the attempted murder of Hendrix but, so far, only four people know he's not dead. You, me, Nair and Hendrix himself. And he would have been very dead if you hadn't let go with the Uzi when you did. It was a matter of a split second.'

'What are you getting at?'

'Supposing he doesn't join the others? Supposing he stays dead? That's going to confuse the hell out of somebody.'

'Which somebody?'

'How the devil would I know? But six Tanzanians don't deliberately try to murder the inheritor of three million pounds just for kicks. The average Tanzanian wouldn't even know Hendrix existed. Somebody, somewhere, must have given the orders. Now, that somebody will think Hendrix is dead as per orders. He might be mystified about the disappearance of two Tanzanians, but Hendrix will have disappeared, too. The survivors of the group will tell their tale and it will all add up to Hendrix's death because, if he isn't dead why doesn't he show up? But I'll have him. He's not a trump card but a joker to be played at the correct time.'

Chip stared at Stafford for a long time in silence. Eventually he said, 'You don't want much, do you?' He ticked off points on his fingers. 'One, we kidnap Hendrix; two, we have to smuggle him out of the Mara because he can't go through any of the gates; three, we have to keep him alive with food and water while all this is going on; four, we have to find a place to put him when we get him out of the Mara; five, that means guards to be supplied; six . . .' He stopped. 'You know; a man could run out of fingers this way.'

'In the past you've always proved to be a resourceful chap,' Stafford said engagingly.

Chip gave him a thin smile. 'All hell is going to break loose,' he said. 'This is going to make headlines in the world press. An American multi-millionaire kidnapped and killed – a first-rate front page story full of diplomatic dynamite. The Kenyan government will be forced to protest to Tanzania and the American government will probably join in. So what happens when we finally turn him loose? Then our heads are on the chopping block.'

'Not at all,' Stafford said. 'He won't say a damned thing. He *can't* say a thing. You're forgetting that he isn't really Hendrix.'

'I'm forgetting nothing,' said Chip coldly. 'All I know is what you've told me. You haven't proved anything yet.'

Stafford turned his head and looked at Hendrix. 'Let's ask him his name,' he proposed.

'Yes, but not here. Let's get out of Tanzania.'

Stafford hesitated because he was worried about the tour

group, particularly the Roches. 'The others,' he said. 'Will they be all right?'

'I told you; Adam will take care of them,' said Chip impatiently. 'They'll be all right. Look, Max; we'll be able to make better time on our own. We can get back to Keekorok and have cars sent to pick them up on the border. And on the way you can have your talk with Hendrix.'

Put that way it was a good solution. 'All right,' Stafford said at length. 'Let's get going.'

'But I promise nothing until you prove your point about Hendrix,' said Chip. 'You have to do that.'

15

So they went back into Kenya but not the same way they had come out. They changed direction and headed north-west, in the direction of Mara New Bridge. Chip said, 'Whatever happens we'll have to come up with a story for the police, and it will have to be a story with no guns in it. Dr Robert Ouko isn't going to take kindly to civilians who make armed incursions into Tanzania.'

'Who's he?'

'Minister for Foreign Affairs. He'll be sending a strong diplomatic note to Dar-es-Salaam and he won't want it weakened by talk of guns.'

'How are you going to keep Hendrix's mouth shut?'

'Don't think it isn't on my mind.'

On the way they concocted a story. After sending Curtis back to Keekorok to raise the alarm they had courageously and somewhat foolishly chased after the Tanzanians. On realizing they were about to infringe Tanzanian territory they stopped and turned back, only to lose their way. After several hours of wandering in the dark they had finally found the road near Mara New Bridge and were now reporting like good citizens to the Police Post.

A thin story and not to be carefully examined. It also presupposed the total absence of Hendrix which cheered Stafford because it seemed that Chip was tacitly accepting his proposal to keep Hendrix under wraps. But he suspected that Chip was busy in the construction of another yarn should he have to write Hendrix back into the script.

Meanwhile they marched steadily through the bush until nightfall, with Hendrix protesting at intervals about the speed, and wanting to know who the hell they were, and various other items that came to his mind. He was silenced by Nair who produced a knife; it was the *kirpan*, the ceremonial knife carried by all Sikhs, but by no means purely ornamental, and the sight of it silenced Hendrix as effectively as if Nair had cut out his tongue with it.

They stopped as the last of the light was ebbing from the sky. There was still enough to march by but Chip's decision to halt was coloured by the fact that they discovered a small hollow or dell which was screened from all sides. 'We can build a small fire down there,' he said. 'It won't be seen.'

'Where are we?' Stafford asked. 'Kenya or Tanzania?'

Chip grinned. 'A toss of the coin will tell you.'

So they collected wood to make a fire which wasn't difficult because the bush is scattered with dead wood. The fire wasn't so much for warmth as to keep away animals. Chip said he was worried less about lions and other large predators than about hyenas. 'They'll go for a sleeping man,' he said. They built the fire in such a way so as always to have a burning brand ready to grab for self-defence.

When they got the fire going Chip looked at Stafford then jerked his head at Hendrix. 'Your turn.'

'Okay.' He turned to Hendrix. 'What's your name?'

'Hendrix, Henry Hendrix. Folks call me Hank. Who are you?'

'That doesn't matter,' said Stafford. 'And you're a liar.' He was silent for a moment. 'I notice you haven't thanked anyone for saving your life.'

Hendrix's eyes glimmered in the light of the flames. 'Hell; every time I opened my mouth I was told to shut it.'

'We want you to talk now. In fact, we'll positively encourage it. Who is Gunnarsson?'

'A friend. And, okay; thanks for doing what you did. I really thought I was dead back there. I really did.'

'Think nothing of it,' said Chip dryly.

'Who is Hamsun – Olaf Hamsun?' asked Stafford.

'Never heard of him,' said Hendrix.

'You might know him better as Biggie.'

'Oh, Biggie! He's a guy I knew back in L.A. What's with the questions?'

'Who is Hardin?'

'Never heard of the guy.'

'You ought to know him. He took you from Los Angeles to New York.'

'Oh, him. I never knew the guy's name.'

'You went from Los Angeles to New York with a man and never knew his name? You'll have to do better than that. You'll be telling us you don't know your own name next. What is it?'

His eyes flickered. 'Hendrix,' he said sullenly. 'Look, I don't know what you guys want but I don't like all these questions.'

'I don't care what you like or don't like,' Stafford said. 'And I don't care whether you live or die. What does Biggie wear around his neck?'

The switch in pace caught Hendrix flat-footed. 'What the kind of a goddamn question is that? How in hell would I know?'

'You were his friend. Where did you meet Gunnarsson?'

'New York.'

'Where's the hole in your shoulder?'

Hendrix looked startled. 'What the hell are you talking about?'

Stafford sighed. 'You took a bullet in your shoulder back in Los Angeles. Hardin bound it up. You should have a hole in you so where is it?'

'I heal real good,' said Hendrix sullenly.

'You're the biggest liar since Ananias,' said Stafford. 'You ought to have your mouth washed out with soap. You're not Hendrix, so who are you?'

He hesitated, and Nair said, 'Why did someone want you dead? Is it because your name is Hendrix?'

'That's it,' said Chip. He laughed. 'There's an open season on Hendrixes. Of course, it's illegal; game shooting is prohibited in Kenya.'

'But not in Tanzania,' said Nair. 'It's legal there. They could get away with it.'

'Maybe someone wants a stuffed Hendrix head on his wall,' said Chip. 'A trophy.'

'The eyes would have to be glass,' said Nair. 'Could they match the colour?'

'I believe they're using plastic these days,' said Chip. 'They can do anything with plastic.'

The crazy crosstalk got to Hendrix. 'Shut up, you nigger bastard!' he shouted.

There was a dead silence before Chip said coldly, 'You don't talk that way to the man with the gun.' In the distance there was a coughing roar and Hendrix jerked. 'A lion,' said Chip. 'Maybe we should leave him to the lions. Maybe *they* want a trophy.'

A choked sob came from Hendrix. Stafford said, 'You've been under observation ever since you left the States. We *know* you're not Hendrix. Tell us who you are and we'll leave you alone.'

'Dear Jesus!' he said. 'Gunnarsson'll kill me.'

'Gunnarsson won't get near you,' said Stafford. 'Leave him to us. And what the devil do you think nearly happened by the river? You stay being Hendrix and you're a dead man.'

The night noises in the bush were growing in intensity. The lion roared again in the distance and, from quite close, something snarled and something else squealed appallingly. The squalling noise was cut off sharply and Chip put another tree branch on the fire. 'A leopard caught a baboon,' he said. Nair picked up his rifle and stood up, staring into the darkness.

It got to Hendrix; his eyes rolled and he shivered violently. He'd had a hard time that day. He'd been kidnapped, nearly murdered, and now he was being interrogated by armed strangers who apparently knew everything about him except his name and in a place where animals were murdering each other. No wonder he cracked.

'You'll keep me safe from Gunnarsson. You guarantee it?'

Stafford glanced at Chip who nodded. He said, 'We'll put you in a safe place where no one will know where you are. But you'll have to co-operate. Tell us.'

Hendrix still hesitated. 'Anyone got a cigarette?' Chip took a packet from his pocket and shook one out, and Hendrix lit it with a burning twig from the fire. He took a long draught of smoke into his lungs and it seemed to calm him. 'All right. My name's Jack Corliss and Gunnarsson propositioned me a few weeks ago. Christ; I wish he'd never come near me.'

The story was moderately simple. Corliss worked in a bank in New York. He was a computer buff and had found a way to fiddle the electronic books and Gunnarsson had caught him at it. From then on it was straight blackmail. Stafford did not think Gunnarsson had to try too hard because Corliss was bent already.

'I had to read a lot of stuff about Hendrix,' said Corliss. 'About his family. Then there were tape recordings – a lot of them. Hendrix talking with Gunnarsson. I don't think Hendrix knew he was being taped. Gunnarsson got him to talk a lot about himself; it was real friendly. Gunnarsson got him drunk a couple of times and some good stuff came out.'

'Good for anyone wanting to impersonate Hendrix,' said Chip.

Corliss nodded. 'It looked great. Hendrix was a loner; he had no family. Gunnarsson said it would be dead easy.'

'Dead being the operative word,' said Stafford. 'What else was he offering you, apart from the chance of staying out of jail?' Corliss avoided his eyes. 'Let's have it all.'

'A quarter of a million bucks,' he mumbled. 'Gunnarsson said I'd have to have a hunk of dough to make it look good afterwards.'

'One twelfth of the take,' Stafford said. 'You taking the risk and Gunnarsson taking the cream. What a patsy you were, Corliss. Do you think you'd have lived to enjoy it?'

'For Christ's sake! I had no goddamn choice. Gunnarsson had me by the balls.'

'Where is Hendrix now?'

'How would I know?' demanded Corliss. 'I never even met the guy.'

'Terminated with extreme prejudice,' said Chip. 'That's the CIA expression isn't it?'

Stafford nodded. 'No one knew he was in New York except Hardin. I think that's why Hardin was fired, and I think Hardin was bloody lucky – it could have happened to him. But Gunnarsson underestimated Hardin; he never thought resentment would push Hardin into going to England.'

'What happens to me now?' asked Corliss apathetically.

'Chip and Nair will take you away and put you in a safe place. You'll have clothing and food but no freedom until this is all over. After that we'll get you back to the States where you'd better get lost. Agreed, Chip?'

'If he co-operates and makes no trouble,' said Chip. 'If he does anything foolish there are no guarantees any more.'

'I'll make no trouble,' said Corliss eagerly. 'All I want to do is to get out of this damn country.' He listened to the night noises and shivered, drawing the fatigue jacket closer to him although it was not cold. 'It scares me.'

'There's one more thing,' Stafford said. 'People don't usually get shot for no reason at all. Who'd want to kill you, Corliss? Not Gunnarsson; he wouldn't want to kill the goose that lays the golden eggs. Who, then?'

'I don't know,' said Corliss violently. 'No one would want to kill *me*. I don't know about Hendrix. You guys said it was open season on Hendrix.'

'That was a manner of speaking,' said Stafford.

Corliss shook his head as thought in wonderment at what was happening to him. He said, 'I had an auto accident in Cornwall, but I'm not that bad a driver. The brakes failed on a hill.'

Stafford shrugged. 'It doesn't have to be guns.'

'*Cui bono?*' said Chip, unexpectedly breaking into Latin. He grinned at Stafford's expression, his teeth gleaming in the firelight. 'This nigger bastard went to university. Who inherits from Hendrix?'

Stafford thought about it, then said slowly, 'The next of kin, I suppose. Corliss, here, says Hendrix had no family but, of course, he had, although he didn't know it. His next of kin would be his cousin, Dirk Hendriks, assuming that Henry Hendrix made no will.'

'I think we can accept that assumption,' said Chip dryly.

Stafford shook his head. 'It's impossible. Dirk went back to England with Farrar. How could he organize a kidnapping into Tanzania? That would take organization on the spot. Anyway, he's inherited three million himself. What's the motive?'

From the darkness on the other side of the fire Nair said, 'Six is better than three. Some people are greedy.'

'I don't see it,' said Stafford. 'Hendriks has no Kenyan connections; he's a South African, damn it. He'd never been in the country until he came with Farrar. How could a man, not knowing either country, organize a kidnapping in Kenya by Tanzanians? I'd say South Africans are a damn sight more unwelcome in Tanzania than they are in Kenya.'

'Yes,' said Chip. 'We're a tolerant people. We don't mind South Africans as long as they behave themselves. The Tanzanians aren't as tolerant.'

They batted it around a bit more and got nowhere. At last Stafford said, 'Perhaps we're barking up the wrong tree. I know that no tourists have been killed in these Tanzanian raids but it was bound to happen sooner or later when people carry guns. Perhaps this attempt on Corliss was a statistical inevitability – a Tanzanian aberration.'

'No,' said Chip. 'I can understand a gun going off and killing someone. I can understand one man going round the bend and killing someone. But two men deliberately took Corliss and, as you said, it was the nearest thing to an execution I've witnessed. It was deliberate.'

'Jesus!' said Corliss.

'But why?' Stafford asked.

No one could tell him.

* * *

The fire had to be kept going all night so one man stood watch while the others slept and Stafford stood first watch. By unspoken agreement Corliss did not stand a watch; no one was going to sleep having him loose with two rifles and a sub-machine-gun. When his time wås up Stafford stretched out on the ground not expecting to sleep, but the next thing he knew Nair was shaking him awake. 'Dawn,' he said.

When Stafford stood up he was stiff and his bones creaked. In his time in the army and in the Sahara he had slept on the ground in the open air many times, but it is a game for a young man and as he grew older he found that it ceased to be fun. He looked around, and asked, 'Where's Chip?'

'He left at first light – ten minutes ago. He said he'll be back in an hour, maybe two.' Nair nodded towards Corliss. 'We have to make arrangements about him. He can't be seen by anyone, including the police.'

Stafford stretched. 'I know that you pair display an amazing efficiency but I'd like to know how Chip is going to fix that. The KPU must still have a lot of pull.'

Nair raised his eyebrows. 'The Kenya People's Union no longer exists. How can it have influence?'

'All right, Nair; have it your own way.'

'Max,' he said, 'a word of warning. It would be most un-wise of you to talk openly about the KPU. Loose talk of that nature could put you in prison. It is still a touchy subject in Kenya.'

Stafford held up his hands placatingly. 'Not another word shall pass my lips.' Nair nodded gravely.

It was two and a half hours before Chip came back and he brought with him two men whom he introduced as Daniel Wekesa and Osano Gichure. 'Good friends,' he said.

'Just good friends?' Stafford said sardonically. 'Not brothers-in-law?'

Chip ignored that. 'They'll look after Corliss and get him out of the Mara.'

'Where will they take him?'

'We'll come to that later. The tourists haven't come back yet, and the border is alive with police on the Kenyan side.' He stroked his chin. 'The tour group is probably still in Tanzania. Bare European feet make for slow going. Still, they should come in some time this morning if I know Adam.'

'Which you do.'

'Yes. I want to talk to him. I want to know exactly how the Tanzanians picked him up. I also want breakfast, so let's go.'

Chip talked to Corliss, told him he'd be looked after if he behaved himself, and then they went, again heading north. They left the rifles and the Uzi with Chip's good friends and he made Stafford empty his pockets of ammunition. 'If the police find so much as a single round you're in trouble,' he said.

On the way he said he had seen the police. 'Just stick to the story we arranged and we'll be fine.'

Chip proved to be right. They walked for an hour and then saw a vehicle coming towards them, bumping through the bush. It contained a police lieutenant and a constable, both armed. They spun their yarn and the lieutenant shook his head. 'It was very unwise to follow those men; it could have been dangerous. I am glad that Mr Chipende had the sense to stop you crossing the border.'

Stafford scowled at Chip who was now a virtuous citizen. The lieutenant smiled. 'I hope this has not spoiled your holiday, Mr Stafford. I assure you that these incidents are rare. Certain wild elements in our neighbouring country get out of control.'

'Is there news of the tour group?' asked Nair.

The lieutenant looked bleak. 'Not yet. They will be given a warm welcome when they arrive. Jump in; I'll take you back to Keekorok in time for a late breakfast.'

So they rode back to the Lodge at Keekorok and got there inside half an hour; not long but long enough for Stafford to wonder if it was habitual for Kenyan police officers to administer a mild slap on the wrist for transgressions such as theirs. He had expected a real rocket and here was the lieutenant actually apologizing for a spoiled holiday. Perhaps it was his view that it was normal for a European tourist to be an idiot.

Their arrival was the occasion for a minor brouhaha. Although the manager met them and tried to ease them into their rooms quietly they were spotted and mobbed by a crowd eagerly asking questions in assorted accents. It was known they had been out all night and that there was another party still missing and, from the look on the manager's face as they briefly answered queries, it was definitely a case of bad public relations.

And Curtis was there, his face set in a wide, relieved smile. He put his broad shoulders between Stafford and a particularly importunate American, and said, 'I hope the Colonel is all right.'

'Tired and a bit travel-worn, that's all Sergeant. Just point me towards breakfast and a bed.'

'The manager's arranged for you to have breakfast in your room, sir. He thought it would be better.'

'Better for whom?' Stafford said acidly. His guess was that the manager was wishing they would vanish instantly so as not to infect the other guests with the virus of bad news. And it would get worse when the others came back; having tourists kidnapped was not good for the image of Keekorok Lodge. It would get still worse when one tourist didn't come back at all, and even worse than that when the tourist was identified as an American millionaire. The manager wouldn't know what had hit him.

Over breakfast Stafford said, 'I took your advice, Sergeant,' and brought him up to date. 'We separated Hendrix from Gunnarsson.'

Curtis was normally an imperturbable and phlegmatic man but the story made his thick, black eyebrows crawl up his scalp like a couple of hairy caterpillars until they threatened to eliminate his bald patch. When Stafford finished he thought in silence then remembered to close his mouth. 'So we've got Hendrix – I mean Corliss. Where?'

Stafford buttered some toast. 'I don't know. Chip whistled a couple of characters out of nowhere and they went off with him.' He took a bite and said indistinctly, 'Sergeant, I think I'll have to rechristen you Aladdin; you've rubbed a lamp and conjured up a genie. My slightest wish is Chip's command and I don't know how the hell he does it. Sheer magic.'

Curtis said, 'Something's just come to me.'

'What?'

'You remember when we came to the Masai Mara and stopped at the gate. Chip got us in. You have to pay to get into a Reserve – any Reserve.'

Stafford nodded. 'He said we were his guests.'

'But he didn't pay,' said Curtis. 'No money passed. He showed a card and signed the book.'

Stafford was tired and looked longingly at the bed. 'Maybe a season ticket,' he mumbled, but a season ticket for four wasn't likely.

16

Curtis woke Stafford. 'I'm sure the Colonel would like to know that the other group has come in.'

He came wide awake. 'You're damned right. What time is it?'

'Just after two.' Stafford blinked disorientedly at the closed curtains and Curtis added gently, 'In the afternoon, sir.'

Stafford dressed in shirt and shorts with swimming trunks beneath and thrust his feet into sandals. Curtis said, 'I'm going with Nair to see Corliss if the Colonel doesn't mind.'

'Why?'

'Chip said they're short of food so we're taking it.' He paused. 'It would be good for us to know where he is, sir.'

Stafford nodded. 'Carry on, Sergeant.'

The lobby was a hubbub of noise and crammed with a welcoming committee of the curious – those guests who had not gone game spotting. There were a lot of them. Stafford suspected that game spotting in the Masai Mara would be a depreciating part of the tourist industry until this storm had blown itself out. Game spotting was one thing and the risk of being kidnapped was another.

He joined Chip who was leaning against a wall. 'How are they?'

'I haven't seen them yet, and we won't be able to talk to them for a while. There's a heavy police escort.'

The rescued tourists came in, spearheaded by a phalanx of police. Six of them – the Roches, Gunnarsson, Kosters and Adam Muliro. They did not walk well, but their feet had been bandaged and clothing had been issued, ill-fitting and incongruous but necessary. The crowd pressed around, shouting questions, and the police kept them back, linking arms.

A senior police officer held up his hands in one of which he held a swagger stick. 'Quiet please! These people are not well. They need urgent medical attention. Now, make way, please.'

There was a brief hush, then someone called, 'There are only six. Who's missing?'

'Mr Hendrix has not yet appeared. We are still looking for him.'

As photo-flashes began to pop Stafford watched Gunnarsson. He had a baffled almost defeated, expression on his face. So that's how a man looks when he's been cheated of six million dollars. It must have been how many a man looked in New York in the crash of 1929 just before jumping out of the skyscraper window – an expression of unfocused anger at the unfairness of things. Not that Gunnarsson would commit suicide. He was not the type and, anyway, he had not lost the money because he had never had it. Still, it was a hard blow.

Stafford lost sight of him as the party was led away. Chip made a motion of his hand as Adam Muliro went past and Adam nodded almost imperceptibly. Chip said, 'We won't see them for a while. Let's have a swim.'

It was a good idea, so after waiting for the crowd to thin they walked towards the pool. Halfway there someone ran after them. 'Mr Stafford?' He turned and saw the man who had asked who was missing. 'Eddy Ukiru – the *Standard*. Can I have a word with you?'

Behind Ukiru a man was unlimbering what was obviously a press camera. Stafford glanced at Chip who said, 'Why not?'

And so Stafford gave a press interview. Midway through Ukiru was joined, to his displeasure, by another reporter from the rival newspaper, *Nation*, and Stafford had to repeat some of the details but essentially he stuck to the prepared story which Chip corroborated. Ukiru showed minor signs of disbelief. 'So you turned back at the border,' he said. 'How did you *know* it was the border? There is no fence, no mark.'

Stafford shrugged. 'You will have to ask Mr Chipende about that.'

So he did, and Chip switched into fast Swahili. Eventually Ukiru shrugged his acceptance, the photographers took their pictures, and they all went away. Stafford said, 'They got here damned quickly. How?'

'The manager will have telephoned his head office who will have notified the police in Nairobi. Plenty of room for leaks to the press there. They'll have chartered aircraft. There's an airstrip here.'

'Yes, I've seen the airstrip,' said Stafford. 'But I didn't know about the telephone. I've seen no wires.'

Chip smiled. 'It's a radio-phone in the manager's office. And we can't have wires because the elephants knock down the telegraph poles. Let's have that swim.'

* * *

Stafford wanted to put himself next to Gunnarsson and found the opportunity during the pre-dinner cocktail hours. All the rescued tour group was there in the bar with the exception of Adam Muliro and they were being quizzed about their experience by the other guests. There was an air of euphoria about them; much laughter from the Roches and Kosters. Now saved, their adventure verged somewhat on unreality and would be something to dine out on for years to come. Adventure is discomfort recollected in tranquillity.

Stafford talked with Kosters and Michele Roche and got their account with no great difficulty, then said with an air of puzzlement. 'But what about Hendrix? What happened to him?'

The euphoric gaiety disappeared fast. 'I don't know,' said Kosters soberly. 'They took him away and there was shooting.'

'You think he's dead?'

Michele's voice was sombre. 'He hasn't come back. We didn't see him again.'

Stafford looked across at Gunnarsson. There was no

157

euphoria about him. He sat with his legs stretched out, gloomily regarding his bandaged feet. Someone had found him a pair of carpet slippers which had been slashed to accommodate the bandages. Stafford took his drink and walked over to Gunnarsson. 'You've had a nasty experience. Oh; my name is Stafford.'

Gunnarsson squinted up at him. 'Stafford? You the guy who tried to come after us?'

'We didn't get very far,' Stafford said ruefully. 'We just got lost and made bloody fools of ourselves.'

'Let me top up your drink.' Stafford sat down. 'I'm John Gunnarsson.' He turned and looked at Stafford, then shook his head. 'You wouldn't have done any good, Mr Stafford – those guys were a walking arsenal – but thanks for trying. What will you have?'

'Gin and tonic.'

Gunnarsson beckoned to a waiter and gave the order, then sighed. 'Christ, what an experience. I've been in some tough spots in my time but that was one of the toughest.'

'They tell me it's happened before,' Stafford said casually.

'Yeah. These damned half-ass Kenyans ought to beef up their border force. You know what was the worst? There's nothing takes the steam out of a guy faster than to strip him ballock naked.' He gave a small snort. 'Well, not quite; they let us keep our underpants.' He brooded. 'It was bad coming back what with the sun and the thorns. My feet feel the size of footballs. And there was the goddamn hyena . . .'

'A hyena?'

'A big son of a bitch. It trotted parallel with us about a hundred yards off, I guess. Waiting for someone to lag or drop out. If it wasn't for the nig . . . the black guy, Adam Somebody, I don't think we'd have made it. He was good.'

'I hear somebody didn't make it,' Stafford said.

'Oh, Jesus!' Gunnarsson's neck swelled.

'What happened to him? Enderby, wasn't it?'

'Hendrix.' Gunnarsson glowered. 'There were six of us,

six of them, and Adam, the driver. Trouble was, they were armed. Kalashnikovs. Know what they are?'

Stafford shook his head. 'Things like that don't come my way.'

'You're lucky. They're Russian-made automatic rifles. We couldn't do a goddamn thing. Helpless.' He made a fist in his frustration. 'Then a couple of them took Hendrix away and later there was firing and the four black guys with us burst out laughing. Imagine that.'

'I can't,' Stafford said soberly. 'Were these men in uniform?'

'Yeah. Camouflage gear. A real military set-up. Jesus, but there's going to be trouble when I get back to Nairobi. Nobody's going to get away with doing this to an American citizen.'

'What are you going to do?' Stafford asked interestedly.

'Do! I'm going to raise hell with the American Ambassador, that's what I'm going to do. Hendrix was a real nice young guy and I want him found, dead or alive. And if he's dead I want blood if I have to take it all the way to the United Nations.'

Stafford contemplated that statement. If Gunnarsson was prepared to raise a stink at that level it meant that the real Hendrix was not around to object. Terminated with extreme prejudice, as Chip had said. The killing of a newly made American millionaire was certain to find its way into New York newspapers if Gunnarsson was prepared to push it so far, which meant that Gunnarsson thought he was safe.

'Had you known him long? Hendrix, I mean.'

'A while – not long.' said Gunnarsson. 'But that's not the point, Mr Stafford. The point is they can't get away with doing this to an American citizen and I'm going to scream that loud and clear.'

Yes, it was his only chance if Hendrix/Corliss was still alive and in the hands of the Tanzanians. Only strong diplomatic pressure put on Tanzania by Kenya and the United States could get back Gunnarsson's walking treasure chest. It would take nerve but Gunnarsson had that in plenty.

'I wish you well,' Stafford said. 'Let me buy you a drink.'

So he bought Gunnarsson a drink and presently took his leave. As he walked by the back of Gunnarsson's chair he said, 'Good luck,' and clapped him on the shoulder. Gunnarsson jumped a foot in the air, let out a scream and banged both feet on the floor, whereupon he emitted another piercing yell. Stafford apologized, professing to have forgotten his sunburn, and made a quick getaway.

17

They left for Nairobi next morning and so did a lot of others but for different reasons. After seeing the condition in which the tour group had come back from their unwanted, brief sojourn in Tanzania the front desk was busy as the fearful paid their bills. The manager was gloomy but resigned.

Again they drove that spine-jolting, back-breaking road to Narok and then sat back with relief as they hit the asphalt which led all the way to Nairobi, and pulled into a parking slot in front of the Norfolk Hotel in comfortable time for lunch. There Stafford received a surprise. On opening the door of his room he found an envelope on the floor just inside. It contained the briefest of messages: 'I'm back. Come see me. Room 14. Ben.'

He dumped his bags, went to room 14, and knocked. A guarded voice said, 'Yeah; who is it?'

'Stafford.'

There was the snap of a lock and the door opened and swung wide. He went in and Hardin said, 'Where the hell have you been? I've been telephoning every two hours for the last two days and getting no answer. So I jump a plane and what do I find? No one.' He was aggrieved.

'Calm down, Ben,' Stafford said. 'We had to go away but it had good results.' He paused and examined that statement, then added, 'If I knew what they were.'

Hardin examined Stafford closely. 'Your face is scratched. Been with a dame?'

Stafford sat down. 'When you've stopped being funny we can carry on. You were sent back for a reason. Did you find anything?'

Hardin said, 'I've just ordered from room service. I didn't

want to eat in public before I knew where Gunnarsson was. I'll cancel.'

'No, I'll join you,' said Stafford. 'Duplicate the order.'

'Okay.' Hardin telephoned the order before opening the refrigerator and taking out a couple of bottles of beer. 'Jan-Willem Hendrykxx – an old guy and a travelling man. I've been spending a lot of your money, Max; ran up a hell of a phone bill. And I had to go to Belgium.' He held up his hand. 'Don't worry; I flew economy.'

'I think the firm can stand it.'

Hardin gave Stafford an opened bottle and a glass. 'I've written a detailed report but I can give you the guts of it now. Okay?'

'Shoot.'

He sat down. 'Jan-Willem Hendrykxx born in 1899 in – believe it or not – Hoboken.'

Stafford looked up, startled. 'In the States!'

'It got me, too,' Hardin admitted. 'No, the original Hoboken is a little place just outside Antwerp in Belgium. Parents poor but honest, which is more than we can say of Jan-Willem. Reasonable education for those days but he ran away to sea when he was seventeen. Knocked about a bit, I expect, but ended up in South Africa in 1921 where he married Anna Vermuelen.'

He rubbed his jaw. 'There was a strike in Johannesburg in 1922, if that's what you can call it. Both sides had artillery and it sounds more like a civil war to me. Anyway, Jan-Willem disappeared leaving Anna to carry the can – the can being twin babies, Jan and Adriaan. Jan is the father of Dirk Hendriks, and Adriaan is the father of Hank Hendrix, the guy I picked up in Los Angeles. Follow me so far?'

'It's quite clear,' Stafford said.

'Jan-Willem jumped a freighter going to San Francisco, got to like the Californian climate, and decided to stay. Now, you must remember these were Prohibition days. Most people, when they think of Prohibition, think of Rum Row off Atlantic City, but there was just as much rum running on the West Coast, either from Canada or Mexico, and Hendrykxx got in on the act. By the time Repeal came he was well entrenched in the rackets.'

'You mean he was a genuine dyed-in-the-wool gangster?'

Hardin shrugged. 'You could put it that way. But he made a mistake – he never took out US citizenship. So when he put a foot wrong he wasn't jailed; he was deported back to his country of origin as an undesirable alien. He arrived back in Antwerp in April, 1940.'

Stafford said, 'You've been busy, Ben. How did you discover all this?'

'A hunch. What I found out in Belgium made Hendrykxx a crook. He was supposed to have been killed in Jo'burg in 1922 but we know he wasn't, so I wondered where he'd go, and being a crook he'd likely have a record. I have some good buddies in the FBI dating back to my CIA days. They looked up the files. There's a hell of a dossier on Hendrykxx. When he came to the attention of the FBI they checked him very thoroughly. That's where the phone bill came in; I spent about six hours talking long distance to the States.'

The room waiter came in with lunch and set it on the table. Hardin waited until he had gone before continuing. 'I don't know whether it was good or bad for Hendrykxx that he arrived in Antwerp when he did. Probably good. The German offensive began on May 10th, Holland and Belgium fell like ninepins and France soon after. Antwerp was in German hands about two weeks after Hendrykxx got there. His wartime history is misty but from what I've picked up he was well into the Belgian rackets, the black market and all that. Of course, in those days it was patriotic but I believe Hendrykxx wasn't above doing deals with the Germans.'

'A collaborator?'

Hardin bit into a club sandwich and said, with his mouth full, 'Never proved. But he came out of the war in better financial shape than he went into it. Then he started import-export corporations and when the EEC was organized he went to town in his own way which, naturally, was the illegal way. There was a whole slew of EEC regulations which could be bent. Bargeloads of butter going up the Rhine from Holland to Germany found themselves relabelled and back in Holland with Hendrykxx creaming off the subsidy. He could do that several times with the same bargeload until the damn stuff went rancid on him. He was into a lot of rackets like that.'

'The bloody old crook,' said Stafford.

'On the way through the years there was also a couple of marriages, both bigamous because Anna was still alive back in South Africa. In 1974 he retired and went to live in Jersey, probably for tax reasons. By then he was pretty old. Last year he died, leaving close on a hundred million bucks, most of which went to the Ol Njorowa Foundation in Kenya. End of story.'

Stafford stared at Hardin. 'You must be kidding, Ben. Where's the Kenya connection?'

'There isn't one,' said Hardin airily.

'But there must be.'

'None that I could find.' He leaned forward. 'And I'll tell you something else. Hendrykxx never was all that big time and crooks like him are usually big spenders. I doubt if he made more than five million dollars in his whole life. Maybe ten. Of course, that's not bad but it doesn't make him into any kind of financial giant. So where did the rest of the dough come from?'

'Every time we find anything new this whole business gets crazier,' Stafford said disgustedly.

'I checked a couple of other things,' said Hardin. 'I went to Jersey and saw Hendrykxx's death certificate in the Greffe – that's their Public Record Office. The old guy died of a heart attack. I talked to the doctor, a guy called Morton, and he confirmed it. He said Hendrykxx could have gone any time, but . . .' Hardin shook his head.

'But what?' asked Stafford.

'Nothing to put a finger on definitely, but I had the impression that Morton was uneasy about something.' Hardin refilled his glass. 'Back in London I checked on Mandeville, the lawyer who handled the London end of the legacy business. Very right wing. He's making a name for himself defending neo-Nazi groups, the guys who find themselves in court for race rioting. But I don't see that has anything to do with us.'

'No,' agreed Stafford. 'Did you talk to him?'

'I couldn't. He's vacationing in South Africa.' Hardin drank some beer. 'What's new with you?'

Stafford told him and by the time he had finished it was late afternoon and the undrunk coffee had gone cold. Hardin listened to it all thoughtfully. 'You've had quite a time,' he commented. 'Where's Corliss now?'

'Curtis saw him yesterday,' Stafford said. 'He was in a remote tented camp in the Masai Mara, but I wouldn't want to guarantee he's there now. What do you think of the line Gunnarson pitched me?'

'Righteous anger isn't Gunnarsson's style,' said Hardin. 'He sure as hell wants Corliss back and if that's the way he's going about it you know what it means – Hendrix is dead.'

'I'd already got that far,' said Stafford.

'But there's more.' Hardin took out his wallet. 'I got this at *poste restante* in London. Jack Richardson sent it, and he got it from Charlie Wainwright in Los Angeles. Charlie remembered I'd been interested in Biggie.'

He took a newspaper clipping from the wallet and passed it to Stafford. It was a brief report from the Los Angeles *Examiner* to the effect that a disastrous fire had broken out in a house in Santa Monica and that all the occupants had died, six of them. The fire was believed to have been caused by an over-heated pottery kiln which had exploded. The names of the dead were given. Five of them were unknown to Stafford, but the sixth was Olaf Hamsun. Biggie.

He looked at Hardin and said slowly, 'Are you thinking what I'm thinking?'

'If you're thinking that Gunnarsson plays for keeps.

'Ben; you're a bloody lucky man. How did Gunnarsson miss you?'

'You've just said it – sheer goddamn luck. Jack Richardson sent a letter with that clipping; he told me that the rooming house I'd been living in had burned up. Maybe I'd slipped to London just in time.' Hardin rubbed his jaw. 'On the other hand it might not have been Gunnarsson at all. In the Bronx they have a habit of burning buildings for the insurance money. The whole damn place is falling apart.'

Stafford held up the clipping. 'Was this the whole of the commune?'

'Just about, I reckon.'

'Then that means that you are possibly the only person who definitely knows that the Hendrix who claimed the estate is a fake. What's more, it means that Gunnarsson, if he's going to make a big song and dance at the Embassy, is sure that you won't pop up to prove him wrong. If Gunnarsson thinks you're out of the game – and that's the way he's acting – then that gives us an edge.'

'What do I do? Dress in a white sheet and scare him to death?'

'We'll think of something. Let's get back to the main issue. Who would want Hendrix dead? Chip asked the question – who benefits? The answer to that is his cousin and sole relative, Dirk Hendriks. I argued that he couldn't have organized it because he was in England, but these days one can get around really fast.'

'He was in England,' said Hardin. 'I forgot to tell you. He was on the same plane that I came in on this morning.'

'Was he?' said Stafford.

'It's okay, Max; he's never met me. Besides, he travelled first class, and the guys up front don't mix with the *hoi polloi* in economy.'

Stafford said sarcastically, 'I'm mixing with a real egg-head crowd. First Chip with Latin, now you with Greek.'

Hardin scratched the angle of his jaw. 'You've had a funny

feeling about Hendriks all along, haven't you? Mind telling me why?'

'I'm suspicious about everyone in this case,' Stafford said. 'The more I know about it the stranger it becomes.' He shrugged. 'As for Dirk I suppose it's a gut feeling. I've never really liked him even before you came along and blew the whistle on Gunnarsson.'

Hardin looked at him shrewdly. 'Something to do with his wife?'

'Good God, no! At least, not in the way you're thinking. Alix means nothing to me apart from the fact that we're friends. But you don't like to see friends get hurt. She's a wealthy woman and Dirk is battening on her, or was until this Hendrykxx thing blew up. He's too much the playboy type for my liking.' Stafford changed the subject. 'When you were with the CIA how long did you spend in Kenya?'

'A couple of years.'

'Would you know your way around now?'

'Sure. It hasn't changed much.'

'Do you still have contacts?'

'A few, I guess. It depends on what you want.'

'What I want is to find out more about Pete Chipende and Nair Singh, particularly Chip. I've noticed that he tends to give the orders and Nair jumps.'

Hardin frowned. 'What's the point? They're helping plenty judging by your account.'

'That's just it,' said Stafford. 'They're helping too damn much, and they're too efficient. When we wanted Corliss taken off our hands Chip just pushed off into the bush in the middle of nowhere and turned up two of his friends very conveniently. And there are a few other things. One is that they know soldiering – they're no amateurs at that. In fact, they're thorough all-round professionals. There's also something you said just before you went to England.'

'What was that?'

'You said there'd be others behind Chip and Nair. You said they might not show but they'd be there. I think you're right, and I also think there's an organization, a complex organization, and I want to know what it is before we get into this thing over our heads. Chip is helpful all right, but I'd like to be sure he doesn't help us right into a jail – or a coffin. I don't want to get into any political trouble here.'

Hardin pondered for a moment. 'I don't know who is on the CIA station here right now. I think I'll go along to the Embassy and see if there's anyone there I know.'

'Will they talk to you?'

He shrugged. 'It depends. The CIA is no different than any other outfit; some are bastards, others are right guys.' He grimaced. 'But sometimes it's difficult to tell them apart. Gunnarsson turned out to be a bastard.'

'All right,' Stafford said. 'But don't go to the Embassy until we're sure that Gunnarsson isn't there. I'll see Chip about that.' He smiled. 'He can be helpful in that way as much as he likes. I'll have him check Gunnarsson and let you know.'

* * *

Stafford went back to his room to find the telephone ringing. It was Chip. 'Where have you been?' he asked. 'You walked into the hotel and then disappeared off the face of the earth.'

Stfford looked at his watch. Exchanging information with Hardin had taken most of the afternoon. 'I had things to do,' he said uninformatively.

If silence could be said to have surprise in it then that silence had. At last Chip said, 'Some items have come up. I'd like to see you.'

'Come up.'

When Chip came in he said, 'What have you got?'

'Brice,' said Chip. 'You wanted to know about Brice in Zimbabwe. But it was Rhodesia then. Harry and Mary Brice farmed near Umtali on the Sabi River. They had a son, Charles Brice. When UDI came and Rhodesia became independent Charles Brice had a quarrel with his parents and left the country. Later, when the guerillas became active, the farm was destroyed and Harry and Mary Brice were killed.'

Stafford said, 'That checks out with Brice's story.'

'Exactly,' said Chip.

'Where did you get it?'

'I told you. The brothers in Zimbabwe are co-operative. You asked to have Brice checked there. He was checked.'

'And he comes out whiter than white.' Stafford did not spend much time thinking about that expression because he was thinking of this, yet another spectacular example of Chip's efficiency. He said, 'Chip, you must have quite an organization behind you. A while ago you needled me because you said I was withholding information. Now, just who the hell are you?'

'Some questions are better not asked,' Chip said.

'All the same, I'm asking.'

'And some questions are better not answered.'

'That's not good enough.'

'It's all you're going to get,' Chip said bluntly. 'Max, don't stir things up – don't muddy the water. It could cause trouble. Trouble for you, for everybody. Just let it slide and accept the help. We have helped, you know.'

'I know you've helped,' said Stafford. 'But I don't know why. I want to know why.'

'And I'm not going to tell you. Just study Kenyan history since the British left and draw your own conclusions.' He paused. 'I believe you brought up a certain subject with Nair and he told you to keep your mouth shut. It's advice I strongly advise you to follow. Now let's get on with it. Dirk Hendriks flew in from London this morning. He's staying at the New Stanley. Do you still want him watched?'

'Yes. How did you know he came in this morning?'

'As I once said, I have friends at the airport. We check the passenger list of every London flight – every European flight, come to that. That's how we know that your Mr Hardin came in this morning.'

Stafford sat up straight. 'Are you having us watched, too?'

Chip laughed. 'Simmer down. My friend at the airport relayed the information as a matter of course. Is that where you've been all afternoon; talking with Hardin? I ought to have guessed. Did he find out what you wanted to know?'

Two could play at withholding information. Stafford said, 'It was a cold trail, Chip. Hendrykxx was an old man. You can't unravel an eighty-year life all that quickly. Ben is an experienced investigator, I know, but he's not that bloody good.'

'A pity,' said Chip.

'Where is Corliss now?'

'Not far. If you want him we can produce him inside an hour.'

'But you're not going to tell me where he is.'

'Correct. You're learning, Max.' He looked at his watch. 'Gunnarsson will be here before sunset – back in the New Stanley. You know, it's going to be hard to pin him down.'

'What do you mean?'

'Neither he nor Corliss has committed a crime against Kenyan law. Hendrykxx's will was drawn up by a Jersey lawyer and presumably will come under Jersey law. If Gunnarsson puts Corliss in as a substitute for Hendrix that is no crime here; no Kenyan has been defrauded. We can't hold either of them on those grounds. So how are you going to go about it?'

'I don't know,' Stafford said glumly. 'All I know is that you're talking like a lawyer.'

'How do you know I'm not a lawyer?' said Chip.

'I don't. You're a bloody chameleon. If the Kenyan authorities can't hold Gunnarsson then there's nothing to stop him leaving. I don't think he will leave, not until he knows what's happened to Corliss, but he might. It would be nice if something were to stop him.'

'He could always lose his passport,' offered Chip. 'It wouldn't stop him, but it would delay him until he got papers from the American Embassy.'

'And how would he lose his passport?' Stafford asked.

Chip spread his hands. 'People do all the time. Strange, isn't it? It causes considerable work for the consular staffs.' He stood up. 'I must go; I have work to do, arrangements to make. Take it easy, Max; don't work up a sweat.' He turned to go, then dropped some newspapers on the table. 'I thought you might like to read the news.'

He went and Stafford lay on the bed and lit a cigarette. If Chip was a member of the Kenya People's Union he certainly would not come right out and say so, and he had not. On the other hand, if he was not a member why would he imply that he was? Or had that been the implication? Had Stafford read too much into Chip's equivocations?

But there was more. Whether he was or was not a member of a banned political party why was he being so bloody helpful to Max Stafford to the point of kidnapping Corliss and stealing Gunnarsson's passport, both of which were criminal acts? Stafford was damned sure it was not at the behest of some Indian back in London who liked Curtis.

He picked up the newspapers and scanned the front pages. The kidnapping of the tour group and the disappearance of Hendrix had made headlines in both the *Standard* and the *Nation*. Perhaps, if it had not been for Hendrix, the story would have been played down; Stafford suspected that government pressure would suppress anything that made for a bad public image. But Hendrix made it different – no one had vanished before.

An editorial in the *Standard* called for an immediate and extremely strong note of protest to the Tanzanian government and demanded that Hendrix be returned, dead or alive. Someone from the *Nation* had tried to interview the American Ambassador but he had not been available for comment. The inevitable unnamed spokesman said the American authorities regarded the matter in the most serious light and that steps were being taken. He did not say in which direction.

In neither newspaper was there a report of the interview Chip and Stafford had given to Eddy Ukiru, the reporter from the *Standard*, and his companion from the *Nation*. No mention of Stafford, of Chip, of Nair, of Curtis. No photographs. It was as though their part in this nine day wonder had never happened. Of course, they were pretty small beer compared to Hendrix but it seemed sloppy journalism to Stafford. He tossed the newspapers aside with the thought that perhaps Ukiru and his mate had not met their deadline.

It was only when he was on the verge of sleep that night that he realized he had never told Chip at any time that Hendrykxx's will had been drawn up in Jersey. So how did Chip know?

18

Dirk Hendriks drove down the winding road of the escarpment towards the Rift Valley and Naivasha and towards what he always held in his mind but never mentioned aloud – *die Kenya Stasie*. Not that it was fully operational yet but it would be once this business was over. Still, Frans Potgeiter had done a good job considering the slim funding that had been available. He was a good man.

He passed the church at the bottom of the hill which had been built by Italian prisoners during the war and turned towards Naivasha. His eyes flitted over the signpost that indicated the road to Narok and he smiled. Potgeiter had succeeded in the Masai Mara, too, after others had failed miserably. There had been too much bungling, too much interference. As the English proverb said: 'too many cooks spoil the broth'. But everything was coming right at last.

He turned off the main road short of Naivasha and took the road which ran back along the lake edge past the Lake Naivasha Hotel and on to Ol Njorowa. It was precisely midday when he pulled up outside the gatehouse and blew a blast on his horn. The gate keeper came running. 'Yes, sah?'

'Mr Hendriks to see Mr Brice. I'm expected.'

'Sah.' The gate keeper went back and the gates opened. As Hendriks drove through, the gate keeper shouted warningly '*Pole pole!*' Hendriks did not know what that meant until he hit the first sleeping policeman at a speed which jarred his teeth. He slowed the car and reflected that he had better learn Swahili. It would be useful in the future.

He parked outside the Administration Block and went inside. In the cool hall he approached the reception desk behind which sat a muscular young black who was dressed neatly in white shirt and shorts. Another young Kenyan was sitting at a side desk hammering a typewriter. 'Mr Hendriks to see Mr Brice,' Hendriks repeated.

'Yes, sir; he's expecting you. Come this way.' Hendriks followed, passing through a wicket gate and along a corridor towards Brice's office. He nodded approvingly. Potgeiter had it organized well; no one was going to wander about the place unobserved.

Brice was sitting behind his desk and looked up with a smile as Hendriks came in. The Kenyan left, closing the door behind him, and Hendriks said, *'Goeie middag, meneer Potgeiter; hoe gaan dit?'*

The smile abruptly left Brice's face. 'No Afrikaans,' he said sharply. 'And my name is Brice – always Brice. Remember that!'

Hendriks smiled and dropped into a chair. 'Think the place is bugged?'

'I know it isn't.' Brice tapped on the desk for emphasis. 'But don't get into bad habits.'

'I'm a South African,' said Hendriks. 'I'm supposed to know Afrikaans.'

'And I'm not,' snapped Brice. 'So stick to English – always English.'

'English it will be' agreed Hendriks. 'Even when we're conspiring.'

Brice nodded – a gesture which closed the subject. 'How did you get on in London?'

'All right. That old fool, Farrar, is making the distribution next week.' Hendriks laughed. 'He gave me a cheque for a hundred thousand pounds on account as soon as we got back. Your coffers should be filling up soon.'

'And about time,' said Brice. 'I'm tired of working on a shoestring.' He shook his head. 'The way it was set up in Europe was too complicated. We ought to have had direct control. Farrar asked some sticky questions when he was here.'

'It had to be set up in Jersey,' said Hendriks. 'Do you think

174

we wanted to pay the British Treasury death duties on forty million pounds? This operation wasn't set up to give money to the Brits. As for Farrar, Mandeville kept a tight rein on him. Farrar is a legal snob; he likes working with an eminent British barrister. And Mandeville is a good man. The best.' Hendriks smiled thinly. 'He ought to be considering what we pay him.'

Brice made a dismissive gesture. 'I never understood the European end of this and I didn't want to. I had my own troubles.'

You had troubles! thought Hendriks bitterly, but said nothing. His mind went back to the moment when Alix happily announced that she was pregnant. That had come as a shock because if the child was born before Hendrykxx died it would automatically become one of his heirs and that could not be allowed. The kid would inherit two million of their precious pounds and it would bring Alix right into the middle of the operation.

He had thought of having the will changed and had talked it over with Mandeville but Mandeville had said they would not get it past Farrar. Hendrykxx was then senile and not in his right mind, and Farrar was rectitude itself. So Hendrykxx had to go before the baby was born. It had been risky – murder always was – but it had been done. And all that was on top of the trouble caused by Henry Hendrix who had dropped out of sight in America. Still, that problem had been solved – or had it?

Brice said, 'Your cousin Henry was one of your problems you wished on me. Why the hell was he allowed to come to Africa?'

'We lost him,' said Hendriks. 'And Pretoria was asleep. By the time they woke up back home to the fact that Henry was important because the old man was dead Farrar had employed an American agency and was looking for him himself. The agency man got to Henry about ten minutes before we did.' He snorted. 'Ten minutes and three inches.'

Brice raised his eyebrows. 'Three inches?'

'Our man took a shot at him. Hit him in the shoulder. Three inches to the right and Henry wouldn't have been a problem ever again.'

'Well, he's no problem now,' said Brice. 'I've seen to that. Have you read the papers lately.'

Hendriks nodded. 'It made a couple of paragraphs in the English papers.' He leaned forward. 'You're wrong, Brice. Henry is still a problem. Where's the bloody body? We need the body. His three million quid is tied up until death is proved. We don't want to wait seven years to collect. As it is he's just disappeared.'

Brice sighed. He stood up and went to the window. With his back to Hendriks he said, 'He's not the only one to have disappeared. Two of my men didn't come back.'

'What!' Hendriks also rose to his feet. 'What did you say?'

Brice turned. 'You heard me. I've lost two men.'

'You'd better explain,' Hendriks said tightly.

'It all went exactly the way I planned. You've read the newspaper reports. The stories those tourists told were exactly right except for one thing. They were supposed to see the body and they didn't. It wasn't there – and neither were my men.'

'Could Henry have jumped them and got away? How were they armed?'

'Standard Tanzanian army gear. Kalashnikovs.'

Hendriks shook his head. 'I don't think Henry would have the stuffing in him to tackle those. In any case if he got away he'd be back by now.' He thought for a moment. 'Perhaps the Tanzanians got him. The real ones, I mean.'

'I doubt it,' said Brice. 'The Legislature is in an uproar and the Foreign Minister is putting pressure on the Tanzanians. Some of my boys are on the border with a watching brief. The Tanzanians are scouring the area south of the Masai Mara. Why would they do that if they already had Henry – or his corpse?'

Hendriks said coldly, 'So that leaves one answer. Your men are cheating on you.'

'Not those boys,' said Brice decisively. 'They're two of my best.' He paused, then added, 'Besides, they've got their families back home to think of.'

'So what's the answer?'

'I don't know.' Brice rubbed his eyes and said sourly, 'Who dreamed up this crazy operation, anyway?'

'We did,' said Hendriks flatly. 'You and me.'

Brice said nothing to that but merely shrugged. 'Well, we'll get most of the money in soon.'

'That's true,' said Hendriks as he sat down again. 'But it irks me to have three million tied up. I worked damned hard to get this money in here.' He changed the subject. 'Why did you announce an inheritance of only seven million? Isn't that risky?'

Brice spread his hands. 'Who is going to check back to Jersey? Hell, man; I'll bet not one in a hundred Kenyans even knows where Jersey is. One in a thousand.'

'But what if somebody does?' persisted Hendriks.

'No problem,' said Brice. 'I'll say I was misquoted – mis-understood. I'll say that the seven million is the estimated annual income after the main fund has been invested. We have everything to gain and nothing to lose.' He checked the time. 'We'll have lunch and then I'll show you around. I didn't show you the real stuff last time you were here. Farrar stuck closer than a leech.'

'I'll stay for lunch,' said Hendriks. 'But the rest can wait. I have got to get back to Nairobi and raise a stink. My long lost cousin has been lost again and what the hell are they doing about it? I must do the grieving relative bit to make it look right. Let's go and eat. I'm hungry.'

19

In Nairobi Gunnarsson was angry. His feet hurt and his back was sore but that was not the reason for his anger. What riled him was that he was being given the runaround in the American Embassy. 'Damn it!' he said. 'I've been kidnapped and my friend is still missing. If I can't see the Ambassador who the hell can I see? And don't fob me off on any third clerk. I want action.'

The clerk behind the counter sighed. 'I'll see what I can do.' He moved away and picked up a telephone. 'Is Mr Pasternak there?'

'Speaking.'

'There's a guy here called Gunnarsson wanting to see the Ambassador. He has some crazy story about being kidnapped by Tanzanians and says his friend is still missing. I think he's a nut, but I can't get rid of him.'

An incredulous silence bored into his ear, then Pasternak said, 'Gleeson; don't you read the papers? Watch TV? Listen to the radio?'

'I've been on safari for two weeks,' said Gleeson. 'Just got back this morning from my vacation. Why? Something happened?'

'Yeah; something happened,' said Pasternak ironically. 'Don't let that guy get away; I'll be right down. And catch up on the goddamn news for God's sake.' He hung up, opened his desk drawer to check that his recorder had a tape ready to go, then went downstairs to meet Gunnarsson.

Gunnarsson was still simmering so Pasternak applied the old oil. 'Sorry you've been kept waiting, Mr Gunnarsson, and sorrier that you've been inconvenienced by idiocy.

Won't you come this way?' He slowed his pace to Gunnarsson's hobble as he led the way to the elevator. 'I guess you had a tough time.'

Gunnarsson grunted. 'You guessed right. What's your position here?'

'Nothing much,' admitted Pasternak. 'Third Secretary. You'll realize we're all busy on this thing, especially the Ambassador. He's talking with the Kenyan Foreign Minister right now, trying to get some action. And the rest of our work has to carry on – guys losing their credit cards and traveller's checks and so on.'

'This is more important,' said Gunnarsson acidly. 'You've lost an American citizen.'

Pasternak said, 'We're doing all we can, Mr Gunnarsson; and we're sure you can help.' They left the elevator, walked along a corridor, and he opened the door of his office. 'In here. Would you like coffee?'

'Thanks.' Gunnarsson sat before the desk, thankfully taking the weight off his feet, as Pasternak picked up the telephone and ordered a jug of coffee.

Pasternak sat down, opened his desk drawer and unobtrusively switched on the recorder before taking out a notepad and laying it on the desk. He picked up a pen. 'I've read the newspaper reports,' he said. 'But you know what newspapers are. I'll be glad to hear a first-hand report. If you hadn't come to us, Mr Gunnarsson, we'd have been camping on your doorstep. Now, I'd like you to tell it as it happened. Don't leave anything out even though you might think it irrelevant.'

So Gunnarsson told his story while Pasternak made largely unnecessary notes and dropped in a question from time to time. 'You say these men were in uniform. Can you describe it?' Then again: 'You say the rifles were Kalashnikovs; how do you know?'

'I'm a gun buff back home. I know a Kalashnikov when I see one.'

He got to the end when he said, 'And then we got back to

179

Keekorok and that was that. But Hank Hendrix didn't come back.'

'I see.' Pasternak laid down his pen. 'More coffee?'

'Thanks. All this talk is thirsty work.'

Pasternak poured the coffee. 'What's your relationship with Hendrix?'

'We're business associates,' said Gunnarsson. 'And friends, too.'

Pasternak nodded understandingly. 'Yes, you'd naturally be disturbed about this affair. What business are you in, Mr Gunnarsson?'

'I run Gunnarsson Associates; we're a security outfit based in New York. We run security for corporations and do some investigative work. Not much of that, though.'

'Investigative work,' repeated Pasternak thoughtfully. 'You're licensed for that in the state of New York?'

'In most states of the Union,' said Gunnarsson. 'We're a pretty big outfit.'

'And what were you doing in Kenya?'

'Well, Hank had some business here. He'd inherited a hunk of dough. I came along for the ride; taking a vacation, you know.' Gunnarsson looked at Pasternak over the rim of his coffee cup. 'The shit's going to hit the fan on this one, Pasternak, because Hank had just inherited six million bucks. The papers will make hay of it back home.'

Pasternak raised his eyebrows. 'The State Department does not run its affairs on the basis of newspaper reports, Mr Gunnarsson. But you interest me. You say Henry Hendrix had inherited six million dollars from Kenya?'

Gunnarsson shook his head. 'I didn't say that. He inherited from his grandfather, but the will said that a condition of inheritance was that Hank was to spend at least one month a year at some charitable foundation here; helping out, I guess.'

'Which foundation?'

'Ol Njorowa,' said Gunnarsson, stumbling over the unfamiliar words. 'It's near Naivasha.'

'Yes,' said Pasternak meditatively. 'I read they'd come into money but I didn't know about Hendrix.' He thought for a moment, then said, 'How long are you staying in Kenya, Mr Gunnarsson?'

Gunnarsson shrugged. 'For a while, I guess. I'll stick around to see if Hank comes back. And I want to goose the Ambassador. An American citizen has disappeared, Pasternak, and no one seems to be doing much about it. I tell you, I'm going to raise hell.'

Pasternak made no comment. He drew the notepad towards him, and said, 'If you'll give me the name of your hotel here, and your home address, I think that's about all.'

'What do you want my home address for?'

'I doubt if you'll be staying in Kenya indefinitely,' said Pasternak reasonably. 'We might want to talk to you again, even back in the States. And if you intend moving about in Kenya we'd like to know your itinerary in advance.'

'Why?'

'We might want to get hold of you in a hurry. For identification purposes, for instance.' Again it was a reasonable request. Pasternak wrote down the addresses, then pushed a button and stood up. 'That's all, Mr Gunnarsson. Thanks for coming in.' He held out his hand. 'We'll do our best to find what happened to Mr Hendrix.'

'You'd better find him,' said Gunnarsson. 'There's a lot riding on Hank.'

A man entered the room. Pasternak said, 'The messenger will escort you downstairs.' He smiled. 'If you're in the security business you'll realize why we don't like people wandering around the building.'

Gunnarsson grunted and left without saying another word. Pasternak opened the drawer and stopped the recorder, then rewound it. He played it, skipping back and forth, and listened to one part several times. Would a gun nut know a Kalashnikov when he saw one? There were precious few of those floating about loose back home. True, an enthusiast might study illustrations in books. And Gunnarsson was in something known amorphously as 'security' which could be

181

a euphemism for something more dangerous. A couple of loose ends which needed tidying up. He played the tape yet again and frowned when he noted that both he and Gunnarsson had consistently referred to Hendrix in the past tense.

Pasternak turned to the typewriter and wrote a request for any known information on John Gunnarsson, giving the address in New York. He took it to the code room himself.

The telex was addressed to Langley, Virginia.

* * *

An hour later Pasternak was interrupted again. The telephone rang and Gleeson said 'Mr Hardin is asking for you.'

Pasternak frowned, hunting in his mind for a connection, then his brow cleared. 'Not Ben Hardin?'

There was a pause and a few mumbled words, then Gleeson said, 'Yes; Ben Hardin.'

'Have him brought up.' Pasternak depressed the telephone cradle and dialled. 'Send in some more coffee.' When Hardin entered the room he stood up and smiled. 'Well, hello, Ben. It's been a long time. What are you doing in Kenya?'

They shook hands and Hardin sat down. 'A sort of working vacation,' he said. 'I haven't been here in years. Nairobi has changed some but the country hasn't. I thought I'd drop in to see if there was anyone I knew from the old days.'

'And you found me.' Pasternak smiled. 'It's certainly been a long time. What are you doing these days?'

'Working for a British outfit.' Hardin shrugged. 'A guy has to earn a living.'

'I'd stick in Kenya,' advised Pasternak. 'I wouldn't go into Tanzania. You'll still be on a list after what you did in Dar-es-Salaam. I know it was years ago but those guys have long memories.'

'I'm not going anywhere near Tanzania,' said Hardin. 'Not even to the border. I hear it's not safe even for tourists.'

'You heard about that?'

'It made the London papers,' said Hardin. 'I read about it over there.'

'It will have made the New York papers, too,' agreed Pasternak gloomily. 'If it hasn't yet, it will. One of the guys who was kidnapped has just been in here bending my ear. The other American, the one who came back. Gunnarsson has been threatening to raise Cain.'

'Gunnarsson!' Hardin showed surprise. 'Of Gunnarsson Associates in New York?' Pasternak nodded. 'Well, I'll be a son of a bitch!'

'Do you know him?'

'I used to work for him after I left the Company. He's ex-Company, too.'

'I didn't know that,' said Pasternak. He poured a couple of cups of coffee while he thought. That would explain the recognition of the Kalashnikovs, but it did not explain why Gunnarsson had lied about how he knew unless he did not want to advertise his one-time connection with the CIA. A lot of the guys were sensitive about it. But Gunnarsson had not looked the sensitive type. 'What sort of a guy is he?'

'A 22-carat bastard,' said Hardin, and hesitated. 'Look, Mike, I'd just as soon Gunnarsson doesn't know I'm around. We parted on bad terms and now I'm working for the competition. He won't like that.'

Pasternak shrugged. 'No reason for me to tell him, Ben. Who are you working for?'

'Stafford Security Consultants of London. I joined them when Gunnarsson fired me.'

The facts in Pasternak's mind rearranged themselves into a different pattern. Another security crowd! 'You said "a working vacation." How much is work and how much vacation?'

'About fifty-fifty,' said Hardin. 'Max Stafford, my boss, is in Nairobi too. We're giving Kenya the once-over to see if it's ripe for us to move in.' He thought for a moment. 'Damn it; I'll bet that's why Gunnarsson is here. I'll tell Stafford.' He sipped his coffee. 'Getting any action around here?'

Pasternak smiled genially. 'You know better than to ask that, Ben. You're not in the Company any more and, even if you were, I wouldn't tell you a damned thing and you know it.' He leaned forward. 'I've got the idea you aren't here just to talk about old times, so why don't you spill it?'

'You always were sharp,' said Hardin with a grin. 'It's like this. Stafford has Europe pretty much tied up. Our clients are the multinational corporations and a couple of them aren't happy about their security out here, so they want Stafford to set up shop in Kenya. Well, he's not going to do it blind, and he'll need more than two clients to make it profitable, so he's here to see for himself. Follow me so far?'

'You're doing fine,' said Pasternak dryly. 'Come to the point.'

'We ran across a couple of guys who seem to be the cat's whiskers in our line, very smooth and efficient. Trouble is that Stafford thinks they're connected with the Kenya People's Union and that's bad. If Stafford is thinking of setting up a permanent office here he can't afford to be mixed up with a banned political party.'

'It would be the kiss of death if it came out,' agreed Pasternak soberly. He reached for a pen. 'Who are these guys?'

'A black Kenyan called Pete Chipende and a Sikh, Nair Singh. Know them?'

Pasternak was so taken by surprise that his pen made a scrawled line on the pad. He controlled himself and wrote down the names. 'No, but I guess I can find out, given time.' His mind was busy with the implications of what he had just heard. 'What kind of a guy is Stafford?'

'Not bad – so far,' said Hardin judiciously. 'He hasn't cut any corners yet, not that I know of.'

'Maybe I'll meet him some time,' said Pasternak. 'What about a drink together?'

'Why not? We're staying at the Norfolk.'

'I'm busy today, but maybe I'll give you a ring tomorrow. Okay?'

'That's fine. Stafford's an interesting guy; he was in British army intelligence – a colonel.'

'Was he? I look forward to meeting him.'

Hardin took his leave and Pasternak seated himself before the typewriter again and composed another request for information. This time the subject was Max Stafford and the telex was to be sent, after coding, to the American Embassy in London. After a moment's thought he wrote another request for information on Hardin and addressed it to Langley.

Kenya was becoming livelier, thought Pasternak.

* * *

Gunnarsson was in the Thorn Tree café at the New Stanley hotel having drinks with Dirk Hendriks. As he had been leaving the American Embassy he had heard a man saying to the marine guard, 'My name is Dirk Hendriks. Where do I go to find out about Henry Hendrix, the man who was kidnapped into Tanzania?'

The marine pointed. 'Ask at the desk, sir.'

Gunnarsson touched Hendriks on the arm. 'Are you Hank Hendrix's cousin?'

Hendriks turned and looked at Gunnarsson in surprise. 'Yes, I am.'

'I'm John Gunnarsson. I was there.'

'You were where?'

'With your cousin when he was kidnapped.' Gunnarsson jerked his thumb towards the inquiry desk. 'You'd better talk with me before you butt your head against that brick wall.'

Dirk looked at him interestedly. 'You mean you were kidnapped, too?'

'Yeah. That's why I'm not too sharp on my feet. They made us walk out and I was stuck full of thorns.'

'I've got my car here,' said Hendriks. 'No need to walk. Where shall we go?'

'I'm staying at the New Stanley,' said Gunnarsson. 'We can have a drink at the Thorn Tree.'

The Thorn Tree was a Nairobi institution, being an open air cafe serving light refreshments. In the centre grew a large acacia, tall and spreading wide to give pleasant shade and which gave the Thorn Tree its name. The peculiarity which made the Thorn Tree different was the notice board which surrounded the trunk of the tree. Here it was the custom to leave messages for friends and it was a commonplace to say, 'If you want to find out where I am I'll leave a message on the thorn tree.' A local beer company even provided message pads, and it certainly did no harm to the profits of the café.

They sat down at one of the few available tables and Hendriks caught a waiter on the fly and ordered drinks. He resumed the conversation they had been having in the car. 'And that was the last you saw of my cousin?'

'Yeah. Then we heard shots and the guys around us laughed.'

'But you didn't see his body.'

Gunnarsson shook his head. 'No, but there was something funny about that. They herded us downriver, three of them, leaving one guy to guard the loot. We went maybe half a mile and then they got excited, jabbering away to each other.'

'What were they excited about?'

'I wouldn't know. Maybe because they couldn't find Hendrix. Two of them stayed with us and the third, the guy with the sergeant's stripes, went away. After a while he came back and they had a conference, a lot of talk.' Gunnarsson shrugged. 'They shooed us away then. The sergeant pointed up the hill and the others poked at us with their rifles. We were glad to get away.'

Hendrix frowned. 'The two men who took my cousin away; were they around at that time?'

'I didn't see them.'

The waiter brought their drinks. Hendriks picked up his glass and pondered. 'Could Henry have got away?' he asked. 'But if he did why hasn't he come back?'

'I've thought about that,' said Gunnarsson. 'He might have got away and the shooting might have missed. The two Tanzanians would be chasing him, of course. Still, he might have got away.' Gunnarsson certainly hoped so.

'Then why hasn't he come back?'

'Have you been out there?' asked Gunnarsson rhetorically. 'It's the damnedest country, and every bit looks like every other bit. Hank might have got lost like the guys who followed us in. And remember he was stripped like us. He may still come back, though, if the Tanzanians didn't catch up with him.'

'Who followed you in?' asked Hendriks alertly.

'Another tourist crowd found our abandoned truck and tried to find us. They didn't; they got lost and spent a night in the bush.'

Hendriks was pensive. 'I didn't read about that in the newspapers.'

'I talked to one of them when we got back,' said Gunnarsson. 'A guy called Stafford. He said that . . .'

'Max Stafford!' said Hendriks unbelievingly.

'He didn't tell me his other name.' Gunnarsson stopped, his glass halfway to his lips as he was arrested in thought. The only Max Stafford he had heard of was the boss of Stafford Security Consultants back in London. Now just what the hell was going on?

Hendriks was also thoughtful. Stafford had said he was taking a holiday in Kenya. But was it coincidental that he had been involved in the search for Henry Hendrix? He said, 'Do you know where Stafford is now?'

'No; he left Keekorok and I haven't seen him since. You know the guy?'

Hendriks nodded abstractedly. 'Yes, I think so.'

'Now isn't that a coincidence,' said Gunnarsson.

'Isn't it?' Hendriks badly needed a telephone. He said, 'Glad to have talked with you, Mr Gunnarsson. Are you staying here at the New Stanley?'

'Yeah.'

'Then perhaps you'll have dinner with me before you leave. I'll give you a ring tomorrow morning. I'd like to know more about my cousin's disappearance but right now I have an appointment. Will you excuse me?'

'Sure.' Gunnarsson watched Hendriks get up and walk away. Something goddamn odd was happening but he was not sure what it was. If the Stafford he had talked to at Keekorok was the Max Stafford of Stafford Security then there was definitely no coincidence. He decided he needed a telephone and hoisted himself laboriously to his feet.

* * *

Stafford dined with Curtis at the Norfolk that evening and they were halfway through the meal when Hardin joined them. He said, 'I've just seen Chip. He says that Gunnarsson and Dirk Hendriks had a drink and a chat at the Thorn Tree this afternoon.'

Stafford put down his knife and fork. 'Did they, by God?'

Curtis grunted. 'That's not good for the Colonel.'

'No.' Stafford looked at Hardin. 'Ben, do you remember when you followed Gunnarsson and Corliss to Mandeville's chambers in Lincoln's Inn? Did Gunnarsson meet Dirk there?'

Hardin looked up at the ceiling and gazed into the past. He said slowly, 'Gunnarsson and Corliss went in then Gunnarsson came out.' He snapped his fingers. 'Gunnarsson came out just as Dirk and Alix went in – they passed each other in the entrance.'

'Any sign of recognition?'

'Not a thing.'

'Then how did they get together here?' asked Stafford.

'I talked to Chip about that and maybe it can be explained,' said Hardin. 'Gunnarsson went to the police and then on to the American Embassy to raise some hell about them dragging their heels on the Hendrix case. I saw Mike Pasternak and he told me about it.' Hardin retailed his discussion with Pasternak. 'Chip says that Hendriks and Gunnarsson met in the lobby of the Embassy apparently by chance.'

'It's unlucky for us,' said Stafford. 'If Gunnarson mentioned my name to Dirk in connection with the disappearance of Hendrix then he's going to be suspicious.'

'Suspicious about what?' demanded Hardin. 'I don't know what you have against Dirk Hendriks – he's just a guy who's inherited a fortune. It's Gunnarsson and Corliss who are trying to put one over on the estate.'

Stafford was about to reply when he was interrupted by a waiter who handed him a note. 'From the gentleman at the corner table, sir.'

Stafford saw a man looking towards him. The man nodded curtly and then addressed himself to his plate. Stafford opened the folded paper and read, 'I would appreciate a moment of your time when you finish dinner.' There was an indecipherable scribble of a signature below.

He looked across the room again and nodded, then passed the note to Hardin. 'Do you know him?'

Hardin paused in the middle of ordering from the menu. 'A stranger to me.' He finished ordering, then said, 'Mike Pasternak phoned half an hour ago. He'd like to meet you. Is four o'clock tomorrow okay?'

'I should think so.'

'He'll meet you here by the swimming pool. Maybe he'll be able to tell you who Chip really is.'

'Perhaps.' Stafford was lost in thought trying to fit together a jigsaw, taking a piece at a time and seeing if it made up a pattern. It was true he had nothing against Dirk beyond an instinctive dislike of the man but suppose . . . Suppose that Dirk's meeting with Gunnarsson at the Embassy had not been by chance, that they already knew each other. Gunnarsson had been established as a crook so what did that make Dirk? And then there was Brice at Ol Njorowa who had unaccountably lost tens of millions of pounds. If Dirk talked to Brice and found that Stafford had been at Ol Njorowa *and* Keekorok then he would undoubtedly smell a rat.

Stafford shook his head irritably. All this was moonshine – sheer supposition. He said, 'What else did Dirk do today?'

'He went out to Ol Njorowa, stayed for lunch, then came back to Nairobi where he went to the police and then on to the American Embassy.'

'Where he met Gunnarsson. Did he see anyone at the Embassy?'

'No,' said Hardin. 'He went with Gunnarsson to the Thorn Tree.'

'Could have been pre-arranged,' said Curtis.

'You're a man of few words, Sergeant,' said Stafford, 'but they make sense.'

'But why meet at the Embassy?' persisted Hardin. 'They're both staying at the New Stanley -- why not there?'

'I don't know,' said Stafford, tired of beating his brains out. He finished his coffee and nodded towards the corner table. 'I'd better see what that chap wants.'

He walked across the dining room and the man looked up as he approached. 'Abercrombie-Smith,' he said. 'You're Stafford.'

He was a small compact man in his early fifties with a tanned square face and a neatly trimmed moustache. There was a faint and indefinable military air about him which could have been because of the erect way he held himself. He slid a business card from under his napkin and gave it to Stafford. His full name was Anthony Abercrombie-Smith and his card stated that he was from the British High Commission, Bruce House, Standard Street, Nairobi. It did not state what he did there.

'I've been wanting to meet you,' he said. 'We've been expecting you at the office.'

Stafford said, 'It never occurred to me.'

'Humph! All the same you should have come. Never mind; we'll make it the occasion for a lunch. There's no point in having the formality of an office meeting. What about tomorrow?'

Stafford inclined his head. 'That will be all right.'

'Good. We'll lunch at the Muthaiga Club. I'll pick you up here at midday.' He turned back to his plate and Stafford assumed that the audience was over so he left.

20

Stafford was ready when Abercrombie-Smith arrived on the dot of midday to pick him up. Hardin and Curtis had taken a Nissan and gone off to the Nairobi Game Park situated so conveniently nearby.

Abercrombie-Smith drove north through a part of Nairobi Stafford had not seen and made bland conversation about the sights to be seen, the Indian temples and the thriving open markets. Presently they came to a suburb which was redolent of wealth. The houses were large – what little could be seen of them because they were set back far from the road and discreetly screened by hedges and trees. Stafford noted that many had guards on the gates which interested him professionally.

'This is Muthaiga,' said Abercrombie-Smith. 'A rather select part of Nairobi. Most of the foreign embassies are here. My master, the High Commissioner, has his home quite close.' They turned a corner, then off the road through a gateway. A Kenyan at the gate gave a semi-salute. 'And this is the Muthaiga Club.'

Inside, the rooms were cool and airy. The walls were decked with animal trophies; kongoni, gazelle, impala, leopard. They went into the lounge and sat in comfortable club chairs. 'And now, dear boy,' said Abercrombie-Smith, 'what will it be?'

Stafford asked for a gin and tonic so he ordered two. 'This is one of the oldest clubs in Kenya,' he said. 'And one of the most exclusive.' He looked at the two Sikhs across the room who were engrossed in a discussion over papers spread on a table. 'Although not as exclusive as it once was,' he observed. 'In my day one never discussed business in one's club.'

Stafford let it ride, content to let Abercrombie-Smith make the running. His small talk was more serious than most. He expatiated on the political situation in Britain, ditto in America, the dangers inherent in the Russian interference in Afghanistan and Poland, and so forth. But it was still small talk. Stafford let him run on, putting in the occasional comment so that the conversation would not run down, and waited for him to come to the nub. In the meantime he assessed the Muthaiga Club.

It was obviously a relic of colonial days; the chosen, self-designed watering hole of the higher civil servants and the wealthier and more influential merchants – all white, of course, in those days. It was probably in here that the real decisions were made, and not in the Legislative Council or the Law Courts. The coming of Uhuru must have been painful for the membership who had to adapt to a determinedly multiracial society. Stafford wondered who had been the brave non-white to have first applied for membership.

They finished their drinks and Abercrombie-Smith proposed a move. 'I suggest we go into the dining room,' he said. He still had not come to any point that was worth making. Stafford nodded, stood up with him, and followed into the dining room which was half full of a mixed crowd of whites, blacks and Asians.

They consulted the menu together and Stafford chose melon to start with. 'I recommend the tilapia,' said Abercrombie-Smith. 'It's a flavoursome freshwater fish from the lakes. And the curry here is exceptional.' Stafford nodded so he ordered curry for both of them, then said to the waiter, 'A bottle of hock with the fish and lager with the curry.' The waiter went away. Abercrombie-Smith leaned across the table. 'One cannot really drink wine with curry, can one? Besides, nothing goes better with curry than cold lager.'

Stafford agreed politely. Who was he to disagree with his host?

Over the melon they discussed cricket and the current Test Match; over the fish, current affairs in East Africa.

Stafford thought Abercrombie-Smith was coming in a circumlocutory manner to some possible point at issue. But he was right; the tilapia was delicious.

As the curry dishes were placed on the table he said, 'Help yourself, dear boy. You know we really expected you to come to us after that unfortunate incident in the Masai Mara.' He cocked an eyebrow at Stafford expectantly.

Stafford said, 'I don't know why. I had no complaints to make.' He spooned rice on to his plate.

'But, still; a kidnapping!'

Stafford passed him the rice dish. 'I wasn't kidnapped,' he said briefly. The curry had a rich, spicy aroma.

'Um,' said Abercrombie-Smith. 'Just so. All the same we thought you might. Would you like to tell me what happened down there?'

'I don't mind,' Stafford said as he helped himself to the curry, and gave a strictly edited version.

'I see,' he said. 'I see. You say you turned back at the border. How did you know it was the border? As I recollect there are no fences or signs in that wilderness. No fences because of the wildebeest migration of course, and the elephants tend to destroy any signposts.'

'Like the telegraph poles,' Stafford said, and he nodded. Stafford sampled the curry and found it good. 'You'll have to ask Pete Chipende about that. He's the local expert.'

'Try the sambals,' Abercrombie-Smith urged. 'They do them very well here. The tomatoes and onions are marinated in herbs; not the bananas, of course, and certainly not the coconut. The coconut, I assure you, is perfectly fresh; not the nasty, dried-up stuff you get in England. I recommend the mango chutney, too.' He helped himself to curry. 'Ah, yes; Chipende. An interesting man, don't you think?'

'Certainly an intelligent man,' said Stafford.

'I would tend to agree there; I certainly would. How did it come about that he was with you?'

Abercrombie-Smith was being too damned nosey. Stafford said, 'He offered to act as guide and courier.'

'And Nair Singh? A courier also?' His eyebrows twitched upwards. 'Wasn't that a little overkill, dear boy?'

Stafford shrugged. 'Chip wanted Nair along as driver. He said Nair was the better driver.' That was the exact truth but he did not expect to be believed.

Abercrombie-Smith started to laugh. He laughed so much that he was speechless. He choked on his curry and it was quite a time before he recovered. He dabbed his mouth with his napkin and said, still chuckling, 'Oh, my dear chap; that's rich – rich, indeed.' He put down the napkin. 'Didn't you know that Mr Peter Chipende entered the East African Safari Rally three years in succession? He didn't win but he finished every time and that is an achievement in itself.'

Stafford had heard of the East African Safari Rally; it was supposed to be the most gruelling long-distance motor race in the world and, judging by the condition of the road between Narok and Keekorok, he could very well believe it. He cursed Chip for putting him in such an intenable position and said, 'I wouldn't know about that; I'm a stranger in these parts.'

'So that's what Chipende told you, is it? Well, well.'

Stafford decided to give him back some of the malarkey he had been handing out. 'This curry is really very good; thanks for recommending it. Do you think I could get the recipe from the chef? I pride myself on being a good cook.'

Abercrombie-Smith's eyes went flinty. He knew when someone was taking the mickey as well as the next man. However, he held himself in. 'I would think it's the chef's family secret, dear boy.' He fiddled with his napkin. 'You haven't been here, long, Stafford; but you've mixed with some very interesting people. Interesting to me, that is.'

Stafford thought it would be rather more interesting to MI6 or whatever funny number they gave to foreign espionage these days. He said, 'Who, for instance?'

'Well, Peter Chipende and Nair Singh, to start with. And then there are a couple of ex-CIA agents, Hardin and

Gunnarsson. Not to mention Colour Sergeant Curtis, but he's small fry and you did bring him with you.'

'This curry is so good I think I'll have some more.' Stafford helped himself. 'You seem to be taking an inordinate interest in me, too.'

'Colonel Max Stafford,' Abercrombie-Smith said meditatively. 'Late of Military Intelligence.'

'Bloody late,' Stafford observed. 'I left the army ten years ago and, by the way, I don't use my rank.'

'Still, you were a full colonel at the age of thirty-five. You ought to kn w which end is up.'

'Come to the point. What do you want?'

'I want to know what you're doing here in Kenya.'

'Taking a much needed holiday,' Stafford said. 'I haven't had a holiday for three years.'

'And I know about that one,' said Abercrombie-Smith. 'You take holidays in peculiar places. That was when you went to the Sahara and came back with a bullet in your shoulder.'

Stafford put down his fork. 'Now this be damned for a lark.' He was trying to keep his temper. Besides, he wanted to string this joker along for a while. He was silent for a moment. 'What else would you want to know? There's sure to be more.'

'Of course,' Abercrombie-Smith said easily. 'Principally I'd like to know more about Chipende.' Who wouldn't? Stafford thought. 'And, of course, I'd like to know if Hardin and Gunnarsson really are ex-CIA as they claim. And I'd like to know your interest in the Ol Njorowa Foundation.'

Stafford said deliberately, 'And can you give me any reasons why I should do all this?'

Abercrombie-Smith drummed his fingers on the table. 'What about patriotism?' he suggested.

'Patriotism is not enough, as Edith Cavell said. And as Sam Johnson added, patriotism is the last refuge of a scoundrel.'

'Samuel Johnson was a self-opinionated old fool,'

Abercrombie-Smith snapped. 'And I'm not here to bandy literary criticism.'

Stafford grinned at him. 'I didn't think you were.'

Abercrombie-Smith stared at Stafford. 'So patriotism is not enough. I suppose that means you want money.'

'The labourer is always worthy of his hire,' said Stafford. 'But, as it happens, you're wrong. You know what you can do with your bloody money.'

'Damn it, Stafford,' he said. 'Can't you be reasonable?'

'I can; if there's anything to be reasonable about. As it is I resent you probing into my affairs, as you seem to have done quite thoroughly.'

'Well, *I'll* try to be reasonable. Don't you recognize that you are in a most sensitive position? Stafford Security Consultants runs security on a dozen defence contractors back home.' He reeled off the names of half-a-dozen. 'Of course we've had you investigated. We'd have been fools not to. Under those circumstances we couldn't take the risk of you being turned. You do see that, don't you?'

Stafford saw. His own dealings with the intelligence establishment had been with the counter-espionage crowd of MI5 and the police Special Branch. They were thin on the ground and could not possibly undertake the detailed work Stafford guaranteed when he took on a contract. Consequently they were distantly pleased and recognized that Stafford Security was largely on their side. But Stafford could see that they would want to guarantee he was safe. Many a one-time agent has been turned in the past.

Abercrombie-Smith said, 'Well, there you are. I think you'll see the advantage of co-operation now because, if you don't, your firm back in England could get into considerable difficulties.'

He paused as the waiter began to clear dishes from the table. Stafford welcomed the interruption because Abercrombie-Smith's eyes were shifting around as plates were swept away, and he did not see the expression on Stafford's face as he contemplated this naked piece of blackmail.

When the waiter had gone Abercrombie-Smith said, 'I recommend something to take away the taste of curry before we have coffee. What do you say to lychees? They're fresh, dear boy; not like those tinned monstrosities you get in England.'

'Yes,' Stafford said mechanically. 'I'll have lychees.'

So they had lychees and then went into the lounge for coffee. On the way there Stafford excused himself and went into the entrance hall where he found the hall porter and asked him to order a taxi. 'How long will it take?'

'Five minutes, sah; no longer.'

'Let me know as soon as it arrives. I'll be in the lounge.'

'Yes, sah. Immediately.'

When he returned Abercrombie-Smith offered him a cigar which he declined. Abercrombie-Smith produced a silver cutter and nipped the end from his cigar and proceeded to light it with great concentration. When he had got it going to his satisfaction he put the cutter away and said, 'Now, my dear boy; I think we can get down to business.'

'I thought you didn't discuss business in your club.'

'Pah!' he said. 'I was referring to commercial business.'

'You mean the sordid business of making money.'

'Precisely. This is different.'

Stafford put some sugar into his coffee and stirred. 'Sam Johnson, whom you seem to despise, had something to say about that. He said that there are few ways in which a man can be more innocently employed than in getting money. Is the proposition you have just made to me in your club any less sordid than commerce?'

Abercrombie-Smith raised his eyebrows. 'My dear chap; I see your are a moralist. Scruples? I would have thought scruples to be undesirable in your profession; positively a hindrance.' His voice sharpened. 'I suggest you address yourself to self preservation and the protection of your – er – business interests since you seem to have such a high regard for money getting.' He was openly contemptuous.

His contempt Stafford could survive. 'I'm Max. Do you

mind if I call you Anthony?' He sipped the coffee.

The switch took Abercrombie-Smith by surprise. 'If you must,' he said stiffly. He came from the formal world of English public schools and London Clubland in which the informality of the use of Christian names is looked down upon.

Stafford said, 'Well, Tony; you're nothing but a cheap blackmailer – a common criminal. If the security of the United Kingdom has to depend on you, or the likes of you, then God help us all. I have nothing against blackmail, of course, but clumsiness is intolerable. Your approach to me had all the subtlety of a Soho whore.'

Abercrombie-Smith was taken aback as though he had been attacked and bitten by a newborn lamb. He reddened and said, 'Don't talk to me in those terms.'

'I'll talk to you in any way I damn well like.'

'So you won't co-operate. That could be dangerous as I have pointed out.'

Stafford put down the coffee cup and leaned back. 'I like your idea of co-operation, but I doubt if it's an acceptable dictionary definition. Do what I say or else – is that it?' He leaned forward. 'I've built up quite an organization in the last ten years. Stafford Security Consultants is primarily a defensive organization but it can be used for attack. If I find any change for the worse in the way I do my business I have the capability of finding the reason. If you are the reason I'll smash you. Not your department or whatever idiot employs you but you, personally. Personal ruin. Do I make myself quite clear?'

Abercrombie-Smith was apopleptic. He gobbled for a moment then said breathily, 'This is outrageous. I've never been spoken to like that before; not by anyone.'

'A pity,' Stafford said, and stood up as the hall porter came into the lounge. 'You might have made a half-way decent man if someone had taken you in hand earlier.' He held up his hand. 'Don't get up. I'll find my own way back.'

* * *

By the time the taxi deposited him in front of the Norfolk he had cooled down somewhat. As he paid off the driver he wondered if he had made a rod for his own back. Stafford had always deemed it a virtue not to make unnecessary enemies and he had been hard on Abercrombie-Smith. Still, the man had been nauseating with his casual assumption that he had but to crook a finger and Stafford would come to heel. Stafford reflected that he had better look to his defences.

He picked up his key at the desk and found a message from Hardin saying he was at the hotel pool. He walked through the courtyard, past the aviaries with their twittering and chirping birds, and through the archway to the pool. There he found Hardin who said, 'Where have you been? Pasternak rang again, and said he'd have to make it earlier. He'll be here any minute.'

'I've been having my brains washed,' Stafford said sourly. 'Pasternak wouldn't be boss of the Kenya CIA station by any chance?'

'He might be,' said Hardin with a grin. 'But he's not saying.'

'Tell me more,' Stafford said.

'I didn't know Pasternak when I was here but I knew him from Langley. We weren't really buddy-buddy in those days but we had a drink together from time to time. It's useful that he's here.'

'Where's Curtis?'

'He went downtown.' Hardin looked over Stafford's shoulder. 'Here's Pasternak now.'

Pasternak was a lean, rangy man with a closed look about his face. As they shook hands he said, 'Mike Pasternak. Good of you to see me, Mr Stafford.'

'It's no trouble,' he said. 'But I don't know that I can tell you much. I'm a security man and it's my job to keep secrets. Care for a drink?'

'I'll get them,' said Hardin. 'Beer, Mike?'

Pasternak nodded and Hardin went to the poolside bar. Pasternak said, 'Ben tells me you're interested in Pete Chipende.'

'That's right.' Stafford gestured. 'Let's sit.'

They sat face to face across a table and Pasternak looked at Stafford thoughtfully. 'I'd give a whole lot to know *why* you're running with Pete Chipende.'

'Didn't Ben tell you?'

'Yeah.' Pasternak smiled wryly. 'I didn't believe him. I'm hoping you'll tell me.'

'I'm afraid it's my business, Mr Pasternak.' said Stafford.

'I thought you'd take that attitude. I'm sorry. I hope you know what you're getting into.' Pasternak lit a cigarette. 'Ben tells me you're in the same line as Gunnarsson, but in Europe. He also told me you were in British army intelligence at one time.'

'That's correct. It's a matter of record. And you are CIA but you won't admit it outright.'

Pasternak smiled. 'Would you expect me to?' The smile faded. 'Now, here's a funny thing. Hendrix, a newly hatched millionaire, and Gunnarsson, ex-CIA, are in a party kidnapped into Tanzania. Along comes Stafford, again an ex-intelligence guy, and he chases after the kidnappers together with Chipende and Nair Singh. Then I see Ben, also ex-CIA. Don't you think it's strange, Mr Stafford?'

Stafford said, 'Do you know a man called Abercrombie-Smith from the British High Commission?'

Pasternak straightened. 'Don't tell me he's in on this? Whatever it is.'

'I had lunch with him. And now you are here. Perhaps we'd better hire the Kenyatta Conference Centre for a secret service congress,' Stafford said dryly. 'But what's *your* interest in Chipende?'

Pasternak gave Stafford a strange look. 'Are you kidding?'

'I never kid about serious matters, Mr Pasternak. I really would like to know.'

'It seems as though I'm wasting my time after all,' he said. 'And probably wasting yours. Here's Ben with the beer. Let me put it on my expense account.'

'Don't bother,' Stafford said. 'Just tell me about Chipende.

Abercrombie-Smith wants to know, too. He tried to twist my arm this afternoon.'

'Successfully?'

'He got a flea in his ear.'

'I don't want to get the same treatment, Mr Stafford,' said Pasternak. 'So just let's concentrate on the beer.'

Hardin came up with a tray which he placed on the table. They drank beer and chatted about inconsequential subjects such as the necessity for adjusting the carburettor of a car when driving from Mombasa at sea level to Eldoret which is at an altitude of nearly 10,000 feet. Hardin was baffled, as Stafford could see by the odd looks he received.

Pasternak drained his glass. 'I must be going,' he said, and stood up. 'Nice to have met you, Mr Stafford.'

'Come again,' said Stafford ironically.

He walked with Pasternak through the courtyard. Pasternak stopped by one of the aviaries and said, 'Have you noticed that there are no songbirds in Africa? They cheep and chirp but don't sing.' He paused. 'Do you mind if I give you some advice?'

Stafford smiled. 'Not at all. The great thing about advice is that you needn't follow it.'

'Watch Gunnarsson. I got a report on him this morning. That guy is bad news.'

'That's the most superfluous advice I've ever been given,' said Stafford chuckling. 'But thanks, anyway.' They shook hands and Pasternak went on his way.

Stafford turned to go to his room and met Hardin who said, 'Were you two talking in code or something? That meeting was supposed to be about Chip.'

'Ben, I know where I am now.' Stafford clapped him on the back. 'Bismarck was reputed to be silent in seven languages, but I'll bet his silence told more than his speeches. It was what Pasternak didn't say that interested me.'

'Nuts!' said Hardin disgustedly.

21

Next morning after breakfast Stafford said to Hardin, 'Ben I'm tired of this pussyfooting around; we're going to do some pushing.'

'Who are you going to push?'

'We'll start with Chip. Sergeant?'

Curtis stiffened. 'Yes, sir.'

'You've been liaising with Chip. I want him in my room by ten o'clock.'

'Yes, sir.' Curtis pushed back his chair from the breakfast table and left the room.

Hardin said, 'Why Chip? He's on our side.'

'Is he?' Stafford shook his head. 'Pete Chipende is on no side other than his own. What's more, he has Corliss hidden somewhere and that gives him leverage should he want to use it. You uncovered Corliss but Chip has got him and I don't like that one little bit.'

'You have a point,' acknowledged Hardin. 'But I don't think he'll push easy.'

'We'll see,' said Stafford.

At nine-thirty Curtis reported back. 'Chip will see the Colonel at ten as requested. He asked what the Colonel wanted. I said I wasn't in the Colonel's confidence.'

'You are now,' said Stafford, and told Curtis what he wanted him to do.

Hardin said, 'Max; are you sure about this?'

'Yes, Pasternak told me.'

'I didn't hear him.'

'He didn't say anything,' said Stafford, leaving Hardin baffled.

He spent the next half hour guarding his back.

He wrote a letter to Jack Ellis in London asking that the resources of Stafford Security Consultants be put to investigating thoroughly one Anthony Abercrombie-Smith from the time of his birth to the present day; his schools, clubs, work, friends if any, investments and anything else that might occur to him.

As he put the sheet of notepaper into an envelope Stafford reflected on Cardinal Richelieu who had said, 'If you give me six lines written by the most honest man, I will find something in them to hang him.' That surely would apply to Abercrombie-Smith should he have to be leaned on.

He had just sealed the envelope when Chip arrived. 'You want me?'

Stafford glanced at Hardin and Curtis. 'Yes. Where's Corliss?'

'He's quite safe,' assured Chip.

'No doubt. But where is he?'

Chip sat down. 'Don't worry, Max. If you want Corliss at any time he can be produced within half an hour.'

Stafford smiled gently. 'You keep telling me not to worry and that worries the hell out of me.' He apparently changed the subject. 'By the way, Abercrombie-Smith sends his regards.'

Chip paused in the act of lighting a cigarette, just a minute hesitation. He continued the action and blew out a plume of smoke. 'When did you see him?'

'We had lunch in the Muthaiga Club yesterday.'

'What did he want?'

'Ostensibly he wanted to know why I hadn't reported in to the High Commissioner's office after the kidnapping. He really wanted to know about you.'

Chip's eyebrows lifted. 'Did he? What did you tell him?'

'What could I tell him? I know nothing about you.'

Hardin stirred. 'True enough.'

Chip said, 'Do you know who he is?'

Stafford smiled. 'He'll be listed as a trade advisor or something like that, but really he's the MI6 man in Nairobi, serving the same function that Mike Pasternak does for the CIA.'

Chip sat on the bed. 'You've been getting around. Have you talked to him, too?'

'We had a chat over a beer. Nothing important.'

'For a stranger in the country you get to know the most interesting people.'

'I didn't go out of my way to find them,' said Stafford. 'I attracted them as wasps to a honeypot. We seem to be stirring up some interest, Chip. When can we expect the KGB?'

'It's not a matter for joking,' he said soberly. 'I don't know that I like this.'

'Oh, come *on*,' said Stafford. 'It's not that bad. They approached me openly enough. Hardin knew Pasternak years ago so Pasternak couldn't deny he's a CIA man. As for Abercrombie-Smith, he's a bad joke.'

'Don't be fooled by Abercrombie-Smith,' warned Chip. 'You may think all that "dear boy" stuff is funny but underneath he's as cold as ice. Max, why should you attract the attention of the foreign intelligence services of two countries?'

'I don't know that I have,' said Stafford. 'They didn't seem to be all that interested in me. I think *you* are attracting the attention. They both wanted to know what you are doing.'

Chip smiled sourly. 'And all I'm doing is what you tell me to do. Did you tell them that?'

'I forgot to,' said Stafford apologetically. 'It slipped my mind.'

'Very funny.'

'I'm noted for my sense of humour,' agreed Stafford. 'Here's another sample. Which branch of Kenyan Intelligence are you in, Chip?'

Chip stared at him. 'Are you joking?'

'Not two intelligence services, Chip – three. And maybe another to make four.'

Hardin said, 'You're losing me fast, Max.'

Chip said; 'He's already lost me.' He laughed.

Stafford ticked off points on his fingers. 'One; you could get us rooms at the drop of a hat in any hotel or game lodge I might suggest at the height of the tourist season. That takes pull. Two; you got the information on Brice from Zimbabwe too fast. Three; you could put Adam Muliro into Corliss's party as courier and driver at short notice. Four; in the Masai Mara you could whistle up support to take Corliss into custody at equally short notice. Five; you're too well aware of the identities of foreign agents operating in Kenya to be any ordinary man. Six; when I was talking to Pasternak he rattled off a string of names, all in intelligence, and your name and Nair's were included. I made a crack that we hold a secret service congress and Pasternak didn't disagree. Seven; we were interviewed and photographed by journalists but nothing appeared in the press, and that takes pull too. I'm not surprised you didn't want your picture in the paper – the well-known secret service agent is a contradiction in terms. Eight . . .' Stafford broke off. 'Chip, as you said in the Mara – a man can run out of fingers this way.'

'I didn't say I had no organization,' said Chip. 'The Kenya People's Union . . .' He stopped. 'But I'm not going to talk about that.'

'You'd better not,' said Stafford grimly. 'Because you'd be telling me a pack of lies. I'm saving the best until last. Eight; when we entered the Masai Mara you didn't pay; a little bit of economy which was a dead giveaway. You showed some kind of identification which you probably have on you now. Sergeant!'

Before Chip knew it Curtis had stepped from behind and pinioned him and, although he struggled, he was no match for Curtis who had mastered many an obstreperous sailor in his day. 'Okay, Ben,' said Stafford. 'Search him.'

Hardin swiftly went through Chip's pockets, tossing the contents on to the bed where Stafford checked them. He searched Chip's wallet and found nothing, nor did he find any form of identification, except for a driving licence, among the scattering of items on the bed. 'Damn!' he said. 'Try again, Ben.'

Hardin found it in a hidden pocket in Chip's trousers – a plastic card which might have been mistaken for any credit card except that it had Chip's photograph on it. 'All right, Sergeant,' he said mildly. 'You can let him go.'

Curtis released Chip who brushed himself down, straightening his safari suit. Stafford clicked his finger nail against the card and said, 'A colonel, no less,' then added dryly, 'I probably have seniority. Military Intelligence?'

'Yes,' said Chip. 'You shouldn't have done that. I could get you tossed out of the country.'

'You could,' agreed Stafford. 'But you won't. You still need us.' He frowned. 'What puzzles me is why you were interested in us in the first place. Why did you latch on to us?'

Chip shrugged. 'There *was* a KPU connection. The address Curtis got in London was a KPU safe house. It wasn't as safe as all that because we'd infiltrated and we intercepted Curtis. Naturally we were most interested in why you, a one-time British intelligence agent, were investigating something with the help of the Kenya People's Union. At least you seemed to think you were working with the KPU. As time went on it became even more interesting. Complicated, too.'

Hardin snorted. 'Complicated, he says! Nothing makes any goddamn sense.'

'Tell me,' said Stafford. 'Who were those two men you conjured up in the Masai Mara to take care of Corliss?'

Chip smiled slightly. 'I borrowed a couple of men from the Police Post on the Mara and put them into civilian clothes.'

'And where is Corliss now?'

'About two hundred yards from here,' said Chip calmly 'In a cell in police headquarters on the corner of Harry Thuku Road. I told you he was quite safe.' He lit another cigarette. 'All right, Max; where do we go from here?'

'Where do you want to go?'

'I'm quite prepared to go on as before.'

'With me picking your chestnuts out of the fire,' said Stafford sarcastically. 'Not as before, Chip. There'll be no secrets and we share information. I'm tired of being blind-folded. You know, there's more to this than Gunnarsson trying to push in with a fake Hendrix. There's a hell of a lot at stake.'

'And what is at stake?' asked Chip.

Stafford stared at him. 'You're not stupid. Suppose you tell me.'

'About twenty-seven million pounds,' he said easily. 'The money Brice didn't declare from the Hendrykxx estate.'

'Balls!' snapped Stafford. 'It's not the money and you know it. But how did you get on to that?'

'Because you were inquisitive about the Ol Njorowa Foundation so was I,' said Chip. 'I rang the Kenya High Commission in London and had someone look at the will. Quite simple, really. But tell me more.'

Stafford said, 'I could kick myself. It's been staring me in the face ever since Ben, here, came back from investigating old Hendrykxx and said there was no Kenya connection. That really stumped me. But then I saw it.'

'Saw what?'

'The bloody South African connection,' said Stafford.

'Bull's eye!' said Chip softly. 'But tell me more.'

'Everywhere I've looked in the case the South African connection has popped up. Old Hendrykxx lived there. Dirk Hendriks is a South African. Mandeville, the English QC, is a right-winger who takes holidays in South Africa. He's there now. I think Farrar, the Jersey lawyer, is a cat's paw and I'll bet it was Mandeville who drew up the will.' Stafford drew a deep breath. 'Brice made a mistake in underestimating the size of the Hendrykxx estate – he was greedy. Are you sure he's in the clear, Chip? Because I'm betting he's another South African.'

* * *

For the next hour they hammered at the problem trying to fit the bits and pieces of their knowledge together without a great deal of success. At last Chip said, 'All right; we've got a consensus of opinion; we think that Dirk Hendriks might be a South African intelligence agent, and the same could apply to Brice. What we can't see is where Gunnarsson fits in and who has been trying to kill Corliss.'

'Not Corliss,' said Hardin suddenly. 'Hank Hendrix. Someone took a shot at Hank in Los Angeles and that was before Gunnarsson made the substitution.'

'So you think whoever is trying to kill him is unaware that Gunnarsson made the switch?' queried Stafford. 'It could be.' He looked at Chip. 'That business on the Tanzanian border seemed authentic in the sense that such kidnappings have happened before. What do you think, Chip? How easy is it to lay hands on Tanzanian uniforms and Kalashnikovs?'

Chip smiled thinly. 'Given enough money you can buy *anything* on the Tanzanian border. As for Kalashnikovs, Kenya is surrounded by the damn things – Tanzania, Somalia, Ethiopia, Uganda. There'd be no problem there. You think the kidnapping was a put-up job to lay the blame on the Tanzanians?' He nodded thoughtfully. 'That could very well be.'

'Then Brice would have organized it,' said Hardin. 'Dirk Hendriks was in England at that time.'

'But all this is supposition,' said Stafford. 'We're not sure of a damned thing. What move will you make now, Chip? It's your country, after all.'

'We can't move openly against the Foundation,' said Chip. 'That would make waves. Newspaper stories and too much publicity. I'll have to take this to my superior officer.' He held up his hand. 'And don't ask who he is.'

Curtis stirred. 'Would the Colonel mind a suggestion?'

'Trot it out, Sergeant,' said Stafford. 'We could do with some good ideas.'

'Give Corliss back to Gunnarsson. Then stand back and see what happens.'

'You've got a nasty mind,' said Hardin. 'That would be like setting him up in a shooting gallery.'

'But we'd stand a chance of seeing who's doing the shooting.' Stafford looked at Chip. 'What do you think? He'd need a good cover story.'

'No cover story would stand up,' said Chip. 'We've had him too long. In any case he's a bad liar; we'd be blowing our own cover.' He thought for a moment. 'No; we've got to get someone inside Ol Njorowa to have a look around.'

'And maybe not find anything,' said Hardin morosely.

'I think there's something to be found,' Chip stubbed out a cigarette. 'Since you drew my attention to Ol Njorowa I've been looking at it carefully. The security precautions are far beyond what's needed for an agricultural college.'

'The Hunts explained that away,' said Stafford. 'Judy said things were being stolen; she said mostly small agricultural tools which didn't matter very much, but when it came to experimental seed it was different. And Alan Hunt came up with a story of a leopard.' He thought about the Hunts. 'Chip, the whole damned staff can't be in South African intelligence. The Hunts are white Kenyans and Dr Odhiambo is an unlikely agent.'

'There's probably just a cell,' agreed Chip. 'Coming back to Hendriks – how long has he lived in England?'

'I don't know,' said Stafford. 'He came into my life two years ago when he married Alix.'

'If he is in South African intelligence he'd be a sleeper planted in England and the Brits wouldn't like that. I think some liaison with London is indicated; and on a high level.' Chip stood up. 'And I'll see if I can get a man into Ol Njorowa.'

'Wait a minute,' said Stafford. 'Dirk knows I'm in Kenya – I told him I'd be taking a holiday here and that I might see him. I think I'll invite myself to Ol Njorowa. Besides, I have an invitation from the Hunts to go ballooning.'

'Going alone?' asked Hardin.

'No, I'll take the Sergeant.' Stafford smiled at Curtis. 'How would you like to go ballooning, Sergeant?'

The expression of disgust on Curtis's face was an eloquent answer.

* * *

The air of tension in Brice's office was electric as Hendriks said, 'Why the hell didn't you tell me that Stafford was mixed up in this?'

'Because I didn't know,' snapped Brice.

'Christ, he'd been here! You'd met him, damn it!'

'So how would I know who he was?' Brice asked plaintively. 'You'd never mentioned him. All I knew then was that he was a friend of the Hunts; they were dining together at the Lake Naivasha Hotel with an Indian, a Sikh called Nair Singh.'

'Who is he?'

'A friend of Alan Hunt. They were at University together.'

'And then Stafford turned up in the Masai Mara chasing after Hendriks. Couldn't you put two and two together?'

'I didn't hear about it. It wasn't reported in the press. Who is Stafford, anyway?'

'A friend of Alix,' said Dirk broodingly. 'And he's sharp, Brice; damned sharp.' He told Brice exactly who and what Stafford was. 'It's not coincidence that he's popping up here and there at critical times and places. Did he mention me when he was here?'

'No.'

'Why not?' demanded Dirk. 'He knew I was coming.' His mind was busy with possible implications, then he said explosively, 'Good God!'

'What's the matter now?' said Brice tiredly.

'He's seen the bloody will, that's what's the matter,' said Dirk viciously. 'A man called Hardin came to see Alix when I was in South Africa.' He told Brice about it, then said, 'I never met Hardin. Alix said he'd gone back to the States.'

'And you never thought to tell me about this?' said Brice acidly.

'I was too busy thinking about what to do with Hendrix. But that doesn't matter now. What matters is that Stafford knows the Foundation has inherited a hell of a lot more than seven million.'

Brice shrugged. 'We've got a cover for that. I told you about it. I'll just have to report the full extent of our windfall. A pity, but there it is.' He stood up and began to pace. 'This is a damn funny tale you're telling me. Hardin, an American, tells your wife that you had an unknown cousin. Further, Hardin has taken the trouble to get a copy of the will. Why should he do that?'

'He said he was suspicious of the man he was working for according to Alix. I told you I never met the man.'

'And who was he working for?'

'A private detective agency in New York.'

'The name?'

'I don't know. Alix didn't say.'

'Who employed the detective agency?'

'Farrar, the Jersey lawyer.'

Brice stopped his pacing and faced Hendriks. 'Now tell me something,' he said coldly. 'How did Farrar know there was an American heir?' Dirk was silent. Brice said, 'How many people knew there was an American heir?'

'Pretoria knew,' said Dirk. 'I knew, but I didn't go near Farrar. Mandeville knew, of course.' He stopped.

'Mandeville knew,' repeated Brice. 'The eminent Queen's Counsel knew. Do you know what happened, Hendriks? While Pretoria was chasing Hendrix in Los Angeles he was also being chased by American detectives employed by Farrar at the instigation of Mandeville. Pretoria nearly got Hendrix but he was rescued by Mandeville's crowd. What a balls-up! Hasn't anyone heard of co-ordination and liaison? We've been fighting ourselves, you damned fool.' His tone was cutting. 'What made Mandeville go off half-cocked like that?'

'He always said Pretoria was slow off the mark,' said Dirk. His voice was sullen.

'I think you'd better talk to Mandeville. Find out if our reasoning is correct. If it is, you tell him never to do anything without orders again.' He picked up the telephone. 'Find out the delay on London calls, please.' As he put down the telephone he said, 'And you might ask him for the name of the American detective agency.'

'Why? It doesn't matter any more.'

'How do you know that? Have you got crystal balls?' Brice slammed his hand on the desk with a noise like a pistol shot. 'There's been too much going wrong on this operation. I haven't been sweating blood here to see it torpedoed by inefficiency.' He sat down. 'Now tell me more about Stafford? How did he come to see the will?'

'Hardin had a copy and took it to Alix. I was in South Africa so Alix asked Stafford for his advice. Hardin showed him the will.'

'So he knows the extent of the will, he's been prowling about here, and he was in the Masai Mara when Hendrix was snatched. This man you met . . . er . . . ?' Brice snapped his fingers impatiently.

'Gunnarsson.'

'Gunnarsson told you that Stafford had followed the raiders. Is that it?'

'That's right. Afterwards Stafford told him that his party got lost in the bush.'

'Got lost, did they? I wonder.' Brice cocked a raised eyebrow at Hendriks. 'I lost two men and your cousin is still missing. We discussed it before but we didn't know about Stafford then.' He rubbed his jaw thoughtfully. 'I can see we'll have to find out more about Stafford.' The telephone rang and he picked it up. 'Oh!' He covered the mouthpiece. 'Someone for you. Who knows you're here?'

'No one,' said Hendriks. 'After I talked to Gunnarsson I went to the American Embassy but I told no one where I was going after that.'

'Someone knows.' Brice held out the telephone. 'You'd better find out who it is.'

Hendriks took it. 'Dirk Hendriks speaking.'

'Hello, Dirk; so I've tracked you down at last,' said Stafford, and Hendriks nearly dropped the phone. 'Max here. I thought I'd phone Ol Njorowa on the off chance you'd be there. How are you doing?'

'Fine,' said Dirk. He put his hand over the mouthpiece and said in a low voice, 'It's Stafford.'

'Have you been ballooning yet?' asked Stafford.

'What?' said Dirk stupidly.

'Ballooning with the Hunts. They've extended an invitation for me to go ballooning with them tomorrow. I've just been talking to Alan. I'll be staying at the Lake Naivasha Hotel. We must have dinner.'

'Yes, we must,' said Dirk mechanically. 'Hang on a minute.' Again he covered the mouthpiece. 'He's coming here. Some crazy talk about ballooning with someone called Hunt. He'll be at the hotel.'

Brice began to smile. 'Give me the phone.' He took it, and said, 'Hello, Mr Stafford; Charles Brice here. I hear Alan Hunt is taking you up tomorrow. Now, there's no question of your staying at the hotel, we can put you up here. Apart from anything else it will be more convenient for Alan. Yes, I insist. What time shall we expect you? All right, we'll see you then.'

His smile broadened as he cradled the telephone. 'I'd just as soon have him here where I can keep an eye on him. "'Walk into my parlour,' said the spider to the fly".'

22

Gunnarsson lay on the bed in his room at the New Stanley reading a paperback novel in which he had no interest. Several times he had lost the drift of the plot and had to turn back several pages and he was bored and irritable. True, being on his back helped his feet which were still sore, and the doctor had recommended bed rest, but what he was really doing was waiting for a telephone call from London.

The telephone rang and he reached for it. 'Gunnarsson.'

'Mr Gunnarsson, this is George Barbour of Peacemore, Willis and Franks in London. I understand that you want to know the present location of Max Stafford of Stafford Security Consultants.'

'Yeah.'

'To the best of our knowledge Mr Stafford is now in Kenya on holiday. He left London on the eighteenth.'

So the bastard had been waiting in Nairobi, thought Gunnarsson. He said, 'You didn't tip off Stafford Security, I hope.'

Barbour was hurt. 'We know how to make discreet enquiries, Mr Gunnarsson.'

'Okay. Well, thanks.'

He rang off and pulled the telephone directory towards him and began to ring the Nairobi hotels. He struck lucky on his fifth try which was the Norfolk. Yes, Mr Stafford was staying at the Norfolk. No, he was not in the hotel at the moment. It was believed that Mr Stafford was away on safari, although he had retained his room. No, the whereabouts of Mr Stafford were not known. Did the gentleman wish to leave a message?

Gunnarsson did not wish to leave a message so he hung up abruptly and lay back on the bed and tried to sort out his thoughts. He had never met Stafford but had heard much of him from Peacemore, Willis and Franks. There was no Peacemore, nor Willis, nor Franks; the three-barrelled name having been invented by Gunnarsson as having a cosy ring to it suitable for the City of London. The outfit was ram-rodded by Terence Ferney who had been vitriolic on the subject of Stafford Security Consultants from time to time. 'Stafford's halo is getting tight the way his head is swelling,' he once said. 'But he's a good operator, there's no doubt about that. He keeps his security tight and he's recruited good men – Jack Ellis for one.'

Gunnarsson had seen Ferney in London and Ferney had been crowing about how they had got past Stafford Security's guard at Electronomics during the Electronomics takeover and Gunnarsson had cut him short curtly. 'You've won one and lost five. Your record's not good, Terry. Get on the ball.'

So it was Stafford who had followed him in the Masai Mara. What sort of coincidence was that? The boss of one of America's biggest private security organizations is kidnapped and the boss of one of Europe's largest security organizations is conveniently at hand. Nuts!

But how had Stafford got on to him? And had he anything to do with the disappearance of Corliss? Did he know about Corliss – that he was a ringer for Hank Hendrix? And why was he horning in anyway? Gunnarsson picked up the telephone again and dialled. 'I'd like to put in a call to New York.'

* * *

Hardin was also lying down, but on a lounger by the swimming pool at the Norfolk Hotel and acquiring a tan. He lay on his stomach, intently watching the bubbles rise in a glass of Premium beer, and reflected that he could not be said to be earning his pay. Stafford and Curtis had gone to Ol Njorowa, Chip and his myrmidons were keeping an eye on

Gunnarsson, and there was nothing left for Hardin to do. He felt dissatisfied and vaguely guilty.

He lay there for an hour soaking in the sun, then swam ten lengths of the pool before rubbing himself down and changing into street clothes in the change room. He walked through the bird-noisy courtyard towards the rear entrance of the hotel lobby but, as he entered the lobby, he did a smart about turn and retreated into the courtyard. Gunnarsson was at the reception desk talking to the clerk.

He was about to return to his room when Nair Singh walked into the courtyard from the lobby, his eyes half closed protectively against the sudden blast of sunlight. As he put on sunglasses Hardin tapped him on the shoulder. 'Damn it!' he said. 'I nearly walked straight into Gunnarsson. I should have had warning.'

'I phoned your room on the house phone,' said Nair. 'You weren't there.'

'I was at the pool. What the hell is Gunnarsson doing here?'

'I'd say he's trying to find Stafford,' said Nair. 'He knows who Stafford is. He took the trouble to ring London to establish that the Stafford he met at Keekorok is the same Stafford of Stafford Security Consultants.'

'How do you know that?'

'We put a tap on his phone.' Nair smiled. 'Standard procedure. He rang New York an hour ago requesting reinforcements. He's bringing in three men.'

'Who?' demanded Hardin. 'Did he give names?'

Nair nodded. 'Walters, Gottschalk and Rudinsky.'

'Gottschalk I don't know,' said Hardin. 'But Walters is a pretty good man and Rudinsky has worked in Africa before. He's an ex-Company man, too. The pace is hotting up. When are they expected?'

'The day after tomorrow, on the morning flight. Plenty of time to decide what to do. I'll talk it over with Chip; he might have them barred as undesirable aliens.'

Hardin jerked his head towards the lobby. 'You'd better

get on with the job. Gunnarsson might give you the slip.'

'He won't. I have three men out there and there's a radio transmitter in the car. He's still at the reception desk.' Nair regarded Hardin blandly. 'I have a radio in my turban; they miniaturize them these days.'

'Neat,' said Hardin admiringly and looked at the turban with interest. The folds of cloth over Nair's ears even concealed the earphone he must be wearing.

Nair held up his hand for silence and cocked his head on one side. 'He's leaving now – getting into a taxi. We'll see him on his way before we check at the reception desk.'

'I wonder how Gunnarsson got on to Stafford,' mused Hardin.

'Could have been through Dirk Hendriks,' said Nair. 'It doesn't really matter. He's out of Harry Thuku Road now. Let's find out what he wanted.'

They went into the lobby to interrogate the man at the desk. Nair said, 'The man who was here just now . . .'

'Mr Andrews? The American?'

'Yeah,' said Hardin. 'Mr Andrews. Was he looking for someone?'

'He wanted to see Mr Stafford. He's a friend of yours, isn't he? I've seen you together.'

Hardin nodded. 'What did you tell Andrews?'

'I told him where to find Mr Stafford.' The clerk looked at the expression on Hardin's face nervously. 'Did I do wrong?'

'I guess not,' said Hardin, thinking otherwise. 'Where did you tell him to go?'

'Ol Njorowa College. Mr Stafford mentioned it before he left. He said he'd be away for a couple of days but wanted to keep his room here.'

Hardin looked at Nair blankly. 'Thanks,' he said. As they moved away he said, 'That was pretty foolish of Max.'

'He wasn't to know Gunnarsson would come looking for him.' Nair stopped with an intent look on his face as he listened to his inner voice. He said, 'Gunnarsson is getting out of his taxi in Muindi Mbingu street.' He paused. 'He's going into the United Touring Company office. The UTC is a car hire firm among other things.'

There was no discussion. 'I'll pack a bag,' said Hardin. 'Ready in fifteen minutes.' As he walked out of the lobby he saw Nair already reaching for a telephone.

* * *

Again Stafford suffered the ritual of inspection before the gates of Ol Njorowa College opened for him. He drove to the Administration Block, parked the Nissan, and went inside where he gave his name to the black Kenyan behind the counter in the hall. He looked around and saw what he had not noticed on his first visit. Chip was right; security was tighter than one would expect in such an innocent organization.

No one could penetrate anywhere into the building without passing the wicket gate, and he was willing to bet that every time it opened it would send out a signal; at least it would if he had been responsible for security. He looked around with a keen professional eye and detected a soft gleam of glass high in a corner of the hall where two walls and a ceiling met, and guessed it was the wide-angle lens of a TV camera. It was unnoticeable and only to be detected by someone actively looking for it. He wondered where they kept the monitor screen.

The man behind the counter put down the telephone. 'Mr Hendriks will be with you in a moment. Please take a seat.'

Stafford sat on a comfortable settee, picked up a magazine from the low table in front of him, and flipped through the pages. It was a scientific journal devoted to tropical crop production and of no particular interest. Presently Hendriks appeared and came through the wicket, his arm outstretched. 'Max! Good to see you.'

Stafford doubted that statement but he got up and they shook hands. 'Nice of Brice to have me here,' he said. 'I could just as easily have stayed at the hotel. It's not far down the road.'

'Charles wouldn't hear of it,' said Hendriks. 'As soon as he knew we were friends. Why didn't you mention it when you were here last?'

'I didn't have all that much time with Brice, and I was with another party – the Hunts, Alan and Judy. Do you know them?'

'No; but I haven't been here all that long. I've just got back from England.'

'And how are Alix and young Max?' asked Stafford politely.

'Motherhood agrees with her,' said Hendriks, and took Stafford's arm. 'Come and see Charles.' He led Stafford through the wicket gate and along a corridor where he opened a door. 'Max is here,' he said.

Brice greeted Stafford genially. 'So you've come to be an intrepid birdman with Alan Hunt. Rather you than me; I don't trust that contraption – it looks much too flimsy.' He waved Stafford to a chair.

As he sat down Hendriks said, 'Bad news about cousin Henry. You've heard, of course?'

Stafford was ready for that one and had already formulated his reply. 'More than heard,' he said. 'I was there. Not with the kidnapped party but with a group who charged off somewhat blunderingly to the rescue. I didn't know that Henry Hendrix was involved, though, and when we got back to Keekorok I got a shock when I heard the name. In fact, at first I thought it might have been you.'

Brice said, 'Odd that your adventure wasn't reported in the press.'

Stafford shrugged. 'Bloody bad journalism. Have there been any developments?'

'Nothing,' said Dirk. 'I've been to the police and the American Embassy but no one seems to know anything or, if they do, they aren't saying.'

'It hasn't done diplomatic relations between Kenya and Tanzania any good,' remarked Brice. 'Not that they were so sparkling in the first place.' He changed the subject. 'I suspect you'll want to clean up. We have some bedrooms upstairs for VIPs – the Trustees visit us from time to time and sometimes the odd government official. You can have one of those while you're here.'

'It's very good of you.'

'No problem at all. You know, we're a rather ingrown community here – something like a monastery but for the few women among us like Judy Hunt. It will do us good to see a new face and have fresh conversation and ideas. Dirk will show you to your room and then . . . er . . . hunt up Hunt, if you'll pardon the phrase.'

'Right,' said Dirk. 'I'll take you up. You have the room next to mine.'

'And you'll join us for dinner,' said Brice.

As they went upstairs Stafford said to Hendriks, 'You're the real VIP here, of course. What do you think of the place?'

'I haven't seen much of it yet. I've been too busy trying to get some action on my cousin. But what I've seen has impressed me. Here's your room.'

The 'monks' in Brice's monastery lived well, thought Stafford as he surveyed the bedroom which would not have disgraced a three-star hotel. Dirk indicated a door. 'That's the bathroom. If you'll give me your car keys I'll have someone bring up your bags.'

'It's not locked.'

'Right. The staff room is at the far end of the corridor. I'll meet you there in fifteen minutes with Hunt. We'll have a drink together.'

'I know where the staff room is.'

'Oh, yes,' said Dirk. 'I'd forgotten you've been here before.'

He departed and Stafford did not doubt that the Nissan would be thoroughly searched, as would his suitcase. He did not mind; there was nothing unusual to be found. He inspected the room with a experienced eye, looking not for comfort but for bugs, the electronic kind. He had no doubt that the room would be bugged; Brice would be interested in the private conversations of the Trustees and government officials.

The table lamp was clean as was the reading lamp over the bed. There were no strange objects attached beneath the coffee table, the dressing table or the bed. He looked at the telephone doubtfully. It would probably be tapped but that did not matter; any conversation he used it for would definitely be innocuous. However, it might have been gimmicked in another way. He unscrewed the mouthpiece and shook out the carbon button to inspect it. It looked all right so he put it back and replaced the mouthpiece. It had taken him fifteen seconds.

As he put down the telephone there was a knock at the door and the Kenyan who had been at the counter in the hall downstairs came in bearing Stafford's suitcase. He put it next to the dressing table, and said, 'Mr Hunt is in the staff room, sah.'

'Thank you. Tell him I'll be along in a few minutes.' Stafford took his toilet kit and went into the bathroom. When he came out he looked at the picture on the wall which appeared conventional enough. It was a reproduction of a painting of an elephant by David Shepherd, typical of those to be found in the curio shops in Nairobi. He examined it more closely paying attention, not to the picture itself, but to the frame which was of unpainted white wood and which seemed unusually thick. Near the bottom of the frame he found a small knot hole and he smiled.

From his jacket pocket he took a pen torch and examined the hole more carefully. By angling the light and moving it rhythmically he caught a repeated metallic wink from the bottom of the hole – the diaphragm of a miniature button microphone. As he put away the torch he felt relieved. If he had not found a bug he would have been worried because so far all his suspicions about Hendriks and Brice had been built on a tenuous chain of suppositions. But this was the clincher; no innocent organization would bug its own rooms.

Hidden in the thickness of the picture frame would be a

small transmitter and the batteries to power it, and probably somewhere in Ol Njorowa would be a receiver coupled to a sound-actuated tape recorder. It would be simple to put the bug out of order by the simple expedient of inserting a needle into the hole and ruining the microphone but that would not do because it would be a dead giveaway. Better to leave it alone and say nothing of consequence in the room or, indeed, anywhere in Ol Njorowa.

Before leaving the room he took a small pair of field glasses from his suitcase and went to the window. In the distance he could see a section of the chain-link fence which indicated the perimeter of the college. He swept it, the glasses to his eyes, and estimated it to be ten feet high. At the top were three strands of barbed wire. Somewhere on the other side Curtis was making an examination of the fence from the outside, and his briefing had been to make a complete reconnaissance of the perimeter. Stafford put the field glasses away and walked to the staff room with a light heart.

* * *

In Brice's office Dirk Hendriks put down the telephone. He had found it difficult to contact Mandeville in London; the lawyer had been engaged in court and Hendriks had requested a return call with some urgency. Now he had just finished talking to Mandeville and the news he got had knocked the wind out of him.

Brice said, 'What's the matter? What did Mandeville say?'

'The New York agency was Gunnarsson Associates,' said Dirk hollowly.

'*What*?' Brice sat open-mouthed. 'You mean the man you talked with in Nairobi was the man who found Henry Hendrix in the States?'

'It would seem so.' Hendriks stood up. 'There can't be many Gunnarssons around and the Gunnarsson in Nairobi is an American.'

'And he was in the tour group with your cousin. They were travelling together, obviously. Now, why should a private detective still stick around after he's delivered the goods? And to the extent of coming to Kenya at that. And why should Henry Hendrix let him?'

'Perhaps he thought he needed a bodyguard after inheriting all that money.'

'Unlikely.' Brice drummed his finger on the desk.

'Oh, I don't know,' Hendriks objected. 'He'd been shot in Los Angeles and there was the business of the car in Cornwall. He might have become suspicious.'

'I suppose so,' Brice said tiredly. 'Another suggestion is that Gunnarsson and Stafford are tied together.' He thought for a moment. 'Whichever way it is Gunnarsson needs watching. We must find out who he sees, and particularly if he gets in touch with Stafford.'

'Do I go back to Nairobi?' asked Dirk.

'No, you stay here and keep an eye on Stafford. I'll send Patterson.' Brice stood up. 'I'll go to the radar office and send him now. You say Gunnarsson is staying at the New Stanley?'

Dirk nodded. Brice was almost out of the room when Dirk said suddenly, 'Wait a minute. I've just remembered something.' Brice turned back and raised an eyebrow, and Dirk said, 'When I was talking to Gunnarsson in the Thorn Tree I had the odd impression I'd seen him before but I couldn't place him. I can now.'

'Where?'

'Remember when I came to Kenya for the first time with Henry and Farrar? We stayed at the Lake Naivasha Hotel. You joined us there and we had dinner together.'

'Well?'

'Gunnarsson was dining at a corner table alone.'

23

Dirk Hendriks walked into the staff room and found Stafford in conversation with Alan Hunt who was saying, 'I'm going up tomorrow anyway. Jim Odhiambo wants some photographs of his experimental plots. The balloon is useful for that kind of thing.'

Stafford beckoned to Dirk and said, 'Alan, I don't think you've met Dirk Hendriks, the grandson of the benefactor of the Ol Njorowa Foundation. Alan Hunt.'

The two men shook hands and Hunt said, 'Your grandfather's largesse has come just at the right time for me. I want a fraction of that seven million quid for a gas chromatograph.'

Dirk laughed. 'I wouldn't know what that is.'

'Seven million!' said Stafford in simulated surprise. It's more than that, surely.'

'Per annum,' said Dirk easily. 'That's Charles Brice's estimate of the annual return when the capital is invested. I think he's too optimistic. It's before tax, of course, but he's having talks with the government with a view to getting it tax free. The Foundation is a non-profit organization, after all.'

All very specious. 'I must have misunderstood Brice,' Stafford said.

Hunt whistled. 'I certainly misunderstood him, and so did the pressmen. How much did your grandfather leave us?'

'At the time of his death it would have been about thirty-four million, but probate and proving the will has taken some time during which the original sum has been earning more cash. Say about thirty-seven million.'

Hunt gave a sharp crack of laughter. 'Now I *know* I'll get my gas chromatograph. Let's drink to it.'

He ordered a round of drinks and then Stafford said curiously, 'You said you are taking photographs for Dr Odhiambo. I don't see the point. I mean he can see the crops on the ground, can't he?'

'Ah,' said Hunt. 'But this is quicker. We use infra-red film to shoot his experimental plots. Plants that are ailing or sick show up very well on infra-red if you know what to look for. It saves Jim many a weary mile of walking.'

'The wonders of science,' said Hendriks.

'They use the same system in satellites,' said Hunt. 'But they can cover greater areas than I can.'

Stafford sampled his beer. 'Talking about satellites, who owns the satellite your animal movement people use? They couldn't have put it up themselves.'

Hunt laughed. 'Not likely. It's an American job. The migration study boys asked to put their scientific package into it. It's not very big and it takes very little power so the Yanks didn't mind. But the satellite does a lot more than monitor the movement of wildebeest.' He pointed to the ceiling. 'It sits up there, 22,000 miles high, and watches the clouds over most of Africa and the Indian Ocean; a long term study of the monsoons.'

'A geo-stationary orbit,' said Stafford.

'That's right. It's on the Equator. Here we're about one degree south. It's fairly steady, too; there's a bit of liberation but not enough to worry about.'

'You've lost me,' said Hendriks. 'I understand about one word in three.' He shook his head and said wryly, 'My grandfather wanted me to work here part of the year but I don't see what I can do. I haven't had the right training. I was in liberal arts at university.'

'No doubt Brice will have you working with him on the administrative side,' observed Hunt, and drank some beer.

No doubt he would, thought Stafford, and said aloud, 'Which university, Dirk?'

'Potch. That's Potchefstroom in the Transvaal.'

Stafford filed that information away in his mind; it would be a useful benchmark if Hendriks had to be investigated in depth at a later date.

Hunt said, 'Max,' if you're coming with us tomorrow it'll be early – before breakfast. The air is more stable in the early morning. I'll give you a ring at six-thirty.' Stafford nodded and Hunt looked at Dirk. 'Would you like to come? There's room for one more.'

Hendriks shook his head. 'Brice wants to see me early tomorrow morning. Some other time, perhaps.'

Stafford was relieved; he had his own reasons for wanting to overfly Ol Njorowa and he did not want Hendriks watching him when it happened. He did not think the Hunts were mixed up in any undercover activity at the College. They were Kenya born and it was unlikely they would have been suborned by South African intelligence. He thought they were part of the innocent protective camouflage behind which Brice hid, like most of the scientific staff. He had his own ideas about where the worm in this rosy apple lay.

Hunt announced he had work to do, finished his beer and went off. Stafford and Hendriks continued to chat, a curious conversation in which both probed but neither wanted to give anything away. A duel with words ending at honours even.

*   *   *

As Gunnarsson drove to Naivasha he began to put the pieces together and the conclusion he arrived at was frightening. He was a tough-minded man and did not scare easily but now he was worried because the package he had put together in New York was coming apart; the string unravelling, the cover torn and, worse, the contents missing.

Corliss was missing, damn him!

He had been so careful in New York. After Hendrix had been delivered by Hardin no one had seen him because Gunnarsson had personally smuggled him out of the building and to a hideaway in Connecticut. The only person to have laid eyes on Hendrix, apart from Hardin, had been his secretary in the outer office and she did not know who he was because the name had not been mentioned. And he had successfully got rid of Hardin; the damn fool needled so easily and had blown his top, which made his dismissal a perfectly natural reaction.

Gunnarsson tapped his fingers on the wheel of the car. Still, it was strange that when he wanted to find Hardin again he had vanished. Probably he had crawled into some hole to lick his wounds. Gunnarsson shrugged and dismissed Hardin from his mind. The guy was a has-been and of no consequence in the immediate problem he faced.

But Hardin's report had been interesting and valuable. Here was Henry Hendrix, a hippy drop-out with no folks, and no one in the world would give a damn whether he lived or died because no one knew the guy existed. No one except that freaky commune in Los Angeles and, at first, he had discounted Biggie and his crowd.

And so, with Hendrix held isolated, he had the material for the perfect scam, and the hit was going to be big – no less than six million bucks. Hendrix had gone along with everything, talking freely under the impression that his interrogation was for the benefit of a British lawyer and quite unaware of the quietly revolving spools of the tape recorder memorizing every word.

And then there was Corliss. Corliss had been easy because he was weak and bent under pressure. He had been uncovered in a routine check by Gunnarsson Associates and when Gunnarsson had faced him and shown him the options he had folded fast. No one in the organization wondered when he quit his job without being prosecuted because everyone knew computer frauds were hushed up. No bank liked to broadcast that it had been ripped off by a computer artist because it was bad for business. And so Corliss had also been isolated but Gunnarsson made sure that Corliss and Hendrix never met.

Then Corliss was groomed to take the part of Hendrix. It was lucky that Corliss was not unlike Hendrix physically – they were both blond and of about the same age – and the passport was easy to fix. After that something had to be done about Hendrix and Gunnarsson saw to it personally. It was a pity but it was necessary and Hendrix now resided encased in a block of concrete at the bottom of Long Island Sound.

Gunnarsson had second thoughts about Biggie and the commune. The sudden emergence of an overnight multi-millionaire called Hendrix could attract the attention of the media. It might make the papers on the West Coast – it could even be on TV with pictures – something which Biggie might see. So something had to be done about *that* and, again, Gunnarsson saw to it personally.

He smiled grimly as he reflected that Hardin had told him how to do it in his report. If a pottery kiln had blown up once it could blow up again, this time with more serious consequences. Exit Biggie and the commune. It was then that he began looking for Hardin seriously and found that he was living in a fleabag in the Bronx, and another rooming house fire in the Bronx passed unnoticed. It did not even rate a paragraph on the bottom of page zilch. That worried Gunnarsson because he was not certain he had taken out Hardin. Discreet enquiries revealed that the bodies in the rooming house were unidentifiable and a further search for Hardin produced nothing so he relaxed.

After that everything had gone perfectly. Corliss had been accepted in London and that old fool, Farrar, had even anted up two hundred thousand bucks as an earnest of what was to come. That was only a sweetener of course; a morsel before the main meal. Then they came to Kenya and the whole goddamn scheme had fallen apart when Corliss was snatched in Tanzania. What griped Gunnarsson was that he did not know whether Corliss was alive or dead.

'Jesus!' he said aloud in the privacy of the car. 'If he's alive I could be cooked.'

He sorted out the possibilities. If Corliss was dead then

goodbye to six million dollars; he would cut his losses and return to the States. If Corliss was alive there were two alternatives – either he stayed as Hendrix or he spilled his guts. If he had the nerve to stay as Hendrix then nothing would change and everything was fine. But if he talked and revealed that he was Corliss then that meant instant trouble. Everybody and his uncle would be asking what had happened to the real Hendrix. Maybe he could get out of it by fast talking – he could blame the whole schmeer on the absent Hardin. He could swear he had accepted Corliss as the real McCoy on the word of Hardin. Maybe. That would depend on exactly how wide Corliss opened his fat mouth.

But the stakes were goddamn high – six million dollars or his neck. Gunnarsson thumped the driving wheel in frustration and the car swerved slightly. Corliss! Where was the stupid son of a bitch?

And now someone else was butting in – Max Stafford! It was inconceivable that Stafford could be there by chance; there was no connection at all. So Stafford had caught onto something. But how? He thought back to the time when he and Corliss were in London, reviewing what they had done, and could not find any flaw. So what in hell was Stafford doing and how much did he know? Well, that was the purpose of this trip to Naivasha – to find out. But carefully. And for the moment he was short of troops – he needed legmen to nose around – but a couple of days would cure that problem.

He came off the tortuous road of the escarpment and drove along the straight and pot-holed road that led to Naivasha, and he was unaware of the Kenatco Mercedes taxi which kept a level distance of four hundred yards behind him. There was no reason why he should be aware of it because there were two fuel tankers and a beer truck between them.

As he turned off the main road and bumped across the railway track to join the road which led alongside the lake he thought fleetingly of Hardin's report – the bit where it said Hendrix had been shot in Los Angeles. 'Now, what the hell?' he muttered. Had it started – whatever 'it' was – as early as that? What had Hardin said? A couple of guys with un-American accents – possibly Krauts – looking for Hendrix. And then he had been shot. It would bear thinking about.

He turned into the grounds of the Lake Naivasha Hotel, parked and locked his car, and went to the desk to register. As he signed in he said, 'Which is Mr Stafford's room?'

'Stafford, sir? I don't think . . .' After a moment the manager said, 'We have no Stafford here at the moment, sir. I do recall a Mr Stafford who stayed here some little time ago.'

'I see,' said Gunnarsson thoughtfully. Where was the guy?

'I'll send someone to take your bags to your room, sir.'

'I'll unlock the car.' Gunnarsson turned away, brushing shoulders with an Indian as he walked towards the parking lot, and was again unaware that Nair Singh turned to stare after him. He strode towards his car followed by a hotel servant and unlocked it. As his bags were taken out he looked about him and his attention was caught by the taxi some little distance away. His eyes narrowed and he walked towards it.

He stopped about five yards away and surveyed it. One radio antenna was okay – a guy might need music while he travelled. Two radio antennas? Well, maybe; being a taxi it might be on a radio network. But *three* antennas? He knew enough about his own work to know what that meant. He tried proving it by approaching from the driver's side and peering at the dashboard, and he saw an instrument which was definitely not standard – a signal strength meter.

Slowly he withdrew and returned to his own car where he dropped on his haunches and looked under the rear. He passed his hand under the bumper and found something small which shifted slightly under the pressure of his fingers. He wrenched it loose and withdrew it to find he was holding a small anonymous-looking grey metal box from which two stiff wires protruded. He tested it on the bumper and it adhered with a click as the magnet on the bottom caught hold.

Gunnarsson straightened, his lips compressed, and looked across at the taxi. Someone had been following him; someone who so badly did not want to lose him that a radio beeper had been planted on his car to make the task of trailing easier. He walked briskly back to the hotel and went to the desk. 'That taxi back there,' he said. 'Whose is it?'

'A taxi, sir?'

'Yeah, a Mercedes,' Gunnarsson said irritably. 'Owned by Kenatco – least that's what the sign says.'

'It could have been the Indian gentleman who was just here,' said the manager. 'He went that way.'

Gunnarsson ran back quickly but, by the time he came within sight the taxi was taking off at speed in a cloud of dust. He stood there, tossing the radio bug in his hand, then he dropped it on to the ground and crushed it under his heel. Somebody was playing games and he did not know who. It was something to think about before proceeding too precipitately so he went to his room and lay on the bed before ringing the Kenatco Taxi Company in Nairobi, giving the registration number.

As he suspected, the Kenatco people denied all knowledge of it.

24

Stafford was wakened at six-thirty next morning by the ringing of the telephone next to his bed. At first he was disorientated but put together the fragments of himself when he heard Hunt say, 'We leave in half an hour, Max. I'll meet you in the hall.'

Half an hour later Hunt said, 'Don't worry; you'll get your breakfast.' They got into a Land-Rover and Hunt drove out of the College grounds and up a winding unsurfaced road which ran next to the chain-link fence. 'The wind is perfect,' he said. 'I think I'll be able to take you through Hell's Gate. Have you ever been up in a balloon before?'

'No, I haven't.' Stafford did not mention that the suggestion that he go through Hell's Gate on a first flight made him feel decidedly queasy.

Hunt swung off the road and the Land-Rover bumped across open bush country. 'Here we are.'

Stafford got out of the Land-Rover stiffly and saw Judy about fifty yards away, standing next to what appeared to be a laundry basket. 'Is she coming, too?'

'Yes; she operates the camera.'

They walked over to her, and she said, 'Hi! Had breakfast?' Stafford shook his head. 'Good! Breakfast is better after a flight.'

He inspected the 'laundry basket' and found it was the thing they stood in while being wafted through the air. Judy was right; it was indubitably better to have breakfast *after* the flight. Stafford was not scared of many things but he did have a fear of heights. He was prepared to climb a cliff but nothing would ever get him close to the edge while walking at the top. Not an unusual phobia. He wondered how he was going to acquit himself during the next couple of hours.

The edge of the basket was padded with suede, and from each corner rose a pillar, the pillars supporting a complicated contraption of stainless steel piping in two coils which was, Stafford supposed, the burner which heated the air. Beyond the basket the multi-coloured balloon envelope was laid out on the ground. It was bigger than he expected and looked flimsy. Four black Kenyans were stretching it out and straightening wire ropes.

He turned to Hunt. 'It's bigger than I expected.' He didn't mention the flimsiness.

'She's a Cameron N-84. That means she's 84,000 cubic feet in volume. When she's inflated the height from the floor of the basket to the crown of the balloon is over 60 feet.'

'What's the fabric?'

'Close weave nylon treated with polyurethane to close the pores. This envelope is nearly new; the old one became too porous and I was losing air and efficiency. It's the ultra-violet that does it, of course. Even though the fabric is specially treated the sun gets it in the end. A balloon doesn't last nearly as long here as it would in England. I'll give the boys a hand.'

Hunt walked forward and began checking rigging. Stafford turned to see Judy working on the basket. She was clamping a big plate camera on to the side. 'Can I help?'

She smiled. 'I've just finished. We'll be leaving in ten minutes.'

'So soon?' He looked at the flaccid nylon envelope and wondered how.

Hunt came back. 'All right; let's get this thing into the air. Lucas, get the fan. Chuma, you're for the crown rope. You others start flapping.' He turned to Stafford. 'Max, you help us get the basket on its side, slow and easy.'

They tipped the basket over so that the burners pointed to the balloon. Two Kenyans were flapping the nylon, driving air into the envelope. It billowed enormously in slow waves and visibly expanded. Lucas came behind with the fan; it was like an over-sized electric fan but driven by a small

Honda petrol engine. The engine sputtered and then caught with a roar, driving air into the balloon.

Hunt got into the basket and crouched behind the burners. He lit the pilot flames and then tilted the burners towards the balloon. 'All right, Lucas,' he said, raising his voice above the noise of the fan. 'Join Chuma on the crown rope. Judy and Max to the basket.'

Stafford and Judy stood on each side of the basket. He did not know what to do but was prepared to follow her lead. The balloon was filling rapidly and suddenly there was a growling, deep-throated roar and a blue flame, six feet long and nearly a foot in diameter, shot into the open throat of the balloon. It took Stafford by surprise and he started, then looked towards Judy. She was laughing so he grinned back weakly.

The roar went on and on, and the balloon expanded like a blossoming flower caught in time-lapse photography. Hunt switched off the flame, and one of the Kenyans turned off the fan and there was blessed silence. Hunt looked up as the ballon rose above them. 'All hands to the basket,' he said, and sent another burst of flame into the balloon.

The two Kenyans joined Stafford and Judy as the basket began to stir like a live thing. Slowly it began to tilt upright as the flame poured heat into the envelope. Hunt switched off again, and shouted, 'Let go the crown rope.' Immediately the basket became upright as the balloon surged above them. 'All hands on,' said Hunt, and four pairs of black hands clamped on the padded edges. 'Max, get in.'

There was a sort of footstep in the wickerwork so Stafford put his foot in it and swung his other leg inboard. Hunt caught his arm and helped him regain balance. Judy climbed in from the other side. She immediately began to turn a valve on one of the cylinders of which there were four, one in each corner of the basket. Hunt was giving short blasts of flame, a few seconds at a time. It seemed to Stafford as though he was doing some kind of fine tuning. Once he said, 'Hands off,' and then, almost immediately, 'Hands on.'

Lucas was rolling a cylinder along the ground towards the basket. Judy unstrapped the cylinder she had been working on and exchanged it for the one brought by Lucas. Then she tapped her brother on the shoulder. 'Okay to go.'

He released a sustained flame, then said 'Hands off.' For a moment nothing apparently happened and then Stafford became aware that they were airborne. The ground was dropping away as they rose in complete silence, and the slight breeze he had felt on the ground had disappeared.

Hunt said, 'The wind is just right. We'll pass over Jim's vegetable patch, take our pictures, and we're set for Hell's Gate. But we'll get some height for the photographs.' The burner roared and Stafford felt heat on his face as he looked up into the vast, empty interior of the envelope into which the flame was disappearing. When he looked down again the ground was receding even faster and the landscape was opening out.

Hunt pointed. 'The College. We'll pass over it. You ready, Judy?'

She bent down to look through a viewfinder. 'Everything okay.'

Stafford produced his own camera. It was a Pentax 110; not a 'spy' camera like the Minox, but still small enough to be carried unobtrusively in a pocket. It also came with a selection of good lenses.

The noise of the burner stopped. 'We'll still rise a bit,' said Hunt conversationally. 'What do you think of it?'

To Stafford's surprise all his qualms had gone. 'I think it's bloody marvellous,' he said. 'So peaceful. Except for the noise of the burner, but that isn't on all the time.'

'There's Dirk Hendriks down there,' said Hunt. 'Talking to Brice outside the Admin Block.' He waved. 'If we were lower we could have a chat.'

'How high are we?'

'Getting on for 2,000 feet from point of departure. That's about 8,000 feet above sea level. The experimental plots are coming up, Judy.'

'I see them.' She took about ten photographs while Stafford took some of his own and then straightened. 'That's it,' she said. 'The work's done. Now for the pleasurable bit.'

'About the noise of the burner,' said Hunt. 'It's difficult to make a quiet burner; I'd say impossible. This one up here is rated at ten million Btu – that's about 4,000 horsepower. You can't keep that lot quiet when it's ripping loose.'

'You're kidding,' Stafford said unbelievingly.

'No, it's quite true. One of the gas cylinders will provide the average household with two months' cooking – we use it up in less than half an hour. But we're not operating at maximum efficiency, so I reckon we're getting about 3,000 horsepower. In England and America they use propane but that's a bit tricky in the African heat so we use butane which has a lesser calorific value. And we have to add pressure with nitrogen; that's what that little cylinder there is for.'

Stafford found the power of the burner hard to believe. Hunt said, 'This dial tells the temperature – not here, but at the crown of the balloon up there.' He jerked his thumb upwards. 'Optimum temperature is 100 degrees Celsius.'

'But that's the boiling point of water.'

'Quite so,' Hunt said equably. 'If it gets above 110 degrees I'm in trouble – the nylon doesn't like it – so I keep a careful eye on the bloody gauge.'

'We're coming up to the entrance of Hell's Gate,' said Judy. 'Alan, come low over Fischer's Column.'

'Okay, but I'll have to go up after that.' He produced a packet of cigarettes and offered one. As Stafford looked doubtfully at the cylinders of butane surrounding them Hunt smiled, and said, 'Quite safe; it'll just add a bit more hot air.'

They drifted into the gorge of Hell's Gate through a gap in sheer cliffs. Hunt occasionally reached up to the burner controls and gave a short blast. Apart from that it was quiet and Stafford could hear cicadas chirping and the twittering of birds. The smoke from his cigarette ascended lazily in a spiral and he realized that was because they were moving at the same speed as the wind. It was weird.

'There's Lucas in the chase car,' said Judy. He looked down and saw the Land-Rover bucketing along a track on the floor of the gorge and towing a trailer. 'That's one of the problems of ballooning; you have to have a way of getting back to where you started.'

Stafford looked up at the immensity of the envelope above, and then down again at the Land-Rover. It seemed strange that a structure the size of a six-storey office block could be folded up to fit in a small trailer. Ahead, rising from the floor of the gorge, was a big rock pillar, tapering to a needle point. 'Fischer's Column,' said Judy. She opened the lid of a box which was lashed to the side of the basket and took out a pair of binoculars. 'We should see rock hyrax. Believe it or not, they're the nearest relation to the elephant. Cuddly creatures.'

'Not too cuddly,' remarked Hunt. 'They carry rabies.'

They were now quite close to the ground, not more than fifty feet high, and Hunt was maintaining this height by short bursts of flame. For a moment Stafford thought they were going to crash into the rock column but they passed about twenty feet to one side. 'There,' said Judy. 'Those are hyrax.'

They were small animals which he would have taken to be rodents. A couple of dozen of them took fright and dashed for crevices in the rocks and disappeared. As they passed Hunt said, 'That's the closest I've been to Old Man Fischer. It's an old volcanic plug, you know.' He operated the burner control and the flame roared in a sustained burst. 'Up we go. There'll be bigger game ahead.'

The balloon rose and the strange landscape of Hell's Gate spread before them. The cliffs to the east were alive with birds which flew faster than any others Stafford had seen. Judy said they were Nyanza swifts. Ahead there was another, but smaller, rock column which he was told was called Embarta. As they rose above the cliffs the crater of the volcano Longonot came into view in the east and Hunt turned off the flame.

Stafford said, 'What kind of bigger game?'

'Oh, eland, zebra, impala – the usual inhabitants. Giraffe, perhaps.'

He saw them all. The zebra herds wheeled as the balloon shadow passed, and the giraffes galloped off in a rocking-horse canter. But none of the animals moved far away; as soon as the balloon drifted by they resumed their grazing and browsing placidly. Stafford said, 'Is this a game reserve?'

'Oh, no,' said Hunt. 'But there is plenty of game outside the reserves.' They were drifting lower and he had the binoculars to his eyes. 'Look there,' he said, handing them to Stafford. 'That tree by the big rock there. There's a leopard on the branch to the right. I wonder if he's the chap who's been visiting the College.' The leopard looked up incuriously, and yawned as the balloon went silently by.

'There's a lammergeier,' said Judy. There was an odd note of warning in her voice. Stafford looked to where she was pointing and saw a big bird circling.

Hunt said, 'That means our flight is nearly over. When the lammergeier goes up the balloon comes down.'

'Why?' asked Stafford. 'Is it likely to attack us?' He could imagine that a sharp beak and talons could make a few nasty rents in the thin fabric of the envelope.

Both Hunt and his sister went into fits of laughter. 'No,' Hunt said. 'A lammergeier wouldn't attack anything. He's a carrion eater. But when he's in the air it means that the ground has heated up enough to start thermals strong enough for him to soar. And balloons don't like thermals; the ride gets too bumpy and it can be positively dangerous. That's why we fly in the early morning.' He looked ahead. 'Still, we'll make it all the way through Hell's Gate.'

They all fell quiet and Stafford found himself in a dreamlike state, almost a trance. Ahead, on the crest of the pass, were puffs of white smoke drifting in the breeze and, from the ground, came the clear barking of baboons. They were nearly at the end of Hell's Gate and he saw, at last, why it was so named. What he had taken for smoke was steam escaping from a hundred fissures, and the violent hissing noise competed with the rumble of the balloon's flame.

'This is it,' said Hunt. 'Prepare for landing. Show Max how, Judy.'

She said, 'When Alan says "Now" crouch down in the basket and hang on to these rope handles – like this.' She demonstrated.

They passed over the steam jets and the balloon danced a little. There were flows of jagged lava which Stafford thought would do the balloon envelope a bit of no good should the balloon land among them. They went over those at a height of about fifty feet towards the open grassland beyond. Hunt said 'Now!' and Judy and Stafford crouched, but not before he had seen an eland looking at him with astonishment.

The basket made contact with the ground and he twisted his head to see Hunt yanking on a line. Above him the whole top of the envelope seemed to tear apart and he could see blue sky. Then the basket tipped on to its side and he was thrown on to his back alongside Judy. Everything was still and they had stopped moving.

'End of ride,' she said, and crawled out.

Stafford rolled out and stood up. Behind were the lava flows and steam clouds; ahead was the balloon envelope, looking very much as it had when he had first seen it, inert and dead upon the ground. In the distance the Land-Rover was driving towards them over the grass. Hunt was standing by the basket. He grinned and said, 'What does it feel like to be a hero of the sky?'

Stafford said slowly, 'I think that was the best damned experience I've had in my life.'

'You've not finished yet,' Hunt said. 'There's more to come. But first help me get the gas cylinders out.'

They took out the cylinders and rolled them aside. The Land-Rover drove up and Lucas and the other Kenyans got out. Lucas came over carrying a hamper. 'Breakfast!' said Judy with satisfaction. She opened the hamper and took out plastic boxes. 'Cold chicken; boiled eggs, fruit. I hope I put the salt in – I can't remember.'

'You're forgetting the most important thing,' said Hunt, and stooped to pick up a large flask. 'It's an old ballooning tradition that anyone making a first flight ends up drinking champagne.' He opened the flask and took out a bottle. 'Nicely chilled,' he commented, and smiled. 'That's why we like to take up first-time passengers; that way we get to drink champagne, too.'

They sat on the empty cylinders eating breakfast and drinking champagne while Lucas and his friend packed up the balloon. It folded into a cube with dimensions of under four feet a side. After breakfast they climbed over the lava flows and had a look at the place where the steam was issuing. There was a strong smell of sulphur and the ground was hot underfoot.

Hunt pointed. 'Ol Karia is about two kilometres that way. They're drilling for steam there; gone down over five and a half thousand feet.'

Stafford looked at the steam issuing all around him. 'I don't see the point. Why drill that far down? There's plenty here.'

'Not this flabby stuff; you need high pressure steam to drive a turbine.'

Stafford shook his head. 'I don't think I'd like to live in a volcanic area. I prefer my *terra* to be *firma*.'

'Oh, it's fairly stable around here,' said Hunt. 'There was a quake in the Valley about four years ago but it didn't hurt much apart from taking out a piece of the road coming down the escarpment from Nairobi.'

Stafford turned and looked across at Longonot. The crater showed quite clearly. 'Is that an active volcano?'

'Not so as you'd notice. A few fumaroles, that's all. I'd call it quiescent. I've climbed into the crater. There are caves, some quite large, where gases have blown out. There are active volcanoes further south of here in Tanzania, notably Ol Doinyo Lengai.'

They turned to walk back to the Land-Rover and Stafford saw a taxi drawn up next to it and, much to his surprise, Hardin and Nair standing by. Hunt said in surprise, 'Now what are they doing here?'

Nair stepped forward and held the Hunts in conversation leaving Hardin to talk privately with Stafford. 'Things began happening yesterday,' Hardin said. 'We didn't know how to contact you but Nair had the bright idea of following the balloon. You gave us quite a chase.'

He related the facts about Gunnarsson, and Stafford looked at the taxi with its array of antennas. 'You were a damn fool to try a trick like that on an old pro like Gunnarsson. Now he's alerted.'

'It was Nair – not me,' protested Hardin.

'Look, we must have a conference; you, me, Nair, Curtis and Chip, if he's around.' Stafford took the camera from his pocket and extracted the film cassette. 'We'll hold the conference as soon as you get this developed and prints made.'

'How can we let you know?'

'I can see the fence from my bedroom,' said Stafford. 'There's a place on the other side of the fence about a hundred yards long where the grass has been burned over. Curtis will know where it is; he's been scouting the perimeter of Ol Njorowa. In the middle of the burned area there's an acacia. When you're ready have someone take a fairly big sheet of newspaper and stick it on one of the thorns as though it's been blown there. That will be the signal. Where are you staying?'

'I couldn't stay at the Lake Naivasha hotel,' said Hardin. 'Gunnarsson is there. I booked into a place called Safariland.' He told Stafford where it was.

'Then that's where we'll talk.'

'What about?' said Hardin.

'About using you to spook Gunnarsson and drive him towards the wolves.' Stafford smiled. 'The wolves being at present located at Ol Njorowa.'

25

Stafford spent the rest of the morning wandering over the grounds of Ol Njorowa, at first with Hunt and then with Dirk Hendriks. He was shown the propagation sheds, the soil testing laboratory, the fertilizer testing laboratory, the this laboratory and the that laboratory, and the scientific terms were pumped remorselessly into one ear only to escape from the other. However, he managed to keep his end up by showing a halfway intelligent interest while keeping his eyes open.

He came to a few conclusions, the first of which was that Hunt was probably not in Brice's pocket. All the time he was in Hunt's company he noted that they were under discreet surveillance by three men, two blacks and a white, who apparently had nothing better to do than potter about in the middle distance. When Hunt excused himself to go about his business they vanished, too, and Hendriks took over the guided tour. The conclusion was that Hunt was not trusted to steer Stafford away from dangerous areas but that Hendriks was.

A second conclusion was that he was being conned and, had it not been for the bugged picture frame in his bedroom, he might have fallen for it. It was being demonstrated to him with some assiduity that Ol Njorowa was an open book in which he might read from any scientific page. The trouble was that science was a foreign language to him and he could have done with a translator.

At last Dirk looked at his watch. 'Well, that's about it, Max. It's nearly lunchtime. I think you've seen about everything.' He laughed. 'Not that I'm qualified to show you. I don't know all that much about the place myself. Brice was going to give you the tour himself but something came up.'

'Yes,' said Stafford. 'He must be a busy man.' He looked around. 'How big is this place?'

'About six hundred hectares.' Hendriks paused to figure it out. 'A little over two square miles.'

Stafford smiled. 'I couldn't have worked it out so quickly.'

'We have the metric system in South Africa now. It makes you bilingual in mathematics.'

As they strolled in the direction of the Admin Block which was about a quarter of a mile away Stafford thought glumly that one could hide a hell of a lot in two square miles. But could one? Assuming that Ol Njorowa was a going concern as a genuine agricultural college then most of the staff would be genuine agricultural specialists. They would be wandering all over the place and could quite easily stumble across something illicit and wonder what it was. No, thought Stafford; hiding something at Ol Njorowa would not be as easy as all that.

They went into the dining room and threaded their way among the tables to where Brice sat. Judy Hunt was sitting with her brother and waved to him as he passed. He waved back as Dr Odhiambo caught his arm. 'Are you enjoying yourself, Mr Stafford?'

'Very much so,' Stafford assured him.

They sat at Brice's table and Stafford looked around the room which was noisy with animated conversation. Brice said, 'Did you enjoy your flight with Hunt?'

'It was great.' Stafford tasted the soup which was placed before him. 'Alan says hot air ballooning is becoming popular in England. I might take it up when I get back.'

Brice grimaced. 'I don't think I'd like a sport where every landing is a crash landing. And when are you going back to England?'

'Any day now. As it is I've been away too long. I have a business to take care of, you know.'

'Yes.' Brice buttered a slice of bread. 'Dirk has been telling me something of what you do. It must be interesting and adventurous.'

'You mean cloak and dagger?' Stafford laughed. 'Not much adventure behind a City desk, Mr Brice.'

'Oh, please call me Charles.' Brice looked up as a waiter came to the table and gave a card to Hendriks who glanced at it and passed it to Brice. They had a brief conversation in murmurs and Hendriks excused himself and left the table. 'An . . . er . . . acquaintance of yours has just arrived,' said Brice casually. 'Perhaps he'll join us for lunch.'

'Oh?' Stafford raised his eyebrows. 'Who can that be? I know few people in Kenya.'

'I believe you met him in the Masai Mara at Keekorok. An American called Gunnarsson. I wonder what he wants. Never mind; no doubt we'll find out. And what do you think of Ol Njorowa after your morning's exploration?'

Stafford managed to convey a spoonful of soup to his mouth without spilling a drop. 'A truly remarkable place,' he said. 'You're doing good work here.' As he pushed away his soup plate he thought that the next few minutes would probably prove interesting.

'We'll be able to really push it now we have the Hendrykxx inheritance. It's been a hard slog up to now.' Brice looked up as Hendriks and Gunnarsson came into the dining room. 'Would that be Mr Gunnarsson?'

'Yes.' Stafford watched Gunnarsson's face intently and caught the instant change of expression as Gunnarsson saw him sitting next to Brice; from blankness it changed to apprehension and then suspicion.

He and Brice stood up and Hendriks introduced them. 'This is Mr Brice, the Director of the Foundation, and Max Stafford I think you already know.'

'I sure do,' said Gunnarsson as Brice ordered another place set at the table. 'We met at Keekorok.' There was something of a baffled look in his eyes as he stared at Stafford.

'That's right,' said Stafford. 'How are your feet, Mr Gunnarsson?'

Gunnarsson grunted as he sat down. 'Better.' He looked around the table: at Hendriks who was finishing his soup; at Brice who, with bottle poised, was asking blandly if he would like wine; at Stafford who was leaning back to allow a plate to be put before him. Here they all were and what the hell was going on?

Hendriks said, 'I went to the American Embassy and did no better than you, Mr Gunnarsson; a complete blank wall. Have you heard any further news of my cousin?'

'No,' said Gunnarsson briefly. He started on his soup. 'What are you doing in Kenya, Mr Stafford?'

'I'm on holiday,' said Stafford easily.

Gunnarsson grunted. 'If you're like me you don't take vacations.' He looked at Dirk. 'Do you know who he is?'

Hendriks looked surprised. 'Yes; he's Max Stafford.'

'But do you know what he does?'

'We were discussing it before you came in,' said Brice. He sipped his wine. 'Must be very interesting work.'

'Mr Gunnarsson is in the same line of business,' observed Stafford. 'But in the United States. You might say that we're competitors, in a way. Or will be.' He smiled at Gunnarsson. 'I'm thinking of expanding my operations.'

'Thinking of moving into the States?' asked Gunnarsson. His smile had no humour in it. 'It's tough going.'

'It can't be worse than Europe,' said Stafford equably.

'Or Kenya.' Gunnarsson finished his soup. 'Funny things happen here, apart from people going missing. The latest is that my car was bugged. A bumper beeper.'

Stafford raised his eyebrows. 'Now who'd do that?'

Gunnarsson shrugged. 'You have the know-how.'

Stafford put down his knife and fork. 'Now look here. I told you I was in Kenya on holiday. Apart from that I'm a friend of the Hendriks family. You would say that, wouldn't you, Dirk?'

'Of course.' Hendriks smiled. 'Especially since my wife named our son after you.' His tone was a fraction sour.

Brice said coolly, 'We know all about Mr Stafford. What

we don't know is why *you* are in Kenya, Mr Gunnarsson. You found Henry Hendrix in Los Angeles and delivered him to London. Why should you then accompany him to Kenya where he mysteriously disappears?' He tented his fingers. 'It would appear that you have to make the explanations rather than Max Stafford.'

Gunnarsson looked at him. 'I don't know that I'm required to give an explanation, Mr Brice, but, since you ask, Hendrix wanted me to come with him.' He smiled. 'He's a nice, young guy and we got on well together when I found him. You might say we became friends and I came with him to Kenya at his request.'

Brice shrugged and turned to Stafford. 'Will you really take up ballooning, Max?' He was obviously changing the subject.

'I might. It seems a great sport.'

The conversation became general with Brice holding forth enthusiastically on the future of the Ol Njorowa Foundation now that it was in funds. Gunnarsson made the odd comment from time to time but his main attention seemed to be on his plate. He was aware of an interplay of tensions about the table but was unable to identify the cause. However, it was enough for him to make up his mind that there was something odd about Ol Njorowa. As he put it to himself, it was 'something phoney'. It was not what was said that drew his attention – it was what was not said. For instance, Brice and Hendriks had not said much about the disappearance of Hank Hendrix.

As Stafford sipped his coffee he had a sudden thought. He could put the picture frame bug to some use – a use that Brice could not have foreseen. He put down his cup, and said, 'Mr Gunnarsson; I'd like to have a few words with you.'

'What about?'

'Well, you know that Stafford Security is broadening its activities. I'd like to discuss a few . . . er . . . ground rules with you.'

Gunnarsson snorted. 'Ground rules!' He smiled grimly. I'm willing to talk, sure.'

'After lunch, in my room?' suggested Stafford.

Gunnarsson drained his coffee cup. 'After lunch is now.'

Stafford said to Brice. 'I hope you'll excuse us. It's not my usual policy to talk business in these circumstances, but since Mr Gunnarsson is here and I have the unexpected opportunity . . .' His voice tailed off.

'Of course,' said Brice. 'One must always take opportunity by the forelock.'

Stafford rose and left the table followed by Gunnarsson. There was a moment's silence before Brice said, 'I'd like to hear that conversation. Let's go.' They both stood up.

At the door Stafford cast a glance backwards. He saw Gunnarsson following and, beyond, Hendriks and Brice were just rising from the table. He smiled slightly as he went up the stairs two at a time towards his room. He went in and stood aside to let Gunnarsson enter, then he closed the door. Gunnarsson swung around. 'Stafford; what are you trying to pull?'

'Sit down,' said Stafford. 'Take the weight off your feet.' He looked thoughtfully at the Shepherd print on the wall and thought he had better give Hendriks and Brice time to get settled in their listening post so he took out a packet of cigarettes. 'Smoke?'

Gunnarsson took a cigarette and Stafford snapped on his lighter. He lit the cigarettes, taking his time, blew out a plume of smoke, and said, 'Is it true what Brice said? That you delivered Henry Hendrix from the States to London?'

Gunnarsson glowered. 'What's it to you?'

'Not a damn thing. But if it is true then you have some explaining to do.' He held up his hand. 'Not to me, but questions will certainly be asked. Dirk Hendriks will probably go to the police and they'll be asking the questions. They'll want to know why you came to Kenya after delivering the heir. You'd better have some good answers. I don't believe the yarn you spun to Brice.'

'I'm not here to talk about me,' said Gunnarsson. 'Wha
about you? What are you doing in Kenya? You were in the
Masai Mara when Hank was kidnapped, and now you're
here. It's too goddamn coincidental.'

'You heard about that downstairs,' said Stafford tiredly
'I'm a family friend of the Hendriks's.' He paused. 'Well, no
really. I'm more of a friend of Alix Hendriks. I might have
married her at one time, and Dirk knows it. I don't think he
likes me much.'

'Is it true his wife named the baby after you?' When
Stafford nodded Gunnarsson said, 'Yeah, I guess he could
be sore about that.' He pulled on his cigarette. 'But you were
at Keekorok at the right time and pulling heroics. And now
someone is trailing me.'

'When did you discover that?'

'Yesterday – about midday at the Lake Naivasha Hotel.'

Stafford spread his hands. 'Then it wasn't me. I was already
here talking to Alan Hunt about a balloon trip. You can go
down and ask him; he's in the dining room.' He flicked ash
into the ashtray. 'I have no interest in you, Gunnarsson
But you must have been doing something for someone to
take notice of you, and it's my guess that it's connected with
your coming to Kenya with young Hendrix.'

'Aw, hell!' said Gunnarsson. 'It's like this. Here's this
young guy still wet behind the ears who's just inherited six
million bucks. He talked to me about it. He was worried
see? Hank wasn't exactly stupid; just inexperienced. He
talked me into coming along as protection.'

'As a bodyguard?'

'Yeah; something like that.'

Stafford laughed. 'Gunnarsson, this is Max Stafford you're
talking to. Better men than you have tried to con me. The
boss of Gunnarsson Associates wouldn't take on that job
himself; you'd assign it to one of your goons. Now let's have
the real story.'

Gunnarsson sighed. 'Okay, why not? The truth is that I
was standing right next to six million bucks and I was trying

248

to figure a way to cut me a slice. I talked Hank into letting me come along with him to Kenya.'

'You were going to con him into something,' said Stafford flatly.

'I guess I was. I just didn't know exactly how. I was trying to work out a scam when he was kidnapped and maybe killed. How do you like that?'

Stafford got up and walked to the window. Gunnarsson sounded properly aggrieved and his story was cleverly near the truth. All that Gunnarsson had left out was that he had substituted Corliss for Hendrix in the United States. Stafford hoped that Brice and Hendriks were absorbing all this.

He looked out over the grounds of Ol Njorowa and stiffened when he saw the sheet of newspaper caught against the acacia on the other side of the fence. Nair had wasted no time in getting the prints developed and that meant they were ready to hold the conference.

He turned and said, 'Well, all this has nothing to do with me.' He picked up his suitcase, put it on the bed, and opened it. He took his toilet kit and began to put away his shaving tackle.

Gunnarsson said, 'What are you doing?'

Stafford zipped the leather case closed and dropped it into his suitcase. 'What does it look as though I'm doing? I'm packing. I came here for the sole reason of having a balloon flight with Alan Hunt. I had the balloon flight this morning so that's it. When I've got this suitcase packed I'll be going down to say goodbye to Brice, Dirk and the Hunts. Then I'm going back to Nairobi. If you want a lift you're welcome.'

'I have my own car.'

Stafford became sarcastic. 'And if you want notice of my further movements I'll be leaving for London on the flight tomorrow morning or the day after, depending on whether I can get a seat. Does that satisfy you?'

Gunnarsson watched him folding a shirt. 'Why should you want to satisfy me?'

'I wouldn't know,' said Stafford. 'But this was intended

to be a holiday, the first I've had for three years, and it hasn't really turned out that way. I became involved, quite accidentally, in the kidnapping of a group of tourists, and since then everyone has been questioning my motives. Even Charles Brice has been asking pointed questions. Well, I've had enough. I'm going home.' He opened drawers to make sure he had packed everything, then closed his suitcase hoping that Brice was taking it all in.

He said, 'Gunnarsson; what do you think happened to young Henry Hendrix? You were there.'

'I don't know what to think. How about you?'

'I think the group was kidnapped by Tanzanians. It's happened before. I think Hendrix was killed, probably accidentally, and buried. Probably not even buried – the scavengers would take care of him. And I think you're wasting your time, Gunnarsson. You've lost out on your con game. Why don't you go home as I'm doing?'

Gunnarsson regarded Stafford sardonically. 'It'll be a long, long day before I take advice from you. There's something goddamn phoney going on here, and if you can't see it then I can. I'm sticking around to do some probing.'

Stafford shrugged and picked up his case. 'Suit yourself.' He walked to the door. 'I suppose we'll meet again, probably in New York. Brace yourself for a fight.'

'I fight rough,' warned Gunnarsson.

'I don't mind that.' Stafford stood at the door, his hand on the handle. 'Are you coming down or do you think you've inherited this bedroom?'

'Go to hell!' said Gunnarsson, but he stood up and followed Stafford down the stairs. On the ground floor they parted, Gunnarsson going back into the dining room and Stafford to the Nissan to deposit his suitcase. As he walked back to the entrance of the Admin Block he was well satisfied. The conversation he had had with Gunnarsson had been really aimed at Brice and Hendriks and he hoped the picture frame bug had been in working condition.

On his return to the dining room he saw Brice and Hendriks at their table talking to Gunnarsson. As he sat down Brice said, 'Mr Gunnarsson tells us you're leaving.'

'That's right. I'm here to say goodbye and to thank you for your hospitality.' Stafford looked at Hendriks. 'Sorry about your cousin, Dirk. Keep in touch and let me know what happens. I might be moving around when I get home but letters addressed to the office will find me.'

'I'll do that.'

Brice said, 'Did you and Mr Gunnarsson resolve your differences? I hope so.'

Stafford laughed. 'We have no differences – not here.' A waiter put down a cup before him and filled it with coffee. 'Those will begin in New York.' Gunnarsson snorted, and Stafford said evenly, 'That's why I told Dirk I'd be moving around.'

'You think you can muscle in while I'm away?' Gunnarsson chuckled. 'Not a chance, buster.'

Stafford drank his coffee, then turned to Brice and held out his hand. 'Nice to have known you, Mr Brice – Charles. I hope your plans for Ol Njorowa turn out well.' They shook hands and Stafford got up and went around the table. He clapped Hendriks on the shoulder. 'When do you expect to be back in London, Dirk?'

'I don't know. I seem to have my hands full here.'

'You don't mind if I pop in to see Alix and my godson, do you?'

'Of course not. She'll be glad to see you.'

Stafford looked across the room. 'I'd better catch Alan Hunt before he leaves. Goodbye, and thanks for everything.'

With a wave he went striding across the room to intercept Hunt at the doorway of the dining room. 'Alan, I'm going now. Thanks for the balloon flight.'

'I only did it for the champagne,' said Hunt with a grin.

Stafford put a hand on Hunt's elbow and steered him towards the entrance hall. 'I'd like to have a word with you. You were born in Kenya, weren't you?'

'That's right.'

'So it's your native country. What do you think of the way it's run.'

'On the whole not bad. The government makes mistakes, but what government doesn't.' Hunt frowned. 'What are you getting at, Max?'

They walked down the steps into the sunlight and towards Stafford's Nissan. He said, 'Would you consider yourself a patriot?'

'That's a hell of a question,' said Hunt. 'You mean dying for my country and all that?'

'I'd rather you lived for it,' said Stafford. 'Look, Alan; a problem has come up. Do you know where Safariland is?'

'Of course.'

Stafford checked the time. 'Could you meet me there in half an hour. There's a few people I want you to meet.'

'I suppose so,' said Hunt uncertainly. 'What's this all about?'

'You'll be told when you get there.' Stafford opened the door of the Nissan and got in. 'I'd rather you didn't tell anyone where you were going. Maybe you'd better invent a shopping errand in Naivasha.'

Hunt smiled faintly. 'It sounds very mysterious – but all right.'

'I'll see you there.' Stafford reversed out of the parking slot, waved, and drove towards the gates of Ol Njorowa very slowly because of the sleeping policemen. He looked in the mirror and saw Brice walking from the Admin Block to meet Hunt. He hoped Hunt had sense enough to keep his mouth shut as he had been told.

26

Stafford had expected to see Hardin at Safariland but instead he was met by Curtis who walked forward as the Nissan drew to a halt. He got out, and said, 'Good afternoon, Sergeant. Where is everyone? What's the drill?'

Curtis said, 'Colonel Chipende thought it advisable to hold the meeting on Crescent Island. That's an island in the lake, sir. If the Colonel will follow me I have a boat ready.'

Stafford smiled. Now that Chipende was revealed, Curtis was giving him full military honours. He said mildly, 'I think we'll still call him Chip, Sergeant.' He looked at his watch. 'We can't go yet. I'm expecting someone else. Perhaps fifteen minutes.'

So they waited and presently Hunt arrived and, somewhat to Stafford's consternation, he had brought Judy. They got out of the car and Stafford said, 'I told you not to tell anyone else.'

Hunt gave a lop-sided grin. 'I wanted a witness.'

'And I'm a patriot, too,' added Judy. 'What's going on, Max? It's all very mysterious.'

Stafford stood undecided for a moment then he shrugged. 'Very well. You might as well come along.'

'That's not very gracious,' she said.

'It wasn't intended to be,' he snapped, and turned to Curtis. 'Carry on.'

Curtis led the way to the edge of the lake where there was a rough timbered jetty alongside which was moored an open boat with a black Kenyan sitting in the stern. They got in and the Kenyan started the outboard engine and soon they were cruising at a respectable speed towards an island which lay about a mile offshore. 'Why are we going to Crescent Island?' asked Judy.

'I don't know, but we'll soon find out,' said Stafford. He nudged Curtis. 'Who's there?'

'Col . . .' Curtis swallowed and began again. 'Chip and Nair, and Mr Hardin. And there's another man. I don't know who he is.'

Stafford grunted and wondered about that but did not let it worry him. The time to worry was when he thought it might cause trouble. Hunt said, 'Do you mean Nair Singh?'

'Yes,' said Stafford shortly, and watched the island ahead.

At last they drew alongside the rocky foreshore and were able to land. Chip came down to meet them. He looked at the Hunts and frowned, then said to Stafford, 'Could I have a word with you?' Stafford nodded and they walked out of earshot. 'I don't think this is a good thing, Max. Why did you bring them?'

'I didn't bring *them*,' said Stafford irritably. 'I wanted Hunt along; his sister came without invitation.'

'But why even Hunt?'

'We've got to have someone on the inside and I elected Hunt,' said Stafford. 'I have my reasons and I'll justify them. Curtis tells me you've brought along your own surprise.'

Chip nodded. 'You'll forgive me if I don't introduce him. He's here . . . er . . . incognito.'

'One of your bosses?'

Chip smiled. 'Could very well be.'

'So that's why we're here on an island,' said Stafford. 'All right; let's get on with it. We have a lot to discuss.'

Chip hesitated, then nodded. 'All right; let's go.'

Stafford jerked his head at Curtis and the Hunts and they all followed Chip up a slope which led down to the beach, walking among trees. Once Stafford was alarmed as a big animal broke away from quite close and he saw a white-ringed rump as it plunged away from them. 'Waterbuck,' said Curtis dispassionately.

'They do very well here,' said Chip. 'They swim across from the mainland. The big cats don't like water very much, at least not to the extent of swimming a mile, so the water-buck are safe from predators.' Stafford thought with some humour that even now Chip could not resist acting the courier, but became alert when Chip said, 'Watch out for snakes.'

They pressed on and eventually came to a piece of level ground on which were the foundations of a building. Whether the building had fallen down or whether the builder had just got as far as putting in the foundations Stafford could not decide. Here, waiting for them, were the others – Nair, Hardin and a stranger. He was an elderly black Kenyan with greying hair and an expressionless face. Chip went over to him and talked in low tones.

Stafford walked over to Hardin. 'Hello, Ben. Who's the old man there?'

'He doesn't say – neither does Chip. I'd say he's top brass. He doesn't talk so you'd notice.'

'He's come to assess the evidence,' said Stafford. 'I have some to give him.'

Chip stepped forward and said to the Hunts, 'I think we ought to introduce ourselves. I'm Pete Chipende, but call me Chip. This is . . .'

'No!' said Stafford sharply. 'Let's not pussyfoot around.' He looked at Alan Hunt. 'This is Colonel Peter Chipende of the Kenyan Army.' There was a flash in Chip's eyes which he ignored. 'You already know Nair but you don't know his rank and neither do I.'

Nair stepped forward. 'Captain Nair Singh, at your service.'

Hunt raised his eyebrows. 'I didn't know you were in the army, Nair.'

'You still don't know,' said Chip flatly. 'This conversation isn't happening. Understand?'

Stafford said, 'Ben Hardin you've already met, and this is Curtis. That gentleman over there I don't know, and I don't think I want to know. Chip is right. What you learn here you keep under your hats.'

Judy laughed nervously. 'All very portentous.'

'Yes,' said Hunt. 'Very cloak and dagger. What's it all about?'

'Tell him, Chip,' said Stafford.

Chip said, 'We have reason to believe that Ol Njorowa is not as it seems, that it is an illicit base in Kenya for a foreign power -- a centre for espionage.'

'You're crazy,' said Hunt.

'Alan, you haven't heard the evidence. Wait for it.' Stafford turned to Nair. 'Have you got the photographs?' Nair gave them to him and he said, 'You produced these damned quickly.'

'My brother-in-law is a photographer. He did them.'

Stafford grimaced. 'That joke is becoming pretty thin, Nair.'

'But it's true,' protested Nair. 'My brother-in-law really is a professional photographer in Naivasha. He says because he did them so quickly they won't last; the colours will fade. He's doing a more permanent set now.'

Stafford flipped through them. 'These will do for now.' He sat on the edge of the crumbling concrete foundation and began to lay them out. As he did so he said, 'Has anything happened I ought to know about, Chip?'

'Not much, except that someone was inquiring about Gunnarsson at the New Stanley. He wasn't there, of course; he was already in the hotel here.'

'Who was being inquisitive?'

'We don't know yet. It's being followed up.'

Stafford had got the photographs spread out. 'Right. These are pictures taken of Ol Njorowa during an overflight in Alan's balloon this morning. Anyone got any comments?'

He drew back to let the others inspect them. They crowded around except for the elderly Kenyan who had seated himself on a nearby rock and was placidly smoking a pipe. There was silence for a while then Hardin said, 'Yeah; this tower here. What is it?'

'That's the water tower,' said Hunt. 'The water is pumped up there and then distributed by gravity.'

Curtis coughed. 'Perhaps I could point out to the Colonel that the water tower is in the wrong place.'

'Why, Sergeant?'

'The natural place to build a water tower would be on the highest point of land.' Curtis pointed at another photograph. 'Which would be about there.'

Hunt looked at Stafford curiously. 'Are you a colonel, too?'

'I'm trying to retire but Sergeant Curtis won't let me,' said Stafford dryly. 'All right, a water tower in the wrong place.'

Hardin picked up the photograph. 'It's close to the perimeter fence where it angles. I'd say it's an observation tower. From the top you could cover a hell of a lot of that fence. Good place to put a couple of TV cameras.'

Chip said, 'What about at night? Is the fence illuminated?'

'No; I checked,' said Stafford.

'Could be infra-red,' said Nair. 'You couldn't see that.'

'No infra-red. You're behind the times, Nair. *If* there is TV coverage of the fence they'd probably use photo-multipliers – the things they use as night sights in the army. Even on a moonless, cloudy night you get a pretty good picture.'

'Are you serious about this?' demanded Hunt.

'Very.' Stafford waved his hands over the photographs. 'Anything else?'

'Yeah,' said Hardin. 'But it doesn't show in these pictures.' He turned to Hunt. 'You said a leopard was getting over the fence and that's why there was an armed guard. Right?'

Hunt nodded. 'Brice had a patrol out. He reckoned the leopard was getting over by climbing a tree which was too near the fence.'

'Yeah, that's what you said.' Hardin jerked his head at Curtis. 'Tell him, Sergeant.'

'Acting on instructions of the Colonel I did a tour of the perimeter from the outside. The vegetation has been cut back on the outside of the fence to a distance of at least thirty feet. There is no tree near the fence. I found evidence of weed killer; there was an empty paper sack. I didn't remove it but I made a note of what it was.' He took a piece of paper and gave it to Stafford.

'Pretty powerful stuff,' said Hardin, looking over Stafford's shoulder. 'It's the defoliant we used in Vietnam, and it's now illegal for commercial use. It looks as though someone wants a clear view along the fence.'

'How long is the fence?' asked Stafford.

'About six and a half miles, sir,' said Curtis.

'A ten foot chain-link fence six and a half miles long,' commented Stafford. 'That's pretty much security overkill for an innocent agricultural college short of funds, wouldn't you say, Alan?'

'I hadn't really thought of it in that light,' said Hunt. 'It was already there when I came to Ol Njorowa.' He shook his head. 'And I hadn't noticed the cleared strip on the outside.'

Chip picked up a photograph. 'This interests me.'

'It interests me, too,' said Stafford. 'In fact, it's the key to the whole bloody situation. What about it, Alan?'

Hunt took the photograph. 'Oh, that's the animal movement laboratory. I don't know much about it. I've never been inside.'

'Tell Chip about the pretty wildebeest,' said Stafford ironically.

Hunt retailed all he knew about the work done there on patterns of animal migration. He shrugged. 'I don't know much more; it's not my field. In any case it's not really a part of the College; we just give them house room.'

'I've been all over Ol Njorowa,' said Stafford. 'I've been given the grand tour; I've been everywhere except inside that so-called laboratory. Alan has been at Ol Njorowa for two years and he hasn't been inside.'

'Well, it's not used all the year round,' said Hunt. 'And the wildebeest migration doesn't begin for another six weeks.'

Judy said, 'We don't see much of those people, anyway. They're not good mixers.'

'So Alan remarked before.' Stafford looked at the sky and said dreamily, 'Up there, a little over 22,000 miles high, is an American satellite for extended weather research, a laudable project and no doubt quite genuine. But it contains equipment used by these people at Ol Njorowa. It occurred to me that a signal sent from that dish antenna to the satellite could be relayed and picked up in, say, Pretoria which is about 25 degrees south. Or possibly somewhere in the Northern Transvaal such as Messina or Louis Trichardt which are about 22 to 23 degrees south.' He smiled. 'I've been looking at maps.'

Hunt said, 'This is all sheer supposition. You talk of TV cameras on the water tower, but you don't know they're there. And all this waffle about signalling to Pretoria is just sheer guff in my opinion. If this is what you've brought me to hear you're wasting my time.'

'Alan,' said Stafford gently. 'Does a respectable establishment bug the guest bedrooms?'

'You're sure of that?' said Chip sharply.

'Dead sure. Microphone and radio transmitter disguised as a picture of an elephant.' He described what he had found.

Chip blew out his cheeks in a sigh of relief. 'Thank God!' he said. 'It's the first firm evidence we've had.'

'That's what I thought,' said Stafford. He recounted the events of the day in detail, then said, 'I manoeuvred Gunnarsson into a private conversation in the bedroom because I was pretty sure that Brice would be listening. All the time I talked to Gunnarsson I was really addressing Brice.' He grinned. 'I needled Gunnarsson into saying that he's going to stick around to investigate Ol Njorowa because he thinks it's a phoney set-up.'

'He always was a sharp operator,' said Hardin soberly. 'I'll give him that. He doesn't have cotton wadding between his ears.'

'Yes, but Brice will have heard him saying it.' Stafford laughed. 'It will be interesting to see what happens now.'

Hunt looked at his sister. 'What do you think?'

'Until Max told about the picture in his room I wasn't convinced,' she said. 'But he's really getting to me now.'

'Have you seen the TV camera in the entrance hall of the Admin Block?' asked Stafford helpfully.

Hunt looked startled. 'No, I haven't.'

'That's not surprising; it's hard to spot unless you know what you're looking for. As you face the counter it's behind and to your left in the top corner. Now, don't go staring at it, for God's sake! Just do an unobtrusive check.'

Hunt shook his head in bewilderment. 'You know, last year Brice showed me a couple of papers in a journal about the work done by the animal migration lab. From what I could see it was really good stuff.'

'No doubt it was. The best cover is always genuine.' Stafford turned to Chip. 'When I was talking to Gunnarsson I indicated I was leaving Kenya and going back to London. Brice might believe it or he might not. Can you do anything to support that story?'

Chip thought about it. 'We don't know yet how big an organization Brice has built up, or how far we've been penetrated. I'll have someone book air tickets in the names of you and Curtis. Let me have your passport numbers, and the records will show that you left tomorrow morning. In the meantime you'll have to go to ground.'

'Why not here?' said Nair. 'Here on Crescent Island. It's close to Ol Njorowa and it's quiet. We can bring a tent and sleeping bags and anything else you might need.'

'We'll need a boat,' said Stafford.

Curtis leaned forward and said in a low voice, 'The Colonel might like to know there's someone coming.'

'Where?'

'Up the slope from the water and moving quietly.'

Chip had caught it. He signalled to Nair and they both headed down the slope, angling in different directions. They disappeared and, for a while, nothing happened. Then they came back, strolling casually, and Chip was tearing open an envelope. 'It's all right; just someone bringing me a message.' He took a sheet of paper from the envelope and scanned it. 'The man who was asking for Gunnarsson at the New Stanley. He's been traced back to Ol Njorowa; his name is Patterson.'

Stafford wrinkled his brow. 'That name rings a faint bell.'

Hunt said, 'He's one of the animal migration team. I suppose that does it.'

'Wasn't he the man with Brice when I met him for the first time at the Lake Naivasha Hotel?'

'Yes,' said Judy. 'Alan, I think Max has proved his point.' She looked directly at Stafford. 'What do you want us to do?'

'Chip's the boss,' said Stafford.

'Not really,' said Chip, and nodded his head towards the grey-haired Kenyan who was knocking out his pipe on the rock he sat on. Stafford had glanced at him from time to time during the conference. His face had remained blandly blank but he had obviously listened to every word. Chip said, 'I'll have to have a private talk first.' He walked to one side and the elderly man put away his pipe and followed him.

Curtis said to Nair, 'If we're staying on this island we'll need essential supplies. Beer.'

Stafford smiled, and Hardin said, 'What do I do?'

'That depends upon what Chip wants to do, and that depends upon the decision of Mr Anonymous over there. Or he could be General Anonymous, since this seems to be an army operation. We'll have to wait and see.'

'You know,' said Hunt. 'I can't believe this is happening.'

'You don't know the whole story yet,' said Stafford. 'You'd find that even more incredible.' He turned to Hardin. 'It seems that Gunnarsson is not involved with Brice or Hendriks. He had a ploy of his own which he'd probably call a scam.'

'Ripping off the Hendrykxx estate with Corliss,' agreed Hardin.

Stafford laughed. 'You started all this, Ben. Did you imagine, back in Los Angeles, that you would uncover an international espionage plot in the middle of Africa? It's only because we were suspicious of Gunnarsson that we got wind of it. You know, it puzzled me a long time. I was trying to fit pieces into a jig-saw and only now have I realized there were *two* jig-saw puzzles – one around Gunnarsson and the other around Ol Njorowa.'

Judy said, 'So what happens now?'

'I suspect we fall into the hands of politicians,' said Stafford. He jerked his head. 'That pair over there are, I think, simple-minded military men. If they have their way they'll climb in to Ol Njorowa and disinfect it. The direct way. The politicians might have other ideas.'

Hunt said, 'Curtis refers to you as the Colonel. Are you still active, and in what capacity?'

'God, no! I got out ten years ago.' Stafford sat up. 'I was in Military Intelligence and I became tired of my work being either ignored or being buggered about by politicos who don't know which end is up. So I quit and started my own civilian and commercial organization. I resigned from *Weltpolitik.*' He paused. 'Until now.'

Hardin lifted his head. 'Chip's coming back.'

Stafford heard the crunch of Chip's footsteps. He raised his head and said, 'What's the verdict?' His eyes slid sideways and he watched the grey-haired Mr Anonymous walk down the slope and out of sight among the trees.

Chip said, 'We wait awhile.'

'I might have guessed it,' said Stafford. He shrugged elaborately as though to make his point with Alan Hunt.

Hunt said, 'What about us?' He indicated his sister.

'You just carry on normally,' said Chip. 'If we need you we'll get word to you. But until then you don't, by any action or quiver of a muscle, give any indication that anything is out of the ordinary.'

Hardin said, 'And me? What do I do?'

Chip blew out his cheeks. 'I suppose you come under Mr Stafford. I recommend that you stay here – on Crescent Island.'

Hardin nudged Nair. 'That means more beer.'

Stafford said, a little bitterly, 'Chip, you've talked to that mate of yours. I suppose he was a high-ranking officer. Am I to take it that he's going for instructions?'

Chip shook his head sadly. 'You know how it is, Max. Wheels within wheels. Everyone has someone on his neck. Any action on this has to be taken on instruction from the top. We're talking about international stuff now – a clash of nations.'

Stafford sighed. He leaned back so that he lay flat, and put his hands over his eyes to shade them from the sun. 'Then get on with your bloody clash of nations.'

27

Brice stood looking out of his window over the grounds of Ol Njorowa. His brow was furrowed as he swung to face Hendriks. 'First Stafford, and now Gunnarsson. You heard them. They're on to us.'

'Not Max,' said Hendriks. 'He's going home.'

'All right. But Gunnarsson suspects something. Who is he?'

'You know as much as I do,' said Hendriks. 'He's boss of the American agency which found Henry Hendrix in California. You heard what he said to Stafford. He tried to cut himself a slice but he failed when he lost Hendrix. He's a bloody crook if you ask me.'

'I don't need to ask you,' said Brice acidly. 'It's self-evident.'

Hendriks held up a finger. 'One thing seems clear,' he said. 'Cousin Henry really must be dead. Stafford certainly thinks so.'

'That doesn't do us much good if there's no body.' Brice sat behind his desk. 'And you heard Gunnarsson. He says he's staying around to investigate.'

'So what is there to investigate?' asked Hendriks. 'He's not interested in us. All he wants is to find Henry – which he won't. After a while he'll get tired of it and go home like Max. There's nothing for him to find, not now.'

'Perhaps, but we'll keep an eye on him.'

'Do that,' said Hendriks. He stood up and walked to the door. 'If you want me I'll be in my room.'

He left Brice and went upstairs. In his room he lay on the bed and lit a cigarette, and his thoughts went back over the years to the time it had all started.

He supposed it began when he was recruited to the National Intelligence Service. Of course in those days it was called the

Bureau for State Security. Joel Mervis, the then editor of the Johannesburg *Sunday Times*, had consistently replaced 'for' with 'of' which resulted in the acronym BOSS. A cheap trick but it worked and was adopted by newspapers all over the world. Hendriks reflected how oddly insensitive his fellow countrymen were in matters of this nature. It took them a long time to get the point and then the name was changed to the Department of National Security which made the acronym DONS. Even that was received with some hilarity and another change was made to the National Intelligence Service. Nothing much could be made of NIS.

He was thoroughly trained and began his fieldwork, working mostly in Rhodesia at that time. South Africa was desperately trying to buttress the Smith government but, of course, that came to nothing in the end. The death of Salazar in faraway Portugal sent a whole row of dominoes toppling. An anti-colonial regime in Portugal meant the loss of Angola and then Mozambique; the enemy was on the frontier and Rhodesia could not be saved. Now the Cubans were in Angola and South West Africa was threatened. It was a bleak outlook.

But that was now. In the days when it seemed that Rhodesia could be saved for white civilization Hendriks had enjoyed his work until he stopped a bullet fired not by a black guerilla but, ironically, by a trigger-happy white farmer. He was pulled back to South Africa, hospitalized, and then given a month's leave.

Time hung heavily on his hands and he sought for something to do. He was normally a mentally and physically active man and not for him the lounging on the beach at Clifton or Durban broiling his brains under the sun. His thoughts went back to his grandmother whom he dimly remembered – and to his grandfather who was thought to have been killed in the Red Revolt of Johannesburg in 1922. But there had been no body and Hendriks wondered. Using the techniques he had been taught and the authority he had acquired he began an investigation, an intelligence man's way of passing the time and searching the family tree. It paid off. He found from old port records that Jan-Willem Hendrykxx had sailed from Cape Town for San Francisco on March 25, 1922, a week after the revolt had been crushed by General Smuts. And that was as far as he got by the end of his leave.

He did not go back to Rhodesia but, instead, was posted to England. 'Go to the Embassy once,' he was told. 'You'd be expected to do that. But don't go near it again. They'll give you instructions on cut-outs and so on.'

So Hendriks went to London where his main task was to keep track of the movements of those exiled members of the African National Congress then living in England, and to record whom they met and talked with. He also kept a check on certain members of the staffs of other Embassies in London as and when he was told.

Intelligence outfits have their own way of doing things. The governments of two countries may be publicly cold towards each other while their respective intelligence agencies can be quite fraternal. So it was with South Africa and the United States – BOSS and the CIA. One day Hendriks passed a message through his cut-out; Could someone, as a favour, find out what happened to Jan-Willem Hendrykxx who had arrived in San Francisco in 1922? A personal matter, so no hurry.

Two months later he had an answer which surprised him. Apparently his grandfather could out-grandfather the Mafia. He had been deported from the United States in 1940. Hendriks, out of curiosity, took a week's holiday which he spent in Brussels. Discreet enquiries found his grandfather hale and well. Hendriks went nowhere near the old man, but he did go to the South African Embassy in Brussels where he had a chat with a man. Three months later he wrote a very detailed report which he sent to Pretoria and was promptly pulled back to South Africa.

* * *

266

Hendriks's immediate superior was a Colonel Malan, a heavily built Afrikaner with a square face and cold eyes. He opened a file on his desk and took out Hendriks's report. 'This is an odd suggestion you've come up with.' The report plopped on the desk. 'How good is your evidence on this Belgian, Hendrykxx?'

'Solid. He's the head of a heroin-smuggling ring operating from Antwerp, and we have enough on him to send him to jail for the rest of his life. On the other hand, if he comes in with us he lives the rest of his life in luxury.' Hendriks smiled. 'What would you do, sir?'

'I'm not your grandfather,' growled Malan. He leafed through the report. 'You come from an interesting family. Now, you want us to give the old man a hell of a lot of money tied up in a way he can't touch it, and he makes out a will so that the money goes where we want it when he dies. Is that it?'

'Yes, sir.'

'Where would you send the money?'

'Kenya,' said Hendriks unhesitatingly. 'We need strengthening in East Africa.'

'Yes,' said Malan reflectively. 'Kenyatta has been crucifying us in the United Nations lately.' He leaned back in his chair. 'And we have an interesting proposition put to us by Frans Potgeiter but we're running into trouble on the funding. Do you know Potgeiter?'

'Yes, sir.'

'Could you work with him?'

'Yes, sir.'

Malan leaned forward and tapped the report. 'Your grandfather is old, but not dead old. He could live another twenty years and we can't have that.'

'I doubt if he will.' Hendriks took an envelope from his breast pocket and pushed it across the desk. 'Hendrykxx's medical report. I got hold of it the day before I left London. He has a bad heart.'

'And how did you get hold of it?'

Hendriks smiled. 'It seems that someone burgled the offices of Hendrykxx's doctor. Looking for drugs, the Belgian police say. They did a lot of vandalism; you know how burglars are when they're hopped up, sir.'

Malan grunted, his head down as he scanned the medical documents. He tossed them aside. 'Looks all right, but I'll have a doctor go over them. The Brussels Embassy wasn't involved, I hope.'

'No, sir.'

'This will have to be gone into carefully, Hendriks. The Department of Finance will have to come into it, of course. And the will – that must be carefully drawn. We have a barrister in London who can help us there. I rather think I'd like to move Hendrykxx out of reach of his friends and where we can keep an eye on him. That is, if this goes through. I can't authorize it, so it will have to go upstairs.' He smiled genially. 'You're a *slim kerel*, Hendriks,' he said approvingly.

'Thank you, sir.' Hendriks hesitated. 'If Hendrykxx doesn't die in time he could always . . . er . . . be helped.'

Malan's eyes went flinty. 'What kind of a man are you?' he whispered. 'What kind of man would suggest the killing of his own grandfather? We'll have no more of that kind of talk.'

* * *

The operation was approved at top level and that was in the days when the South African intelligence and propaganda agencies were riding high. There was money available, and more if needed. Hendrykxx had his arm duly twisted and caved in when offered the choice. He was removed from Belgium and installed in a house in Jersey under the supervision of Mr and Mrs Adams, his warders in a most luxurious jail. Jersey had been chosen because of its lack of death duties and the general low tax rate; not that much tax was paid – when a government goes into the tax avoidance business it takes the advice of the real experts. £15M was injected into the scheme which, at the time of Hendrykxx's death, had magically turned into £40M. It is surprising what compound interest can do to a sum which has proper management and is left to increase and multiply.

Frans Potgeiter went under cover and surfaced as Brice, the liberal Rhodesian, the real Brice having conveniently been killed in a motor accident while trying to do the Johannesburg–Durban run in under five hours. He went to England to establish a reputation, and then moved to Kenya to manage the Ol Njorowa Foundation. Hendriks returned to his undercover post in London.

All was going well when came the débâcle of Muldergate in 1978 and gone were the days of unlimited funds. One by one the stories leaked out; the setting up of the newspaper, *The Citizen*, with government funds, the attempted purchase of an American newspaper, the bribery of American politicians, the activities of the Group of Ten. All the peccadilloes were revealed.

In 1979 Connie Mulder, the Minister of Information, was forced to resign from the Cabinet, then from Parliament, then from the party itself. Dr Eschel Rhoodie, the Information Secretary, took refuge in Switzerland, and appeared on television threatening to blow the gaff. Mulder did blow the gaff – he named Vorster, once Prime Minister and then President of the Republic of South Africa, as being privy to the illegal shenanigans. Vorster denied it.

The Erasmus Judicial Commission of Enquiry sat, considered the evidence, and issued its report. It condemned Vorster as 'having full knowledge of the irregularities.' John Balthazar Vorster resigned from the State Presidency. It was a mess.

Hendriks, in London, read the daily newspaper reports with horrified eyes, expecting any day that the Hendrykxx affair and the Ol Njorowa Foundation would be blown. But someone in Pretoria must have done some fast and fancy footwork, scurrying to seal the leaks. It was not Colonel Malan because he was swept away in the general torrent of accusations and resigned his commission.

Hendriks had worried about his uncle Adriaan whom, of

course, he had never met, and his particular worry revolved about the possibility of Adriaan fathering legitimate off-spring. An inquiry was put in motion and thus he discovered Henry Hendrix, then in his last year in high school. Hendriks wanted, as he put it, 'to do something about it,' a euphemism which Malan burked at. 'No,' Malan had argued. 'I won't have it. We'll do it some other way when the need arises.'

But after Muldergate, when Malan was gone and Hendriks wanted to 'do something', Henry Hendrix had dropped out of sight, an indistinguishable speck of dross in the melting pot of 220 million Americans. From London Hendriks had tried to rouse Pretoria to action but the recent brouhaha of Muldergate had had a chilling effect on the feet and nothing was done.

It was only when Alix became pregnant and it was neces-sary that Hendrykxx should go that Pretoria took action, half-heartedly and too late. Hendrykxx had left £20,000 in his will to his jailers, Mr and Mrs Adams. Mandeville had insisted upon that, saying that the will had to look good. They responded by killing him, a not too difficult task con-sidering he was senile and expected to die any moment, even though he was inconsiderately hanging on to life tenaciously.

Pretoria bungled in Los Angeles and Hendrix got away. He had survived the car crash in Cornwall, too, by something of a miracle, but now Potgeiter had finally solved the prob-lem in a somewhat clumsy way. Or had he?

Hendriks was roused from his reverie by the ringing of the telephone next to his bed. It was Potgeiter. 'Get down here. Gunnarsson has gone on the run. I've sent Patterson after him.'

28

Stafford thought the lake flies constituted the worst hazard of Crescent Island until he nearly broke his neck.

Chip, Nair and the Hunts had departed; the Hunts back to Ol Njorowa, Chip to Nairobi, and Nair to Naivasha to round up supplies. Nair came back in the late afternoon in a boat loaded with provisions and camping gear. They helped him get it ashore, then he said, 'We'll camp on the other side of the island where lights can't be seen from the mainland.'

'Are you staying with us?' asked Stafford in surprise.

Nair nodded without saying anything and Hardin snorted. 'I guess Chip thinks we want our hands held.'

Stafford had a different notion; he thought Nair was there to keep an eye on them. The mystery of Ol Njorowa had almost been solved and all that remained was to bust up the South African operation. But Chip, and possibly others, did not want premature activity and Nair was there to see that Stafford's party stayed put.

They lugged the supplies to the other side of the island, a matter of half a mile, and then made camp. Nair was meticulous about the setting up of the mosquito nets which were hung on wire frames over the sleeping bags, and fiddled for a long time in a finicky manner until he was sure he had got it right. 'Get much malaria around here?' asked Hardin.

'Not here.' Nair looked up. 'Lot of lake flies, though.' He did not elaborate.

Curtis put a burner on to a small cylinder of propane and began to open cans. In a very short while he had prepared a meal, and they began to eat just as the sun was setting over the Mau Escarpment. Over coffee Nair said, 'It's time for bed.'

'So early?' queried Hardin. 'It's just after six.'

'Please yourself,' said Nair. 'But the wind changes at nightfall and brings the lake flies. You'll be glad to be under cover.'

Stafford found what he meant five minutes later when he began to swat at himself viciously. By the time he had got into the sleeping bag and under the safety of the mosquito netting he felt the skin of his arms and ankles coming out in bumps which itched ferociously. Also he found that he had admitted several undesirable residents to share his bed and it was some time before he was sure he had killed the last of them.

Curtis was silent as usual, but from Hardin's direction came a continual muffled cursing. 'Goddammit, Nair!' he yelled. 'You sure these things aren't mosquitoes?'

'Just flies,' said Nair soothingly. 'They won't hurt you; they don't transmit disease.'

'Maybe not; but they're eating me alive. I'll be a picked-over skeleton tomorrow.'

'They're an aviation hazard,' said Nair in a conversational voice. 'Especially over Lake Victoria. They block air filters and Pitot tubes. There have been a few crashes because of them, but they've never been known to eat anybody.'

Stafford lit a cigarette and stared at the sky through the diaphanous and almost invisible netting. There were no clouds and the sky was full of the diamond brilliance of stars, growing brighter as the light ebbed in the west. 'Nair?'

'Yes, Max?'

'Did Chip say anything before he went to Nairobi?'

'About what?'

'You bloody well know about what,' said Stafford without heat.

There was a brief silence. 'I'm not a high ranking officer,' said Nair, almost apologetically. 'I don't get to know everything.'

'They can't stop you thinking. You're no fool, Nair; what do you *think* will happen?'

Again there was silence from Nair. Presently he said, 'This is a big thing, Max. There'll be a lot of talk among the people at the top; they'll argue about the best thing to do. You know how it is in intelligence work.'

Stafford knew. There were a number of options open to the Kenyans which he ticked off in his mind. They could go for a propaganda victory – smash into Ol Njorowa with full publicity, including TV cameras on hand and hard words in the United Nations. Or they could snap up Brice and Hendriks unobtrusively and close down their illicit operation without fanfare. The South Africans would know about it, of course, but there would not be a damned thing they could do. That would give the Kenyans a diplomatic ace up the sleeve, a *quid pro quo* for any concession they might want to wring out of the South Africans – do this for us or we blow the gaff publicly on your illegalities. Stafford doubted if the South Africans would respond to that kind of blackmail.

There was a third option – to do nothing. To put a fine meshed net around Ol Njorowa, to keep Brice, Hendriks and the animal migration team under surveillance and, possibly, feed them false information. That would be the more subtle approach he himself would favour, but he did not give the average politician many marks for subtlety. The average politician's time-horizon was limited and most would go for the short term solution. Had not Harold Wilson said that a week in politics was a long time?

And so there would be a lot of talk in Nairobi that night as factions in the government pushed their points of view. He hoped that Chip and Mr Anonymous had the sense to restrict their new found knowledge of Ol Njorowa to a select few.

He stirred. 'Nair – the men who kidnapped the tour group – do you think they were Tanzanians?'

'In the circumstances I doubt it.'

Stafford leaned up on one elbow. 'Kenyans?'

'Perhaps.'

'But how would Brice recruit them?'

'Some men will do much for money.'

'Even kill, as they were going to kill Corliss?'

'Even that.' Nair paused. 'They could, of course, have been South African blacks.'

Stafford had not thought of that. 'Could a South African

273

black pass himself off as a Kenyan? Could he get away with it?'

Nair said dryly, 'Just as easily as a Russian called Konon Molody could pass himself as a Canadian called Gordon Lonsdale. All it needs is training.'

Stafford mulled it over in his mind. 'But I can't understand why blacks would work for the white South Africans in the first place. Why should they defend white supremacy?'

'The South African army is full of blacks,' said Nair. 'Didn't you know? A lot are in the army for the pay. Some have other reasons – learning to use modern weaponry, for instance. But in the end it all comes down to the simple fact that if a man has a set of views it's always possible to find another man with the opposite set of views.'

'I suppose so,' said Stafford, but he was not convinced.

'The white man finds it difficult to understand how the mind of the black man works,' said Nair. There was a smile in his voice as he added, 'Not to mention the mind of the Indian. Even the white South Africans, who ought to know better, make mistakes about that.'

'Such as?'

'To begin with, the countries of Africa are artificial creations of the white man. The black does not really understand the nation state; his loyalties are to the tribe.'

'Yes,' said Stafford thoughtfully. 'Chip was saying something about that.'

'All right,' said Nair. 'Take Zimbabwe, which used to be Southern Rhodesia, an artificial entity. They had an election to see who'd come out on top, Nkomo, Mugabe or Bishop Muzorewa who ran the caretaker government. No one gave much chance to Muzorewa. The odds-on favourite was Nkomo and Mugabe was expected to come a bad second. Even the South Africans, who ought to have known better, laid their bets that way.'

'Why ought they to have known better?'

'They've been in Africa long enough. You see, there are two main tribes in Zimbabwe, the Ndebele and the Mashona. Nkomo is an Ndebele and Mugabe a Mashona. The Mashona outnumber the Ndebele four to one and Mugabe won the election by four to one. Simple, really.'

'They voted along tribal lines?'

'Largely.' Nair paused, then said, 'If the South Africans could set up a well-financed secret base here they could stir up a lot of trouble among the tribes.'

Stafford extinguished his cigarette carefully and lay back to think. Because of its position in Africa Kenya was a hodge-podge of ethnic and religious differences, all of which could be exploited by a determined and cynical enemy. Nair was probably right.

He was still thinking of this when he fell asleep.

* * *

He awoke in the grey light of dawn and looked uncomprehendingly at something which moved. He lay on his side and watched the buck daintily picking its way across his line of vision. It was incredibly small, about the size of a small dog, say, a fox terrier, and its legs were about as thick as a ball point pen and terminated in miniature hooves. Its rump was rounded and its horns were two small daggers. He had never seen anything so exquisite.

A twig snapped and the buck scampered away into the safety of the trees. Stafford rolled over and saw Nair approaching from the lake. 'That was a dik-dik,' said Nair.

'Have the flies gone?'

'No flies now.'

'Good.' Stafford threw back the netting and emerged from the sleeping bag. He put on his trousers, then his shoes, and took a towel. 'Is it safe to wash in the lake?'

'Safe enough; just keep your eyes open for snakes. Not that you're likely to see any.' As Stafford turned away Nair called, 'There are some fish eagles nesting in the trees over there.'

As Stafford walked to the water's edge he shook his head in amusement. Nair's cover as a courier for tourist groups seemed to have stuck. A herd of Thomson's gazelle drifted out of his way, not hurrying but keeping a safe distance from him. At the shore he sluiced down and was towelling himself dry when Hardin joined him. 'Peaceful place,' Hardin remarked.

'Yes. It's very nice.' Stafford put on his shirt. 'Where's Curtis? His sleeping bag was empty.'

Hardin waved his arm. 'Gone to the top of the ridge there; he wanted to have a look-see at the mainland.'

Stafford smiled. 'Military habits die hard.'

Hardin was staring out into the lake. 'Now, look at that, will you?'

Stafford followed his gaze and saw nothing but ripples. 'What is it?'

'Wait!' Hardin pointed. 'It was about there. Look! It's come up again. A goddamn hippo.'

Stafford saw the head break surface and heard a distant snorting and snuffling, then the hippopotamus submerged again. He said, 'Well, we are in Africa, you know. What would you expect to find in an African lake? Polar bears?'

'Crocodiles, that's what.' Hardin looked around very carefully at the lake shore. 'And I hope Nair was right about lions and leopards not liking to swim too far. We don't have a gun between the lot of us.'

There was an outcrop of rock close by and Stafford thought he would get a better view of the hippo from the top so he walked over to it. As he climbed he found the rock oddly slippery and he had difficulty in keeping his footing despite the fact that his shoes were rubber-soled. At the top he lost his balance entirely – his feet shot from under him and he fell to the ground below, a matter of some ten feet.

He was winded and gasped desperately for breath, and his senses swam. He did not entirely lose consciousness but was hardly aware of Hardin running up to him and turning him on to his back. 'You okay, Max?' said Hardin anxiously.

It was a couple of minutes before Stafford could reply. 'Christ, but that was bad.'

'Anything broken?'

Stafford handled himself gingerly, testing for broken bones. At last he said, 'I think I'm in one piece.'

'It could have been your neck the way you went down,' said Hardin. 'What the hell happened?'

Stafford got to his feet. 'There's something about that rock. It's damned slippery; almost as if it's been greased.'

Hardin took a pace to the outcrop and inspected it visually, then passed his hand over the surface. 'Just plain old rock as far as I can see.'

'Damn it!' said Stafford. 'It was just like walking on loose ball bearings.' He joined Hardin but could detect nothing odd about the nature of the stone surface.

Hardin said, 'If you're okay I'll finish cleaning up.' He returned to the waterside and Stafford waited, watching what he supposed was one of the fish eagles Nair had mentioned as it circled lazily above, and wondering about the curious nature of the rock on Crescent Island.

Hardin finished and they walked back, Stafford limping a little because he had pulled a muscle in his leg. Nair had coffee waiting and gave Stafford a cup as he sat on his sleeping bag. Hardin said, 'Max thinks you have odd rocks here. He took a nasty tumble back there.'

Nair looked up. 'Odd? How?'

'Damned slippery. I could have broken something.' Stafford massaged his thigh.

'Take a look at the soles of your shoes,' Nair advised.

Stafford took off a shoe and turned it over. 'Well, I'll be damned!' The rubber sole was completely hidden by a packed mass of brown seeds.

'You'll be all right walking about in the normal way,' said Nair. 'Just pick your surfaces and don't walk on naked rock or you'll slip.'

All the same Stafford took his pocket knife and de-seeded his shoes after breakfast. The seeds were small and tetrahedron in shape with a small spike at each vertex so that whichever way they fell one spike would be uppermost, rather like miniature versions of the medieval caltrops which were scattered to discourage cavalry charges. Nature got there first, he reflected, and said aloud, 'Now I know why Gunnarsson was hobbling so badly when he got back to Keekorok.' He inspected the sole of the shoe. The remaining small spikes had broken off under his body weight and left a smooth, polished surface as slick as a ballroom floor. He cleaned the seeds out and then looked at the sole of his shoe. It was full of pinholes.

After they had breakfast and done the camp chores such as flattening and burying the empty cans there was nothing much to do. 'Did Chip say when he'd be coming back?' asked Stafford.

Nair shrugged. 'I doubt if he'd know.'

'So we twiddle our thumbs,' said Stafford disgustedly.

Curtis returned to his position on top of the ridge, taking with him Stafford's binoculars, and Hardin elected to keep him company. Nair and Stafford took a walk; there being nothing else to do. 'We'll be at the north end of the island,' Nair told Hardin before they left.

They strolled along, taking their time because they were not going anywhere in particular. As they went Stafford told Nair of his assessment of the Kenyan options and Nair agreed with him somewhat gloomily. 'The trouble with us,' he said. 'Is that we're civilized enough to have intelligence and security departments, but not civilized enough to know how to use them properly. We haven't had the experience of you British. I don't think we're cynical enough.'

It was an odd way of defining civilization, but Stafford thought he could very well be right.

Once Nair stopped and pointed to the ground, ahead of them but to one side. 'Look!'

Stafford saw nothing, but then an ear twitched and he saw a beady eye. 'A rabbit!' he said in astonishment. 'I didn't know you had those in Africa.'

'Not many,' said Nair. 'Too many predators. That's a Bunyoro rabbit.' He moved and the rabbit took fright and bounded away, changing direction with every hop. Nair slanted his eyes at Stafford. 'Too many predators in all of Africa.'

And most of them human, agreed Stafford, but to himself.

It was nearly eleven in the morning when Hardin caught up with them. 'Alan Hunt just landed from a boat,' he reported. 'The Sergeant has gone down to meet him.'

'He might have brought news,' said Stafford. 'Let's go see.'

Hunt, however, had no news. He had been to the service station in Naivasha to replenish the butane bottles for the balloon and to have a pipe welded on the burner and had then decided to see if Stafford knew what was happening. 'We're marking bloody time, that's all,' said Stafford. 'Waiting for the top brass to make up its collective mind – if any.'

'You were right,' said Hunt.

'What about?'

'The TV camera in the entrance hall of the Admin Block. I checked on it.'

Stafford grunted. 'I hope you didn't poke your eye right into it.'

'And your friend, Gunnarsson, stayed over last night. He and Brice seemed quite pally.'

Stafford thought of the directed conversation he had with Gunnarsson in the bedroom. He said, 'Brice is probably measuring him up; assessing the opposition, no doubt.'

Hardin laughed. 'Measuring him up is right. For a coffin, probably.'

Stafford disagreed. 'I doubt it. It's a bad operation that leaves too many corpses around. I don't think Brice is as stupid as that.'

'He wasn't too worried about leaving a corpse on the Tanzanian border,' objected Hardin.

'That was different. There's still no direct connection between Brice and that episode. He's still pretty well covered. I think . . .'

What Stafford thought was lost because a piercing whistle came from the ridge and he looked up to see Curtis waving in a beckoning motion. 'Something's up,' he said, and began to run.

He was out of breath when he cast himself down next to Curtis and thought that this was a job for a younger man. Nair and Hunt were with him, but Hardin was still trailing behind. Curtis pointed to a boat half way across the narrow strait between the island and the mainland, and passed the binoculars to Stafford. 'If the Colonel would care to take a look? It's coming from the Lake Naivasha Hotel.'

Stafford put the glasses to his eyes and focused. In the stern was a young black Kenyan, his hand on the tiller of the outboard motor. And Gunnarsson sat amidships, staring at the island and apparently right into Stafford's eyes.

29

Stafford withdrew from the crest of the ridge as Hardin flopped down beside him. 'What is it?' Hardin asked. He was short of breath.

'Gunnarsson. He's coming straight here as though pulled by a magnet. Now, how the hell does he know where we are?' No one answered him, so Stafford said, 'Ben, you get lost. You, too, Nair; but stay close and available. Curtis and I will form a welcoming committee. Come on, Sergeant.'

'What about me?' said Hunt.

Stafford considered the matter and shrugged. 'That depends on whether you want to get involved. Come if you like.' He peered over the ridge. Gunnarsson's boat was heading straight as an arrow to the roughly-made jetty which formed the landing place.

'I'll come,' said Hunt.

The three of them traversed the ridge heading north and keeping below the crest, then went over at a place where the jetty was screened from view by trees. They moved fast because Stafford wanted to intercept Gunnarsson at the jetty before he set out to explore the island. A waterbuck exploded out of a thicket, panicked by their sudden presence, and went galloping across a glade ahead of them. As they went by it stopped and stared and then, reassured, resumed its browsing.

Stafford slowed his pace as he neared the jetty close enough to hear the puttering of an outboard engine. The jetty came into view, half hidden by a leafy screen. He stopped and moved a branch and saw Gunnarsson getting out of the boat. There was a distant mutter of voices and then the raised note of the motor as the boat pulled away. Gunnarsson stood on the jetty and looked at the boats moored there: the one in which Nair had brought the camp supplies and the other in which Hunt had arrived.

Stafford whispered to Hunt, 'Did you come from the Lake Naivasha Hotel?'

'No – from Safariland.'

Stafford frowned. That made it unlikely that Gunnarsson had been following Hunt, so what had brought him? He watched Gunnarsson inspecting the boats. He got into each and appeared to be searching them thoroughly. Not that there was anything to find.

Gunnarsson climbed back on to the jetty, and Stafford said, 'Let's ask him what he wants.' They left cover and walked along the shoreline.

Gunnarsson had his back to them but, as he heard their approach, he turned. A grim smile appeared on his face and he put his hands on his hips and stood with arms akimbo. They got close enough for conversation and Stafford said pleasantly, 'Good morning, Mr Gunnarsson. How are your feet today?'

'By Christ!' said Gunnarsson. 'Stafford, you are one magnificent liar. You had me fooled, you really did. So you were pulling out and going back to London? And I believed you.'

Stafford was comforted by that. If he had fooled Gunnarsson then he might have also fooled Brice and Hendriks. He said, 'What are you doing here?'

'I'm looking for a guy in a turban, but I suppose you wouldn't know anything about him.' He raised his hand before Stafford could speak. 'And don't tell me you don't know anything about him. I wouldn't believe you now if you told me that the thing shining in the sky is the sun.'

Stafford shrugged. 'That sounds like Nair Singh, our guide.'

Gunnarsson looked at Hunt. 'You're from Ol Njorowa. I saw you at breakfast this morning. So you're in this, too.'

'My name is Hunt. What am I supposed to be in, Mr Gunnarsson?'

Gunnarsson looked frustrated. 'If I knew that I wouldn't be screwing around here in this half-assed manner.' He glanced at Curtis. 'Who are you?'

The reply was characteristically brief and brought Gunnarsson no joy. 'Curtis.'

Gunnarsson's attention returned to Stafford. 'This Hindu guy you say is your guide. Where is he?'

'I wouldn't call him a Hindu; he might take umbrage because he's a Sikh.' Stafford waved his arm. 'He's back there. Do you want to talk to him?'

'Yeah, I want to ask him if he usually drives a phoney taxi equipped to track a beeper bug,' said Gunnarsson with heavy irony. 'It's standing in the hotel parking lot right now. I suppose you don't know anything about that, either.'

'I know now.' Stafford smiled. 'You've just told me.'

Gunnarsson snorted. 'So what is a tourist guide doing with triple antennas and a signal strength meter? Why was he trailing me?'

'Let's ask him,' Stafford proposed. 'I'll lead the way.' He walked away from the jetty and Gunnarsson fell into step beside him. Curtis and Hunt tagged along behind. 'What led you to Crescent Island?'

'That goddamn taxi was in the parking lot when I got back to the hotel this morning,' said Gunnarsson. 'I asked at the desk where the owner was and I was told he'd come here.'

So it had been as easy as that, thought Stafford. Nair had made mistakes; first with the beeper and then not getting rid of the Mercedes. Still, no harm had been done.

They climbed the ridge and went down the other side to the camp site. Stafford shouted, 'Nair!', and Nair got up from where he was unobtrusively lying in the shade of a tree. 'A man here wants to talk to you.'

Nair approached them. 'What about?' he asked innocently.

'Jesus; you know what about!' said Gunnarsson belligerently. 'Why are you so goddamn interested in me?'

'Do you have something to hide?'

Gunnarsson's eyes flickered. 'What's with the double-talk?'

'I think he *has* something to hide,' said Stafford. 'For instance, I'd like to know what happened to Henry Hendrix.'

'We've been through all that before.' Gunnarsson took out a handkerchief and mopped his brow and his neck. 'I'm tired of telling the story.'

'Oh, I don't mean Corliss,' said Stafford casually. 'I know what happened to him. But what happened to Hendrix?'

'Hendrix is . . .' Gunnarsson began, and stopped as the meaning of what Stafford had said sank in. He moistened his lips and swallowed before saying, 'Who is Corliss?'

'Your friend who disappeared in Tanzania.'

'You're crazy! That was Hendrix.'

Stafford shook his head. 'Gunnarsson; you're a bigger liar than I am. The Hendrix you took to London was not the Hendrix found in Los Angeles.'

'Not Hendrix!' said Gunnarsson numbly. 'You must be kidding.' He forced a smile.

'Definitely not Hendrix,' said Stafford. 'And proveable.'

'Look, the guy was brought to me in my office. He had everything right; a pat hand. Everything checked out.' He paused in thought. 'I sent an operative to pick him up in Los Angeles. Could he have pulled a fast one on me?'

'What was his name? This operative?'

'A guy called Hardin. Something of a dead beat. I had to fire him.' Gunnarsson was sweating as he extemporized his story. 'If anyone pulled a fast one it must have been Hardin. He's a . . .'

Stafford cut him short by raising his voice, 'Come out, come out, wherever you are.' As Gunnarsson gazed at him in astonishment Stafford said coolly, 'Why don't you ask him? He's just behind you.'

Gunnarsson whirled and his eyes bulged as he saw Hardin who smiled and said, 'Hello, you lousy cheapskate.'

'You've been under a microscope,' said Stafford. 'Every move you've made has been noted ever since you pitched up in London with Corliss and palmed him off as Hendrix. I won't say we've recorded every time you went to the loo, but damned nearly. And Corliss has been singing as sweetly as any nightingale. The jig's up, Gunnarsson.'

Gunnarsson looked defeated, rather as Stafford had seen him when he hobbled into the game lodge at Keekorok. He mumbled, 'Where is Corliss?'

'Where you'd expect him to be – in a police cell. And that's where you're going.'

To Stafford's surprise Nair stepped forward and produced a pair of handcuffs. 'You're under arrest, Mr Gunnarsson. I'm a police officer.'

Gunnarsson whipped round and began to run. Unfortunately Curtis happened to be in the way and it was like running into a brick wall. Hardin collared him from behind and brought him down. Then Nair manacled him, right wrist to left ankle. 'Best way of immobilizing a man,' said Nair. 'He can't run. His only way of getting around is to roll like a hoop.'

Curtis interrupted the steady flow of obscenities from Gunnarsson. 'If the Colonel doesn't mind I'll get back up there.' He indicated the ridge.

'Very well, Sergeant.' Stafford watched Curtis walk away in his stolid fashion and turned to Nair. 'Are you really a police officer?'

Nair grinned. 'Police reserve. I always carry a spare warrant card. Do you want to see it?'

Stafford shook his head. 'I'll take it on trust.'

Gunnarsson looked up at Hardin malevolently. 'You lousy bastard! I'll have your balls.'

'Talk to me like that again and I'll kick your teeth in,' said Hardin sharply. 'Any injuries can be put down to resisting arrest.'

'Yes,' said Nair. 'I would advise a still tongue.'

Gunnarsson twisted around to face him. 'What's the charge? I've committed no crime in Kenya.'

'Oh, we can always think of something,' said Nair cheerfully.

Hunt wore a baffled expression. 'I don't understand all this.

Who is this man, and what has he to do with Ol Njorowa?'

'His name is Gunnarsson and he has nothing whatever to do with Ol Njorowa,' said Stafford. 'He tried to get some easy money but didn't know what he was getting into. Still, he *did* lead us to the funny business at the College. Hardin will tell you all about it.'

'Yeah,' said Hardin. 'Over a beer. We've got some six-packs cooling in the lake; let's go get them.'

As they walked away Stafford called, 'Take a beer to the Sergeant,' then said to Nair, 'So what do we do about him?' He indicated Gunnarsson.

'Not much. He'll keep until Chip comes back. Of course, we'll have to feed him.'

'Yeah,' said Gunnarsson. 'If there's any beer going I'd like a can. And what's this about Ol Njorowa? I figured the place wasn't kosher but I couldn't put my finger on what's wrong about it.'

'Hardin always said you were smart,' admitted Stafford. 'But not, I think, smart enough. You got in over your head, Gunnarsson. One of my associates described it elegantly as the clash of nations.'

Gunnarsson looked up at him uncomprehendingly.

*   *   *

One of the nations was preparing for its part in the clash.

Brice looked at Patterson stonily. 'So Gunnarsson went out to Crescent Island. Why?'

'I couldn't ask him; he wasn't within shouting distance,' said Patterson acidly. 'But I think he's chasing after some Indian – a Sikh. He was making enquiries about the driver of a Kenatco taxi in the hotel car park and then hired the hotel boat to take him to the island. The boatman wouldn't wait for him because someone wanted to go fishing. He promised Gunnarsson he'd pick him up in a couple of hours.' He looked at his watch. 'That was nearly an hour ago. I left Joe Baiya on watch and came back here to report. You said not to use the telephone in this business.'

'So I did.' Brice tapped a ballpoint pen on the desk and stared unseeingly at Dirk Hendriks. 'A Sikh in a Kenatco taxi. That's something new.'

'And interesting,' said Hendriks.

'It gets more interesting,' said Patterson. 'I had another look at the taxi – a Mercedes just like Kenatco uses, but I don't think it's theirs. It had three antennas and a signal strength meter on the dashboard. A professional trailing job.'

Brice sat straighter in his chair. 'Gunnarsson told us about that. I didn't know whether or not to believe him.' He stood up and paced the room. 'If it isn't one damn thing it's another. We get rid of Stafford and now we've got this man, Gunnarsson pushing in. I'd like to know why.'

'Are we sure Stafford has gone?' asked Patterson.

Hendriks nodded. 'Our man in Nairobi reported in person fifteen minutes ago. Stafford left on the morning flight. He checked out of the Norfolk early and changed his Kenyan money at the airport bank like a good boy. Our man saw the record – he has good contacts at the airport. Both Stafford and his man, Curtis, are on the passenger list.'

'But did anyone *see* them leave?' persisted Patterson.

'Forget Stafford,' snapped Brice. 'Our immediate concern is Gunnarsson and, more important, with whoever is following him. I don't like it.' He stood up. 'Since they're both conveniently to hand on Crescent Island I propose that we find out what they're doing there. Come on.'

The three of them left the office and, on the way through the entrance hall, Brice collected the black who presided behind the reception desk.

* * *

Hunt said, 'That's the damnedest story I've ever heard.'

Hardin chuckled. 'Isn't it, though? Not long ago Max asked me if I thought that running down Biggie and Hank would lead to what's happening here in Kenya. Really weird. If Gunnarsson hadn't tried to pull a switch then the Ol Njorowa crowd might have got away with it. Brice and

Hendriks are damned unlucky.' He rubbed his chin. 'There's one person I'm really sorry for.'

'Who's that?'

'Mrs Hendriks back in London. I liked her – a real nice lady.'

'Perhaps she's in it up to her neck just as much as her husband.'

Hardin drained his beer can and then crushed it flat. 'Max says not, and he's known her for a long time. He knew her before she married Hendriks. Apparently he got her out of a jam once before; some trouble her brother was in. That's why she went to him when I appeared with my story and Hendriks was away in South Africa. If she was in cahoots with Dirk she'd have kept her mouth shut. No, I think this is going to hurt her bad when the news gets out.'

Hunt looked at his watch. 'I'd better be getting back.'

'Okay.' Hardin picked up a beer can and tossed it to Hunt. 'Give that to Curtis on your way. It must be as hot as Hades up there. Tell him I'll relieve him for the afternoon watch. And check with Max before you go. He might want you to do something at Ol Njorowa.'

'Right.' Hunt looked up at the ridge. 'Funny, chap, Curtis. Never says much, does he?'

Hardin grinned. 'The Sergeant is the only guy I know who only talks when he has something to say. Everybody else goes yacketty-yack all the time. But when he does say something, for Christ's sake, take notice.'

Hunt reported to Stafford that he was leaving. Stafford said, 'Alan, is there a way into Ol Njorowa other than the front gate?'

'Not that I know of,' said Hunt. 'You go through the gate or through the fence – or over it.'

'Or under it,' suggested Nair.

Stafford shook his head. 'Brice knew what he was doing when he put up that fence. He's not stupid. My bet is that it's like an Australian rabbit fence and extends four feet underground. Is the animal migration laboratory normally kept locked?'

'I don't know,' said Hunt. 'I've never had occasion to try the door.'

Stafford grimaced. 'Of course not.' He reflected for a moment. 'I don't know if there'll be any rough stuff – nothing like a shoot-out at the OK Corral – normally intelligence outfits don't favour guns. But there may be a bit of trouble when Chip moves in, so my advice is to get Judy out of there. Send her to Nairobi for a week's shopping or something like that.'

'I've already tried that and she's not buying it,' said Hunt.

'Well, tell her to keep her head down.' They shook hands and Hunt departed and Stafford walked over to where Nair was interrogating Gunnarsson. 'Now,' he said. 'You were about to tell us what really happened to Hank Hendrix.'

'Go screw yourself,' said Gunnarsson.

Curtis turned his head as Hunt approached and slid down from the top of the ridge. He accepted the can of beer gratefully. 'Thanks. Just what the doctor ordered.'

'Hardin says he'll relieve you soon,' said Hunt.

'He needn't bother.'

Hunt regarded him curiously. 'Have you been with Max Stafford long?'

Curtis swallowed beer, his Adam's apple working vigorously. He sighed in appreciation. 'A couple of years.'

'Were you in the service together.'

Curtis nodded. 'In a way. A long time ago.'

Hunt decided that making conversation with Curtis was hard work. The Sergeant was polite and informative but brief as though words were rationed and not to be squandered. If brevity was the soul of wit Curtis was the wittiest man alive. But surprisingly Curtis came up with a question. 'Are hippos dangerous?'

'That depends, said Hunt. 'I wouldn't go too near in a boat and I certainly wouldn't choose them as swimming companions.'

'This one's ashore.' He pointed. 'Landed about an hour ago over there.'

Hunt looked to where Curtis pointed and saw nothing. 'They don't usually venture ashore in daylight. And, yes, they're bloody dangerous. They can move a lot faster than you'd think, certainly faster than a man can run, and those tusks can kill. The thing to remember is never to get between a hippo and the water.'

'I'll tell the Colonel,' said Curtis.

Hunt nodded. 'I'm going back to Ol Njorowa.'

Curtis eased himself to the top of the ridge and picked up the binoculars. Hunt was about to walk past him when Curtis held up his hand. 'Wait!'

Hunt stopped. 'What's the matter?'

'Get down off the ridge – off the skyline.' Curtis was intently watching something below as Hunt dropped beside him. He said, 'A boat coming. Five men; three white, two black.' He paused. 'One is Dirk Hendriks. I don't know the others.' He passed the binoculars to Hunt.

Hunt focused and the approaching boat suddenly jumped towards him. 'Brice and Patterson,' he said. 'And Joe Baiya – he's a sort of handyman around Ol Njorowa – with Luke Maiyani. He's usually behind the desk in the Admin Block.'

Curtis's voice was even. 'You'd better tell the Colonel. I'll stay here.'

Hunt plunged down the hill towards the camp site.

30

Stafford's first reaction was to turn to Nair. 'Is this island big enough to play hide-and-seek?'

'Hide from five men?' Nair shook his head decisively. 'And what about him?' He pointed to Gunnarsson who was stubbornly resisting Hardin's questioning.

'Damn!' said Stafford. Gunnarsson was a real stumbling block; if he was left manacled Brice was sure to find him, but if he was freed he might run straight to Brice and blab all he knew, and he knew too much for comfort. Stafford damned the men in Nairobi who were talking instead of acting.

He strode over to Gunnarsson and dropped to his knees. 'Do you want to live?' he asked abruptly.

Gunnarsson's eyes widened. 'That's a hell of a question.'

'Look, I'm not interested in your tricks with Corliss,' said Stafford. 'That's small time stuff compared with what Brice is doing.'

'Yeah', said Hardin. 'You were ripping off a lousy six million bucks. Brice was going for broke – maybe a hundred million.'

'He's coming here now,' said Stafford, and heard Hardin make a muffled exclamation. 'And he's bringing his troops. A few lives are nothing compared to what he has at stake.'

'He wouldn't risk murder,' said Hardin. 'Shots could be heard from the mainland.'

Stafford thought of the man he had killed in Tanzania. 'Who said anything about shooting? There are other ways of killing and the evidence can be buried in the belly of a crocodile,' he said brutally, and Gunnarsson flinched. 'As you are now you wouldn't stand a chance so I'm going to release you, but just remember who is doing you the favour.'

'Sure,' said Gunnarsson eagerly. 'Just let me run.'

Stafford signalled to Nair who shrugged and produced the key of the handcuffs. When Gunnarsson was free he stood up and massaged his wrist. 'This true?' he asked Hardin. He jerked his head at Stafford. 'This guy was talking about something else before.'

'It's true,' said Hardin. 'We've run against South African intelligence and those guys don't play patty-cake. You ought to know that. We've got in the way of one of their big operations.'

'Then I'm fading,' Gunnarsson announced.

'You'll do as you're bloody well told,' snapped Stafford. He was looking at Curtis up on the ridge. 'You said five men? That all?'

'All I saw,' said Hunt. 'There could be another boat coming along behind.'

'Curtis hasn't signalled anything about that,' commented Stafford. 'What do you think, Ben? The odds are better than even if Gunnarsson comes in. Six to five.'

'You mean a straight fight for it?' Hardin made a wry face. 'We'd lose,' he said flatly. 'Look at us – middle-aged men except for Alan and Nair here, and I wouldn't think Alan has had the training for it. Dirk Hendriks is a husky young guy, and Brice looks as though he eats nails for breakfast. I don't know about the others.' He looked at Hunt.

'Patterson's a toughie and I wouldn't like to tackle Luke Maiyani without a club in my hand,' said Hunt frankly.

'Then if we can't use force we must use guile,' said Stafford.

Gunnarsson said, 'And we can't waste time standing here yapping.'

Nair said suddenly, 'Why is Brice coming here?' It was a rhetorical question because he answered it himself. 'I think Gunnarsson has been followed, probably by Patterson. It was Patterson who went looking for him in Nairobi. And Gunnarsson was following me. I think Brice expects to find only the two of us.'

'Makes sense,' said Hardin. 'And that means . . .'

'Yes,' said Stafford.

Gunnarsson found himself the centre of a circle of eyes. 'Now wait a minute. If you guys expect me to stick my neck out after the way you've treated me you're crazy.'

'Mr Gunnarsson,' said Nair politely. 'You and I are going across the island to meet Brice. On the way we'll think of something to tell him. I'm sure your imagination will be up to it.'

'Keep them occupied while we get rid of this stuff,' said Stafford. He waved his hand at the evidence of the camp site. 'Say ten or fifteen minutes. Then draw them out of sight of the boats at the jetty. We'll be coming in on the flank. And send Curtis down here.'

* * *

The engine note altered as the boat neared the jetty. Brice said, 'Two boats here. All right; one brought the Sikh but the boat which brought Gunnarsson went back, you said.' He turned to Patterson. 'So whose is the other?'

Patterson looked at his watch. 'The boatman must have come back for Gunnarsson. Just about time.'

Brice nodded briefly as the boat drifted in and touched the jetty. Baiya and Maiyani held it steady as he went ashore. He turned and said, 'Baiya, you stay here. The rest come with me.'

Baiya lashed the painter around a cleat on Hunt's boat and the others went ashore. Hendriks looked around. 'Where do we start?'

'We'll find them,' said Brice confidently. 'It's not a big island.'

'No need to go far,' said Patterson. 'They've found us. Look!' He pointed up the hill to where two figures stood silhouetted on the ridge.

'Good; that saves time,' said Brice. 'Let's go to meet them. I'd like to know what this is about – but let me do the talking.'

They walked up the hill and met Nair and Gunnarsson on the level base of the foundations of the old building. To Brice's surprise he saw handcuffs on Gunnarsson's wrists.

'What's going on here?' he demanded. 'Why is Mr Gunnarsson handcuffed?'

Nair Singh looked at him sternly. 'Do you know this man?'

'I had breakfast with him this morning.'

'I am a police officer.' Nair took a small leather case from his pocket and flipped it open. 'Nair Singh. This is my warrant card. Mr Gunnarsson is under arrest.'

Brice turned to look at Hendriks who was plainly shocked. He turned back to Nair. 'May I know the charge?'

'He has been arrested but not yet charged,' said Nair. 'You say you had breakfast with Mr Gunnarsson this morning. May I know your name, sir.'

'Brice. Charles Brice.'

Nair's face cleared. 'Of Ol Njorowa College?'

'Yes. Now what's this all about?'

'Ah, then I think you'll be pleased to know that we caught this man before he did too much damage. He's under arrest for fraud.'

'It's a goddamn lie,' said Gunnarsson. 'Look, Mr Brice, do me a favour. Ring the American Embassy in Nairobi as soon as you can. This is a put-up job; I'm being framed for something I didn't do.'

'The American authorities will be informed,' said Nair coldly.

'Now hang on a minute,' said Hendriks. 'What sort of fraud?'

Nair looked at him. 'Who are you, sir?'

'Hendriks. Dirk Hendriks. I'm staying with Mr Brice at Ol Njorowa.'

Nair looked oddly embarrassed. 'Oh! Then you will be an heir to the estate which has benefited Ol Njorowa?'

'That's correct.'

Brice said impatiently, 'Who is Mr Gunnarsson supposed to have defrauded?'

Nair was playing for time. He said to Hendriks, 'Then it was your cousin who disappeared in Tanzania.'

Hendriks and Brice exchanged glances. Hendriks said,

'Yes; and nothing seems to have been done about it. Was Gunnarsson mixed up in that business? Is that it?'

'Not quite,' said Nair. 'How long had you known your cousin, Mr Hendriks?'

The question seemed strange to Dirk. 'What's that got to do with anything? And what's it got to do with Gunnarsson?'

'How long?' persisted Nair.

'Not very long – a matter of weeks. He was an American, you know. I met him for the first time in London.'

'Ah!' said Nair, as though suddenly a light had been shone into darkness. 'That would explain it.'

'Explain what?' said Brice in sudden irritation.

'Henry Hendrix came back across the border two days after he was kidnapped,' said Nair. 'And . . .'

Brice and Hendriks broke in simultaneously and then stopped, each looking at the other in astonishment. Brice said sharply, 'Why was no one told of this? It's monstrous that Mr Hendriks here should have been kept in ignorance. He's been worried about his cousin.'

'As I said, Henry Hendrix came back,' continued Nair calmly. 'But he was delirious; he had a bad case of sunstroke. In his delirium he talked of certain matters which required investigation and, when he recovered, he was questioned and made a full confession. I am sorry to tell you that the man known to you as Henry Hendrix is really called Corliss and he has implicated Gunnarsson in his imposture.'

'It's a lie,' cried Gunnarsson. 'He screwed me the same way as he screwed everyone else.'

'That will be for the court to decide,' said Nair. He studied Brice and Hendriks, both of whom appeared to be shell-shocked, and smiled internally. 'The American Embassy has, of course, been kept acquainted with these developments and agreed that a certain amount of . . . er . . . reticence was in order while the matter was investigated. Mr Gunnarsson will have a number of questions to answer when we get back to Nairobi.' He looked at his watch. 'And now, if you gentlemen will excuse me . . . ?'

There was something wrong here which Brice could not fathom. He watched Nair and Gunnarsson pass by and felt obscurely that somewhere he was being tricked. He said, 'Wait a moment. Have you been following Gunnarsson in that Kenatco taxi?'

Nair paused and looked back. 'In the line of duty.'

'Then why did it happen in reverse? Why did Gunnarsson follow you here to Crescent Island?'

'I tempted him,' said Nair blandly.

'Yeah, he suckered me all right,' said Gunnarsson in corroboration.

Suddenly Brice saw – or, rather, did not see – the missing piece, the missing man. If Gunnarsson had come to the island and the boatman had gone away and had then returned to pick him up, then where the hell was he? Where was the boatman? And if there was no boatman then whose was the other boat? Brice jerked his head at Patterson and stepped forward. 'Look!' he said sharply, pointing at nothing in particular.

Both Nair and Gunnarsson turned to look and Brice hooked his foot around Gunnarsson's leg and pushed. Gunnarsson went flying down the slope and instinctively put out his hands to save himself. In that he succeeded but the handcuffs went flying away in a glittering arc to clink on a rock, and Brice knew he had been right.

* * *

Stafford watched Curtis ghost through the trees to his left and then turned his head to watch Hardin on his right. He knew he did not have to worry about a couple of old pros who knew their business, but Hunt was different; he was a civilian amateur who did not know which end was up, which is why he was directly behind Stafford with strict instructions to walk in the Master's steps. 'I don't want a sound out of you,' Stafford had said. Hunt was doing his best but flinched when Stafford turned to glare at him when a twig snapped underfoot.

Curtis held both hands over his head in the military gesture indicating an order to stop. If he had had a rifle he would have held it, but he had no rifle, which was a pity. He beckoned to Stafford who, after stopping Hunt dead in his tracks, made his way to Curtis in a walking crouch.

Curtis pointed and said in an undertone, 'They've left a man at the boats.' He knew enough not to whisper. Nothing carries further than the sibilants of a whisper.

'Where are the others?'

'Somewhere up the hill. I heard voices.'

Stafford turned his head and gestured to Hardin who crept over. 'There's a guard on the boats,' he said. 'And Nair hasn't decoyed Brice away yet. They're still within hearing distance so they can probably see the boats.'

'Tricky,' said Hardin.

'Would the Colonel like the guard removed?' asked Curtis.

'How would you do it?'

Curtis indicated the water glimmering through the trees. 'Swimming.'

'Goddamn!' said Hardin. 'What about crocodiles?'

'I'd poison a crocodile,' said Curtis solemnly and without the trace of a smile.

'I don't know,' said Stafford uncertainly.

'I've been watching the water's edge from the ridge,' said Curtis. 'I haven't seen any crocodiles.' He was already taking off his shoes.

'Well, all right.' said Stafford. 'But you go when I say; and you incapacitate – you don't kill.'

'I doubt if we'd get trouble if he did,' said Hardin. 'We've proved our point and the Kenyans aren't going to be worried about a dead South African agent.'

'Ben, that man there could be an innocent Kenyan brought along just to drive the boat. We can't take that chance.' Stafford went back to Hunt. 'When you answer keep your voice down. Any crocs in the lake?'

Hunt nodded. 'Usually further north around the papyrus swamp.'

'And here?'

'Could be.'

Stafford frowned. 'We might be making a break for the boats in a few minutes. You follow us and your job is to get an engine started. You do that and you don't bother about anything else. We'll know when you've succeeded. And we want to take *all* the boats so we take two in tow.'

'I'll start the engine in my own boat,' said Hunt. 'I know it best. It's the chase boat we use when the balloon blows over the lake.'

Stafford nodded and went back to Curtis who had taken off his trousers and was flexing a leather belt in his hands. 'Where's Ben?' Curtis silently pointed up the hill to the right.

Presently Hardin came back. 'They're still yakking away up there. I couldn't get close enough to hear what they're saying.'

'Can they see the jetty from where they are?'

'I reckon so.'

That was not good, thought Stafford. Only if Nair could decoy Brice away would they stand a chance. Normally he would have sent Curtis off by now to take out the guard at a signal, but the longer he was in the water the greater the risk, and he would not do that. The only thing to do was to wait for an opportunity.

It came sooner than he expected in the form of a distant shout. He said to Curtis, 'Go! Go!' and Curtis slipped quietly into the water to disappear leaving only a lengthening trail of bubbles. There were more shouts and the man in the boat stood up to get a better view.

Stafford, lurking behind a screen of leaves, followed the direction of his gaze but saw nothing until Hardin nudged him. 'Look! Nair and Gunnarsson are on the run over there.'

Gunnarsson and Nair were sprinting desperately, angling down the slope away from the jetty with Gunnarsson in the lead, and Patterson and a black came in sight in full chase. Then Brice and Hendriks appeared. Brice threw up his arm and he and Hendriks changed direction, running down to the shore on the other side of the jetty. They all vanished from sight.

'Now!' said Stafford, and broke cover to run towards the jetty a hundred yards away, and was conscious of Hardin and Hunt behind him. The guard heard the crunch of their feet and turned in some alarm. He froze for a moment when he saw them and was about to turn back to shout for help when something seemed to tangle his feet and he toppled overboard with a splash.

Stafford ran up and jumped into the boat. He leaned over the side. 'Come on, Sergeant,' he said and took Curtis's arm to help him aboard. Hardin had seized an oar and was pushing the boat away from the jetty and from Hunt's boat there came a splutter as the engine balked. Stafford left Curtis gasping on the floor boards and was just in time to grab the painter of the third boat. He fastened it to a cleat and then had time to look around.

Hunt was rewinding the starter cord on his outboard engine and Stafford said harshly, 'Get that bloody thing started.' He was thinking of Nair. Hardin had pushed off vigorously with the oar and the boats were now drifting about ten yards offshore where the guard was standing dripping wet and already raising an outcry. Stafford looked along the shore line and saw Brice and Hendriks turn to look back.

Hunt's engine caught with a stuttering roar, then settled down to an even purr. Stafford shouted, 'Further out and then go south – after Nair.' The note of the engine deepened and the small convoy increased in speed. He bent down to Curtis, 'You all right, Sergeant?'

'Yes, sir. Nothing wrong with me.'

Hardin was staring at the shore. 'Brice looks mad enough to bust a gut.'

Brice and Hendriks had stopped and were motionless, looking at the boats which were now a hundred yards away and moving parallel with the coast. Brice said something to Hendriks and they began to run again. Stafford said, 'Where are Nair and Gunnarsson?'

'Should be on the other side of that point there, if they haven't been caught.'

Stafford raised his voice and shouted to Hunt in the lead boat. 'Open that thing up! Get a bloody move on!'

Curtis had got up and was in the stern, already starting the engine of their own boat. Hardin hauled on the painter of the other boat to bring it alongside, then he jumped in. One by one the other engines started and Stafford cast off the boats so they could operate independently. He said to Curtis, 'Cut in close to the point. I'll watch for rocks.' He signalled to the others that he was taking the lead.

'Hey!' shouted Hardin, and pointed ashore, and Stafford saw that Patterson was in sight but had fallen. He tried to get up but collapsed when he put weight on his leg. Curtis grunted. 'Broke his ankle with a bit of luck, sir.'

Nair thought his lungs would burst. He risked a glance backwards and saw the black about twenty yards behind – and no one else. Ahead Gunnarsson was running steadily but slowing. Nair got enough breath to shout, 'Gunnarsson! Help!' and stopped to face his pursuer.

Luke Maiyani was taken by surprise. The prey was supposed to run, not stand and fight against odds. By the time he had come to this conclusion he was within five yards of Nair so he also came to a halt and looked back expecting to see Patterson but there was no one in sight. It was this small hesitation that cost him a broken jaw because Nair picked up a rock in his fist and when Maiyani turned to look at him again Nair swung with all the force he could. There was a crunch and Maiyani dropped in his tracks.

Nair turned and found that Gunnarsson was still running along the shore. He stood there with his chest heaving and became aware of shouting from offshore. He looked out at the lake and saw three boats coming in with Stafford in the bows of the leading boat waving vigorously. Behind, Hardin was pointing with urgency and he turned his head and saw Brice and Hendriks just rounding the point.

Without further hesitation he ran for the water and the

approaching boats. He was splashing through the shallows when Hendriks pulled out a gun with a long barrel and took careful aim. There was no report but Nair staggered and fell. He rolled over in the water until it was deep enough to support him and started to swim, striking out with his arms and using one leg.

Gunnarsson's attention, too, had been attracted by the shouting. He stopped to look out into the lake and Hunt yelled, 'Swim for it!' Gunnarsson hesitated, then made up his mind as he became aware of Brice and Hendriks advancing upon him. Hunt steered closer to the shore and waved encouragingly then stopped in mid-wave.

'Oh, Christ!' he said.

As Gunnarsson ran towards the water there was a movement from behind him and a vast grey shape burst out of the trees. Hunt shouted, 'Sideways! Run to the side, Gunnarsson!' but he was ignored. The bull hippopotamus behind Gunnarsson was advancing at a steady yard-eating trot, running much faster than the man. It caught him just as he reached the water's edge. Hunt saw the mouth open in a cavernous gape edged with white tusks which closed in a quick snap. Then the hippo was in the lake and there was no sign of Gunnarsson except for a swirl of bloodied water.

Hunt wrenched the tiller over and opened the throttle, speeding to get between the hippopotamus and Nair who was swimming weakly. He heard no gunfire and did not know what it was that whined past him like an angry hornet to hit the outboard motor. The rapid beat of the engine faltered and then it stopped and the boat lost momentum.

Stafford's boat passed him. Stafford was standing in the bows holding an oar, and shouted, 'Get down – you're being shot at!'

'Watch for the hippo!' Hunt replied and twisted around to look for it but could not see it. But he saw a peculiar wave on the surface of the water and knew the hippopotamus was running on the bottom of the shallow lake. The displacement wave rippled towards Nair but was intercepted by Stafford's boat which lurched violently, almost throwing Stafford off his feet.

Hardin was coming in fast on the other side towards Nair as the hippo surfaced next to Stafford's boat. He raised the oar and struck at its head and as the tough, flexible wood shivered violently in his hands he knew he had got in a good blow. For a moment the hippopotamus looked at him with an unwinking eye then breathed mightily and submerged.

Curtis swung over the tiller and Stafford looked for Nair and was relieved to see Hardin helping him into the boat. A miniature fountain rose quite close to him and Stafford said to Curtis, 'For God's sake, let's get out of here.' He waved to Hardin, pointing out into the lake, as Curtis headed towards the boat in which Hunt drifted.

He slowed as they came alongside and Hunt jumped for it. Even as he jumped Curtis was opening the throttle again and swinging to head out into the lake away from shore. Stafford looked back just in time to see the boat Hunt had abandoned rise bow first and then capsize as the hippopotamus attacked it. There was a splashing and a frothing of water and then the boat had gone leaving only a few shattered timbers floating on the water.

The shore of Crescent Island receded and when they were a good half mile away Stafford said, 'Let's join Hardin and see if Nair is all right.' He looked at Hunt and said quietly, 'That was a bloody bad two minutes.'

Curtis throttled back as he came alongside Hardin and the two boats drifted placidly. Nair had slit his trousers and was examining his leg. Hardin said, 'Nair reckons he was hit in the leg, but I didn't hear any shooting.'

'It was Hendriks,' said Stafford. 'He must have had a silencer. Is it bad, Nair?'

'No, just a hole in the fleshy part of the thigh. The bullet must still be in there; there's only one hole.' He held up his right hand. 'And I broke a finger; maybe two.' He looked around. 'Where's Gunnarsson?'

'Yeah,' said Hardin. 'Where is the son of a bitch?'

'The hippo got him,' said Hunt.

'I didn't see that,' said Stafford. 'I was too busy trying to get to Nair. What happened to him?'

'It bit him in half.' Hunt shivered involuntarily.

'Jesus!' said Hardin. 'I didn't like the bastard but I wouldn't wish that on my worst enemy. Are you sure?'

'I'm sure,' said Hunt. 'I saw it. There was a lot of blood in the water.' He looked at the sky and added dully, 'They've been known to bite crocodiles in half.'

'I'd have reckoned Gunnarsson to be tougher than any crocodile,' said Hardin in a heavy attempt at jocularity, but the humour fell flat.

'We'd better get on,' said Stafford. 'Nair needs a doctor. Any other injuries?'

No one admitted to being hurt, but Curtis said mournfully, 'I left my belt back there. It was a good belt, too. Snakeskin.'

'You left more than that,' said Hardin. 'You left your pants.'

'Yes, but my Amy gave me that belt.'

There was a moment's silence before Stafford said, 'That lot are marooned back there. I think we ought to move into Ol Njorowa now.'

'Chip won't like it,' warned Nair.

'Chip doesn't know the circumstances. How much staff does the animal migration lab have, Alan?'

'I don't know,' said Hunt. 'It varies. I didn't think there was anyone there now until I saw Patterson.'

'Then there's a good chance that it's empty,' said Stafford as though arguing with himself. 'I don't think Brice can have really got going yet. So far he's been working on a shoestring and waiting for the Hendrykxx money. This *must* be the best time to bust him, while he's out of the game. Sergeant; head for the shore.'

'To Safariland,' said Hunt. 'I think I know of a way to get you into Ol Njorowa.'

31

Francis Yongo was boatman at the Lake Naivasha Hotel and Francis was worried. He had promised to pick up Mr Gunnarsson from Crescent Island and he had not done so because someone had taken his boat. He talked to the crayfish fishermen by the lake and asked if they had seen it. One said he thought he had seen it going out across the lake with a number of men in it. No, he had not seen where it was going; it had been of no interest.

Dispiritedly Francis walked up to the hotel to report to the manager who spoke acidly about inconsiderate tourists and got on the telephone. An hour later he called Francis into the office. 'I've traced the boat, Francis. It's lying at Safariland – just come in. You'd better take your bike out there and pick up Mr Gunnarsson on the way back. I doubt if he'll be pleased.' He went on to fulminate about thoughtless joyriders while Francis listened patiently. He had heard it all before. Then he went to get his bicycle.

* * *

Nair leaned heavily on Stafford as he hobbled up from the dock at Safariland towards the manager's office. Stafford said, 'What went wrong back there? How did Brice catch on?'

'It was Gunnarsson,' said Nair. 'I thought it best to stick close to the truth so I told Brice I'd arrested him. That meant Gunnarsson had to be handcuffed but he wouldn't wear them; he said he wanted to be free if anything went wrong so he faked it. Then he stumbled and they fell off.'

'And that was a tip-off to Brice.' Stafford shook his head. 'In a way you could say Gunnarsson killed himself. Will you be all right, Nair?'

'As soon as you've gone I'll phone Chip, then I'll get a doctor.' He sat on one of the chairs on the lawn. 'I don't suppose I can stop you?'

'It's the right time,' said Stafford positively.

'Perhaps, but I have to convince Chip.' Nair took a bunch of keys from his pocket. 'Go to the Lake Naivasha Hotel first. There's a pistol and a spare magazine clipped under the front seat of the Mercedes.' He tossed the keys to Stafford. 'Don't use it unless you have to.'

'Thanks. The others will be waiting. I still have to find out from Hunt how we're to get into Ol Njorowa.'

It was to prove ridiculously easy. He found Hunt, Hardin and Curtis waiting for him in the car-park, standing next to Hunt's Land-Rover. Hunt pointed to the trailer attached to the rear. 'You go in there.'

'Is there room?'

'It's empty apart from a few butane bottles and the burner,' said Hunt. 'I left the envelope and the basket at Ol Njorowa when I took the burner in for repair this morning. God, but that seems a long time ago.'

'Aren't you stopped at the gate?' queried Hardin.

'I never have been. Staff members can move freely.'

'Yes, they'd have to,' said Stafford. 'There's a limit to Brice's bloody security. It would look pretty queer if the staff of an agricultural college were searched every time they went in. That reinforces my contention that whatever there is to be found will be in the animal migration laboratory. All right; let's go.'

'I'll put you right outside the door of the lab,' said Hunt. 'But I can't promise it will be unlocked.'

Hardin said, 'Just deliver us; we'll see to the rest.'

Hunt opened the trailer and Stafford, Curtis and Hardin climbed in. Hunt hesitated. 'I usually keep it locked,' he said. 'There's a deal of petty pilfering.'

'Do as you do normally,' said Stafford, so Hunt locked them in, walked around the Land-Rover and drove off slowly.

Nair's police warrant card had secured him a telephone and

the privacy of the manager's office. But when he spoke to Chip he had his back to the window and so did not see Francis Yongo cycle past somewhat unsteadily on his way to the dock.

* * *

Hunt stopped at the gate of Ol Njorowa, gave a blast on the horn, and waved to the guard. The gate opened and he drove through, keeping his speed down, past the Admin Block and onward to the building surmounted by the dish antenna which lay a little over half a mile further. Ahead there was a car driving equally slowly and, as he watched, it stopped outside the animal migration laboratory. A man got out, unlocked the front door, and went inside. Hunt stopped the Land-Rover and got out.

He looked about him. Everything was calm and peaceful; there were a few distant figures in the experimental plots but no one nearer. He went back to the trailer and tapped on the door. 'Stafford! Can you hear me?'

A muffled voice said, 'Yes. What is it?'

'We're near the lab. Someone just went in.'

'Let us out.'

Hunt unlocked the trailer and Stafford crawled out followed by Hardin and Curtis. They stretched, easing their cramped limbs, and Stafford looked over to the building nearby and noted the parked car. 'Who was it?'

'I don't know,' said Hunt. 'I just got a glimpse of him.'

Hardin looked up at the dish antenna. 'Science!' he said somewhat disparagingly.

'Let's find out.' Stafford waved and the four of them walked to the front of the building. He put his hand on the handle of the door and tested it. To his surprise the door opened. 'We're in luck,' he said quietly.

He opened the door and was confronted by a blank wall three feet in front of him. He raised his eyebrows in surprise and then went inside to the left along a narrow passage and emerged into a room. His hand was in his pocket resting on the butt of the gun.

There was no one in the room but there were two doors, one in the wall opposite and another to the right. There were tables and chairs and, in one corner a water cooler and a coffee machine together with an assortment of crockery. On the walls were large photographs of animals; wildebeest, hippopotamus, elephant. This he took to be the Common Room where the staff relaxed.

He walked slowly into the room. The polished floor was slick and slippery. He went to the door on the right and motioned to Curtis and Hardin who stationed themselves on either side of it. Gently he opened the door and peered inside. Again, this room was empty so he went in. It was an office complete with all the usual equipment one might expect; a desk and swivel chair, a telephone, a reading lamp, a photocopier on a side desk. Total normality.

There were maps on the wall which were covered with a spiderweb of red lines. He inspected one and could make nothing of the cryptic notations. There were also maps on a large side table which had shallow drawers built into it. Again he could make nothing of those on a cursory inspection.

He left and, on an inquiring look from Hardin, shook his head and pointed to the other door. This, again, was unlocked and again the room was empty. It was a big room with no windows and along one wall, running the whole length, were banks of electronic equipment -- control consoles and monitor screens gleaming clinically under the lights of overhead fluorescent tubes. It reminded Stafford of Houston space centre in miniature. He looked about him and saw no other door.

'This is crazy,' said Hardin behind him. 'Where did the guy go?'

Stafford withdrew into the Common Room and said to Hunt, 'Are you sure a man came in here?'

'Of course. You saw the car outside.'

'Three rooms,' said Stafford, 'and one door. There's no back door and no man.' He went to the window and looked out, his shoulder brushing aside curtains. As he turned away his attention was caught by something and he stiffened. 'You know,' he said. 'This place is built like a fortress. A blast wall at the front door, and look here . . .' He pulled aside the curtain. 'Steel shutters to cover the windows.'

'Ready for a siege,' commented Hardin.

'Certainly not innocent.' Stafford looked at Hunt. 'You know more about this scientific stuff than any of us. Take a look round and see if there's anything odd, anything out of place that shouldn't be here. Anything at all.'

Hunt shrugged. 'I don't know much about the electronic stuff but I'll take a look.'

He went into the back room and Stafford returned to the office where he opened drawers and rummaged about, looking for he didn't know what. Hardin checked the Common Room and Curtis stood guard by the front door. Ten minutes later they assembled in the Common Room. 'Nothing in here,' said Hardin.

'All the electronic stuff looks standard to me,' said Hunt. 'But it would take an expert to be sure. I found nothing else out of the ordinary.'

'Same with the office,' said Stafford in a dissatisfied voice. 'But I might have missed something. Take a look at those maps, Alan.'

Hunt went into the office and Hardin said, 'We might have made a big mistake, Max.'

'I'd have sworn on a stack of Bibles six feet high that what we're looking for is in here,' said Stafford savagely.

'So what do we do if it's kosher?' asked Hardin. 'Apologize?'

'It can't be. Not with that damned blast wall and the shutters.'

Hunt came back. 'Standard maps of Kenya,' he reported. 'I'd say the lines are animal movements as recorded by the electronic thingummy on the roof. I told you Brice had shown me papers in a journal. The same stuff.' He saw a strange look on Stafford's face. 'What's the matter?'

Stafford was looking at the door leading into the back

room. It was open and a man stood there. Stafford plunged forward and the man slammed the door in his face and it took him a moment to open it as his feet slipped from under him. He yanked it open and then lost his footing completely and fell on his back just as there was the sharp report of a shot

He rolled over and looked around. The room was empty

He got up slowly and took Nair's pistol from his pocket. He turned carefully looking at every part of the room and saw nothing. 'It's all right, you can come in.' He picked up one foot and felt the sole of his shoe. 'Damned seeds!' he said, and kicked off the shoes.

Hardin appeared at the door. 'Where did the guy go?'

Stafford pointed with the gun. 'He was standing there when I fell.'

'That prat fall maybe saved your life,' observed Hardin. 'That goddamn bullet nearly hit me.' He fingered a tear in the side of his shirt and looked around warily. 'What's the trick?'

'I caught sight of something,' said Stafford. 'Just before I fell. Something big and square.'

'What was it?'

'I don't know. It doesn't seem to be there now.' Stafford studied the floor which was covered with a plastic composition in a checkerboard pattern. Set into it at his feet was a metal plate about three inches square. He bent down and found he could prise it upwards and that it moved on a spring-loaded hinge. Beneath the plate was a three-pin socket for an electric plug.

Hardin said, 'Most of this electronic equipment is mounted on castors. That's why they need floor plugs.'

'Yes,' said Stafford absently. He walked over to where he had last seen the man and found another metal plate. He bent down and lifted it. 'Bingo!' he said softly because it opened to reveal not an electric socket but a metal ring. 'There's a bloody cellar – this is a trap door.'

He ran his fingers along a hairline crack and found the hinge. The trap door was square and it must have been what he saw when it was standing open. 'Take cover, Ben, and warn the others. He might pop off again.' He pulled open the metal flap, put his finger through the ring, and lifted. The door opened easily and he had lifted it about nine inches when there was another shot and a bullet ricochetted from the wall.

Stafford let the door drop and stood on it. Hardin stepped forward from where he had been pressed against the wall. 'Looks like a Mexican stand-off. We can't get down and he can't get up. But if he has a telephone down there he'll be calling for reinforcements.'

Stafford had not thought of that. 'Sergeant!' he shouted. 'If you find any telephone wires cut them, and keep a watch out there.' Hardin was right, he thought. Unless there was another way out of the cellar which he thought unlikely. The entrance to the cellar on which he stood was cleverly disguised; another entrance would double the chances of the cellar being discovered.

He snapped his fingers suddenly. 'Got it! I know how we can winkle him out. Go with Hunt and bring his balloon burner and a couple of butane bottles. We've got a flame thrower of sorts.'

'Jesus!' said Hardin. 'That's nasty.'

'We'll tickle him up, just enough to put the fear of God into him. He'll come out.'

'Okay.' Hardin turned to go, but stopped at the door and looked back. 'I wouldn't stand there,' he advised. 'If he shoots through the door you're likely to lose the family jewels.'

Stafford hastily stood aside and, while waiting for Hardin to come back, he wheeled a console across so that two of its castored legs stood on the trap door and held it down. He then walked to the door and said to Curtis, 'Any signs of activity out there?'

'Nothing here, sir; except that Mr Hardin and Mr Hunt are coming back.' Curtis turned away from the window. 'I'll check the other side.' He crossed the room and walked into the office.

Hardin came in carrying the burner and Hunt followed, staggering under the weight of a butane cylinder. They went into the back room and Hunt put down the cylinder. Stafford said, 'Can you rig this thing?'

'Yes.' Hunt hesitated. 'But I don't know that I want to.'

'Look!' said Stafford, on the verge of losing his temper. He stabbed his finger down at the trap door. 'That man has been shooting at us. He shot on sight -- didn't even stop to say "Hello!". He could have killed any one of us, and Christ knows what he's doing now. I want him out. Now get that damned contraption rigged.'

'Take it easy, Max,' Hardin said quietly. He looked at Hunt. 'Can I help you?'

'No; I'll do it.' Hunt bent to the burner and Hardin watched him with interest.

'Max was telling me about this,' he said. 'When we were idling on the island. He says it's pretty powerful. Is that so?'

Hunt was connecting tubes. 'It's rated at ten million Btu, but it probably delivers about three-quarters of that.'

'I've never figured out what a British Thermal Unit is,' said Hardin. 'I must have been at a ball game when that came up in class.'

'The amount of heat to raise the temperature of a pound of water by one degree Fahrenheit.'

'And you've got ten million of them in that thing!' Hardin looked across at Stafford. 'Did you say you'd tickle him?'

Stafford smiled slightly. He had cooled down and he knew what Hardin was doing; as an army officer he had done it himself when men were in a jumpy condition. Hardin was soothing Hunt as a man might soothe a fractious horse. Stafford said lightly, 'Quite a cigarette lighter, isn't it?'

The burner consisted of two coils of stainless steel tubing mounted in a rectangular frame so that they could swivel. Hardin said, 'Looks as though you have two burners there. Why?'

'Belt and braces principle,' said Hunt. 'If I'm in the sky and a burner fails I want to have another quickly.' He turned a cock on the butane cylinder then lit a small pilot burner. The pilot flame burned blue. 'I'm ready.'

Stafford said, 'I'll operate it.'

'No,' said Hunt. I'll do it. I know exactly how it works.'

'Better think of what's going to happen when you lift that trap,' said Hardin. 'The first thing that'll come through is a bullet.'

'Anyone got a knife?' asked Stafford. Hunt produced a pocket knife and Stafford cut a length of electric wiring from a table lamp. He lifted the small metal flap on the trap door and knotted the end of the wire around the ring beneath. He said, 'I'll pull up the trap from here, standing behind it. The trap door itself will protect my legs from the flame. Let the door be open at least a foot before you let go, Alan; and you'd better lie flat on the floor behind the burner. Bullets travel in straight lines so you should be safe. Ben, move that stuff off the trap and then get clear.'

Two minutes later he looked at Hunt. 'Ready?' Hunt nodded. 'Give it a good long burst,' said Stafford, and hauled the trap door open.

There was a shocking series of chattering explosions as soon as the trap started to move and a stream of bullets came through the opening to strike the ceiling and ricochet around the room. Lights went out as some of the overhead fluorescents were smashed and a monitor screen imploded when hit. Stafford flinched and was about to drop the trap door when Hunt cut loose with the burner. The room was lit by an acid-blue light as a six-foot long flame stabbed down into the basement. The shooting stopped and all that could be heard was the pulsating roar of the burner which seemed to go on interminably.

At last Hunt switched off and the room was quiet. Stafford dropped the trap door back into place and looked around. 'Everyone all right?'

Hardin was clutching his upper right arm. 'I caught one, Max. What the hell was that? A machine-gun?'

'I don't think so,' said Stafford. 'My guess is that it was a

Kalashnikov on automatic fire.' He looked at the blood on Hardin's hand. 'A ricochet, Ben. If you'd stopped a direct hit at that range it would have torn your arm off. This is beginning to get bloody dangerous.' He looked down at Hunt. 'Are you all right?'

Hunt was pale but nodded. He said, 'The shooting stopped.'

'But was it because of us?' asked Stafford. 'Or did his magazine run out?' He looked up and saw Curtis standing in the doorway. 'Get back on watch, Sergeant. That doorway is in the line of fire.'

'Yes, sir,' said Curtis smartly, and disappeared from view.

'Are you ready to give it another go?' asked Stafford, and Hunt nodded. 'All right. I'll open the door. If there's no shooting give him a short burst and stop. If he shoots let him have it – a good long blast.' He turned his head. 'Ben, get the hell out of here.'

Hardin jerked his head. 'I'll be behind that bench.'

'Take this then and stay ready.' He gave Hardin the pistol and took up the slack on the wire, nodded to Hunt, and hauled the trap door open. There was silence for a moment and then again the flame stabbed out with a stomach-tightening rumble. Hunt let it play for only a few seconds then turned it off.

Again there was silence.

Stafford shouted, 'Hey! You down there! Come up with your hands empty. You have fifteen seconds or you'll fry.'

There came a distant call. 'I'm coming. Don't burn me.'

Footsteps were heard climbing the stairs and a man appeared. His hair had been burned away and blisters were beginning to show on his face and the backs of his hands. Stafford said curtly, 'Out!' and he climbed up into the room. Hardin moved forward holding the pistol.

'Anyone else down there?' demanded Stafford. The man shook his head dumbly, and Stafford said, 'We'll make sure. Give it another long squirt, Alan.'

'*Nee, man, nee,*' the man shouted. '*Jy kan nie . . .*' His words were lost as Hunt turned on the burner in a long sustained blast. He turned to run but was stopped at the door by Hardin with the pistol. The burner stopped and then things began to happen so fast that Stafford was bemused.

Hardin dropped as though pole-axed as someone hit him from behind. He dropped the pistol which went off as it hit the ground and the bullet screamed past Stafford so close that he ducked involuntarily. When he looked up suddenly Hendriks and Brice were in the room and Hendriks held the pistol with the silencer. 'Everyone freeze,' he said. 'No one move.'

Brice looked at Hunt lying on the floor, his hand still on the blast valve. 'What in hell is happening?' He looked at the scorched man. 'What happened to you, van Heerden?'

'I was down there and they turned that . . . that damned flame thrower on me.' he said. 'Things are burning . . .'

Hendriks gave a choked cry. He thrust his pistol into Brice's hand and ran forward to the trap door, kicking the burner aside as he went. He clattered down the stairs and disappeared from sight. Hardly had he gone when a hand clamped on Brice's wrist from behind and twisted it sharply. Brice screamed as his arm broke and Curtis appeared from behind him to catch the pistol as it dropped.

Stafford expelled a deep breath. 'Get up, Alan,' he said. Hunt got to his feet and turned around. 'See to Ben.' He was about to step forward when there was a muffled thump and the building shook. A dense column of smoke tinged with flame at its centre shot out of the basement through the open trap, and van Heerden screamed, 'It's going to blow up!'

Something fell and hit Stafford on the head and he knew nothing more.

32

'These grapes are not bad,' said Stafford appreciatively. 'Thanks.'

'It is customary to bring grapes to hospital,' said Chip and hitched his chair closer to the bed. 'It is also customary for those who bring them to eat them.' He took a couple of grapes from the bunch and popped them into his mouth. 'When are they letting you out?'

'Another week.' Stafford touched his bandaged head. 'There's nothing broken, but I get double vision when I'm tired. The doctor says it's concussion and all I need is bed rest. How's Nair?'

'He's all right. They took the bullet out of his leg and he's on the mend. He's in a room down the corridor.'

'I'll pop in and see him.'

Chip smiled slightly. 'The population of this hospital has gone up since you began operations. Hardin had concussion like you; Hunt is having a skin graft on his legs – he got scorched.'

'The Sergeant?'

'Nothing wrong with him. He's a real tough one. He'll be coming in to see you soon.'

'All right,' said Stafford. 'What happened?'

'Curtis got Hardin out then went back to help Hunt get you out. Brice got himself out. Hendriks and Miller were both killed.'

'Miller?' said Stafford interrogatively.

'The man in the basement.'

'Oh! Brice called him van Heerden.'

'Did he?' Chip was interested in that and made a note of it. 'His passport was in the name of Miller. A British passport.'

'He spoke a few words of Afrikaans when he was under stress. What did you find in the cellar?'

Chip looked at him oddly. 'Don't you know?'

'I don't know a bloody thing,' said Stafford. 'You're my first visitor.'

'When Nair rang to tell me what you were doing I rounded up some men and commandeered an army helicopter from Eastleigh because I wanted to get to you fast. I thought you were tackling something bigger than you could handle. We were putting the helicopter down next to the building with the dish antenna when it blew up. The helicopter nearly crashed.'

'Blew up!' said Stafford, startled. 'In God's name, what was down there?'

'We've had our forensic people looking at the bits and pieces that are left. Apparently there were a lot of explosives, commercial gelignite for the most part. They say that didn't blow up – it needs a detonator – but it burned hot and that set off the rest of it. They had a small armoury down there, rifles and ammunition, hand grenades and so on.'

'That wouldn't be enough to blow up a building.'

'That's right,' agreed Chip. 'The damage was really done when the fire got to three Russian SAM-7 rockets. We think there were three but it's difficult to tell now.'

'Rockets!' Stafford rubbed his jaw. He was thinking of that hot, blue flame driving heat into the basement. Talk about playing with fire!

'Most of the stuff down there was Russian,' said Chip. 'Probably captured equipment from Angola. The South Africans smuggled it in, probably through Mombasa. We're going into that now.'

'Indirection,' said Stafford. 'What do you think they were going to use it for?'

Chip shrugged. 'There's a lot of talk going on at the top. The general opinion is that the stuff was going to be used to arm various groups in the general interest of stirring up trouble. Those being used would even think they were being paid by the Russians. It could have caused a lot of bad blood.'

'What does Brice say?'

'Brice is saying nothing; he's keeping his mouth shut. Patterson isn't saying much, either. But Luke Maiyani will talk as soon as his jaw is unwired,' said Chip grimly. 'You're going to have visitors, Max. They'll tell you to keep your mouth shut, too. All this never happened. Understand?'

Stafford nodded. 'I think so,' he said wearily. 'How are you going to keep it under cover?'

'I've brought you some newspapers and marked the relevant stories. The matter of Brice hasn't come up yet so it hasn't been reported. I'll tell you what will happen about him. He's under arrest for embezzlement of Ol Njorowa funds; we found enough in his office to nail him on that. He'll go on trial and he'll stand for it because he can't do anything else. We don't know who he is but we do know he isn't Brice.'

'How do you know that?'

'Before Brice left Zimbabwe – Rhodesia – he got into trouble with the Smith government for some reason or other. Anyway, our brothers in Zimbabwe had a look through police records and turned up his fingerprints, and they don't match those of the Brice we've got.'

Stafford began to laugh. 'So Brice goes to jail for embezzlement. He can't do anything else.'

'He'll spend a long time inside, and he'll be deported when he comes out.' Chip smiled. 'We'll probably put him on a plane to Zimbabwe.' He chuckled 'And the Zimbabweans will arrest him for false pretenses and travelling on a false passport.'

'I almost feel sorry for him,' said Stafford.

'Don't,' said Chip in a grim voice. 'We found a safe built into the wall of the cellar. It was strong and fireproof. In it, among other things which I won't go into, we found three passports in the name of Gunnarsson, Hendrix and Kosters.

That pins the Tanzanian attack directly on Brice. The Hendrix passport had been tampered with.'

'They'd replace Hendrix's photo with that of Corliss,' said Stafford. 'What happens to Corliss?'

'We'll give him the passport and send him home,' said Chip. 'He knows nothing of what went on. He's a very confused boy and will never tell a straight story.' He stood up. 'When you get out of here you must have dinner with me and my wife.'

Stafford was somewhat surprised. 'I didn't know you were married.'

'Most people are.' Chip flipped his hand in a semi-salute and left.

Stafford picked up the newspapers and read the articles Chip had marked. An American visitor, Mr John Gunnarsson, had been killed by a hippopotamus on Crescent Island, Lake Naivasha. His body was being returned to the United States. A brief editorial in the same issue commented that this should reinforce the warning to all visitors to Kenya that the animals they saw in such profusion *really* were wild and could not be approached with impunity. While regretting the death of Mr Gunnarsson it could not be the function of the Kenyan authorities to wet-nurse headstrong tourists.

In another issue was an account of the disastrous fire at Ol Njorowa College. The animal migration laboratory had been wrecked, mostly by the explosion of butane cylinders stored in the basement. Several people, including the Director, Mr Charles Brice, had been injured, and Mr Dirk Hendriks and Mr Paul Miller had been killed. Mr Brice was not available for comment but the Acting Director, Dr James Odhiambo, said it was a grave blow to the advance of science in Kenya. The police did not suspect arson.

Stafford was about to reach for another newspaper when there was a tap at the door and Hardin and Curtis came in. Curtis said, 'I have taken the liberty of bringing the Colonel some fruit.' He put a brown paper bag on the bedside table.

Stafford looked at him with affection. 'Thank you, Sergeant. And I understand I have to thank you for getting me out of the lab before it blew up.'

'That was mostly Mr Hunt, sir,' said Curtis imperturbably. 'I'm sorry I let Brice and Hendriks get past me. I had to watch out on two sides and I was in the office when they came in.'

Stafford thought it was not so much an apology as an explanation. He said, 'No harm done,' then amended the statement. 'Only to Hendriks – and Brice.'

'Is there anything I can get for you, sir?'

'Just a new head,' said Stafford. 'This one feels a bit second hand.'

'I felt like that,' said Hardin. 'But you got a bigger thump than me. We'll come back when you feel better.'

'Hang on a minute, Ben. Do you mind, Sergeant?' Curtis left the room and Stafford said, 'Are you still going to work for me?'

Hardin grinned. 'Not if it's going to be like this month. The pay's not enough.'

'It isn't always as exciting as this. How would you like to go to New York? I want someone across there fast – someone who knows the ropes.'

Hardin looked at Stafford appraisingly. 'Yeah, Gunnarsson Associates will be up for grabs now Gunnarsson has gone. That's what you mean, isn't it?'

'Something like that. I need you there; you know the business. With a bit of luck you could get to be the boss of the American end of Stafford Security.'

'Gunnarsson always kept the reins in his own hands,' said Hardin musingly. 'I guess things could tend to fall apart now. Sure, I'll give it a whirl and see if I can pick up a few of the pieces. To tell the truth I've gotten a bit homesick. All this fresh air seems unnatural; I miss the smell of gasoline fumes. Hell, I'd even take Los Angeles right now.'

'Go by way of London,' said Stafford. 'I'll give you a letter for Jack Ellis. Arrange for whatever expenses you need with him.' He paused. 'Talking of Los Angeles, I wonder what happened to Hank Hendrix – the real one?'

'I'll ask around but I don't think we'll ever know,' said Hardin.

When Hardin had gone Stafford felt tired and was beginning to see double again. He closed his eyes and composed himself for sleep. His last waking thought was of Alix Hendriks who would never know the truth about the death of her husband. It occurred to him that every time he helped Alix she got richer and he achieved a few more scars. This time she would inherit her husband's fortune by courtesy of the South African government, and might even get Henry Hendrix's money with a bit of luck.

He made a mental note that the next time Alix appealed for help or advice was the time to start running.